Praise for Luke M

The Ashes of Berlin

'An engrossing mystery… his best yet' – ***Publishers Weekly***

'Tough, gritty and atmospheric – a new Luke McCallin novel is a cause for celebration' – **William Ryan**, author of *The Constant Soldier*

The Man from Berlin

'An extraordinarily nuanced and compelling narrative' – ***New York Journal of Books***

'a good, fast-paced, engaging read full of surprises as well as a more serious meditation on war, loyalty and the complexities of the former Yugoslavia itself' – ***We Love This Book***

'a gripping and atmospheric thriller… a thoroughly involving and worthwhile read' – ***Crime Time***

'I'm reminded of Martin Cruz Smith in the way I was transported to a completely different time and culture and then fully immersed in it. An amazing first novel' – **Alex Grecian**, author of *The Devil's Workshop*

'From page one, Luke McCallin draws the reader into a fascinating world of mystery, intrigue, and betrayal' – **Charles Salzberg**, author of *Swann's Lake of Despair*

'Set in 1943 Sarajevo, McCallin's well-wrought debut… highlights the complexities of trying to be an honest cop under a vicious, corrupt regime… Intelligent diversion for WWII crime fans' – ***Publishers Weekly***

'Reinhardt's character is compelling, as complex and conflicted as the powers that surround him… I look forward to the next Gregor Reinhardt mystery'
– ***Historical Novel Society***

The Pale House

'Very well written and wonderfully descriptive'
– ***Mystery People***

'the tale creates… a complex, exceptional character in action'
– ***Crime Review UK***

'[A] well-executed sequel… Readers who can't wait for Philip Kerr's next Bernie Gunther novel will find much to like'
– ***Publishers Weekly***

'A multilayered tale of war, political upheaval, and fragile hope'
– ***Kirkus Reviews***

'A very engaging thriller series. Reinhardt is both tough and thoughtful, and it's impossible not to get drawn into his emotional depths and root for him. The cast is full of sympathetic characters, the worst of villains, innocents, and everyone in between. The setting is engaging, the characters complicated, and the plot inspired'
– ***Historical Novel Society***

'A very compelling murder mystery that takes place in a seldom talked-about country during WWII, and Mr McCallin paints a vivid picture of Sarajevo, of the people, and [of] the dire conditions everyone had to endure' – ***Fresh Fiction***

THE **ASHES OF BERLIN**

Novels by Luke McCallin

The Man from Berlin
The Pale House
The Ashes of Berlin (aka *The Divided City*)

THE **ASHES OF BERLIN**

THE DIVIDED CITY

A GREGOR REINHARDT NOVEL

LUKE McCALLIN

NO EXIT PRESS

First published in the UK in 2016
by No Exit Press, an imprint of
Oldcastle Books Ltd,
PO Box 394, Harpenden,
Herts, AL5 1XJ, UK
noexit.co.uk
@noexitpress

Published in the USA as *The Divided City*

Published by arrangement with the Berkley Publishing Group, an imprint of
Penguin Publishing Group, member of the Penguin Random House LLC

A CIP catalogue record for this book is available from the British Library.

ISBN
978-1-84344-832-7 (Hardcover)
978-1-84344-833-4 (Trade paperback)
978-1-84344-714-6 (Epub)

2 4 6 8 10 9 7 5 3 1

Typeset in 12pt Minion Pro
by Avocet Typeset, Somerton, Somerset TA11 6RT

Printed and bound by CPI Group (UK) Ltd, Croydon, CR0 4YY

To my wife, Barbara, and my children, Liliane and Julien

Acknowledgments

This one was a difficult one…

Many people helped me through the writing of this novel, with insights and support, with food and good cheer, or with just being there. My deepest thanks and affection to my family, above all, for living through the good times (there were a few, right?!) and the bad times (plenty of those!) as I wrestled with the plot and the writing and a rewarding but demanding full-time job.

Thanks to those who read the drafts and offered comments and advice. To my wife, Barbara, my parents, John and Margaret, and my sisters, Cassie and Amy. Thanks as well to friends and colleagues, in particular to Number One Fan (aka Marina Throne-Holst), Ben Negus, Séverine Rey, and Marina Konovalova, whose insights and comments into Russian and Soviet thinking were invaluable. Franz Boettcher helped out enormously with research on Berlin's locations and infrastructure, and with German history, idioms, and culture. My cousin, Dominic Barrett, helped out with Russian drinking customs! Ion Mills at my British publishers, No Exit Press, was a reliable font of wisdom, good cheer, and culinary destinations in London. Thanks as always to Ryan and Tamara at Geneva Fitness for keeping the bar high; many's the time I literally worked out frustrations with plot and character! A shout-out to the 'dawn patrol' as well (you know who you are!). Lastly, I want in particular to acknowledge the contribution of Chelsea Starling, my friend and website designer extraordinaire, who insisted that Reinhardt had to have something to live for, that his life could not be all wrack and ruin. She was right.

My thanks to my editors, Tom Colgan and Amanda Ng, and to my agent, Peter Rubie, for keeping things on an even keel.

Dramatis Personae

Main Characters

Reinhardt, Gregor	Kripo detective, assigned to Schöneberg; a former officer in the German Army
Bliemeister, Bruno	Assistant Chief of Police in the American Sector
Bochmann, Heinrich	Former executive officer of III./NJG64 (formerly IV./JG56)
Brauer, Rudolph	Former policeman; Reinhardt's best friend and former partner in Kripo
Carlsen	British agent, found murdered
Collingridge, David	American official in the US Occupation authorities
De Massigny, Armand	French lieutenant and archivist, working in the WASt
Endres	Professor of pathology at the Charité hospital complex
Ganz, Hugo	Veteran Kripo detective in Schöneberg; a man of few loyalties
Gareis	Former pilot in IV./JG56
Gieb	A prostitute
Haber	Former air force researcher and scientist
Jürgen	Former pilot in IV./JG56
Kausch	Former SS Sturmbannführer (major); a man with a past to hide

Lassen	Kripo detective in Hamburg
Leyser, Marius	Former Brandenburger (German commando)
Dr Lütjens	Former air force researcher and scientist
Margraff, Paul	Berlin's police president (chief of police), a German soldier captured at Stalingrad and now a Soviet collaborator
Markworth, James	British official in the UK Occupation authorities
Meissner, Hilde	Widow of Tomas Meissner, Reinhardt's former mentor
Neumann, Walter	Chief of police in Schöneberg
Noell, Andreas	Former pilot in IV./JG56
Noell, Theodor	Former air force researcher and scientist
Ochs	Superintendent of Noell's building
Reinhardt, Friedrich	Reinhardt's son, a former Soviet prisoner of war
Semrau	German official working in the WASt
Skokov	Major in the Soviet MGB (state security)
Stresemann	Allegedly Gieb's pimp
Stucker	Former pilot in IV./JG56
Tanneberger, Karl	Chief of detectives in Schöneberg
Uthmann	Tenant in Noell's building
Von Vollmer, Claus	Former commanding officer of III./NJG64 (formerly IV./JG56), now a businessman
Weber	Kripo detective; a surly young man with an unknown past, often seen with detectives Frohnau and Schmidt
Whelan, Harry	British official in the Allied Control Council
Zuleger	Former pilot in IV./JG56

Other Characters
(Elsewhere or Deceased Prior to This Story)

Albrecht, Fenski, Hauck, Meurer, Osterkamp, Prellberg, and Thurner	Former pilots in IV./JG56
Vukić, Suzana	A Yugoslav partisan

Organisations and Locations

Allied Control Council	The military-occupation governing body of the Allied Occupation Zones in Germany, comprised of representatives from the US, USSR, UK, and France, located in the Kammergericht building in the US Sector in Berlin
Berlin Document Center	Central repository of documents relating to the Nazi Party and Nazism, instrumental in the formulation of war crimes investigations and proceedings. Located in Zehlendorf in the US Sector
WASt	Wehrmacht Information Office for War Losses and PoWs: the central repository for information on German servicemen, as well as German and Allied prisoners of war. Located in Reinickendorf in the French Sector

Part One

How Happy the Dead

1

BERLIN, EARLY 1947

MONDAY

Reinhardt had come to prefer the nights.

The nights were when things felt cleaner, clearer. The nights were when his city could sometimes resemble something more than the shattered ruin it was. The nights were when he did not have to look down at the dust and grit that floured his shoes and trousers, the innards of his city turned out and spread wide for all to see. It was the days when Berlin emerged scarred and scorched into the light, when its people arose to chase their shadows through the day, wending their way from who knew where to who knew what beneath frowning escarpments of ruin and rubble which humped up and away in staggered mounds of wreckage, and through which the roads seemed to wind like the dried-out bottoms of riverbeds.

It was very early on a Monday morning when the call came in, a body in a stairwell in an apartment building in the American Sector of Berlin, down in Neukölln. These were bad hours by anyone's reckoning, the hours no one wanted, the hours married men were curled up asleep with their wives, the single men with their girls, when even drunks found a corner to sleep it off. They were the hours those on the chief's blacklist worked. They were the hours they gave the probationers – those too new to the force to manoeuvre themselves a better shift – or those too old but who had nowhere to go.

Reinhardt knew he was closer to the second category than to the first. But however those hours were counted by others, he considered them his best, when it was quiet and he could have the squad room all but to himself, or else wander the darkened streets and avenues, winding his way past the avalanche slides of brick and debris, learning the new architecture the war had gouged across Berlin's façades. He and his city were strangers to each other, he knew. They had moved on in different ways, and these night hours – these *witching* hours, when he would sometimes chase the moon across the city's jagged skyline, spying it through the rents and fissures deep within buildings, watching the play of light and shadow in places it should never have been seen – were what he needed to rediscover it, what it was, and what had become of it.

All this, though, was in the back of his mind as the ambulance followed the dull glow of its headlights down a road swept clear along its middle, pocked and pitted with shell craters and tears in its surface, a suggestion of looming ruin to either side. He spotted the building up ahead, the fitful yellow beams of flashlights wobbling yolk-like in its entrance and casting the shadows of people up the walls and out into the street. He climbed stiffly out of the ambulance, switching on his own flashlight as he turned up the channel cleared between the rubble. He paused. He swung the flashlight at the entrance of a ruined building across the road. Hidden in the shadows, a pack of children watched with glittering eyes, vanishing from view when he held the light on them a moment longer.

An officer in his archaic uniform, complete with brass-fronted grey shako, watched as Reinhardt knocked the dust from his shoes in the building's entry, pocketing his flashlight.

'There we were about to send for the American MPs, but it looks like the Yanks have shown up anyway,' the young officer quipped. 'Which police station are you from?'

'Reuterstrasse,' said the policeman, his face clenching in suspicion.

'I'll speak to whoever's in charge here,' said Reinhardt, holding the younger officer's eyes as he took his hat off.

The officer's face darkened, but he cocked his head inside. 'Sergeant. *Sergeant!*'

A second officer pushed his way out of a crowd of people milling in the entrance. Reinhardt thought he recognised him, a man well into middle age, tall, lanky, with old-fashioned sideburns – although if it was him, the man used to be a lot heftier and bulkier.

'Cavalry's here, Sarge,' the young officer said. Reinhardt ignored him as the older officer threw his colleague a reproachful look.

'Good morning, sir,' he said. 'What Officer Diechle means, sir, is we was about to call the Amis, I mean, the American Military Police. We didn't know if anyone was coming out from Kripo at this hour.'

'Well, some of us detectives are up and about,' Reinhardt said, smiling, his voice soft. 'Inspector Reinhardt, Schöneberg Kripo Division.'

'Yes, sir. No offence at our surprise in seeing you, sir.'

'And why's that?'

'Because they don't usually stir themselves for what seem like accidents or open-and-shut cases,' said Diechle. ''Specially not at this hour.'

'Who says it was either of those?'

'He was drunk, he fell down the stairs,' Diechle snorted. 'That's all it is.'

'Show me what you've found. Sergeant Frunze, isn't it?' Reinhardt suddenly remembered the man's name, feeling it slip onto his tongue from out of nowhere, it seemed. Something in the man's appearance, those old-fashioned side-burns, the accent triggering a memory of a line of struggling, sweating policemen trying to hold apart a seething mass of Nazis and Communists, and Frunze reeling away with blood sheeting his cheeks but a brown-shirted thug caught under his arm, the lout's face turning red inside the policeman's armlock as Frunze calmly recited the man's rights to him.

'That it is, sir. Frunze. Very glad to see you remember, sir,' he said, ignoring the way his younger colleague rolled his eyes. 'This way, sir.'

'Last time I saw you, you were up in one of the Tiergarten stations.'

'Time's moved on a bit, sir. You go where they send you these days,' Frunze replied, a quick glance at Reinhardt. He could not tell what the glance might have meant, but an experienced officer like Frunze, especially one his age, ought not to be running a night shift in a place like Neukölln. It had always been a rough neighbourhood. Left-wing, working class, where the cops had never been welcome, and Reinhardt did not think things had changed much as Frunze led him through the small crowd of people to the bottom of the stairs, over to where the body of a man lay, face up. The light in the entrance was a shifting mix of flashlights, candles, and lanterns held by the policemen and by the cluster of people – men, women, and children – to the side of the stairs. It made for a confusing play of shadows, but there was light enough for Reinhardt to see that the man's nose and mouth were a puffed and bruised welter of blood that fanned the bottom of his face and jaw and had soaked into the clothes on his left shoulder. There were scratches and lesions on his face, on his scalp, and on his hands, the skin of his knuckles stripped raw. Reinhardt's eyes were drawn back to the injuries around the nose and mouth, the wounds framed by black and blue discolourations that indicated he had received them some time before dying. If he got those falling down the stairs, Reinhardt thought, he would have lain here a good long time before dying and there was no pooling of blood, so far as he could see.

'Has forensics arrived, yet?'

'No, sir.'

'It should be Berthold coming. I called him before I left. Any identification on the body?'

'None, sir.'

'Keys? Money?'

'Nothing, sir.'

Reinhardt pulled on a thin pair of old leather gloves, then reached under the man's neck, lifting it gently. The head did not quite follow, slipping from side to side.

'Broken neck, sir?' asked Frunze.

'It would seem so. Anyone find a bottle?'

'No, sir,' Frunze sighed. 'But the man does smell of booze. I reckon he spilled a bit down the front of his clothes. But much as Diechle would like this to be open and shut, I've a feeling it's not.'

'No. Probably not. Who found him, Sergeant?' he asked, gently moving and pinching his way down the man's arms, feeling the heft to the limbs.

'The building's superintendent. Or, what passes for one these days, sir. Here.' Frunze indicated an elderly man in a threadbare dressing gown with a tangled rosette of iron-grey hair running around his head from ear to ear, a scarf bunched tight around his neck. 'Name's Ochs.'

'Mr Ochs,' Reinhardt addressed him as he knelt, his left knee stretching painfully as he did. 'Tell me what you heard and saw,' he said as he ran his fingers down the man's clothes, reaching carefully under the collar of the overcoat. Some men, black marketeers and criminals in particular, had been known to sew razor blades under the lapels, but there was nothing. Reinhardt felt the fabric of the man's coat, his shirt, the tie knotted loosely beneath his chin.

'Yes, sir. Well, it would have been about two o'clock in the morning. I heard a man calling for help, then I heard a terrible thumping. There was another cry, I think as the poor soul hit the bottom, then nothing. I came out of my rooms, just there,' he said, pointing at a door ajar next to the entrance, 'and found him.'

Reinhardt shone his flashlight at the stairs, the light glistening back from something wet about halfway up.

'Have you seen him before?' Ochs shook his head. 'You're sure? He's not a tenant? Not a displaced person the municipality's moved in recently?' Ochs shook his head to all of it.

'He's no DP, sir,' said Frunze. When Reinhardt encouraged him to go on, Frunze pointed at the man's coat, at his shoes. 'Look at that quality. You don't find that in Berlin these days. If he's a DP, he's a well-off one.'

'Thank you, Sergeant,' said Reinhardt, watching Diechle out of the corner of his eye as the younger officer followed their discussion. The man was no displaced person, Reinhardt was sure. His clothes were too good, his fingernails too clean, his hair had been cut recently, and quite well. He had been well-fed, the weight of his limbs and the texture of his skin testament to that. 'These other people,' he said to Ochs. 'The building's tenants?'

'Yes, sir.'

'Any of them hear or notice anything?' he asked both Ochs and Frunze.

'Nothing, sir,' answered the sergeant. 'One or two of them said they were awakened by the noise of the man falling. One of them says she thinks she might have seen him before, though.'

'Bring her, please,' he said to Frunze. 'Is everyone living in the building here, Ochs?'

'Not everyone, sir. There's some who work nights, and one person's away travelling.'

Frunze came forward escorting a woman carrying a young child, two more children in her wake. 'Madam,' said Reinhardt. 'You told the police you might have seen this man?'

'I think so. Once or twice. The last time maybe two days ago, each time on the stairs.'

'Did you say anything to each other?'

'Only a greeting. Nothing else.'

'Did you notice anything about him?'

'Like what?'

'Anything. Was he in a hurry? Did he seem worried?'

'Nothing. We just passed each other.'

'Thank you, madam. We'll have you all back to bed soon,' Reinhardt said, a small smile for the little boy with a tousled head of hair. 'Have you had a look around upstairs, Sergeant?'

'Not really, sir. We didn't want to mess anything up for the detectives.'

'Very well. We'll have a look now. Ochs, you come with me, please. Diechle, please tell the ambulance men to wait for Berthold before moving this body. And Diechle? There's some children outside, probably living homeless across the street. See if you can persuade one or two of them to talk to us. And Diechle,' he insisted, as the young officer's face darkened again. 'No rough stuff. Just ask them.'

Sweeping his flashlight from side to side across each step, Reinhardt started upstairs. He passed the first smears of blood he had seen from the bottom, about halfway up. At the top of the first flight, where the stairs turned tightly around and continued up, there was another spattering on the floor, a streak on the banister, as if a man had stood there, catching his breath, perhaps calling for help, swaying back and forth through his pain. Up to the first floor, his feet crunching in the dust and clots of plaster and rubble that salted the stairs, more stains, more smudges on the wood of the banister. There were two doors on the first-floor landing, and Ochs confirmed the tenants – the woman Reinhardt had talked to with her three young children, and an elderly couple – were downstairs.

Feeling like Hansel following the bread crumbs, Reinhardt continued upstairs to the second floor, the building's smell growing around him, a smell of people too closely packed together, of damp washing and bad food. At the second-floor landing, Ochs told him the tenants – a widow and another family – were also downstairs.

'All the ladies are on the first two floors. As for the third, the building's in a bit of a state, still. It's not been fully repaired, you'll see.'

On the third floor, the building took on a different register, the walls a labyrinthine scrawl of cracks and rents from the damage it had suffered, and the strains it must still be under. The corners of the stairs and landings were rounded with dust and plaster swept and pushed to the sides. A draught swirled down from somewhere up above. Only one apartment on the third floor was inhabited – a man away travelling – the other was boarded shut, war damage rendering the apartment uninhabitable, according to Ochs. The same was true of the two apartments above it, the little superintendent said, puffing behind Reinhardt with his dressing gown bunched in one fist to hold it clear of his slippered feet.

As the damage became worse, the building seemed to become malodorous, dark, a listening dark, a dark that seemed to shuffle quietly back away from him as if cautious, as if the structure was sensitive to the harm men had wrought upon it. On the fourth floor, Ochs pointed to an apartment that was locked up, where the tenant – Mr Uthmann – worked nights on the railways. There was one floor remaining, and Reinhardt paused at the landing, looking at the door that stood ajar, moving slightly back and forth in the draught.

'Who lives there?'

Ochs caught his breath leaning on the banister. 'Mr Noell,' he managed. 'He lives alone.'

'He's not downstairs?' asked Reinhardt, being careful to hide his own breathing. It was very short, and he felt dizzy with the effort of climbing the stairs.

'No. He is out sometimes. I didn't…' Ochs puffed, 'didn't think his absence downstairs anything out of the ordinary.'

'And the body downstairs is not this Noell?'

'No.'

Reinhardt shone his flashlight across the floor, tracking its beam through the fallen plaster and rubble, not knowing if the scuffed pattern showed the tracks of anyone having passed through it all. 'Well, let's see if he knew your Mr Noell.'

Reinhardt drew his police baton, flicking it out to its full extension. With the lead ball at the tip, he pushed the door open. The first thing his light illuminated inside was a streak of blood on the wall, from about head height and down. He saw a light switch and turned it on, watching the room's only bulb come fitfully to life.

One of the windows had glass in its frame, the other a mix of wood and cardboard, most of it from CARE packages, the aid parcels sent over from the United States, through which the wind slipped its insistent way. There was a sofa and an armchair that had seen better days. On a table made from a packing crate stood a bottle and one glass.

Reinhardt walked carefully through into the second room, past a small kitchen area, little more than an alcove with a sink and a hot plate, and into a bedroom with a bed with a pile of blankets and pillows on it pushed up against the far wall next to a lopsided wooden cupboard with a cracked mirror on one of its doors.

There was a body on the floor. Arms and legs spread wide, face turned slackly to the ceiling.

'Oh yes,' said Ochs, as he peered over Reinhardt's shoulder. 'That's Mr Noell.'

2

Reinhardt collapsed his baton, ordering Frunze to send for the MPs, given two bodies had been found in their sector, and to wait for Berthold downstairs. Ochs waited quietly in the little hallway, the old man seemingly unperturbed, and why not, Reinhardt thought as he stepped carefully into the bedroom. Ochs had probably seen plenty of deaths, many worse than this, if he had been living in Berlin these past few years.

'What exactly is it you do, Mr Ochs?' Reinhardt asked, as unbuttoning his overcoat and kneeling by Noell's body, he checked for a pulse.

'I used to be a building superintendent, until my place got destroyed in a bombing raid. I could fix a pipe, change wiring, collect mail, bit of this, bit of that. So they put me in downstairs and asked me to keep an eye on the place.'

'When was that?'

'The municipality moved me in here in, oh, June '45. Right after the war.'

'The Russians put you here?'

'Well. Yes. But I'm not an informer! Not like those, those people in the Russian Sector. Those wardens. Or whatever you call them. Spying on their neighbours and all that and reporting it to the police.'

'I never thought it, Mr Ochs,' Reinhardt replied.

'And nor should you. You should see my place. I could sneeze across it. If that's what informing gets you, I'd hardly think it worth the effort,' Ochs subsided sulkily.

Noell's body was cold, but not quite the tombstone cold of the long dead. He had been murdered in the last few hours, for sure. He was dressed in trousers, a shirt, and a woollen cardigan, a pair of worn slippers on his feet. Reinhardt squirmed around the body on his haunches, and as he did so, his knee dipped into something wet. He ran a finger across the floor, noting the rippled line it left, and inspected his glove for what looked like water. It lay around Noell's head and shoulders. He looked up at the roof, to see if perhaps it had cracked, perhaps a pipe had leaked and it had come from the ceiling, but saw nothing.

He moved the body slightly onto its side, seeing the purplish dappling of hypostasis under the neck, and that the neck was not broken. He lowered the body back, began checking the limbs. Noell had been a very slight man, made almost certainly slighter by the short rations most Berliners lived on these days.

None of the limbs seemed broken. There was no wound evident, no blood. The only thing Reinhardt could find wrong was a mottled bruising around Noell's mouth and nose. He looked at it, cocking his head to the side. On impulse, being careful not to touch the skin, he lowered his right hand over Noell's mouth, fingers to one side of his nose, thumb to the other. He paused, considering, as the place his hand would have come down on seemed to match the mottling. While he was dying, Noell's mouth had clenched tight shut, and Reinhardt drew back, preferring to leave it for the autopsy.

Reinhardt did not want to disturb the body any more than he had to. He pushed himself to his feet, his knee a tight knot of pain as he did so.

'What did Noell do?'

'I don't think he did anything,' Ochs answered stiffly, his pride still hurt. 'At least, nothing I ever saw.'

'His mail?'

'Hardly anything.'

'How long had he been here?'

Ochs hesitated. 'About, oh, six months. Yes. Six months.'

Reinhardt stared at him. Building superintendents, or concierges, call them what you will, they invariably knew everything about their tenants comings and goings. Ochs coloured under Reinhardt's gaze, his hands tightening in the pockets of his dressing gown.

'That's to say, he's not actually here. If you see what I mean.'

'I don't.'

'He's subletting. From another man. The two of them were friends during the war, or something like that, and when this other man left…'

'This man's name?' Reinhardt interrupted.

'Yes, of course. It's a "K" something. Kassel. Kessel! It's downstairs, I'll get it for you. So when this man left, he asked if we could arrange for his old comrade to move in, as a favour. Keeping his name on the lease.'

'A favour,' said Reinhardt. 'With a touch of remuneration.'

Ochs nodded. 'It's hard for people to get a place. You must know that. Doubly hard for them.'

'Them?'

'War veterans.'

'Noell was a veteran?'

'Yes. Ex-air force, I believe.'

A noise at the door announced Diechle, with the news that Berthold had arrived and was examining the body downstairs. The officer had a bruise on the side of his face, and a trail of blood down the angle of his jaw. Reinhardt refrained from mentioning it, only thanking him and telling him to let Frunze know he could start escorting people back into their apartments, family by family, but for them to steer clear of any of the evidence on the stairs. Ochs made to leave as well, but Reinhardt motioned him to stay put.

He opened the cupboard, seeing a few pairs of trousers and shirts, and a couple of jackets on hangers, all of them well-worn. Socks and underwear. One pair of shoes. The only item of note was an old air force jacket. The jacket had no decorations, except a pair of colonel's epaulettes in the pockets. There was nothing else in the bedroom apart from the bed. No shelves, no table, no books. It was a bare room, almost ascetic, and Reinhardt was struck, suddenly, by how ritualistic Noell's body seemed, spread-eagled in the middle of the floor.

'So you've been here just about two years, Mr Ochs. How well do you know the tenants?'

'Well enough.'

'Noell?'

Ochs thought a moment, his mouth moving against his teeth. 'He kept to himself, mostly. He was civil enough, but I know of one or two times he had an argument with the man downstairs about noise, or something like that. And once I saw him on the stairs, and he barely gave me the time of day. Just brushed right past me. Head in the clouds, or something like that, I thought.'

Reinhardt moved past Ochs back to the living room. It was a different place from the bedroom. It felt *lived-in* for one thing, which, Reinhardt supposed, was normal for a place like a living room. But there was something else: an ordered disorder, with books and newspapers, clothes draped over the back of a ladder-back chair. His eyes were drawn again to the bottle and glass on the table. Some kind of schnapps, he sniffed. The glass was full, and he took note of that incongruous touch in this room where at least one man had been killed, and yet what had happened had not disturbed that liquid.

'Head in the clouds, you say? Fitting, for a pilot.'

'I suppose so,' said Ochs, a weak chuckle at Reinhardt's weak attempt at humour.

'Friends?'

'I never saw any. That is, until the other day. He received a letter that seemed to cheer him up immensely. This would have been about, oh, a week ago. Two or three days ago, someone came to visit him. I don't know who it was, but the two of them had quite the party up here until the early evening, then they left together, all dressed up. Or as dressed up as they could manage, I suppose.'

'This was when?'

'Saturday evening. He came back somewhat the worse for wear on

Sunday morning. That was the last time I saw him, poor man.'

There was a heavy tramping on the stairs, the timbre of foreign voices, and a pair of American military policemen breasted into the room, followed by a female interpreter, a narrow lady of middle age. They were big, blocky men, filling the room with their size and their apparent disinterest and disdain for where they found themselves. Reinhardt answered their questions through the interpreter, who kept her head down. Although he found he could follow just about all they said, he made no sign he understood English, wanting them gone as soon as possible, insisting gently through the interpreter that there was no overt Allied connection to the deaths, no evidence of black marketeering, no sign of fraternisation.

The MPs seemed only too happy to agree, muttering back and forth between themselves, banter concerning the goings-on in their unit, the uselessness of being called out to such scenes, and their anticipation of getting off duty. The only question Reinhardt asked of them was if they recognised the body downstairs, to which he got a grunted negative from one of the MPs, translated as a polite and apologetic *no* by the interpreter. They photographed Noell's body, took Reinhardt's details, pronounced themselves satisfied this was an affair the German authorities could handle, but to make damn sure they were informed if it turned out there was Allied involvement, and were gone, a veritable backwash of collapsed, displaced air following them out, the interpreter scudding in their wake.

Reinhardt sighed in relief, echoed by Ochs, who had been all but plastered against the wall as the MPs had filled just about all the space. He scanned the rooms quickly, satisfied the Americans had not disturbed anything, and resumed his careful search of the apartment. He went back to the impression he had had, that this room felt lived in where the other did not. The clothes drew his eyes, draped over the back of a chair. There was a cupboard next door, so why were they here…?

'Noell lived here alone? You're sure?' Ochs nodded, a yawn pulling his mouth down. 'Very well, Mr Ochs. Thank you for your help. You may go, but please give the name of the man who has the lease on this apartment to the sergeant downstairs.'

Alone in the rooms, the only sounds a faint whisper of voices from the lower floors, Reinhardt leant against a wall. His knee ached, terribly. It was getting worse, he knew. All the walking he was doing around Berlin, the cold and damp, the lack of food, was making the knee feel as bad as it did twenty years ago.

When he had caught his breath, he closed the door. It shut quietly, the door fitting quite well to its frame. He pulled it, pushed on it, shaking the door, but it stayed shut. He opened it again, bending to the lock, running his fingers up the door frame, inside and out. There was a key in the lock, and a bolt drawn back and open. There was no sign of damage, no sign of a forced entry.

From downstairs, Reinhardt heard the distinctive bull bellow of Berthold's voice berating someone for something, and let a grin flash across his face. There was no sign of a struggle in the apartment either. Noell's body bore no defensive wounds that he could see, and neither had the man downstairs, although he would have to check with Berthold about that. Nothing in this room looked disturbed or out of place. Nothing broken, or overturned. It was not that big a room. If two men had been assaulted in here, there ought to have been some sign of it, unless the assault had been of devastating speed and surprise, Reinhardt thought, as he went into the kitchen.

The cupboards were bare, or might as well have been. A collection of mismatched plates, cups, glasses, and cutlery, a battered frying pan and an even more battered army cook pot, all of it probably salvaged from some wrecked building, or given out at municipal shelters. There was a half-empty sack of coffee, a bottle of oil that glistened greasily, and an empty cardboard CARE package. A couple of bottles of schnapps that had a homemade feel to them – these few things were all the kitchen contained.

It was clean, though, Reinhardt noticed. A couple of plates were stacked upside down by the sink, together with a glass; a cloth hung from the single tap. The surfaces were clean and dry, although the sink was pearled with water. There was a dustbin under the counter. Reinhardt hooked it out, peering inside at the inevitable slew of potato peelings that made up the staple diet of any German lucky enough to afford vegetables these days. Beneath the peelings was Friday's newspaper. He flicked out his baton, lifting the paper out to have a look through, in case Noell had made any notations, perhaps in the help-wanted section. *That said,* he thought to himself, poking the baton farther down into the rubbish, *most of the content of the papers these days was either want ads or obituaries,* unless you read one of the Allied publications, which were full of upbeat stories about the benefits of Occupation policies or pieces about Nazis and the harm they had done.

His stirring of the rubbish pulled up several thin sheets of paper covered in typing with handwritten notes jotted into the margin. The papers were stained by being in the dustbin, but there was enough of the writing intact that Reinhardt could read most of it. He straightened, his knee a tight knot of pain as he did so.

3

'Reinhardt? You in here?'

'Through here,' Reinhardt called back, hearing Berthold's heavy footsteps and the gravelly base of his muttering.

'Reinhardt, goddamn it, was it you let those damn Amis foul up my crime scene? That stripling of an officer downstairs says you've been letting Americans tramp around up here. Say it's not true.'

'I've been doing my best to save it for you, Berthold. Nice to see you, at last.'

'Well, thank Christ for you, Reinhardt.' Berthold was all curves, a dense, rotund man with thin hair plastered by sweat to his cannonball of a skull. 'If only all our brethren, in what passes for a police force these days, were as discerning as your good self.'

'Flattery, Berthold, will get you nowhere other than out of bed at three in the morning. Seen the one downstairs?'

'Broken neck for sure, but he was pretty badly beaten up before that. Blows to the mouth and nose, one to the throat, one almighty blow to the sternum. We'll hand him over to the Professor for full autopsy, but the fall down the stairs was the least of his problems I'd say, the poor bugger. That blood on the wall his?'

'Probably, but you tell me.'

Berthold swung his bulk back the way he had come. For all his bluster, Berthold was one of the more competent forensic technicians on the force, a remnant from the pre-Nazi days brought back out of premature retirement to provide some much-needed technical skills to Berlin's police. Twelve years of Nazism and six of war had seen

Berlin's police, once one of the world's most advanced forces, regress to levels Reinhardt had seen in the Balkans. Men like Berthold knew what needed doing but struggled to do it with the means left them.

Reinhardt watched the balloon-like curve of Berthold's back as he hunched over the blood on the wall, taking a sample for analysis. He unfolded himself upright, his cannonball head searching for Reinhardt, in his hand a big camera, a veritable prewar antique. Reinhardt backed out of the way as Berthold took a rapid series of photographs of the living room, then squirmed away as Berthold did the same for the kitchen, and then the bedroom.

'What have you got up here, then?' he asked when he was done, packing the camera away.

'Firstly, no forced entry as far as I can tell,' said Reinhardt. 'In here, no sign of a struggle. Bottle and glass, there, maybe some prints. Try the door handle as well, please. Kitchen is clean. I found some papers in the rubbish. I didn't touch them,' he said holding up his baton as Berthold made to open the cavern of his mouth in protest.

'I'll start in the bedroom then,' said Berthold, lugging his case through.

Reinhardt backed into the kitchen, drawn back to the papers. The sheets were of poor quality, with ink that had run and stained, and they were hard to read. One page seemed to be a statement of grievances of a group that Reinhardt could not make out, of their *untenable* situation, reference to the loss of all worth, pride, and benefits, with *benefits* underlined twice. The second was something of a manifesto, or a call for action. There was a heading on the paper in block capitals – RITTERFELD ASSOCIATION. It was the more damaged of the two, creased, spotted and, he realised, bending low over it, someone had spilled alcohol on it. He poked his baton back into the dustbin, searching for more of the same, but came up with nothing.

'Berthold, I'm going to start looking through the living room. I've got gloves,' he said, cutting off Berthold's inevitable protest. He heard the forensics technician subside into a series of tectonic rumbles, muttering under his breath, and Reinhardt grinned again. He began fingering through the piles of books and papers in the apartment. Most of the newspapers were old, stacked next to a cast iron stove as fuel or kindling, most likely. The books were old, too, and the collection was eclectic. Prewar novels, a few histories, a couple of treatises on philosophy, travel guides, children's stories, and a photo album.

Reinhardt's eyes narrowed as he opened it, finding pictures in some of which Noell was recognisable. The wartime Noell had been a bigger, healthier-looking specimen than the one lying in the bedroom. There were photographs of him in what appeared to be bars in Paris, several taken in front of various aircraft, Noell standing grinning with a hand or elbow placed proprietorially on the wing or rim of a cockpit, Noell standing arm in arm with other pilots. Reinhardt put the album to one side, and continued searching the room. He looked under the chairs, ran his fingers down the back of the sofa, and found wadded against the wall as if kicked or thrown there, a crumpled piece of paper. Fishing it out and unfolding it, he found it was another photograph. Another one of Noell, glancing up at whoever had taken the picture, this time in a dress uniform, with another man, both of them stooped over something. Reinhardt could not make out what. Something in some kind of water-filled tank, wrapped in fabric of some sort, wires and tubes attached to it.

He added it to the photo album, although Reinhardt was fairly sure it did not belong there, and continued his search, looking now for what was clearly missing. There was no identification of any kind, and that was a mystery. He went through the clothes, finding nothing. He went into the bedroom and searched through the clothing hanging up, finding nothing again. Noell had been a veteran, so there had to be some kind of identification, at the least a *Wehrpass*, the document all soldiers received upon demobilisation, and he had clearly been eating, so he had to have been getting rations from somewhere, and if he had been getting them, he had to have had identification.

There was nothing in the apartment, though, at least nothing he could find. At the end, he stood in the doorway, taking a last look, brushing his hat against his leg. The unforced door, the undisturbed living room, the ascetic lines of the bedroom… what had happened to the man who had lived here, and what linked that to the other man downstairs?

'Berthold, I'm finished here,' said Reinhardt. The ambulance men were waiting impatiently on the landing. Berthold grunted back at him from where he was brushing down surfaces. 'Can we have the Professor look at the bodies?'

'Yes. That's what I said earlier.'

'Let the ambulance men take the body away when you're ready then. When will your report be finished?'

'Later today if you leave me alone.'

'Consider it done. There's a photo album and some sheets of paper in the kitchen, please take care of those.'

'Right,' Berthold grunted, again, eyes comical behind the bottle as he dusted it down for prints.

'And let me know if you find any ID. I haven't found anything.'

'Right.'

'And I think Gestapo Müller's hiding under the sofa.'

'Very funny, Reinhardt.'

'Just checking you were listening,' said Reinhardt cheerily. He paused on the landing, looking up. The fifth floor was uninhabitable, Ochs had said, but he had a quick look, anyway. It was as Ochs had said, though. The top floor was a ruin, the roof sagging in places, patched and braced, and the two apartments were empty husks flecked with animal tracks and droppings, and an ammoniac reek of urine smothering the smells of damp and dust.

Downstairs, Frunze was waiting with the canvassing report. All the building's tenants were listed and accounted for. Apart from the widow, no one had ever seen the man found dead on the stairs. All of them confirmed Ochs's description of Noell as a quiet and courteous man, but two of them reported that he could at times be surprisingly gruff and distant, passing them on the stairs in the hallway without a word. No one, it seemed, had ever been up to Noell's apartment, and he had never been a guest in any of theirs. The family on the second floor had also mentioned that he had cheered up somewhat in the last few weeks, but did not know why.

'Not much is it, Sergeant?' mused Reinhardt. He took a packet of Lucky Strikes from his pocket and offered one to Frunz, who accepted with a smile. Reinhardt struck a match and lit both of them up, pinching out the match and putting it back in the box. 'Mr Noell. Quiet and courteous, although sometimes rude. Ex-air force. Quite well read. Altogether, something of a mystery man. And he pales in comparison to Mr X, who ended up at the bottom of the stairs.'

'Indeed, sir,' murmured Frunze, as he took a long pull on his Lucky, then stubbed it out, saving the rest for later. 'There is this as well,' he said, handing over a slip of paper with a name – *Mr Kessel*. 'The man from whom Noell was subletting, Mr Ochs said to give it to you.'

'Thank you, Sergeant. This Mr Uthmann, the one who lives below Noell. Ochs reported he had had something of a confrontation with Noell on more than one occasion. He might be worth talking to.'

'Leave a message, with Ochs, sir?'

'Yes.

'There's children living across the street in that ruin.' Frunze nodded. 'I'm going to see if I can talk to them. They may have seen something.'

'Diechle tried already, sir.'

'Yes, I saw that. Where is he?'

Diechle was outside on the building's steps. He straightened as Reinhardt came out. 'What happened, then?' asked Reinhardt, pointing his cigarette at Diechle's face.

'The little fuckers threw rocks at me.'

'For talking to them?'

'I thought I could catch one of them.'

'That was clever.'

'I thought it would be better.'

'I told you to talk to them. That was all,' Reinhardt sighed. He screwed out his cigarette on the wall, leaving the butt on the remnants of the balustrade at the building's entrance, where he knew someone would find and take it. He switched on his flashlight and crossed the street, picking his way carefully into the slew of debris. No one had cleared a path here, and the building in front of him was a checkerboard of holes and spaces that gaped dark and wide, as if they were mouths sucking down the night itself. By the fissure that passed for an entrance, Reinhardt stopped and shook some cigarettes from a packet into his hand. He placed them carefully on a stone with a flat surface, and then stepped well back, leaving his light shining on them, and lowered himself carefully onto the rubble.

'I just want to talk to you,' he called, quietly. 'Just talk.'

There was no answer, no sound, but he could feel he was being watched. He let a few moments pass, then called again.

'The cigarettes are for you. They're good. They're Luckies. The real thing.'

He waited a while longer. Although there were far less of them now, gangs of children still haunted some of the ruins, especially those swaths that had been condemned as uninhabitable, impossible to reconstruct.

'There's three of them. Think of what you can trade for them.'

A grating of rubble, the softest hiss of sound. Something moved in the darkness of the entrance.

'What d'you want, bull?' a girl's voice.

'Just talk.'

'S'never just talk with you bulls.'

'It is with me.'

'You always try to take us away.'

'I won't, don't worry.'

'Turn the light off.'

Reinhardt was plunged into darkness. He felt a moment of apprehension as the rubble seemed to come alive with sounds, small sounds, the whisper of little feet, a low snatch of words. Children they were, and he always wished more could be done for them – even if most of them wanted nothing to do with people like him and this new world and, really, who could blame them for that – but they could be menacing on their own ground, very dangerous if they felt themselves provoked or threatened. He could just make out the shape of something that flitted out of the night, and his cigarettes were gone.

'All right, bull, so talk.'

'What's your name?'

'What's it matter?'

'Nothing. It's nice to know who I'm talking to. My name's Gregor.'

There was silence. 'I'm Leena.'

'You know about what's happened across the street, Leena?'

'Yes.'

'Did you see anything? See anyone?'

'Like what?'

'Anything or anyone strange.'

'Strange?'

'People coming or going. People you've never seen before. The sounds of argument. People fighting.'

Reinhardt waited, hearing the children whispering.

'Sometimes Poles'd come and watch.'

'Poles? How do you know?' Reinhardt asked the night.

'Poles kicked us out of our house in Breslau.' It sounded like a young boy. 'Poles took my mother and my sister. Poles put me on a train. I know Polish.'

'You're saying Polish men came to watch the building?'

'Been a while since they was here. Weeks. They would watch. I heard 'em talking. They were looking for soldiers. From the war. Soldiers that done bad things to 'em.'

'I saw a man I ain't never seen before.' A new voice, another boy.

'When did you see him?'

'I don't know that, bull. I ain't got no watch.'

'S'about midnight,' interrupted the girl. 'The moon was just over the middle of the street.'

'Right. So this man come out of the building,' the boy continued. 'He were all dressed up in his coat like the Ivans wear. And a hat. I never got a good look at him.'

'What did this man look like? Was he big, this man?' Reinhardt asked to the darkness.

'He weren't big, but he… he moved all funny. That's why I spotted him.' More whispering, and the voice came back, feeling aggrieved over something. 'He moved funny,' the boy insisted.

'Funny how?' Reinhardt asked, quietly.

'Like he was part of the night.'

'Only thing funny here's your brain,' a child laughed. A rude name was called, and there was a furious scrabble of feet and cursing, until the girl's voice cut across the noise.

'There's something might interest you, bull, 'side from men who move funny. The last couple of days, s'been a man coming here. First time he came, he watched the building from in here, but he never saw us. About three times he's come. We saw him go in and out. He never stayed long. We saw him go in tonight, but he hasn't come out, yet.'

'Thank you. Is there anything else?'

'That's not enough?' came the belligerent reply.

Reinhardt stood up, asking one more question of his hidden audience, receiving a curt reply. He made his way back across the street, his feet scraping and turning on the detritus. The ambulance men were bringing Noell down and loading him into an ambulance with white sides that glimmered with all the dents and bangs the vehicle had ever had. They protested at Reinhardt's request, finally acquiescing and putting the stretcher with Noell on the ground, and heaving out the other body. They stood there with the stretcher between them as Reinhardt shone his flashlight on the man's face for a slow count of ten.

He stood in the quiet street, waiting, until a voice came out of the dark.

'That was him,' said the girl. 'The one who came before.'

'Thank you, Leena,' said Reinhardt. He shook a few more Luckies from his pack. 'You come and find me at the Schöneberg station if you remember anything more. On Gothaerstrasse. You ask for Inspector Reinhardt. Or if you need anything.'

'We don't need nothing, bull,' came the whisper from out of the night. Reinhardt left the cigarettes on a stone, walking back into the building and not turning at the patter of feet across broken stone.

4

Dawn was breaking across Berlin, the city's wrecked skyline marching torturously across a deepening wash of sky, and Reinhardt felt the tickle of unease he always felt at seeing Berlin by day as the ambulance dropped him off at the Schöneberg police station on Gothaerstrasse, before it continued on to the morgue up in Mitte, in the Soviet Sector. The station was a Wilhelmine-era building, rectangularly rigid. Reinhardt thought of it as a monstrous pile of stone that had come through the war more or less unscathed because it was too obtuse to be damaged. Along with the even more spectacularly proportioned Magistrates' Court opposite, the two buildings towered over the ruins around them. Some people might have found their permanence somehow reassuring, throwbacks to a calmer, more certain era. Reinhardt found them oppressive, purveyors of a false sense of certainty and continuity.

The morning shift was starting to trickle in, but it was still fairly quiet, quiet enough for Reinhardt to start writing up his report with an hour to go before roll call. He kept his head down, and his focus on his papers as he felt the squad room fill up, surprising himself by how far he had got with his notes and how focused he had been when someone jostled him on the shoulder.

'Oh, sorry. Didn't see you there,' said the man who had bumped into him. The man looked down, feigning astonishment. 'Reinhardt? Look, boys, look who it is!' Three detectives, younger men, were standing or sitting around him.

'Bugger me, it's Reinhardt!'

'The Captain!'

'Captain Crow!'

'He *liiiives*!'

The detectives were men Reinhardt hardly knew and barely cared to. They were new men, mostly, men brought in by the Soviets in the months following their conquest of the city, when they did as they wished. By their accents, none of them were from Berlin, and Reinhardt could not tell where the Soviets had found them, nor what any of them had done during the war. They were old enough to have been called up towards the end, and so they were old enough to have faced the Red Army in combat. Most Germans who had, had either been killed, captured, or escaped somehow. So far as Reinhardt could tell, officers like these contributed very little in actual police work, and half of them were barely literate.

To Reinhardt's mind, they were all placemen, put into the police by the Soviets, therefore considered reliable, therefore Communist in outlook, if not in belief. They made a strange complement to the holdovers from the Nazis, or even the pre-Nazi period, men from heretofore antagonistic systems, between them making for a schizophrenic atmosphere. On top of that, the Western Allies, when they arrived in Berlin in July 1945, had not done much to curtail the implicit Soviet influence in the police in their sectors. One might even have said they had made it worse, leaving the Soviet placemen where they were and adding a fair sprinkling of their own.

Reinhardt knew that because he was one of them.

'What on earth are you doing here, Reinhardt?' one of them asked sardonically, the one who had jostled him. His name was Weber. He was a tall, raw-boned young man, all sharp angles and heavy joints, his skin stretched tight around the curves and hollows of his head, all topped off with a shock of poorly cut blond hair that made him look much younger than Reinhardt suspected he was.

'Working,' said Reinhardt levelly, putting his head back down to his notes. 'Why, what are you doing here?'

There was a chorus of *ooh*s and *aah*s from the man's friends, a flurry of elbows poking into ribs as they settled themselves in for a bit of fun.

Weber's jaw tightened. 'Working on what?'

'A murder investigation.'

'A real investigation. Dammit, boys, what did I say?' Weber's eyes glittered. 'Reinhardt always has all the luck.'

'That's because there must be Americans involved. Right, Captain?' asked another officer, his eyes wide with a feigned interest. His name was Schmidt, Reinhardt thought.

'Not yet, no,' he answered.

'Shame. All your friends must have gone home by now, I would have thought.'

'Back across the ocean. To *New York*, or *Chicago*,' one of them gushed. His name was Frohnau. The two of them – Schmidt and Frohnau – were Weber's shadows. 'They don't stay long, do they? Still, you must have made some new ones.'

'As you say,' Reinhardt said equably, feeling the heat rising in his blood at this baiting. It never got any easier to bear, however much he tried to let nothing show.

'Listen to him. "As you say." Is that how you all talked when you were bloody officers? Fighting the good fight?' Weber's jaw was clenched as he stared at Reinhardt.

'You lot playing nicely, I hope?'

It was a newcomer who had spoken. Another detective stood behind Reinhardt. He was an elderly man, stout, even fat, if a Berliner these days could be said to be fat, with a stringy fringe of hair combed over the bald dome of his skull, but a magnificent Hohenzollern-style moustache that frothed and curled around his mouth. Ganz had already been a long-serving detective back in the '20s, during the Weimar years when Reinhardt had first joined the police. Although the detective had retired in 1936, in the last great Nazi reform of the police, it had never seemed to Reinhardt that Ganz had had a problem working for them. That said, he had not worked through the war, and that had to be a point in his favour with Germany's new masters. When Reinhardt had come back to Berlin he had found Ganz back out of retirement, a chief inspector, second in command of the division's detectives.

'Everything all right, Reinhardt?' Ganz asked.

'Fine,' Reinhardt said, shortly.

Ganz said nothing, just stood over Reinhardt's desk until he looked up at him. 'Something strange must be going on to see you here, Reinhardt, I thought to myself,' said Ganz, reaching out one finger to rest on Reinhardt's baton, which he had left on his tabletop, rolling it from side to side. 'Then I heard you got called out. Where did you *get* this? I didn't think there were any of them still around.'

'In the ruins of the Alex, down in one of the armouries,' Reinhardt replied. He got up and went to the back of the room where an urn of coffee had just been brought in by one of the kitchen staff, his ear catching the mutter of conversation behind him. He poured himself a cup, eschewing the powdered milk, and even if there had been any sugar it would not have made the coffee any better. He stood quietly a moment, remembering Sarajevo and the coffee he used to take on Baščaršija, the sun on his face as he watched the city ebb and flow, and waiting for the moment when the muezzin would cry the call to prayer from the mosque on the corner of the square.

Ganz followed him, pouring himself a cup.

'Something the matter, Reinhardt?'

'I'm always surprised to see you back on the job, Ganz.'

'Yes? Well, no timid dog ever got fat, eh?' Ganz replied, straight-faced. For a second, he sounded just like Becker, and Reinhardt froze, remembering the sound Becker had made as he died in that hut in the Bosnian forest, the laugh that had fallen back in his throat, choking out the last of his breath. Becker and Ganz had been, if not friends before the war, then close, Reinhardt remembered. Ganz had often taken the younger Becker under his wing, covering for him more than once. Why had he remembered that?

'Something the matter, Reinhardt? You look like you've seen a ghost.' Reinhardt stared at him unseeing, until his eyes focused, and he swallowed. Had he spoken aloud, had he panicked? That memory had been so vivid… Ganz was watching him with those beady eyes, and Reinhardt knew that behind their glitter they were calculating, considering, probing for weakness. 'So? Nothing you want to share?'

'Nothing.'

Someone made a cawing sound, like a crow's, a bray of laughter from behind turned him round. Ganz turned to look as well, his face expressionless, but his eyes gleamed over the swell of his cheeks. If the detectives around Reinhardt's desk were taking their cue from him, Ganz was doing a good job of hiding it.

'Well, whatever you say, Reinhardt. Tanneberger will want you to brief at roll call. You ready?'

'Yes,' Reinhardt said. He walked back to his desk, and he knew he must be colouring. His old nickname, Gregor the Crow, had surfaced, and Reinhardt knew it had to be one of the older men who had resurrected it. Captain Crow they called him, sometimes, making a mockery of his old army rank, as so much was made a mockery of that had had anything to do with the armed forces. To hear people now, officers were a gang of criminals who had either failed to kill Hitler or who had managed to lose the war. Reinhardt subscribed to neither view, and his war was not one he would willingly share with anyone, but faced with this constant level of hostility and mockery, he too often found himself, in his mind, taking the side of those who had, indeed, been criminals or who had acted like them.

It was a defensive reaction, he knew. There was no doubt for him about the army's role – and the officer class's in particular – in the horrors of the war, and too many men like him either thought they had done nothing wrong and would do it all again – preferably with the British and Americans at their side – or refused to think of it at all. He shunned their company whenever and wherever he came across them, but yet found himself prodded into thinking for them and against what he knew when faced with the antagonism of those he worked with. It was only proof of being human, he supposed, a man alone could not help but turn inward, seek reassurance in whatever way he might find. But Reinhardt could not help thinking there was something instinctively weak in himself that he thought that way.

The squad room's door opened, and Tanneberger walked in.

'Roll call,' Ganz shouted, pointing at the detectives' small meeting room. Reinhardt rose, gathering his papers. He squeezed past the desks, and somehow he knew that Weber would put his foot out, try to trip him. He felt as much as saw it happening, such that he pointed his foot and kicked hard and sharp at Weber's ankle, watching the other man's face change from a feigned surprise to a real twitch of pain.

'How clumsy of me,' Reinhardt murmured as he walked past.

5

Reinhardt sidled up against the back wall in the small meeting room, favouring his left leg. The room was packed with plainclothes policemen wrapped in a fug of cigarette smoke. Around the room, men caught his eyes. Most looked away, disinterested, but here, there, those who remembered Reinhardt, whom Reinhardt remembered from before the war, looked at one another across the heads and shoulders of their colleagues, and in the lacklustre gleam of their eyes, they remembered other times, other days, other places, even if one or two of them nodded civilly enough to him.

Tanneberger was up at the lectern, a sheaf of papers in his hand. He blinked at the room, then down at his papers, and launched into a droning recital of the happenings the day before and overnight, a monotonous litany of really nothing very much at all: a black market ring broken up, prostitutes dragged in, drunks sleeping it off downstairs. Reinhardt listened with half an ear, shifting his weight to ease the pain of his knee, more interested in what was not mentioned. No missing persons. Nothing of relevance from the Soviet Sector.

Tanneberger held the rank of police councillor. Ostensibly, he was the Schöneberg division's chief of detectives, placed here by the Allies in the big police reform of October 1946. Reinhardt remembered Tanneberger vaguely from before the war as some mid-level bureaucrat in Berlin's police administration, and Reinhardt did not know what Tanneberger had done during the war. The man had been dredged up from somewhere, and his *Fragebogen* – the denazification document any and all Germans had to complete for any kind of posting in government – must have passed Allied vetting and the subsequent bickering on the Allied Control Council as each of the occupying powers manoeuvred their men into position. Ganz, who stood next to Tanneberger, was the one who really ran the detective squad, and Reinhardt could still not figure him out.

Tanneberger invariably deferred to him on anything operational and technical. The two went well enough together, Reinhardt admitted, Ganz never contradicting Tanneberger in public, and Tanneberger rarely overruling the way Ganz kept things moving. They made for one of those schizophrenic instances that seemed to characterise the police, though: both of them in their different ways Nazi-era holdovers, both of them now in higher positions of authority under the Occupation than they had ever attained, or ever would have. Reinhardt had left Berlin's police before the war to escape the Nazis. He had come back after it to a police force dominated by communists instead, but there were still too many faces he remembered, who seemed to have that ability he had never had. The ability to bend with the wind, to find accommodation with whatever force or power that held sway and serve all with equal excesses of zeal. Or the minimum needed to get through the day, like he used to do, he remembered, and was in danger of doing again. His gaze drifted to Ganz. Ganz had to have some kind of political connection or line, either to the Soviets or to the Americans, but if it was to the latter, Reinhardt had never discovered it and it had never been revealed to him.

On the other hand, Reinhardt's own American connections were all too painfully obvious.

As if he heard Reinhardt's thoughts drifting, Ganz looked back at him, and there was a sardonic gleam in his eyes, such that Reinhardt knew straight away something was wrong.

'Reinhardt!'

He straightened, realising he had missed something. Tanneberger was looking at him. The whole room was looking at him.

'Reinhardt?'

'Chief.'

'I know you're usually tucked up in bed at this time, Reinhardt.' A low chuckle ran around the room, like a wave washing over a pebbly shore. 'But perhaps you might like to fill us in on your case, seeing as you're the only one who seems to have had any excitement lately.'

'Yes, sir. I responded...'

'Up front, Reinhardt. Up here,' Ganz interrupted.

'Two bodies in a building in the US Sector,' Reinhardt said, looking out over the rows of seated officers, at those standing along the back wall, feeling the lodestone weight of Tanneberger and Ganz behind him. He felt nervous, and his tongue stroked the gap in his teeth where the Gestapo had knocked one out. 'One found dead at the foot of the stairs, a broken neck sustained in an apparent fall, but the man had been badly injured before then. Upon inspecting the building, I discovered a second body. From what I could tell, this second victim had been asphyxiated. In the apartment, which showed no signs of disturbance, there was a streak of blood on the wall that I suspect was blood from the man found on the stairs. I was told by the building's supervisor that the apartment's tenant, the man I found asphyxiated, was named Noell, although I found no identification for him anywhere. The man on the stairs remains unidentified. Forensics is going over the apartment, and Professor Endres will autopsy the bodies.'

'Theories, Reinhardt?' interrupted Ganz, from where he stood to one side.

'Too early to tell. I did have an impression, though...'

'Yes?' Ganz's face was flat.

'Noell's murder had an air of ritual about it. The way his body was laid out on the floor, with water around his head. I think, although I can't be sure, but it reminds me of something I have heard or read recently.'

'Ritual?' repeated Weber. His voice was lazy, but the sparkle in his eyes glittered the lie of his apparent disinterest, as did the way they roved left and right, gathering in support. There was a shift in the room, heads coming up, a charge in the air like the expectation of a confrontation.

'Ritual,' Reinhardt said, again. 'I think it would be useful to look into other, similar cases.'

'If there are any,' murmured Weber.

'Any leads?'

'Several. Noell's neighbour works nights. I will go back to question him. As well, Noell was sub-letting the apartment from a Mr Kessel. We need to find him and question him.'

'Anything else?' asked Tanneberger, eyes down on his papers.

Reinhardt knew he was being goaded, made fun of, but there was no way to avoid it, so he simply continued. 'There is a group of children, probably orphans, living in the ruins opposite the building. I managed to talk to them. They said they had seen the unidentified man on several previous occasions over the past several days.'

'And?'

'I suspect this man knew or was meeting with Noell, or was looking for him.'

'Ritual *and* suppositions,' Weber carped. '"Suspect" this and "believe" that.'

'They may also have seen the murderer and gave me a description of what they saw,' said Reinhardt, dreading the next question.

'And?' prodded Ganz.

'All they could tell me was he walked in a strange manner. From the description of the children, it sounds like a man used to using cover, and that he wore what sounds like a Russian quilted jacket.'

There was a silence as each man examined the desirability of a Russian being the prime suspect in these murders.

'A war veteran, surely,' snorted Weber explosively. 'An officer, probably, walking with a rod up his backside or with wounds *honourably* gained in defence of the Fatherland. Veterans *and* Allies. This is perfect!'

'Have you called social services about those children?' Tanneberger asked suddenly.

'No, sir.'

'Do you intend to?'

'No, sir.'

'Why not?' Tanneberger lifted his face from his papers. Next to him, Ganz's face was expressionless, but Reinhardt knew he would be frustrated at this nit-picking.

'I will mention them in my report, but I believe that they can take care of themselves well enough for now.'

'For now?'

'For the time we need to concentrate on this investigation.'

'I'm surprised, Reinhardt. I did not expect such callousness from you.'

'Maybe he wasn't so softened up by the Americans as we thought,' Ganz said, taking back the initiative. Most of the men grinned, as they were supposed to, a few more looked uncomfortable.

Tanneberger grinned, a quick twitch of his mouth. 'Where are you with the report?'

'It needs to be typed up, and I need Berthold's and Endres's findings.'

'Very well. Let me have it as soon as it's done.

'Yes, sir. There is one more thing. The unidentified victim seemed to me too well-dressed, too well-fed, and too clean to be a Berliner. Or if he is one, he is very well-connected.'

The room was silent.

'Meaning?'

'There may be an Allied connection, sir.'

The room shifted. Someone groaned.

'Allied?' Tanneberger asked.

'Yes, sir.'

'Who?'

'Americans. Who bloody else with Reinhardt?' Weber muttered.

'Quiet!' Ganz growled. 'Reinhardt?'

'I have no idea. As I said, it is an impression.'

'Because he was well-fed?'

'And he was found in the US Sector,' offered Ganz, his eyes like two cherries pushed into dough.

'I'm sorry, what's that you're saying, Ganz?' asked Reinhardt, stung into a reaction. 'Are you saying the people in the US Sector are better off than in others? The Soviet Sector, for example?'

There was a hiss of laughter, and Ganz reddened, made to say something, but Tanneberger cut him off.

'Enough, the pair of you. The US MPs were called?' Reinhardt nodded. Tanneberger looked at him with his blank face. 'And they had nothing to say? No surprise, there. Well, if they saw nothing to worry them, I see nothing for us to worry about. I will let Bliemeister know,' Tanneberger finished, referring to the assistant chief of police of the American Sector. He looked at Ganz, and something unspoken passed between them.

Reinhardt hesitated a moment. 'One of the children also said he'd seen Poles watching the building. From what I could gather, these Poles may have been searching for war criminals.' The room was very quiet.

'Sterling work, Reinhardt,' Ganz said, 'to land us with an investigation possibly involving the Allies.' There was a smattering of laughter. 'And, of course, not forgetting your impression this might have happened before. So. Circulate the victims' information to the other precincts, and make sure the Allied military police command is informed as well. Then get some rest and be back in later. You're off night shifts until this is cleared up. Some sunlight should do you some good. You look like a bloody corpse.'

6

Reinhardt left the station with his head spinning from lack of sleep. The sun was well up, and Berlin was well awake. The streets were spotted with people, dark-clothed for the most part, although here and there were splashes of colour on women, among the younger ones especially. The young recovered faster, and made more efforts to appear normal. He felt terribly old as he thought that, walking past people huddled around the window displays in the few shops that were open, and there were already queues in front of the bakeries and butchers.

A few cars, mostly Allied vehicles, moved along the main roads, which had been largely cleared and above which the stark façades of the ruins reared their gashed and scored faces from skirts of debris. All the surfaces seemed sanded down, even clean, somehow, paint and stonework chipped and blasted away.

The destruction, as titanic as it was, was not what repelled his eye and mind as he walked under the empty-socketed stare of the buildings. It was that the city seemed deaf and blind. There was almost no noise. No crowds, no traffic. And it was the lack of windows, although that knowledge, that impression, had not come easily or quickly, and until it had, Berlin had left him with a feeling of wrongness at odds with the colossal damage that had been wrought on it. There was no light, no reflections. There was almost no glass, so the light seemed to vanish into the gaping fissures of the ruins. Reinhardt did not know what other people thought of the face of their city, but he could not get used to it, could not draw his eyes away from the jigsaw jumble. The only time it had become something more than a tangle of ruins was in winter, when the snow had turned the ruins into cathedrals, lining broken walls and brick like lace.

He walked down Grunewaldstrasse and took the steps to the underground station at Bayerischer Platz. The atmosphere on the platform was frosty with humidity, the tang of unwashed people, wet brick, stagnant water. A train came eventually, the yellow square of its frontage flickering through the crowds that then surged forward into the carriages. He squeezed in and swayed and jostled with the rest of the passengers. He let himself be wedged up against the wall of the carriage, his eyes lost somewhere else – some when else – but he was not so lost he did not feel the little fingers that tried to worm into his pockets. He clamped his hand around a thin wrist, looking down at a boy. A pickpocket. The boy blinked up at him with eyes hard as glass, the ripple of a snarl on his face. Reinhardt shook his head, lifted a finger to say 'wait', and fished a couple of Luckies from his pack, handing them over. The boy stared at them, then snatched them and was gone as the train's doors opened onto Kurfürstenstrasse station.

Reinhardt lost sight of him almost immediately, wishing the little boy some measure of luck in this ruined world, where crime had taken on dimensions never before seen in Berlin. Theft, assault, rape, extortion, black marketeering, corruption… everything and anything that the malicious could foist on the desperate, and that the desperate could get away with, most of it committed by Berliners on Berliners while the occupying forces passed immune through it all. Not many would dare raise a hand to one of them, but he knew there were few things a Berliner would not do to win the favour of an Allied soldier. Especially the women. Widows and young women. German women and Allied soldiers. It provided the women with money or chocolate or cigarettes, but he knew it fuelled a cycle of violence within families and communities. People could not help but look with condescension and contempt on such behaviour. Time-bound conservatism was hard to shift at the best of times. Desperate times strengthened them, and he knew some men were driven to savagery at what their womenfolk did, or what they suspected they did.

Another time-honoured stricture, for a man to take his failings out on his woman or children.

The train carried on east and he alighted at Hallesches Tor, walking up to Belle-Allianz-Platz, where, in place of the prewar circle of elegant, classical buildings, there was nothing, just a suggestion of space bounded by heaps of ruin. He had worked here, once, in the CID offices at No. 5. They were gone. Totally gone, and because the memories of those years were not good, he had nothing to hold him, and his steps led him on, almost without him thinking, away from the main thoroughfares, paralleling the Landwehr Canal off to his right, where Berlin's defenders had made one of their last stands against the Soviet advance, and eventually into a ruined street, all but deserted, many of the buildings simply gone and reduced to stone and rubble. Times and places like this, Reinhardt knew it was not a lack of words to describe the damage, it was simply a new language, a new alphabet that was needed to quantify it, and to what it had done and was doing to those who lived here.

Even among ruin so immense, here and there smoke spiralled up from the piles of debris, and washing hung limply on sagging lines, evidence of life still going on somewhere down below all this. People picked across the ruins, poking with sticks, from time to time stooping to pick something up and place it in a bag. Children chased each other across mounds of masonry, the older ones leaping fleet-footed, the younger ones picking their more cautious way. Where walls still stood, they were covered in scrawled messages that families and friends had left one another, desperate and forlorn announcements of their safety, their location in the aftermath of the war's end.

He paused outside one such building, messages and addresses scribbled densely up and over the archway of its entrance. The arch, and a few feet of wall to either side and over it, was about all that remained of the apartment building that had once stood here. Reinhardt walked under it, his feet crunching on stone and plaster, past where a staircase lurched up to end abruptly in a splintered mess of wood, looking up and across the hewed piles of rubble where the building had collapsed in on itself. He made his careful way across it, stepping aimlessly, seeing how his shoes were powdery with dust. His eyes roved across the ruins, over shattered stone, blackened timber, over the straight lines and the curved, as if searching for something. He would lean down, sometimes, his eye drawn by a spot of colour, a piece of wood, trail his fingers across the dust on a scrap of fabric, but whatever he found, he left, and whatever he looked for, he did not find.

After a while, he brushed clean a stretch of wall and sat, folding his coat around him, and lit one of his Luckies. His eyes kept moving, finding nothing, as always, but he could not help this pilgrimage, the urge that pulled him nearly every day, here, to where he used to live. To where he had once lived with Carolin, his wife, and with Friedrich, the son he had lost to the Nazis, and who had vanished on the Eastern Front at Stalingrad. Somewhere, down there, under all this, there must be a trace of her, of them, for he had nothing, now. He remembered the last time he had seen Friedrich, before his son had stormed out and left for the army. It had been the day his wife died. He had sat at the kitchen table and made tea in the blue pot she always would use. Was it down there, he wondered? Under all this? Had someone else come into the apartment, seen it, maybe used it, used it carefully… just a blue teapot, a china teapot bought for a few marks in a Berlin department store, but he could not stop thinking about it.

He sat, smoking slowly, making the cigarette last. He did not have that sense of being watched. The last few times he had come, he had thought someone else was here, and once, he was sure he had seen a shape passing, but it was usually at night that he came, and he was not sure anyone was there at all. Places like this, moods like his, you could hear and imagine anything.

When he finished, he resumed his walk through the wakened city, his steps slow and dragging for all that he wanted to be off the streets. The sun was low in the east and its light lay in a sawed line down the middle of the street. Like the moon, the sun shone past and into places it never should have, glimmering and shining through the ruins in ways that probed and startled. He took the southbound C line U-Bahn to Paradestrasse, not far from Templehof airfield. A crocodile file of children wound down the street, escorted by Swedish nurses, probably on their way to breakfast in one of the schools. He put his head into one or two shops, but the shelves were empty where there were no queues, and would be soon where the queues had formed. A man bumped into him as he came out of a butcher's, a flattened piece of meat flopping over the scrap of greaseproof paper he held in his palm. The man ducked his head in apology, pulling his purchase closer to his chest.

'There's meat?'

'If you can call it that,' the man answered. He summoned up a smile from somewhere. 'You know what they say, right? It'll be peace when the butcher asks "and can I offer you a quarter pound more…?"'

'Or they increase fish rations, only to run out of newspaper to wrap them in.'

Across the street from the butcher's, Reinhardt spotted a small crowd in the entrance to an alleyway and when he peered past heads and shoulders, he saw a woman, probably a farmer from the countryside, selling produce from a suitcase. He shouldered through the crowd, ignoring the menacing gaze of the man who stood behind the farmer holding an iron-bound club in his hands, and exchanged some Luckies for six eggs and some ham, and a small pot of cream. The eyes of the crowd pricked into him as the goods changed hands, richness that almost none could afford anymore.

He kept an eye out that none of them sought to follow and rob him. He folded himself into a corner on a tram and rode it most of the rest of the way back to where he lived. He was very tired now, his mind slowly running down as the ruined buildings began to fall away outside the windows, the destruction lessening as the tram squealed onward. The buildings became smaller, until they were houses, standing in rows and on little plots, perhaps one of the last vestiges of the Weimar vision of Berlin as a garden-style city, all individual homes and gardens.

He left the tram, walking down a quiet street and unlocking the front door of a small house with white walls and a high peaked roof of red tiles. The house was quiet inside, and despite the war and the poverty it somehow maintained a deep smell of wax and wood, and the heavy odour of old fabrics and air left still. Somewhere further into the house, a clock ticked remorselessly. In the kitchen at the back, light shone thickly through the tall windows, slanting and breaking around the leaves of the plants that clustered along the sills. An old lady sat at a table, a mug in front of her, a scent of mint in the air and a newspaper folded open. She looked up as he came in taking off his hat, slight surprise on the austere lines of her face.

'Good morning, Mrs Meissner.'

'Good morning, Gregor,' she replied. 'Will you have some tea?'

'Thank you, no.' If she was offering tea, it meant there was nothing to eat. He put what he had bought on the table. Meissner's face stayed steady, but her eyes blinked as she looked things over. The rations were very low and his salary, although regular enough, did not bring enough extra in, not on black market prices. Without his cigarettes, without the largesse of his American friends, they would be far worse off. 'Nothing for me but some rest. I will check the garden first, though.'

'I did it already,' she replied. 'Nothing is missing.' Reinhardt shrugged out of his coat as he went quietly upstairs, opening the door of his room. It was dark, the curtains drawn, only the sound of slow breathing to disturb the stillness. He draped the coat over the end of what passed for his bed – a child's mattress laid atop some empty ammunition crates – jacket and tie following as he sat and heeled off his shoes. He sat there, elbows on knees, eyes nodding closed, then fluttering open to look across the room where, curled like a dog into a corner, lay Brauer.

Reinhardt looked at him a long moment, before lying back on his bed, a long, low sigh escaping as he did so, fingers cupping the flame of his knee. He lay awake, eyes open on the ceiling, listening to the harsh rasp of his oldest friend's breathing. Reinhardt's stomach rumbled, and he turned in the bed, the wood of the crates creaking. Perhaps disturbed by Reinhardt's movement, Brauer cried out in his sleep, turning in distress. Reinhardt craned his head up, seeing Brauer with his eyes open, but he knew he was not awake.

'It's not our war, is it?' Brauer called hoarsely. 'It's not. So why?'

Reinhardt slipped across the room, putting a hand on Brauer's shoulder, smelling the alcohol on his breath, and rocked him back onto his side.

'No,' he murmured. 'It's not our war.'

He stayed there a moment, his hand on Brauer's shoulder, feeling how thin he was, before going back to bed, lying down quietly. He lay awake some time, listening to Brauer's breathing, before he, too, eventually found sleep himself.

The Feldjäegers stood in ranks four deep beneath a warm sun on a field of green grass. As places went, Reinhardt thought, looking at the Americans, drawn up in their own ranks, it was as good a place as any for it to end, and these were men good enough for it to end with. He watched the General step out in front of the Feldjäegers. Opposite him, an American General mirrored his movement.

The end. At last.

The German saluted the American, received a salute back. He turned to face his men, looking across the ranks of Feldjäegers. Two Germans stepped out to face him, one of them the colonel. Scheller. More words, then Scheller was moving down the ranks towards where Reinhardt stood with Lainer and Benfeld, with the others who had fought all the way up from Bosnia to here, this field in southern Germany.

Scheller faced his men, his eyes roving back and forth.

'Feldjäegers. My friends. My comrades. It has been a long war. A year longer than it might have been. Than it should have been. But we have reached the end, when so many of us have not, and now, this day, this month of June, this year of 1946, it is over for us. It is time to lay down our arms. It is over.'

Over, Reinhardt thought, as he unstrapped his pistol belt and laid it on the ground. Around him, Feldjäegers were doing the same. Over, he thought again. He remembered November 1918. That war had ended for him in a hospital bed, seemingly bereft of purpose, but there had been a light then, a sudden light that was Carolin. There was nothing here, now.

What would he do? What would any of them do…?

On a shouted command, the Feldjäeger ranks about-faced, and marched back, leaving their weapons piled on the grass. Another command, and they turned to face their general. He was in trouble, Reinhardt knew, looking at him. Something had happened in Greece, Reinhardt was not sure what. The war might be over, but what had happened in it would follow him.

It would follow them all, in its different ways.

There was a last salute, echoed by the Americans, and then it really was over. The ranks broke up, men separating, coalescing. Lainer stood alone, looking far away. Benfeld had gone somewhere, as had Scheller.

'Smoke?'

Collingridge stood next to Reinhardt, a captain of the American Military Police. He shook Lucky Strikes from a packet, lit them both up. They smoked quietly, surrounded by Feldjäegers and Americans, moving and mixing together.

'Long road, right?'

'It has been a long road,' Reinhardt answered around a mouthful of smoke, his English slow and precise.

'You're a free man, now, Reinhardt. Now what?'

'I do not know.'

'Where will you go?'

'I do not know that, either.'

'It's gotta feel good, no?'

Reinhardt put his face to the sun. They began walking, boots swishing slowly through the grass. 'It feels... something,' he replied. He felt lighter. As if a load had been lifted. As if traces he had worn a long time had been lifted off, but his English was inadequate to the moment. Collingridge seemed to feel it, and switched to German.

'What about home?'

'I do not know where that is anymore.'

'Aren't you from Berlin?'

'I am. But there is nothing there for me.'

'You used to be a policeman, didn't you? The city could use a good cop, from what I hear.'

Reinhardt stopped, looking at Collingridge. The American had been a good enough colleague. The war had ended in May last year, but the Feldjäegers had not surrendered along with the rest of the army. Rather, their surrender had not been accepted. The Americans had used them to help maintain law and order, guarding prison camps and securing roads, ensuring a valuable link between the hundreds of thousands of prisoners of war and their captors. Whatever help the Feldjäegers had given, it was no longer needed, now. The camps were almost empty. Reinhardt and the others would join the ranks of the demobilised, the aimless.

'Are you trying to tell me something, Captain?'

'Call me David, please.' Reinhardt smiled, but waited. 'I'm going,' Collingridge said, eventually. 'To Berlin. I'm being reassigned.'

'To what?'

'To the Allied Control Council. I'm to work on the law-and-order committee. Something glorified like that.' He spoke of it lightly, yet it was clear to Reinhardt that Collingridge felt it differently. He was a man who saw longer shadows everywhere other than the one he himself threw. And why not, he wondered? There was work, even great work, to do in this Germany. Shadows were everywhere. People cast them. People lived under them. Perhaps this was a

chance for Collingridge to cast a long shadow of his own.

'Good luck to you, David,' said Reinhardt. 'You will do well.'

Collingridge smiled, finished his cigarette with a long, slow draw.

'Think hard about it, Reinhardt. About what you're going to do. It's a tough world out there now. Men like you,' he said, gesturing at Reinhardt and the other Feldjäegers, 'you're not popular. No ex-officer is.'

'Defeat is an orphan. An unloved only child.'

'A redheaded stepchild,' Collingridge quipped.

'As you say,' said Reinhardt, not understanding. 'I have been here before, in a way, David. In 1918. We were not popular then either. Us officers.'

'It's a different world now.'

'I don't doubt it.'

'I mean it's really different. The army no longer exists. In any form. You have no rights, you veterans. The people hate you. The officers most of all. Listen, Reinhardt. You've been a good man to work with. I've appreciated our cooperation. You did good work with us in the prisoner-of-war camps. We wouldn't have solved that case of the Sudeten Germans without your help. What I'm saying is, I can help you. If you want.'

He was, to Reinhardt, a painfully young man, smooth-faced, his hair carefully brushed. A man with many answers, but precious few questions, it sometimes seemed. A lawyer more than a soldier.

'What are you trying to say, David?'

'I'm saying think about Berlin, Reinhardt.'

'Think about the police, you mean?'

'Not only that.'

'But mostly that.' Collingridge looked away a moment, and Reinhardt wondered how much of this was genuine and how much was Collingridge following an order or a suggestion. 'You mean I can be of use to you.'

'Yes.'

'But I can decide what I want.'

Collingridge shrugged. 'Of course.'

'Because I am a free man now,' said Reinhardt.

'Yes.'

But Reinhardt knew otherwise. He could feel the traces coming back on. Different. Seemingly lighter. But traces just the same, and after all, he thought, everyone wore them. It was just they hung heavier on some than on others. And Reinhardt remembered. He remembered 1918. We called ourselves free, then, too, he thought, but freedom was not much use on an empty belly.

Part Two

By His Work Is a Craftsman Known

7

Reinhardt slept a few hours, sleep that did little to refresh him, waking to hear the big clock in the house eating away the hours with every tick. He lay in bed, smoking, letting the smoke dull the taste of too little sleep from his mouth. Downstairs he found Brauer staring outside where Mrs Meissner was pottering around, tending the rows of plants and vegetables that grew thickly along the length of the garden. There was mint tea and honey, which Reinhardt spooned thickly into his mug, relishing the sweetness, feeling more awake for it. Meissner had boiled the eggs, and he ate one slowly with a slice of the ham.

Brauer sat with him, embarrassed, like he always was after nights like that. Reinhardt knew that what had happened at the end of the war was still haunting him. Brauer's wife had been killed in a bombing raid that had injured him, rendering him unfit for front-line service but not unfit for being drafted into the Volksstürm, the citizen army of old men, cripples, and boys that the Nazis had cobbled together at the very end to defend Berlin to the death. The way Brauer told it, he had been given a rocket-propelled grenade and a pistol older than he was, lined up with a dozen other men, then put under the command of a boy in the Hitler Youth and told to go out and hunt Soviet tanks.

'I've caught a case.'

Brauer spluttered into his tea. '*You?*'

Reinhardt smiled, happy for that momentary spark of life in Brauer. He remembered Brauer as so much more than this: a wiry, upright man, a strong but simple sense of right and wrong, but he left soon after Reinhardt came down. Brauer had done something at the end of the war, but he would not say what. It was not that he had survived, nor that he had survived by running away like, as he said, a beaten dog. Reinhardt knew there was more, but Brauer would say nothing, changing the subject instead to ask about Reinhardt's work.

He glanced at the newspaper Mrs Meissner had left on the table, folded open to a story about looted art. A former director of Berlin's Museum of Decorative Arts, Hilde Meissner had resigned in horror at the Nazis' continent-wide theft of artworks. Only her husband's position in the Foreign Ministry had protected her from the repercussions of her resignation, and she now avidly followed news of the attempts to find and restore plundered art. Reinhardt scanned the article, a story about various commissions – French, Belgian, Dutch, Italian, Polish, even a Yugoslavian one – being formed to try and track down what the Nazis had stolen. He read it desultorily, leaving it to stand and watch the old lady at her digging and weeding.

On his way out of the house, Reinhardt paused, then walked quietly into the living room. All its old, heavy furniture was gone, stolen at the end of the war or smashed or broken up for firewood. That deep smell of fine, aged fabric and wood was gone. The fireplace was cold, but he remembered how it had been that last time, before the war. He had sat just *there* on the floor by the fire, and Meissner, his former colonel, had sat just *there* in his leather armchair; that night Reinhardt had finally decided to abandon the police and return to the army.

'Will you go back in?' Meissner had asked.

'I'll do it for you, sir. For nothing else.'

Meissner had sighed softly, then nodded, the fire playing across his white hair. 'Thank you.'

The chair was gone, although his mind's eye could still see it angled towards the fireplace. Tomas Meissner was gone, too. He had not survived the war, he and the other members of his resistance group, swept up by the Gestapo in the aftermath of the July plot against Hitler in 1944. They found out later he had been executed just a day before the Americans would have liberated the prison he was held in.

The warders had executed a dozen men that day. One might have put it down to a paroxysm of violence and vengeance; the last throes of a dying system that simply could not let things go. But no, it was far more mundane than that. It was simply that those prisoners had been scheduled for execution on that day, and so on that day they were executed, and the next day the Americans had come and everything had changed. So sharp and fine are the lines that divide us from one state to another, Reinhardt knew. He made to go, but found Mrs Meissner standing behind him, a pair of gardening gloves in her hand. Her eyes were very calm in the porcelain of her face.

'I remember you and him, in there. You miss him.'

Reinhardt blinked, uncomfortable, so used to the woman's reticence. 'I somehow feel… somehow feel like I failed him. Like I was not there for him. At the end.'

'You must not think that. Tomas loved you,' she said. Her eyes were very calm, but she threaded the gloves through her hands. 'Come and sit with me in the kitchen. Just a moment. We've only talked a little since you came back. You've told me so little of what happened to you.'

'I told you… I told you of Bosnia.'

'Yes. Tomas told me he saw you there. And you have told me of the end.'

'"The end",' Reinhardt snorted. 'My pièce de résistance.'

'Why so cynical, Gregor?'

'I am sorry. It's just… I look at what happened here. I think of what happened everywhere. And I wonder whether what I did amounted to anything.'

'You acted. You fought back. You found respect, and love.' Reinhardt's lips clenched as he shook his head. 'Respect and love in the ranks of the enemy. That is not such a small thing. Why are you back, Gregor?' she asked, suddenly.

'Where else…? What else could I do?' Reinhardt replied, flustered.

'Times change. This is not the place you knew. You could have gone elsewhere.'

'Who I am… what I do… it's what I know.'

'Be someone else. If not for you, for someone else.' Reinhardt frowned, confused, at a loss for what to say. Mrs Meissner seemed to sense it, and she gave a little smile and a shake of her head. 'You know, I am happy you are here. I was happy when you arrived, out of nowhere. You saved me. You and Rudi. I don't think I could have managed another winter alone.'

'You survived the fall of the city well enough,' he interrupted, gently.

'I escaped what happened to most women, yes. But you mustn't feel that you owe me, Gregor.'

'I do. I owe you both. So much.'

'Don't listen to me, Gregor. I'm just an old lady, lost in her dreams and her weeding. And you must go. I shall see you later.'

Outside, even though he knew Brauer would have done it, Reinhardt made a tour of the house to check that the fences and barbed wire he had installed were intact. He'd put them up after the last time Mrs Meissner's vegetable patch had been raided. He thought again about Tomas Meissner's fate.

Life from death.

Good luck from bad.

Friends from enemies.

At Gothaerstrasse, hoping that Berthold might have finished his report, Reinhardt went upstairs to his desk. Late morning, and the squad room was largely empty, much to his relief. Only Weber and Schmidt were there, Weber glancing up from his work as Reinhardt passed across the room. Their gazes slid across each other, no words exchanged, but a latent antagonism was there between them. Berthold's report was waiting for him, as promised, but there was no address for Kessel, the man from whom Noell had been subletting. Reinhardt gathered up the file and made to leave, but as he reached the door, running the gauntlet of Weber's hostility, the detective spoke.

'Off somewhere interesting?'

Reinhardt ignored him.

'Just in case anyone asks. You know. I'm only looking out for you.'

He heard the pair of them laugh as he headed back downstairs. The bodies had been taken to the main police mortuary in the Charité hospital complex on Hannoversche Strasse, in Mitte. But aside from the fact it was in the Soviet Sector, it was a long and sometimes halting journey on the U-Bahn to get there.

The Charité had been badly damaged at the end of the war and, despite extensive repairs by the Soviets, was still not completely functional. Professor Endres ran the police pathology facilities in the morgue. Whereas Reinhardt had jumped before he was pushed out of the police by the Nazis, Endres had clung tenaciously to his position in the medical services until he was fired, and had spent the last two years of the war in a concentration camp following his arrest for allegedly treasonous activities. Liberated by the British, he had turned up back at the mortuary, looking, as one man said, like he belonged on a slab, not standing over one, and wishing to resume work as if nothing had ever happened. With the morgue bombed out and not liking what he saw going on, Endres had made his opinions clear as to what he thought of the new Berlin police force's levels of professionalism, but he had put his heart and soul into getting the facilities back up and functioning, and somehow the new police administration and the Soviets had left him to it. Together with Berthold and a handful of other men, including, Reinhardt liked to sometimes think, himself, Endres had brought a much-needed sense of calm and professionalism back to police work.

'I've been waiting for you, Reinhardt,' Endres said, when Reinhardt found him in his small office below ground, next door to the autopsy facilities. Endres was tall and cadaverous, an impression worsened by his austere black suit and white doctor's overcoat. He had never stood on ceremony and he did not now, rising out from behind his desk. 'I must tell you that your superior has been looking for you.'

'Tanneberger?'

'He called and left a message you were to report to him.'

'When?'

'Momentarily.'

Reinhardt's mouth tightened as he quietly cursed Weber, but he was here now, and he might as well finish, as he said to Endres.

Endres nodded, ushering Reinhardt back down a corridor and into the autopsy room where two bodies lay on tables under bright light. The hospital was a priority for electricity, so the power was usually on, and the refrigeration units still worked, although they had taken a battering during the war and were badly in need of repair and spare parts. Reinhardt recognised Noell and the still unidentified second man, the scars left by the autopsies riding livid up and across the bodies, which seemed strangely sunken in on themselves. Reinhardt shivered, drawing himself tighter, feeling, as he always did, how the air felt colder than it actually was in places like this, and was reminded how much he detested hospitals.

'I should thank you, Reinhardt. This was interesting. The first real case I've had in quite some time.'

'You're most welcome, Professor,' said Reinhardt, not at all flippantly. Endres was infamous for having no sense of humour at all, only a blade-bright understanding of professionalism that time and his experiences had not dulled. Reinhardt shook a couple of Luckies from his packet and offered them to the Professor, who tucked them into the breast of his white coat. 'May I ask a question before you begin? Thank you. The time of death?'

'I would say sometime between midnight and one o'clock in the morning. For both of them. Shall we look at the unidentified body first?' Endres asked. Reinhardt nodded politely, knowing the Professor had not really asked a question. Endres stood at the body's head. Under the harsh light, his scalp shone pinkly through the thin weave of his silver hair. 'Observe,' he said, 'a very serious blow to the sternum. Extremely powerful. Observe further,' pointing to the body's left eye, down across the nose to the collarbone. 'You see the discolouration? It forms a line. Eye, nose, shoulder. A second blow, here, across the throat, that crushed and damaged his cartilage.' Endres's finger pointed to a bruised line of flesh, as if someone had laid an iron bar across the man's throat and pushed.

'Then, his assailant tried to break his neck. He did break it, in fact, except that the spinal cord was not quite severed. Breaking someone's neck is always difficult to do, or in any case, much harder than people think, and in this case the man survived, just. Perhaps it was luck. Perhaps it was because he was incapacitated, and he seemed dead.' Endres spoke in a calm, measured voice, toasted and caked by decades of cigarettes, his eyes steady on the body laid out in front of him. 'In any case, his attacker knew that to break a neck, you do so by whipping it from one side to the other, fast, and applying precise force. You can see the bruising on his jaw, there,' he pointed, 'and there's some discolouration of the scalp on the opposite side. A push, and a pull,' he mimed, his hands coming up, spiderlike, one hand resting on Reinhardt's jaw, the other behind his head. 'Push,' he murmured, tilting Reinhardt's to one side, 'pull,' his hands moving Reinhardt's head back the other way with the slightest of jerks, fingers coming away and spread into the air. 'Done fast. Done precisely. The tissue, muscle, and tendon damage is quite conclusive. His spinal cord was ruptured at the C2 vertebra, up here, then it finally broke in his last fall.'

Reinhardt shivered. Endres had a way of demonstrating his findings on you, and although he had never liked it, it was always instructive. He opened Berthold's file to the photographs showing where they thought the man had lain after being attacked. 'The evidence suggests an attacker who used a lot of force, and knew how to use it.'

'Yes. From the wounds, I suspect the attacker used his forearms to strike.' Endres raised his right arm as if it were a club, and swung it down slowly at Reinhardt's head. The Professor's hand rested lightly on Reinhardt's brow, the length of his forearm along Reinhardt's face. He pushed, lightly, drawing his arm down, his hand rasping softly across Reinhardt's skin. He stepped back, and then mimed swinging his arm back across Reinhardt's throat. 'All blows were extremely forceful and precise. They would have caused severe pain and disorientation, probably even loss of consciousness. He would have been in terrible pain when he awoke. The blow to his sternum would have made it difficult to breath. His neck was broken, his balance would have been off, and his voice box was crushed. He would have been disoriented and confused, so not surprising he fell down the stairs, where the fall finished off what the blows had not.'

'His blood work?'

'It was O positive.'

'The same as the blood found upstairs in Noell's apartment,' said Reinhardt, reading from Berthold's report. He looked up. 'Alcohol level?'

'Low. Certainly not enough to have him falling down the stairs. And no sign of drugs. There was more alcohol on his clothes than in his system.'

'And no sign of defensive wounds?' said Reinhardt, his eyes on the man's jaw, and he shivered again, imagining the killer's hands closing on him. Whoever he had been, he had been a fairly young man, well-built, clean-shaven, and with dark hair cut short.

'None.'

'And the other one?'

'Mr Noell. Yes. Quite interesting. Observe again,' he said, pointing out the huge bruise that purpled Noell's sternum and then the bruising on each arm above the elbows. 'Whoever attacked Noell, it was very fast, and very precise, leaving him no time to defend himself. Whoever did it, again, the person knew how to incapacitate someone fast and efficiently.'

'The same man?'

'In my opinion?' Reinhardt nodded. 'Undoubtedly.'

'Cause of death?'

'Asphyxiation. The signs are clear, around the nose and mouth, a hand clasped tight, fitting like the tightest of lids.' Lifting the back of Noell's head, he showed Reinhardt where the scalp was bruised and bloodied from the head being pressed into the floor by the weight of the assailant, and presumably the victim shaking his head from side to side in a vain attempt to throw the attacker off. The bruising on the arms was from the weight of the assailant bearing down on Noell, holding him to the floor. Both of them were silenced by the mental images this threw up, until Endres cleared his throat. 'But I have not shown you the most interesting thing yet.'

He showed Reinhardt a jar, filled with a cloudy fluid.

'It is water,' Endres said.

'You took it from Noell's lungs,' Reinhardt guessed, remembering what he had seen and felt under his feet as he moved around Noell's head.

'Yes. This,' Endres continued in his elegant, throaty voice, 'would have been poured down Noell's throat while he was still alive. It was ingested into the stomach, and it was in the lungs. The killer held him down to choke and suffocate. To drown, in essence. I would think – indeed, I would hope – that Noell was all but unconscious when it started, due to the blow to his sternum. But the act of suffocating – of drowning – would have roused him, thus the signs of restraint around his mouth, the bruising to the back of the head, and the bruising on the arms. I found bruising to the back of the throat and the oesophagus consistent with something like a funnel being pushed in. Without that, I don't think the killer would have been able to force Noell to ingest as much as he did, and there would have been far more of a mess around the body than you say you found.'

'My God,' Reinhardt murmured. 'So the attack was fast, but his death was not.'

'Most definitely.'

With that, Endres seemed to lapse in on himself. Reinhardt recognised it as a sign he was finished talking. The Professor lit one of the cigarettes Reinhardt had given him, leaning back against the autopsy table with a long, satisfied sigh. Another of his little habits, to smoke when he was finished talking. Reinhardt felt momentarily and absurdly comforted by the gesture, as if it were a firm anchor to the past, to a different, a better, time.

Reinhardt, leaving Endres to smoke, looked from body to body and to Berthold's report. 'Professor, is it just me, or is one of Noell's legs thinner than the other?'

'It is. It's polio, a mild case of it.'

Precision, Reinhardt thought. 'And intimacy,' he said, aloud. Endres turned his head, the light running up and over the thin strands of his hair. 'Apart from the precision of the blows, with Noell there is the intimacy of the act. The killer would have had to have knelt over the body, holding it down, coming close to Noell's face as he suffocated him… Professor, have you ever heard of anything like this?'

'Before the war, never,' Endres answered eventually, his eyes on the tip of his cigarette. 'Since then, anything is possible. The difficulty would be in finding anything in this city anymore that could pass for records. I can check for you, if you would like.'

'I very much would, Professor. I have a feeling that something similar has indeed happened, but I cannot seem to remember what, or when. Or even where. There is one last thing. This photograph was found at the scene. Balled up and thrown down the back of a sofa. It looks like the victim. Like Noell. Wearing what I think's an air force uniform. The rest, I can't make out…'

Reinhardt offered the file to Endres, who leant over to look, and something strange happened. The cigarette stopped halfway to his mouth, and he did not breathe for a long moment. 'You found this at Noell's apartment?'

Reinhardt nodded. Endres looked at Noell's body, then slowly put the cigarette in his mouth and finished it in one long drag.

'Berthold's report says Noell's prints were on it, as were others. Not his,' Reinhardt said, gesturing at the other body. 'Do you know what it is?'

'No, but that is a man in the water, inside that… thing. That suit.' Endres looked at the photograph a long moment, his eyes roving to Noell's body, then lit another cigarette. 'There were rumours in the camps,' he said, finally, 'of things done during the war. Terrible things. To prisoners. Rumours of human experimentation. I never saw anything like the rumours, so I don't know if they were true or not, but I believe them, nonetheless. If only half of what we hear, and what the Allies tell us, is true, then anything could have happened. And probably did,' he finished. He looked away, taking another deep draw of his cigarette.

'How would one follow up on this?' Reinhardt asked.

Endres shook his head, breathing smoke up and away. 'You could try the Berlin Document Center,' he said, referring to the location where the Allies had stored all the Nazi party and SS materials they had captured at the end of the war. 'That photograph shows something that looks like it could have been linked to party-sanctioned activities. Legal, then, illegal now. But they don't let just anyone into the Center. However,' he said, pausing, his mouth moving. 'I think I know someone who might be able to help. Give me a day or so, will you?'

An attendant put his head into the room. 'Professor, there is someone…'

'Not now, Gerd.'

'Yes, now, Professor.' Ganz pushed his way into the room, a second man on his heels. Ganz's eyes fixed Reinhardt where he stood. 'You. Did you or did you not receive messages we were looking for you?'

'Only recently. From the Professor,' Reinhardt answered, hating the tone and wishing the words back as soon as he had said them.

'Who is that?' Endres asked, pointing at the man who had come in with Ganz. He was a compact man in a dark overcoat belted around his waist, a head of black, closely cropped hair runnelled with grey. He walked with a rolling limp to stand over the body of Noell, then over to the unidentified man, tilting his head to look down at him. The man's mouth twisted, then he nodded at Ganz.

'Professor, your records for these autopsies. Reinhardt, you are coming with me back to Gothaerstrasse.'

'What is going on, Ganz?' Endres demanded.

'Nothing to concern you, Professor. Reinhardt, if you've quite finished playing forensics, you've got friends waiting,' said Ganz, his eyes narrowing at the other man, who was still looking at the body of the man found on the stairs. 'The Allies have arrived.'

8

The Allies in question had a car, a big American vehicle with seats as wide and deep as a sofa. A British sergeant drove, the other man sitting in the front, Reinhardt in the back with Ganz. No one spoke all the way back to the station, and Reinhardt was content enough to sit and be driven, watching Berlin unfurl in front of him. The driver sped down Luisenstrasse, then through Pariser Platz and under the Brandenburg Gate, past the Soviet sentries, skirting the eastern edge of the Tiergarten Park, which, devoid of its trees and with its vast expanse turned over to cultivation, looked profoundly wrong. They swung across and through the blasted acreage of Potsdamer Platz, round the swirling edges of the permanent black market, and then the driver floored it down Potsdamer Strasse, and finally back to the station in Schöneberg.

They followed Ganz up to the chief's office, which occupied a corner of one of Gothaerstrasse's upper floors, in one of the building's corner turrets looking across the road to the Magistrates' Court. It was spartan in terms of decoration – just a desk, a pair of chairs in front of it, an old table for conferences, nothing on the walls – and it usually gave a sense of space, but not when Reinhardt stepped into it followed closely by Ganz and the other man.

Tanneberger sat near one end of the conference table, Ganz taking the place to his right. The other man took a seat on the side that ran down the wall, where another man was already sitting. He placed Berthold's and Endres's files in front of him. Between the two of them sat a young woman with a purse on her lap, the lines of her body and clothes severe, straight, all seeming to rise up to the point at the back of her head where her hair was tightly bound back. A third man was sitting with his back to him, but Reinhardt knew him anyway from the roundness of his shoulders to the brilliantined sheen of his hair.

Two other men made up the group. Walter Neumann, Schöneberg's chief of police, and Bruno Bliemeister, the sector assistant chief. Neumann was a grizzled old copper, a no-nonsense character who had walked a beat in Weimar Berlin and had been a bit of a living legend when Reinhardt was a young detective. Bliemeister was a political appointee, one of four assistants the Allies had imposed upon Margraff – upon the Soviets, if truth be told – during the big reform of the police in October 1946, the same reform that had brought Reinhardt back. The assistants were supposed to stay out of operational police work, but they did have a responsibility to keep an eye on issues of potential concern to the Allied sector commanders. The pair of them, Bliemeister and Neumann, had been dredged up out of the pre-Nazi past where the Allies went looking for anyone perceived to be uncorrupted or untainted. If Bliemeister was here, whatever this was that Reinhardt had been called to was political, or had the potential to be.

'Reinhardt, at last,' Tanneberger barked. 'Sit there, please,' he pointed at the end of the table. The supplicant's place, all eyes focused upon him. 'These gentlemen have been waiting to speak with you.'

'No harm, no foul, Councillor,' the man with his back to Reinhardt drawled, his German heavily accented. He turned and flashed a smile at Reinhardt, his teeth very white and even, as the woman whispered a translation to the two other men. 'The inspector and myself are old friends.'

'That's right, you and Mr Collingridge know each other,' said Tanneberger. Ganz said nothing, his chin sunk on his chest as he stared at Reinhardt. If Collingridge noted anything in the mood of the Germans, he ignored it, carrying on brightly.

'I'm just here as a courtesy, purely a courtesy,' smiled Collingridge.

'And as a liaison,' murmured Ganz, his head still sunk low.

Bliemeister said nothing, his face stiff. He looked, to Reinhardt, like a stenographer in a court. Right in the middle of it all, but detached.

'That, too, seeing as the bodies were found in the US Sector. Inspector Reinhardt, these are two esteemed colleagues from the British authorities.' Collingridge smiled at them, his hand coming palm up towards the man who had already been waiting for them when they arrived.

'Harry Whelan,' he said, around a slight cough, as if he were uncomfortable. He was a middle-aged man, hefty and round in a tweed suit, his cheeks flushed high over a tightly knotted tie, banded in what Reinhardt took to be regimental colours.

'James Markworth,' the third man introduced himself, looking up from the files. He sat very still with his eyes steady and narrow on Reinhardt, before dropping them back down to his reading. His eyes were peculiarly hard, like chips of stone or coloured glass. His skin was quite tight across his face and his hands hard-edged where they lay next to the files. Markworth's right hand was rippled with scars along the outer edge, from the tip of his little finger to where his sleeve began, as if his hand had been held to a fire.

'A pleasure, gentlemen,' said Reinhardt. He had only a vague idea of what was going on. 'What exactly is it you do in the Occupation authorities?'

As the woman translated, Markworth's head came up from the files, his eyes heavy, a deep glitter of consideration in them.

'I work for the British representative on the Public Security Committee of the Allied Control Council in the Kammergericht,' answered Whelan through the translator, referring to the old Prussian Supreme Court building where the council met.

Reinhardt's eyes flicked to Markworth, who was still looking back at him, and there was a different cast to them, as if he challenged Reinhardt to question what Whelan had said. 'Are we to wait for a French and Soviet representative as well?' he asked, somewhat disingenuously. He watched Bliemeister as he said it, but the old man showed no reaction, even as Neumann's jaw clenched at Reinhardt's insolence and Tanneberger coloured. Collingridge chuckled.

'Gentlemen,' Neumann said, his voice deep and scratchy, 'I do apologise for keeping you waiting while we searched for Inspector Reinhardt.'

'That's quite all right. I understand you have the investigation into those murders last night, Inspector,' said Whelan. His translator kept her eyes on the table as she talked, keeping very still. Whelan glanced at Markworth, who nodded, his eyes leaving Reinhardt finally to go back to the files. 'What you do not know is that the man you have not identified was, in fact, a British officer. His name was David Carlsen. And it is something of an embarrassment that he was found where he was, and the way he was.'

There was a silence around the table, the Germans looking at one another. Reinhardt waited for any of them to say something, for Tanneberger or Ganz to say something, but they all remained silent, seemingly content to wait on Reinhardt.

'Before I ask why it might be embarrassing,' he said, after a moment, 'may I ask how you found out about this?'

'Well, that would be us, Reinhardt,' said Collingridge as he laid a silver cigarette case and lighter on the table. He flipped the lid open and offered it round. 'Our MPs had their own photos, and your police department also circulated information throughout the city. Our MPs talked to the Royal Military Police, and they figured out pretty quick that one of your stiffs was Carlsen.'

'And he is British?' asked Reinhardt.

'Yes,' said Whelan.

'Is there a "yes, but" in there, somewhere?'

'Reinhardt!' Neumann snapped. The translator twitched at the noise, sitting up straighter as she talked quietly.

'It's quite all right, Chief,' said Whelan, a placatory hand raised, but Markworth's head came up from the files again, and this time his eyes stayed focused on Reinhardt. 'No, there is no "yes, but," Inspector. Carlsen worked for us in the Occupation authorities. He was a military lawyer. Rather a good one, worked very hard, but had a bit of a weakness for the bottle, and the ladies, you see. They sort of went to his head.' He paused.

'All that freedom and responsibility,' said Reinhardt.

'Quite. All that. I shall have to write to his father. Poor chap,' Whelan said again, although if he was referring to Carlsen or Carlsen's father was not clear.

'Bottles and women?' prompted Reinhardt into the short pause.

'Why do I get the sense you are being rather flippant about this, Inspector?'

It was Markworth who spoke, and his voice was a bit like the way he moved: restrained, but with a coiled impression of energy behind it. Markworth's eyes were very hard now, and Reinhardt knew them for judging eyes, eyes that measured him, people like him, Germans, and found them wanting every time. He stared back, stared past, through Markworth, his mind working over the fact that Markworth had spoken before the translator had.

'Indeed,' spluttered Neumann. 'Please accept my apologies.'

'No, it's quite all right,' said Whelan, for the third time. The eternally apologising Englishman, Reinhardt thought, distantly, as he struggled to push back the weight of Markworth's eyes. The woman, confused, translated hesitantly, her words falling out into silence.

Whelan gave his little cough, shifted in his chair. 'So we'd like to help you with your inquiries, Chief. Councillor,' he said, his eyes moving between Neumann and Tanneberger.

'We appreciate that,' said Tanneberger.

'Very much so,' said Reinhardt. 'Perhaps I can start by asking why Carlsen was in the apartment of the other victim. Mr Noell?'

'I can give you no clue as to why he was there, but he most probably wasn't,' said Markworth, firmly, closing the files, glancing at the translator for a moment. He took a sheet of paper from his coat and his eyes hesitated across the Germans, not knowing to whom it should go. He handed it to Bliemeister, eventually. The elderly man, who still had not said a word, handed it silently to Neumann. The chief glanced at it before handing it to Tanneberger, as if he wanted nothing to do with it. 'That is a signed statement by one Rosa Gieb, a prostitute, given to our military police, who swears Carlsen was with her on Sunday night, until well past midnight.'

'What about the blood? In the apartment?' interrupted Reinhardt, then bit his tongue as he realised he had spoken before the translator, and had revealed he had at least some English.

'A smear of blood is no proof of anything, least of all that it was Carlsen's. Your Professor Endres only confirms it was the same blood type.' If Markworth had noted Reinhardt's lapse, he paid it no attention. He had a very different manner to Whelan's, a kind of blunt efficiency about his speech and movements that cut straight to the point and came clearly through the translator's words. 'Mrs Gieb stated that when Carlsen left her, he was rather drunk. For Carlsen, that meant not very much. The man could not hold his alcohol. Endres confirms there was some in his system. Gieb claims he got into an altercation with another customer at a bar they had a habit of frequenting, that he was insulting. The last the prostitute saw, Carlsen was arguing with this man.'

'And you think…?' prompted Reinhardt.

Markworth moved slightly, his hard-edged hands folding over each other atop the files. 'I think, Inspector, that Carlsen got himself into trouble. The kind that leaves you beaten to death on a flight of stairs.'

'Where was this bar?'

Markworth named a bar on a street a few blocks away from where Carlsen's body was found.

'That's a bit off the beaten track for an Allied officer,' said Reinhardt.

'I rather think that was the point, Inspector,' said Whelan, a faint blush to his cheeks.

'Discretion,' murmured Bliemeister. His first words. Whelan gave him a tight smile of thanks as Neumann's jaw clenched hard.

Reinhardt ignored them.

'How did he get where he was found?'

'I have no idea, Inspector,' said Markworth, quietly, the translator echoing him quietly. 'That would be your job. To find out. Maybe Gieb took Carlsen to a room there, or nearby. Maybe the man followed them.'

'Any idea who this "man" is?'

Markworth's eyes narrowed, as if he heard Reinhardt's emphasis of the words. 'Ask Mrs Gieb. But judging from what she does and where she does it, what she told me, and what we know of circumstances in this city, we suspect the man was either one of her regulars, or a pimp, or a member of a criminal gang engaged in protection or extortion.'

'Has she said as much herself?' Reinhardt egged Markworth on, sensing Neumann winding himself up.

'No. Probably because she is too scared, or too cautious.'

'So protect her.'

'That would be your job.'

'And you feel Mrs Gieb is familiar with criminal gangs?'

'She's a prostitute.'

'Your point being?'

'It's all about tact, gentlemen,' Whelan intervened. 'Just a little tact.' He gave a small wince of a smile at the translator, who gave a small wince of a smile back. 'Carlsen was a bit of a wild card. The poor chap just needed to work off steam from time to time.'

'And he was allowed to do it on German women,' Reinhardt interjected, Collingridge snorting out a cloud of smoke.

'*Reinhardt!* For the *last* time,' snapped Neumann, but Ganz's head came up, and he looked carefully at Reinhardt.

Whelan's expression was now distinctly distasteful as he looked at Reinhardt. 'We're rather keen to avoid any embarrassment, you see. Yes, Carlsen had a habit of drinking, and… well, yes, he liked the ladies.'

'He's talking about fraternisation, Reinhardt,' supplied Collingridge, grinning from behind a cloud of smoke.

'Precisely. Well, yes,' muttered Whelan, another glance at the translator. The eternally embarrassed Englishman, Reinhardt added in his mind. 'Allied personnel are not encouraged to fraternise with German women, and Carlsen knew that. Added to which he occupied a sensitive position.'

'You can say that again,' murmured Collingridge, stubbing out his cigarette.

Whelan blushed as the American sniggered at his own double entendre. Markworth seemed unmoved, and he had not shifted the weight of his gaze from Reinhardt. 'The description of this man offered by the prostitute is, I will admit, somewhat anodyne, but you are free to interrogate the prostitute yourselves. Her name and address are on the statement, as is the address of the bar they were at.'

'Are you giving us orders?'

There was a silence around the table, broken finally by Whelan as he leaned forward to speak with Bliemeister and Neumann. 'I regret if this appears peremptory, but the British demand the German police's attention to this case. A British officer has been killed and although we do not suspect it is political, what we do not want is a great deal of publicity. We want efficiency and transparency. Consider it a test of your new credentials as a police force worthy of this new Germany. We will not interfere and will render what assistance we can, but we will require regular reports, and close liaison. Mr Markworth, here, will be our point of contact, and you are required to keep us informed of any further developments that might cast new light on Carlsen's death.'

'The Americans would also appreciate being kept informed,' drawled Collingridge into the sudden silence, sweeping his cigarettes and lighter off the tabletop. 'Seeing as these bodies have popped up in our sector, you understand.'

'That is quite acceptable, of course,' said Bliemeister, but his eyes flickered at Neumann, as if checking or asking permission. Ganz, though, had his eyes fixed on Reinhardt, and what was that in them? Permission? Encouragement…?

'Why is it acceptable, sir?' asked Reinhardt.

'What?'

'Why are the German police doing the Allies' work for them?'

'Reinhardt…' snapped Tanneberger.

'Are they going to want to know about Noell's death as well? I presume not, seeing as Noell and Carlsen never met, according to them.'

'This Noell's death is of no particular concern to the British authorities,' said Whelan.

'Germans should do whatever's asked of them,' grated Markworth over Neumann's squawk of protest, 'and be thankful they are not living in the Soviet Zone.' That coiled energy in Markworth's voice licked out, just a little, and its touch was caustic. The British rose to their feet, Whelan shrugging his arms into an expensive-looking, fawn-coloured gabardine overcoat. 'Although, I'll be honest,' said Markworth, as if only he and Reinhardt were in the room. 'There's some bite in your bark, Inspector. It makes it a pleasure from working with the other spineless wonders who call themselves men in this city.'

Bliemeister and Neumann followed them out. At the door, Neumann turned, his jaw clenched tight and his eyes fixed and hard on Tanneberger. 'Him,' he said, pointing at Reinhardt. 'Sort him out.'

9

Tanneberger closed the doors and swung on Reinhardt, his face suffused with his anger.

'Reinhardt, I swear to God, I will have your badge if you do that again.'

'Do what?'

'What? *What?* Embarrass me like that, you idiot.'

'That was not my intention, sir.'

'What were you trying to do, Reinhardt? Convince us you are not an American stooge? Look good in front of Bliemeister? We all know you are Collingridge's creature.'

'Sir! I…' Reinhardt thought he was inured to this type of accusation, but nevertheless he still seemed to feel its bite as keenly every time.

'Be quiet, Reinhardt. This is not a conversation. I have had my doubts and suspicions for long enough. I have to put up with you, and that's bad enough. I don't have to sit and watch you pretend ignorance about what Collingridge and the Britishers wanted. Well, I'll have no bloody American stooges in this force.'

'As opposed to what? Soviet ones?' snapped Reinhardt. Tanneberger's mouth dropped open and he flushed. 'Exactly what are you accusing me of, here?'

'Of informing the Allies about this investigation. Of bringing them into it.'

'The Allies heard about it through their own channels. You heard them.'

'Please, Reinhardt, do not treat me as if I was born yesterday.

The last thing we need is a politicised investigation.'

'And that's *really* the last thing you can think of that we need?'

'*Inspector* Reinhardt,' Tanneberger spluttered.

'What now, Reinhardt?' Ganz asked.

'I intend to pursue my inquiries into Noell's murder,' Reinhardt answered.

'What about Carlsen? And that prostitute?'

'I will, of course, look into that if you feel it necessary, but perhaps you might assign another officer, as we seem to be faced with two separate investigations. That way, there can be no accusations of collusion on my part.'

He had them there, he realised, watching them glance at each other. Reinhardt wanted this conversation over, wanting at least the chance to get after those British agents.

'Tanneberger,' Ganz murmured, his eyes fixed on Reinhardt. 'I think it would be best for all if Reinhardt was kept off the investigation into Carlsen's murder. I think he can be relied upon to follow up on the death of Noell instead.'

'Do you think so?' Tanneberger replied, apparently eager to grasp the way out offered by Ganz.

'Besides which, I am concerned that if the Carlsen investigation gets rough – which I suspect it will if we have to go digging around in the criminal world – then I will need officers I can rely on fully.'

'Yes. Reinhardt, you focus on Noell,' agreed Tanneberger.

'Thank you, sir, and I am awfully sorry if I embarrassed you,' Reinhardt said, standing up and laying it on thick. If he had had his hat with him, he would have twisted it nervously in front of him, he thought. Anything to augment an image of contriteness that Tanneberger would have related to. 'I apologise unreservedly. May I be dismissed?'

Tanneberger's mouth moved, and he flicked a glance at Ganz.

'Very well,' Ganz said.

Reinhardt took the stairs back down as fast as his knee would let him. Back outside, and the street was dotted with people, figures in dark clothes moving left and right, cars, trucks, a horse-drawn wagon, and no sign of the British, no sign of… *there*. Up towards Grunewaldstrasse. That fawn-coloured coat across Whelan's broad back, next to him Collingridge as they walked down the street, the translator a few steps behind, probably heading back to the Kammergericht. Reinhardt kept well back from them, an elderly couple serving as cover while they walked carefully down the splintered pavement, not sure what he was looking for, nor why he was following them. They stopped next to a Jeep parked next to a shiny black car with British plates. Whelan, Collingridge. Two of them. Where was…?

Reinhardt felt someone watching him, and turned quickly, only spotting Markworth as he stepped out of the shadows of the archway that ran along the front of the Magistrates' Court. Markworth crossed the road slowly, a deliberate rhythm to his steps, as if he were trying to ignore his limp. It was his left leg, Reinhardt saw, that dragged. The two of them stared at each other, both outwardly calm, but Reinhardt felt that crackling energy from Markworth, almost as if it was something personal.

'*What are you doing?*' Markworth asked in English.

'Why pretend you can't speak German?' Reinhardt answered back.

Markworth smiled, a crack across the stone of his face, but said nothing.

'Do you really believe your own story?' Reinhardt continued.

'What's so hard to believe about it?' Markworth answered back.

'Everything.'

'Everything?' Markworth repeated. 'What would you prefer? That perhaps Carlsen fell victim to some nefarious plot? Disgruntled Nazis? Perhaps the Soviets? Something nice and political perhaps?'

'I didn't say that. I just find it hard to believe Carlsen's and Noell's deaths are not linked.'

'No? Ask yourself, then. Are Carlsen's prints in that apartment? Are they on the glasses? Are they on the tap in the kitchen? On the door handle? Anywhere? Well, are they?'

'The pathologist is sure the same man killed them.'

'Or two men trained in the same way.'

Reinhardt floundered a moment. 'It still does not make sense,' he managed, finally. 'A prostitute. An assailant in a bar. Carlsen dead in a stairwell.'

'You did not know Carlsen. I did. He was my friend. He did stupid things.'

Reinhardt felt he wanted to squirm, feeling the ferocity coiled back inside Markworth that the steady level of his gaze could not hide. 'Have you considered that whoever killed Carlsen knew exactly who he was?'

'How so?'

'Carlsen's body had been stripped of all identification. Whoever did it, did it to delay him being identified.'

'And…?'

'You're the one who mentioned criminal gangs. Was he investigating them? Was that his job?'

'Now who's the one complicating things? It's simplicity, isn't it? Isn't that what it often boils down to? A man who realises he's killed a British official, wouldn't he panic? Wouldn't he strip him of his identification?' Markworth's German was slow, somewhat ponderous, as if he considered each word before pronouncing it.

'Had Carlsen been reported missing?'

'What?'

'How did you find out so quickly about his death? Don't tell me the US MPs' photographs moved that fast.'

'Why is that so hard to believe?'

'And even if they did, what are the odds anyone would recognise Carlsen as British? Was anyone looking for him? Had he been reported missing?' Markworth shook his head, frowning. 'He was your friend, you said. Were you looking for him?'

Markworth shook his head, again, moving closer to Reinhardt, the glass chips of his eyes very cold. Reinhardt drew himself in and up, a sudden, reflexive move, as if in the face of sudden danger. 'You're a persistent fucking bull, aren't you?'

10

Then he was gone, a compact man weaving himself into the crowd, leaving Reinhardt behind on the street, perplexed and wondering, Markworth's last word in his mind. *Bull.* Berlin slang for a policeman. Not a word, Reinhardt thought, that a foreigner might pick up easily. And there was something else, maybe something else that Markworth had said, but whatever it was it would not come back to him. *Perhaps later,* he thought, but whatever further thoughts Reinhardt might have given the matter, the rhythm Tanneberger and Ganz had begun to demand of the detectives engulfed him.

The two of them ordered all officers into the briefing room and laid out the situation, ordering Weber out to question the prostitute, and other pairs of detectives and patrolmen to see if anything could be found out about Carlsen's mystery man and possible attacker, and to generally start to shake things up. There were mug shots posted on the corkboard at one end of the room, blurred and grainy images of men with flat faces and hard eyes. Mug shots of criminals, gangsters, pimps, real and suspected, all men who fitted the description given in Mrs Gieb's statement, or who were close enough, or who the police would haul in anyway, given half a chance. Reinhardt was surprised to see one or two faces he recognised from before the war, feeling a sudden disconnect from where he was, back to who he had been. And he again wondered why he seemed to find Noell's death familiar. What was it about it? Where had he heard of something like it…?

He stopped himself from musing overmuch, however, and as Ganz finished reading out the assignments, Reinhardt raised his hand.

'Yes, Reinhardt?' Tanneberger frowned. Heads twisted round on shoulders to look at him, and more than a few grins were cracked. 'You wish to form part of this manhunt, Reinhardt? I thought this was beneath you.'

'I never said…' he began, but Tanneberger interrupted him.

'You are free to concentrate on following up your leads on the murder of Noell. Report to me regularly, especially should you discover links between the two deaths. However, you will understand if the priorities and resources of this division are focused on Carlsen's death.'

In other words, he was on his own, he knew, as the briefing ended and officers and detectives streamed out of the room past him. It was no more than he had asked for from Tanneberger and Ganz, because he wanted to stay focused on Noell and had never had any taste for these roughhouse tactics, the broadsword to his rapier. But to have it rammed down his throat in public was a humiliation he did not need, even though he knew they felt compelled to deliver it. Thankfully, there was a keen edge of excitement in the air, in the crude bursts of speech the men used among themselves, otherwise Reinhardt was sure more fun would have been made of him. It was all somehow depressingly familiar, Reinhardt thought, watching the eager stride of the younger officers.

When the room had emptied, he walked up to the corkboard to look more closely at the mug shots. He read the names, recognising two of them. Both of them had worked for Leadfoot Podolski, one of prewar Berlin's more notorious gangsters, whom Reinhardt had helped arrest. Fischer had been a leg breaker, a man Podolski sent round to storekeepers and bar owners who did not pay their protection money on time. Kappel had been a courier for stolen items, usually small ones, like jewelry and watches. He thought of Podolski, not seeing his photo on the wall and wondering what had become of him, and turned to leave.

Ganz was standing at the briefing room's door, Weber just behind him.

'Something to add, Reinhardt?'

Reinhardt shook his head. 'I remember these two from before the war.'

'And?'

Reinhardt looked at Ganz, remembering. Although both had been violent, Fischer especially, neither had been killers, and although the courier had possessed a certain weasel cunning, neither of them had taken a step without being told when and where to go.

'I don't see either of them beating a man to death like someone did to Carlsen. They weren't like that then. And they were neither of them into pimping.'

'Wars change people, don't they?'

Reinhardt nodded, conceding the point.

'So that's all?' asked Ganz.

'That's all.' Except it was not, but it was only his intuition that told him Carlsen's and Noell's murders were linked.

'Then I haven't much use for you. Do what you want with Noell.'

Ganz's eyes seemed to measure Reinhardt to some cut and cloth that only he knew of, and then he was gone. Weber lingered a moment, a grin sparking across his face before he, too, left.

11

Reinhardt felt Ganz's dismissal eddy across the room, something that sloshed his emotions from side to side and brought a sudden clap of shame to his neck. He breathed deep, surprised he could still feel this way about people he cared little to nothing for, then put it aside, walking back to his desk through the pool of officers and detectives organising themselves to go out into the city, troubled more than ever by the impression he had heard of something like Noell's murder before. Of something like it, and besides, he felt the need to focus and anchor himself. Suspicion from within, derision from without, all this, he realised suddenly, on his first real investigation since rejoining the police back in October 1946.

There was, he knew, more than just a little truth to Tanneberger's accusations about American backing for Reinhardt, and to Ganz's suspicions. And knowing it had been there, that it still was, in a way, made Reinhardt uncomfortable. It was American influence that had got him back in, Collingridge's influence, really, albeit he had come back at a rank lower than the one he used to have. But then, nearly everyone in the police these days owed his position to luck or patronage of some sort, and almost none of them gave it any thought. But Reinhardt had never wanted to be anyone's man, save for those he himself had chosen. There had been Meissner, long ago, his colonel from the first war, a man to whom he had owed his life and with whom he had trusted it. There had been something close to that with Scheller, his commander in the Feldjäegerkorps. There had been almost no one else, no one for him to look up to, to respect, only those who had had power and authority over him.

His habitual introspection, he realised with a start, coming back to himself in the squad room, quieter of a sudden now that most of the officers had left. Introspection, and more than a hint of arrogance, he knew. Most men never had a chance to choose those whom they allowed to have power over them, and most men lived well enough regardless. So why would he think himself any different? Some good old-fashioned, solid paperwork was what was needed – and he thought how long it had been since he had pursued a case through paper and records.

The records were in a parlous state, he knew. So much had been destroyed in the bombing and during the Soviet assault, and the new records were not up to the standard of what had been kept before the war. One of the secretaries showed him to the newspaper archives. She started to leave after pointing him into the room, at stacks of cases and boxes, newspapers, leaflets and magazines heaped and piled on tables and on the floor, all yellow under the weak light. He stopped her, told her what he wanted, and she sighed, beckoning in a couple of her friends while he left her to it.

Back up in the almost empty squad room, he checked the time, then allowed himself a mug of coffee from the urn that someone had refilled, picking up the photograph album from Noell's apartment. The inside cover had a name – Andreas Noell – in a rich hand, and a date – September 1939. The date the war had started. He began to leaf through the photos, slipping one or two out of the folder to see they had notations on the back. Some were simple, like *Paris, 1940*. Some of them were more complex, a series of numbers and letters, along with dates and places. On a couple, he spotted that the notations on the back corresponded to elements of the photographs themselves. In one, a group of officers posed beneath something like a regimental shield, and in another, Noell stood with a pilot in front of a fighter plane with a series of numbers on its tail. The numbers on the shield, and those inscribed on the back of some of the photos corresponded – IV./JG56.

The numbers made no sense to Reinhardt, but he reasoned it might well have been the designation of Noell's former unit. Musing to himself, he wondered who here could make sense of them, or who he knew that might, and in the middle of all that, an elderly woman walked into the squad room, saw Reinhardt, and strode determinedly through the jumble of chairs and desks to plant herself in front of his desk.

'Inspector,' she said firmly, the light glistening along the curves of her iron-grey hair, drawn tightly into a bun at the back of her head.

'Mrs Dommes,' he replied, rising to his feet and inclining his head courteously.

'You've got my girls sorting through old newspapers.'

'That's correct.'

'Did you have authorisation to have them do this?'

'Authorisation, Mrs Dommes?'

'Yes, Inspector. Authorisation. From me. You don't think that's all they needed to do, today, do you?'

Schmidt and Frohnau and a couple of the other younger detectives still in the squad room at an adjacent table paused in what they were doing to watch, grins on their faces.

Reinhardt drew a long, slow breath. Dommes was the redoubtable head of Gothaerstrasse's secretaries and assistants. It did not pay to circumvent her, and Reinhardt had simply forgotten to go through her as he should have done when asking for the records check earlier that day.

'I'm terribly sorry, Mrs Dommes. You are correct, of course. I should have arranged things with you. I simply forgot.'

'You forgot, did you?'

'I did. Shall I accompany you to set things straight?'

Dommes's mouth pursed as she looked back at him, and she seemed to unbend, perhaps mollified by his admission of error. 'No. That is all right. Just see that it does not happen again, Inspector.'

'I will be very sure not to overstep my mark again, Mrs Dommes.'

'Hey, Reinhardt,' said Frohnau in a stage whisper. 'Will you be all right? Do you want some help to take care of things?'

'We're right behind you, Reinhardt!'

Dommes ignored them as she ignored the flush that rose in Reinhardt's face. She came round his side of the desk, flattening a piece of paper on the desk. 'You asked the girls to check the newspapers and police bulletins for the last six months for references to murders or reports of deaths that involve water. Is that right?'

'That is correct. I am interested in cases of asphyxiation that were reported as suspicious, or as sensationalist. But I'm not interested in drownings in lakes or rivers or the like.'

'Across the country?'

'Not limited to Berlin, in any case.'

'You do realise this may take some time?' Reinhardt nodded. 'Very well, then, we'll see what we can find.'

'Well done! You can handle her, Cappie!'

Dommes drew herself up, turning a withering glare on the detectives. *'Gentlemen,'* she snapped. 'You could do worse – far worse – than to emulate the courtesies of a man such as Inspector Reinhardt. Haven't you anything better to be doing?'

'What, like solving a murder?' retorted Schmidt, but the man looked more than a little shamefaced at talking so to a woman who could have been his grandmother.

'Just think,' Reinhardt said to them, pulling on his coat, 'every minute in here, you could be out there canvassing.'

'Don't worry, granddad. We've got plenty of good guys out there.'

'You're right. With you in here, there's a much better chance things don't get screwed up.'

The harsh caw of a crow followed him out of the squad room. He left Gothaerstrasse and made his way back to Noell's apartment, taking the U-Bahn to Kottbusser Tor, then a southbound D line to Schonleinstrasse, from where he walked.

Neukölln had never been the prettiest of Berlin's boroughs, and a combination of Allied bombing and the Soviet ground assault that had rolled over it had done nothing for its looks. It had always been resolutely working class, and before the Nazis came to power, it had been a Communist bastion, so much so that he was often surprised it was now part of the American Sector instead of the Soviet.

He exchanged a few words with the elderly policeman who had been stationed in front of Noell's apartment. All was calm, the policeman reported, only a couple of visitors for Ochs, the superintendent. Upstairs, Reinhardt cracked the police seal, the draft gusting up into his face as he stepped inside Noell's rooms. He stood in the doorway, looking around at the bloodstain on the wall, the bottle on the table, the books, the piled bedding. He walked into the bedroom, putting his head into the kitchen, smelling the faint trace of Berthold's powders. He forced open the window in the living room, looking out and down. There was no fire escape, and the window had had to be wrenched open.

He found himself standing in the middle of the room, his mind drifting back to the police station. To the drive and energy that was passing him by, the solidarity that he was not a part of. He went back into the kitchen. He stood in the doorway, looking into the little alcove. The plates still sat by the sink, next to the glass, and the cloth still hung from the tap. Something was bothering him, though, but he could not put his finger on it. Frowning, hoping whatever it was would come back to him, he went back downstairs and knocked at the apartment under Noell's, then knocked again when there was no answer, calling 'police' through the door. He waited, finally hearing the heavy tread of someone inside, and the door opened on a big man, his hair twisted up and around, and sleep heavy in his eyes.

12

'Mr Uthmann?'

The man nodded, and for someone who worked nights and was woken abruptly, he was civil enough, inviting Reinhardt inside. The apartment was dark and smelled heavy.

'You want to talk about Noell?' Uthmann asked, his mouth turning thickly around his teeth as he worked the sleep out of them. 'I don't know what I can add, really. I didn't know him that well. Knew him by sight, enough to say "hello".'

'Did you ever hear anything from upstairs?'

'You know I work on the trains, right? I'm a track engineer. I mean, when I come home, I sleep, and I'm a heavy sleeper. Not much gets through to me. But when I was up and about, I'd never hear much, if anything, from upstairs. The other night, though, before leaving for work, I heard a fair bit of noise. Sounded like he had company, for once, and I heard him coming home the next day.' That chimed with what others had said, Reinhardt knew, that Noell had had a guest, gone out, and come home early the next morning.

'I hear that you had an argument with Noell on one occasion?'

Uthmann frowned, then nodded. 'The kettle,' he said, gesturing vaguely into the apartment. 'When I come home from work, I like to heat water for washing, and then I boil some for tea. The kettle sometimes whistles before I'm finished cleaning up. The whistle never usually bothered Noell, except once or twice, when he would come downstairs furious, hammering on the door for the noise to stop. He did it just the other day, after the party upstairs.'

'Maybe he had a hangover, and the noise was disturbing to him.'

Uthmann nodded, mouth turning around itself, and he yawned, hugely. 'In any case,' he observed, 'when Noell was angry, he was a changed man. Quite different to his usual self.' Reinhardt indicated for him to go on. 'That's it, really. He was just… changed. Sort of, I don't know. He must have been in a bad way after that party,' Uthmann finished, a small smile on his face.

Reinhardt left him to go back to sleep. Pausing on the landing, he thought a moment, then walked down to the next floor, deciding to canvas the building. He interrupted the ends of meals, doors opening to the flatulent reek of boiling potatoes or cabbage. He saw residual fear at his knocks, too many memories of men in dark coats. He was sent packing in some cases, in others received cordially, in one place even invited in for a drink by a man who looked like he never stopped drinking, and who ventured onto dangerous ground when he began waxing lyrical about the Führer, and how much he had loved the German people and how the German people had let him down. This, as the man sprawled slack-eyed on a sofa with only two legs, and pulled out from under some cushions a portrait of the Führer, his eyes misting over and his words blubbering around whatever emotions moved him.

No one, anywhere in the building, was able to add anything more to what Reinhardt already knew. His last stop was the superintendent's apartment. Ochs answered his knocking eventually. Curled behind his door, he blinked at Reinhardt until recognition filled his eyes after a confused moment.

'Inspector,' he said. 'Back again?'

'Anyone been up in Noell's apartment?'

'What? No one.'

'Are you sure?'

'Yes. I don't know. Not that I saw. But that said, I do remember something, now. About a month ago, maybe a little more, Noell received two visitors. They were both men, and both German, and one of them had a military bearing, sort of "senior officer" type.'

'How would you know what a "senior officer" type looks like?'

'I was in the first war, Inspector. You remember those sorts of things. The man looked down his nose at me, ordered the other one around, who called him "sir".'

'Who was it came to see you earlier today?'

'What? Oh. Just a couple of old friends.'

'Do you remember anything about that man Noell was subletting from?' Ochs blinked at him. 'Kessel?'

'Oh. Yes,' shrugged Ochs, leaning against his doorjamb and breathing heavily. 'Sorry. Nothing. Don't think I ever met the man.'

'The children, living across the street, they say the man found dead on the stairs had come here several times. You're sure you never saw him?'

'I'm sure, Inspector.'

'They said they saw Poles, as well.'

'Poles? I wouldn't put too much faith in what those "children" have to say. Pack of lying and thieving little rats; I wish someone would get rid of them. Can't you do something about them, Inspector?'

Reinhardt looked for the orphans, but their building was empty, no trace of them. He hesitated, intending to make his way back to Gothaerstrasse, but instead he made his way to the bar where Carlsen had supposedly run into trouble. His steps were hesitant, in part because of the stiffness of his knee, but he knew it was more because of the discomfort he felt at all the light and noise. He walked past crowds of people waiting for the irregular public transportation, past a demonstration – mostly women – outside the head offices of the former Nazi welfare organisation, past a gang of 'rubble women' leaning on their shovels and hammers to rest and who wolf whistled as he limped past, some of them so covered in brick dust and grime they resembled statues more than women. Their efforts and their good humour gave him a little lift, and he tipped his hat to them, receiving a flurry of invitations and suggestions in return, one of them flipping up the tails of her grey coat at him in a sweep of dust, before turning her attentions on a man wheeling a little handcart in a zigzag line through the debris-strewn road. Reinhardt smiled as he walked on, but it faded as he thought of what they went through every day.

It was not just the labour, backbreaking as it was. It was not just the risks they took – thankfully, now, the more prosaic risks that came with working in and around damaged buildings, rather than the predatory needs of Soviet soldiers in the initial months of occupation. It was what they found too often down in the rubble. Not a day went by that they still did not unearth bodies – the young and the old, alone, in pairs, sometimes whole families, sometimes whole buildings. Up in Mitte, they were still finding dozens upon dozens of bodies in cellars that had served as air raid shelters and which had been caved in or blocked after the heavy American air raids in February 1945. What these women went through on a day clearing rubble, and then went through with a night of taking care of their families, he had little idea, but they had all the respect he could muster.

He found the bar near the Thielen Bridge, which spanned the grey drift of the Landwehr Canal, little more than a stone's throw from the angle of the American and Soviet Sectors at Lohmühlenplatz. The bar was in the basement of a building that bore its battle scars in scrawls of blackened stonework, and he would have walked past it but for the police handbill on the door, stating that the establishment was closed until further notice. No one answered his knocking, and he was about to leave when he heard someone coughing inside. The door jerked fitfully open to his identification as a police officer, and he stared into the gloom at a man in his middle years, a huge bruise purpling his left eye and another swelling up the side of his mouth.

'Whatchyouwantnow?' he mumbled, glancing at Reinhardt's warrant disc.

'Who did that to you?' Reinhardt asked.

'Fuckinbulls,' he slurred. His words might have been unclear, but there was nothing wrong with the clarity of his eyes. They glittered back at him with suspicion and distrust.

'When were they here?'

The man dropped his head, shook it from side to side. 'Couplevehours… couple of hours ago,' he managed.

'May I come in a moment?'

He said nothing, simply turned back inside. Reinhardt followed him into the bar, into a stink of beer and cigarettes and a floor that stuck underfoot. A mop leaned out of a bucket of water that steamed feebly, and chairs were stacked on tables. The man retrieved a cigarette from an ashtray on the bar and leaned back against it, waiting for Reinhardt.

'This is your place?' The man nodded. 'Pull me a pint, then.' The man hesitated, then went behind the bar. 'Sunday night, were there a couple of Brits in here?'

The man shrugged as he pumped Reinhardt's beer. 'Youshayso.'

'You didn't recognise them? Was there a woman? A prostitute.'

'Lossafuckingprozzies,' the man said, sucking on his cigarette. His face curled in on itself, in frustration, perhaps.

'Her name's Gieb. And speak up, for God's sake.'

'*You* try fuckinspeakin' with a gob fulla brokenfuckinglass.' He slammed Reinhardt's pint on the bar top, beer slopping down the glass's sides. 'Like I told the *others*,' he said, making an exaggerated effort with his words. 'Shecamein… she came *in*, she sat *down*… with this one bloke. With this one bloke…'

'They came together?' The barman nodded. 'Describe him.'

The man sighed, taking a pull on his cigarette. 'Look, like I told the *other* fuckin' bulls, I didn't get a good look at him. Sat with his back… his back to me. Dark-haired. Good coat. Chunky. Biggish, y'know?' he said, puffing out his chest and shoulders. Reinhardt nodded at him to go on. 'He kept his hat on and his back to me. The prozzie bought the beers. They talked… talked a bit. The bloke was a bit drunk. Got drunker. They talked more. He began shoutin'… Some others told him to shurrup. He got upset. Picked a couple of arguments. Picked on a couple of lads who, you know… likely looking lads,' the barman said, gesturing with his cigarette. 'Looked like local thugs. Boys into a bitathisanda… and a bit of that,' he finished, wincing at the pain in his mouth. 'They took it outside. S'all I know.'

'Just an average night in Neukölln.' The barman nodded, ruefully. Reinhardt took a sip of his beer. It was flat and tepid. 'Anyone else see anything?'

'People keep their 'eads down at times like that. Y'know?'

'The prostitute. What did she do? When the trouble started.'

'Nuffin'. Just sat there, smokin'.'

'Describe her.'

The barman sighed. 'Blond. Ratty-lookin'. Like a... like a used rug. Man's got to be desperate to go with a bit of tail like that.'

'You knew her?' The man nodded. 'Where did she live?' The man shrugged. 'What about the two men? Did you recognise them? Seen them before?' The barman shook his head. 'What time was this?'

The man shrugged, glancing at his wrists. 'No watch. No clock. I was knackered. I think it was early morning. I was thinkin' of closin' up. Tha'sall. Look, I'm done in, and I want my bed. You going to pay for that beer?'

'All right, then. What do you want for it?'

'Give me a cigarette, and we'll call it evens.'

Reinhardt allowed a sardonic glint into his eyes as he took a Lucky from his pocket and laid it on the bar top. 'So, a man comes into your bar with a woman you think was a prostitute. You don't get a good look at him. You don't know what time it was.'

'What I said.'

Reinhardt broke the cigarette in two, rolling one half across the bar top.

'You ain't got nuffin' bigger, 'ave you?' the man sneered.

'This man seemed drunk. He picked a fight with who you think were a couple of local thugs. They take it outside. That's it. Did I miss anything?'

'No,' glowered the barman. 'But just be careful the door don't smack you on your fat 'ead as you leave.'

13

Outside Gothaerstrasse, he could tell the other officers had been busy. Policemen lounged up and down the pavement, knots of them clustered in the bare park opposite, many of them smoking, all of them with the eager spring and step of men who were excited, or who had recently come away from something exciting. Gestures were elaborate, voices a little too loud, laughter a little too raucous. Some of the younger detectives laughed and pointed at Reinhardt as he limped past them.

'Captain Crow! You missed all the fun!'

Gothaerstrasse was as on edge inside as it was on the street outside. As Reinhardt walked in, a squad of uniformed officers were manhandling a group of suspects towards the cells on the ground floor. A pair of policemen hauled the all-but-dead weight of a suspect, and Reinhardt saw blood blossom across the white tiles, dripping from the man's head, which hung and wobbled down against his chest. He watched the drops flare across the white tiles, then watched them blurred thin as the man's feet trailed through them, a signpost or sigil towards or from an unknown place.

Going upstairs, Reinhardt pushed past a handful of what could only be lawyers arguing loudly with one of the police administration's legal officers. Policemen clattered up and down, secretaries shouted loudly into telephones, and in the squad room, detectives interrogated surly-looking men who had that air of long suffering, of abused victimhood, that Reinhardt had learned to recognise as a gangster's stock-in-trade. A few of them glanced at him as he made his way through the chaos and fug of cigarette smoke to his desk, and one of them was one of the men whose mug shots he had recognised. Fischer. Podolski's leg breaker. The man's eyes caught his, one of them shining through a purpling welt of skin around his eye socket, and both of them felt recognition catch and flare before the man looked away, back to his interrogator.

'You've had some luck, then?' Reinhardt said, quietly, to the detective at the desk next to his.

The man was not one of the younger ones. He was a Nazi-era holdover, a quiet man who kept his head down, a survivor. The man looked up from a book of mug shots, smoke curling up into his eyes from his cigarette. 'You could say that. They've got that prozzie – Gieb? – upstairs,' he said. 'And they think they've got a lead on the man she fingered. The one who did the beating on Carlsen.'

'Got a name for this man?'

'Stresemann, I think. I'd never heard of him. I'm going through old books now. See if I can find anything.'

'What's with the dragnet, then?'

The detective lifted his head, looking dully across the squad room as he took a long pull on his cigarette before dropping it into a mug of half-drunk coffee, where it hissed briefly. 'Usual suspects. Way things are done. Killing two birds with one stone. Settling old scores. Take your pick. I don't know. Ask someone who gives a shit.'

'Where's the woman, did you say?'

The detective gestured with his head upstairs. 'Tanneberger's offices, I think.'

Reinhardt tried to concentrate on his notes, bringing his evidence, as well as Endres's and Berthold's reports, together. Noell had been an air force pilot, he had been a quiet and courteous man on most occasions, who kept very much to himself, but he could be distant and brusque, even rude, at times. And for a man who kept to himself, he had had quite a few visitors in recent weeks. Two Germans, according to Ochs, the mystery man who had died on the stairs, and the man or men with whom he had celebrated something or other a few days previously. He thought over the barman's story, trying to piece in where what he said he saw fitted the facts as Reinhardt was starting to understand them.

There was too much noise, too much excitement. He could not work, and he was about to pack it in, make his way home, when there was a sudden silence and he looked up. Coming down the stairs were Weber with Schmidt and Frohnau, and with them was a woman. She was young, with a drawn face in which a pair of huge, darkened eyes glittered out at the squad room. The silence seemed to shrink her down into her coat, into the frayed wisps of its fake fur collar, and Reinhardt was moving before the first of the suspects rose to his feet and stabbed his finger at her.

'Fucking bitch!' he yelled. 'Was it you? Was it *you?*'

Walking quickly past him, Reinhardt shoved him back down into his seat, but two other men had lurched to their feet, chairs skidding backwards.

'I'll fuckin' *find* you, you fuckin' '*hore*!' another man screamed.

'Get her out of here,' Reinhardt shouted at Weber, who seemed frozen on the steps. 'Get her out of here!' None of them moved, and Reinhardt bunched his fist into Weber's jacket and yanked him towards the squad room, where pandemonium had erupted, arms and fists flying, the police interrogators trying to get a hold of the situation. 'Sort it out in there. Quickly.' He reached past Schmidt and Frohnau and took hold of Gieb's arm. 'With me, miss. Come with me. *Move,* Weber!'

He urged her down the steps, pulling her into the crook of his arm. Past the backs of the detectives as they fanned out into the squad room, he saw Fischer sitting quite still, just watching. He felt how thin she was beneath the coat, how rigidly she held herself against him, but she did nothing to stop him hurrying her down to the lobby. The bones of her face were stark as if they strained against the constraint of her skin.

'You'll be all right now,' he said, as he stood her in a sheltered corner of the lobby. A group of riot police ran across it and clattered upstairs. 'Cigarette? Have one of these,' he said, offering her a Lucky.

'Thank you,' she managed, but her hands were trembling too much to light it, and so he did it for her, taking her hand in one of his to steady it. 'Thank you,' she said again. She took a pull on the cigarette, a quick peck of her lips, then seemed to let it burn unsmoked. Her lips twitched slightly, her lower lip seeming to rub against her teeth, and she seemed to give little twitches, as if startled by something, but something that only she could hear. She was very pale, as if her heart were rationing her blood.

'We'll have you out of here soon,' Reinhardt said, listening to the racket from upstairs, to the shouting and cursing.

'What?' Her eyes blinked fast. 'Oh. Yes. Thank you.' Her eyes drifted away, again, then she pinched them shut, her brow furrowing. She rubbed her fingertips hard against the wrinkled skin of her forehead, then pushed them through her straggle of thin, dirty blonde hair. She blinked, and the light in her eyes seemed to fall back and in, as if her mind had fallen behind the camber of her gaze.

He looked at her carefully. 'This can't be easy, Mrs Gieb. It was brave of you to come in.'

'What?' she said, again. She seemed to remember the cigarette, and took another quick drag. 'Yes, well…' She yawned, suddenly, a wide gape of her mouth, scrubbing at her hair, curling it back over one ear, and he saw what he thought was a webwork of scars that seamed her scalp.

'Well, what?' Reinhardt prompted her after a moment.

'It was the right thing to do, wasn't it?' She blinked at him, her lower lip rubbing against her teeth. The movement triggered some kind of reflex in him, and he caught himself stroking the gap in his teeth with his tongue, and he clenched his jaw tight. Maybe she noticed something because her eyes seemed to suddenly clear, and she looked at him, actually *looked* at him. '*You* all right?'

Reinhardt managed a smile. 'Shouldn't it be me asking you that?'

'What d'you mean?' she asked, suspiciously.

'Nothing. Did you know Carlsen well?'

'Carlsen?' she managed, her brow furrowing.

'The man they brought you here to talk about.'

'The one that was murdered?' Her eyes glittered up from within dark circles. 'No, I didn't know him that well. He was…' she yawned, again, hugely, showing gaps in her teeth. Then it was as if her mind tripped, fell sideways.

'Mrs Gieb?' he asked, after a moment.

She blinked. 'He was a client. Not even a very regular one. He preferred to talk.'

'Who is Stresemann?'

'Who?'

'The man they're looking for. The one you described in your statement.'

'Oh.' Her face firmed up, and she took a long breath. 'He's a pig, is what he is.'

'How do you know him?'

She stared at him, and there was a flash in her eyes, deep down, far back. 'He was always hanging around me. Wanted to be my pimp.'

'Who is your pimp?'

'Don't have one. Look after myself.'

'How did the British find you?'

'Find me?' Reinhardt nodded.

'Reinhardt!' He turned, seeing Ganz and Weber coming down the stairs, Ganz leaning heavily on the banister as he came down. 'What are you doing with her?'

'She's fine, Ganz, you'll be glad to hear. No thanks to that nincompoop there,' he said, pointing at Weber.

'Yes, well, we'll take it from here. I'm sure Detective Weber is grateful for your assistance.'

Weber said nothing, only reaching past Reinhardt to take Gieb's shoulder. Reinhardt watched her hunch into herself again, but she moved without protest. From upstairs there came a subdued rumble of voices.

'That was all rather careless, not to say needless,' Reinhardt said, watching Gieb as she stood by the door, while Weber talked with a pair of uniformed officers. From where it jutted out from between her fingers, the cigarette spiralled smoke up her arm. Ganz said nothing, only breathing quite heavily after coming down the stairs so fast, and Reinhardt was reminded that Ganz was not a young man, far from it. 'I hear she gave you a name?'

'Man called Stresemann. Walter Stresemann. We've got a few things on him. Extortion, pimping. Suspected armed robbery. We're looking into him now.' Ganz looked at him. 'Ring any bells with you?'

'None,' replied Reinhardt. 'What's her story?'

'Her? Nothing special.'

'You sure?' Ganz said nothing, just looked at him. 'She's distressed about something. I'd put good money on her being a concentration camp survivor.'

'Oh?' asked Weber, coming back. 'And why's that?'

'I think she's suffering from headaches. She's got a problem paying attention. She's missing half her teeth. Her head's been shaved, repeatedly and harshly. Her coat's covered in her hair, meaning it's coming out…'

'Yeah, she's a bit bloody mangy,' Weber interrupted, grinning.

'… and she doesn't protest or resist being manhandled. Not even by you.' Weber flushed, his face hardening. 'She lets her cigarettes burn down to her fingers, and she doesn't notice. I saw the scarring on her fingers, and she's doing it now,' Reinhardt said, pointing to where Gieb stood. He was stung by Weber's attitude. He knew he was saying too much, maybe even showing off, but he did not care. The Lucky Reinhardt had given her had vanished between her fingers, but he could see where it still smoked. 'She's been doing it a while, judging from the state of her fingers. That's a dissociative sign, and that's a complicated word, Weber. More than two syllables.'

'Oh, sod off, Captain bloody Crow.'

Ganz was watching Gieb with a new set to his gaze, light glittering on the sweat that sheened his head. 'What's any of that got to do with concentration camp survivors?'

'Before I was demobilised from the Feldjäegers, when the Americans still had us, I saw a lot of people released from Dachau. I talked to a lot of doctors who treated them. Those were some of the things they described about the survivors.'

'So it's anecdotal, not conclusive. Half of Germany's malnourished.'

Reinhardt shrugged, not interested in arguing, but unable to prevent a tug of frustration at what he saw as Ganz's disinterest. He turned to go back upstairs, then paused. 'Back in the day, we used to call what she's got "shell shock". She stinks of it. The only time she came alive was when I talked to her about Stresemann. I'd place odds he reminded her of someone. If I'm right about her, you might want to check any records you've got for a Stresemann who worked in prison administration, or maybe in a camp. And from her accent, I'm guessing she's a DP from somewhere east. Where most of the camps were. Who did you send down to that bar to rough the owner up?'

Ganz blinked. 'Weber. And a couple of uniforms.'

'Reinhardt, are you saying you went *yourself?*' interjected Weber, almost interrupting Ganz. 'What for? You're not on that case. It's my case,' said Weber.

'It was nearby. I was at Noell's place.'

'And? Get anything useful?' asked Ganz, ignoring Weber.

'No.' Ganz raised his eyebrows. 'The barman's evidence is vague enough to fit just about any story. He saw a man, with a woman, and the man caused trouble with some other men. End of story.'

Weber shook his head. 'Well, thank fucking God we've got you to set us straight, Reinhardt. Christ knows how we managed without you all these years.'

Reinhardt walked past them, back upstairs to collect his belongings, gathering his notes and reports together and locking them into his desk. The squad room was much quieter, most of the disturbance quelled. He felt eyes on him, looked up to see Podolski's henchman – Fischer – staring at him from where he sat handcuffed to a chair. In the harsh lights of the squad room, his face was sheened with a patina of scar tissue along the ridges of his cheekbones and the blunt prow of his forehead. He was looking straight at Reinhardt.

'I know you,' Fischer said. 'I know you from before. You were the one what put Mr Podolski away, wasn't you?'

Reinhardt nodded slowly. 'What can I do for you, Mr Fischer?'

'You remember me. I was sure you did. Couldn't think why those coppers came for me today, unless you fingered me to them. Did you put them on to me?' Reinhardt shook his head. 'Then what'd they want with me?'

'What did they tell you?'

'Like you don't know. You were always a slippery one, Reinhardt. That's what Mr Podolski always said.' Fischer seemed very calm, resigned even.

'And how is Leadfoot these days?'

'Don't be calling him Leadfoot. He never liked it.

'My apologies. How is Mr Podolski?'

'He's dead. Prison done for him. He went and caught tuberculosis inside.'

'I'm sorry to hear that.'

'What do all these coppers want with me?' Fischer's colour was rising, and his breathing with it.

'I don't know, Fischer. They probably wanted to talk to you.'

'Call what they did talking? I'll give you something for free, Reinhardt. With you, back then, it was all talk. None of that rough stuff. Very savvy, you were. Very smooth. He thought you was a gentleman, did Mr Podolski. No hard feelings when you got him. But I saw you with that woman. She's the one behind all this. What you drag me in it for?'

'I didn't, Fischer,' said Reinhardt, holding his eyes.

An elderly policeman poked his head into the squad room, breathing heavily. Reinhardt glanced up at him, the standoff with Fischer breaking like a rope that snapped.

'You're Reinhardt?' The elderly officer paused for breath. 'We've been trying to get through on the lines for a couple of hours, but no luck.'

'There's been some excitement, as you can see. What can I do for you?'

The officer nodded. 'I've a message from Detective Lorenz, at the Zehlendorf CID branch. He thinks he's found another one.'

'Another one?'

'Like the body you found. Another one.'

14

Reinhardt hitched a ride with the morgue's ambulance again, all the way out to an apartment building in Wilmersdorf, in the US Sector. The body had been found at an address not dissimilar to where Noell's body had been found, a building with a pocked façade of exposed brickwork within rosettes of chipped plaster. There was a policeman waiting outside who escorted Reinhardt up through a darkened and hushed building, past the worried and curious gazes of residents, up several flights of stairs right to the top, to a narrow landing just under the roof. There was a second uniformed officer standing outside a door, together with a younger man in plainclothes.

'Detective Lorenz, you're Reinhardt? I've heard of you. All good, don't worry,' the young man said with a flash of a smile. Reinhardt glanced at the uniformed officers, a pair of middle-aged men with imperturbable expressions on their faces. 'I read the briefing summary from earlier today that was circulated, the one about last night's murders.'

'What do you have, Lorenz?'

'It's a man named Conrad Zuleger.'

'There were identity papers?'

'Yes.'

'Show me.' Lorenz handed Reinhardt a Berlin identity card, a work permit, and a ration card. 'Go on.'

'According to the building's super, Zuleger hadn't been seen in a few days. He was usually out and about, and usually dropped in on the super for a drink. The super decided to check on him as he had not been seen since Friday.'

'That was the last time anyone saw him?'

'Yes.'

That was the night before Noell and his friend had gone somewhere, it seemed, to celebrate something.

'Anything else?'

'Strange men in the neighbourhood?' Lorenz grinned. 'One of the tenants says he saw someone he'd never seen before on the Friday evening.'

'Have the Americans been informed?'

'Yes. We notified the MPs. They've been and gone. They're happy to leave it to us.'

'Go on,' Reinhardt said again.

'The super opened the room, and then… well. Why don't you see for yourself?'

Reinhardt raised an eyebrow at Lorenz, then shrugged. 'Lead on, then.'

Lorenz pushed open one of the doors and stepped back for Reinhardt, who walked into a garret, a small apartment right under the roof, and into a stench like a wall. Despite himself, despite what he knew was coming, he stopped, but refused to recoil or to gag, only shoving his tongue hard against the roof of his mouth and breathing shallowly around it.

The smell found him long before he saw what made it. The company emerged from the woods, picking its cautious way through the widening spaces between the trees where the forest began to peter out. The sun shone down through the branches in splintered columns; light daubed vividly across the greenery, across fronds and branches that waved and snapped in the wake of the men's passing.

Up ahead, the ranks were bunching up, men coming to a stop, craning over the heads and shoulders of those in front of them. A murmuring ran through the column, the whispered susurration of voices pitched low. A man ahead dropped to his knees. Another doubled over and vomited.

'It had to happen sometime,' a grizzled old sergeant muttered, as if to himself. He raised his voice. 'Welcome to the butcher's yard, lads. Come on boys, move it on. Be thankful t'ain't you. It's only Russkies. Come on, boys. By your leave, sir, you too.'

Reinhardt had not realised he had stopped. His head felt as if it had swelled up, the strap of his helmet like an assassin's garrote beneath his chin. The field ahead was mazed with bodies, gunned and shelled, a tangled spread of limbs, strewn like rag dolls left by an impatient child... Reinhardt's mind stammered across the field. There were no words for it. There were no words for what he saw. Bodies in repose, as if they lay in sleep. Bodies in pieces. Bodies with their rumps in the air, faces ground into the dirt. Flesh blackened and swelled, bloated through and around the constriction of belts and clothing, buttons and belts burst asunder.

But, dear God, the stench. It had stolen up on him, all but unannounced. His nostrils flared wide at the fetid ripeness of it, as if to welcome it, even as his mind shied back like a startled horse. It entered him, lying thickly across his mouth, papering his tongue, a patina of rot. He wanted to recoil from the presence of the dead in the air, but could not. He was rooted to the spot as his body rippled with its kinship, its connection, on a level he had not known existed, with the remnants of men out across the field.

This, too, his body seemed to be saying to him. This, too, you will come to be.

He blinked, and the memory was gone. The smell of the dead. He had almost forgotten what it was like, he realised, surveying the angles of the room. Yet once he had lived among it in the trenches, and not more than two years ago, it had been a commonplace part of his life. He had only ever found two ways to deal with it. You could try to ignore it, but it would find a way of coming back at you when you least expected or needed it, or you could just accept it, make it part of who you were and where you were.

Before going any farther in, he noted the key in the lock, and that the door and doorjamb were undamaged. Whoever had come in, he had not forced his way in, just like at Noell's. The apartment was little more than one room, with two tall windows, both of them open and framed in folds of tattered curtains billowing from the wind, both of them giving onto the façade opposite, and down onto the street, several floors below. There was a bed, a table, a cupboard, and a small kitchen in a little alcove, smaller than the one at Noell's. The body lay spread-eagled on the bed, there being no room on the floor or anywhere else for it, and it had the ghastly aspect of a body well into decomposition, the skin beginning to slump back from the bone beneath.

'What made you call it in?'

If Lorenz had wanted to make or prove some kind of point by sending Reinhardt in first, perhaps to see how he might react, he himself did not have the same wherewithal. The detective had a handkerchief clasped tight to his face, his voice coming muffled through it.

'Three things.' Lorenz pointed at the body, at the shirt open down the front. A huge bruise purpled Zuleger's torso. He pointed again, at Zuleger's wrist. 'Ligature marks. He was held down.' Lorenz paused, gagging. 'Cupboard, there,' he managed, before bolting over to the windows.

The stench was pinching hard at the back of Reinhardt's throat as he opened the cupboard, looking at a Luftwaffe uniform hanging from one of the doors. Checking the pockets, he found a *Wehrpass*, flicking it open to see Zuleger's photograph inside. The clothes in the cupboard were old, prewar quality. In a box on the floor of the cupboard, he found a collection of women's clothing, carefully folded, a set of hairbrushes, and a framed photograph of Zuleger and a woman, taken on what looked like their wedding day. Reinhardt looked at it a moment, then put the picture back and carefully closed the box, pushing it back into the cupboard.

The smell clawed its way that little bit farther down his throat, cramping hard at his guts. He felt his bile rise, fought it, mastered it, and walked to the table, which, he saw, was more of a writing desk. There were books and newspapers stacked along the side against the wall, and a folder with dozens of sheets of loose paper. He leafed through the top ones, pausing as he spotted something. Some kind of manifesto, outlining the grievances of veteran soldiers in postwar Germany. Beneath it there was more, some of it printed, some of it handwritten: pamphlets and notices, and what looked like minutes from a meeting.

From the windows, he heard Lorenz coughing, and the stench was starting to get to him as well, but he picked up the file, forcing himself to walk slowly round the bedroom. Zuleger was in pyjamas, and the bedclothes were folded back underneath his body. A dressing gown was draped across the end of the bed. All so very normal and comfortable, but the slippers lay tumbled into the middle of the room, as if they had fallen or been kicked off.

'Did you check the body?'

Lorenz looked over his shoulder, shook his head, his brows creasing. 'What do you mean?'

The body's skin was ghostly white, the bruise on the sternum mottled and disfiguring across the bloated swell of the torso. Gritting himself and steeling his nerves, Reinhardt opened Zuleger's mouth, pushing his finger in, imagining, feeling even, through the leather of his glove, the cold and clammy skin of the corpse. Something, he felt… something that rasped, a faint feeling of roughness, something that should not be there… but the body, disturbed, gave off a sudden, dreadful burst of flatulence. Lorenz gaped, gagged, and ran from the room, even Reinhardt reeled away and stumbled to the window, leaning out to breathe deep of the fresh air. In the space of time between one heaving intake and another, something twitched down on the darkened street, a glimpse – a sense, rather – of paleness that flashed away, as if someone had been looking up and suddenly looked away.

Reinhardt looked at his finger. A bobbled smear of viscous fluids coated the glove, but studded within it were flecks and clumps of what looked like dust or sand. He took a deep breath of fresh air, held it as he walked quickly back through the room and into the corridor, closing the door behind him.

'You again, Reinhardt?' Berthold came stumping up the stairs, filling the space with his rotund bulk, a pair of stretcher bearers just behind. 'What is it this time?'

'Same thing, it would seem.'

'You got my report on the other one?' Reinhardt nodded. 'There were plenty of Noell's prints all over the rooms. There were other prints, too, but without records worth the name, they're useless for comparison.'

'Right. Room's all yours, Berthold. Be warned. He's ripe.'

'Ripe, is he?' Berthold said with some relish as he pulled on a pair of gloves. 'Let's have a look, then.'

One of the uniformed officers pulled the door shut on the forensics technician, his face blanching at the smell. The stretcher bearers stood their poles into a corner of the landing and made themselves comfortable with cigarettes.

'The canvassing report, Lorenz?' Reinhardt asked, as he peeled off his gloves, folding the one he had put inside Zuleger's mouth inside out. 'What do you have?'

'Zuleger had been living here about a year. He was quite well known to everyone,' he reported, 'and seems to have been a decent man, a good neighbour, putting up shelves for one family, unblocking another's plumbing. The apartments to either side of his: one's empty, the occupant's away, the other is an old widow. A bit hard of hearing, but she knew him quite well and she's waiting for you downstairs. Zuleger had a job at a metalworks,' he continued, glancing at his notes. Reinhardt noted down the address, in Charlottenburg-Nord in the British Sector. 'According to his neighbours, he was quite outspoken in his opinions as to the state of Germany's veterans. Apparently he would get into arguments very often with others in the building over it, especially with the widow and a disabled veteran. He's also waiting for you downstairs. Other than that one tenant, no one saw or heard anything suspicious these last two or three days. No one on the stairs, no sounds of arguments. Nothing.'

The widow and veteran were, as Lorenz had promised, waiting for him in the superintendent's small set of rooms. The widow was well into her sixties, and the veteran missing his lower left leg; otherwise they were a pair of forgettable-looking people. Forgettable in so far as Germany's present-day population made them. Both of them repeated the impression of Zuleger as a good neighbour, a kind enough and considerate man but, the widow said, when he had had a few drinks, he opened up a lot more.

'And *theeeen*, he would go on and *oooon* about the *bloody* war, about the army and the humiliations that officers in particular had to put up with.'

'Zuleger was an officer?'

'He was a proper Emil,' said the veteran, using the army slang for pilots. 'Always going on about it. Looping the loop, round and round the clouds like a carousel,' he muttered.

'You?' asked Reinhardt, flicking open Zuleger's *Wehrpass*.

'Infantry. Sergeant in the engineers.'

'You said you saw someone on Friday?'

The veteran shrugged. 'I was coming out of the bog. There's a toilet on the second floor. I came out and walked into this bloke. Never seen him before. Opened the door right into him. There was one of them moments, you know, when you want to get past someone. You both go the same way, you both go back the other way. You grin, you apologise. So he stops, looks right at me, then says, "What's the password, mate?"'

'"What's the password?"' Reinhardt repeated. Then he understood.

'Latrine passwords,' said the veteran. The super and the widow looked on blankly. The veteran grinned. 'Gossip. The kind soldiers would exchange on the thunderbeam.'

'He means on the toilet,' explained Reinhardt.

'You served, did you? Where was that then?'

'What did you say?' asked Reinhardt, ignoring the question.

'I said, "No gossip, just the aches and the runs." Like we always had, right?'

'Then?'

'I lean on the wall for him to go past, and I'm hopping, see, 'cos of my leg, I didn't have it on, and he sees it, and says, "You're proper K.v.h, mate." That was it. He went past me and upstairs.'

K.v.h, thought Reinhardt. It was army slang. It meant 'fit for use in war at home,' but soldiers used it as a pun for 'can convincingly hobble.' For a shirker or a malingerer. The Feldjäegers had used it a lot, he remembered, towards the end, when the front was coming apart and men scattered every which way they could, going anywhere, doing anything to get away. The Feldjäegers would catch them, or stop them. Turn and herd them back.

'Kvh is it? Pull the other one. And it's back you go.'

'You reckon he was an old hare, then?' Reinhardt asked. Something clicked inside. Something to do with hobbling, but he had no idea what, or why.

'He was a veteran, yes.'

By itself, it did not mean much. Most German men were veterans of one war or another. Reinhardt and this ex-sergeant were. Zuleger was another. His *Wehrpass* had him demobilised as a lieutenant in the air force, released from a POW camp in December 1945, near Bremen. 'Describe this man.'

'Not tall. Sort of square. Blocky. Couldn't see much of his face, it was dark, and he had a flat cap. Like a worker would wear. He had a moustache and quite a bit of stubble, like he hadn't shaved much.'

'His accent?'

'Berlin. No doubt.'

'Zuleger had been here a year, you said to the detective?' Reinhardt asked the superintendent.

'About a year, I'd say. Bit less. He said he was released from a POW camp sometime at the end of '45. Came back to Berlin.'

'His *Wehrpass* says he lived in Treptow.'

'I think he mentioned that, yes,' said the superintendent. 'I know it was somewhere in the Soviet Sector for sure.'

'Why would he come back to Berlin?' Reinhardt wondered, half to himself.

'Man's got to come back to somewhere, hasn't he?' muttered the sergeant, half to himself as well.

'He told me he had family here,' the superintendent said. 'A wife. But I think she died in the winter of '45, '46. He didn't talk about her much. Their old place in Treptow had been destroyed during the war, and when she died, wherever they were living, the city authorities must have considered it too big for one man. He can't have been priority for housing. He was a veteran, and he wasn't injured. So they moved him out and put him up there, in that garret. But he was a fairly upbeat fellow. Never let things get him down, except the death of his wife. He'd get all maudlin about that. And he found work, at last, a few months ago.'

'The detective said you and he would drink sometimes.' The superintendent nodded. 'Did he talk about the war? Did you hear the same things from Zuleger?'

'That and more.' The superintendent's mouth worked. 'Look, Zuleger, he was a good enough bloke. He took care of people. Helped out. But we differed on all that wartime stuff. Far as I can tell, and far as I'm concerned, there was an officer clique who helped Hitler take power, who maintained him there, and who then lost the bloody war. Zuleger was emblematic of that clique, obsessed with the wrongs done him and the rights he was owed. He was a good enough bloke, but he wasn't half-obsessed with how bad he thought he had it.'

The superintendent nodded to himself as he finished, folding his arms across his chest as if to hold himself back from more. It sounded trite, somehow formulaic. It sounded like some of the propaganda you would hear the Soviets expounding, that filled the pages of the East Berlin press. Like most propaganda, there was enough truth in it to make its messages stick, but Reinhardt knew there was more than just enough truth in it. The widow nodded vigorously at what the superintendent said, the former sergeant a bit less so, but both were keen to assure Reinhardt they had nothing to do with his death, and no idea who might have done it. Reinhardt heard them out, then left, glad that none of the other detectives were there to offer any pithy remarks about the officer class.

And then whatever it was that had clicked inside clicked again, and became clear. Hobbling. K.v.h. The old army joke. Can convincingly hobble. Noell had had polio. He had had it as a child. So how did he ever pass the fitness requirements to join the armed forces, let alone as a pilot, and rise to the rank of colonel…?

15

Mrs Dommes found him as he trudged wearily up the stairs, and he followed her to the archives where two other secretaries sat exhausted on boxes, their faces sheened with a veneer of dust.

'We think we found something, Inspector,' Dommes said proudly, although from the veiled glances the younger secretaries gave her, and from the impeccable lines of her grey hair, Dommes had had little to do with it. 'Greta, please tell the inspector what you found.'

One of the secretaries held out a newspaper, folded open to an article. The paper was from Hamburg, from January of that year, and described the death of a man a few days previously, a death that had baffled police. The case was being referred to, as Reinhardt saw with some excitement, as that of 'The Man Who Drowned on Dry Land.'

'Hope that's what you need. 'Cos it took forever to find it.'

'Greta,' snapped Dommes. 'Your manners, young lady.'

Reinhardt scanned the article quickly, before looking up at the secretaries. 'Was there anything else? Anything similar?'

'Nothing we could find,' said the other one. 'These here are follow-on articles, from the same paper. The last one's from February.' She handed over a pile of maybe a dozen newspapers.

'Very good,' Reinhardt breathed. 'Very good. Ladies, you have my thanks for all your work. Let me assure you, it was not wasted. If you would allow me,' he said, reaching into his pocket, 'I should like to offer you a little something for your efforts, on me.'

'*Tush*, Inspector! No need for that. They were just doing their jobs. Ladies, you heard the inspector. Such courtesy is rare enough in these days.'

'Yes, Mrs Dommes,' they both said, rising to their feet.

'Mrs Dommes. Perhaps I might ask another favour, if I might escort you to your office?'

He allowed Dommes to precede him out before slipping a few Occupation marks onto one of the boxes by the door, as well as a few Luckies, giving the two secretaries an outrageously exaggerated wink and miming lifting a glass as he left, and seeing the quick flashes of their smiles.

'Now, Mrs Dommes,' he said, as they walked to her office. 'I note in these articles that there is an inspector in the Hamburg police who was leading this investigation, an Inspector Lassen. Do you think your services might try to track him down and arrange a telephone call with him? Perhaps as early as tomorrow morning?'

'Oh, I should think so, Inspector,' Dommes said severely, already considering the challenges of trying to place a telephone call across occupied Germany, and probably dismissing most of them. 'For tomorrow morning, at nine o'clock?'

'Perfect, Mrs Dommes. Perfect.'

Upstairs, Reinhardt added the materials he had found in Zuleger's apartment to the papers and emerging report on Noell's murder. He leafed through the pile and, as the widow and the veteran had indicated, it was made up mostly of all sorts of literature on the situation of Germany's veterans, but one particular paper caught his eye. It resembled the one he had found at Noell's. He spread them out side by side. They were the same, although Zuleger's was in far better condition, Noell's having been found in the waste bin. 'RITTERFELD ASSOCIATION' headed both pages, and he could see from Zuleger's that it was an agenda, or something similar to one, with a number of items laid out. 'The situation of our veterans' was followed by 'Legal status in the various Occupation Zones', 'Pride in the uniform', 'Lessons from captivity', 'The value of solidarity', and other similar items.

Wherever it was and whatever it was, there was neither location nor date.

For the rest of it, there were newspaper articles and clippings, photographs, op-ed columns, obituaries, letters to editors, classified advertisements, all outlining in various details the plight of individual veterans and their families. Many of the obituaries were for suicides, even if the word itself was never used, the implication being that these men had no longer been able to bear their lives. Although, thought Reinhardt with more than a touch of cynicism, that may have had as much to do with what they had done during the war as with what they had been reduced to after it.

The last item he found was an invitation to an event, some sort of gathering on Saturday. That would have made it a day after the estimated time of Zuleger's death, which he and Berthold had estimated at three days ago, based on the state of the body and the last time anyone had seen him. Endres would give them a more exact time, but not before tomorrow. If they were right, the event would have been around the right time for Noell, who witnesses said had gone out in good spirits, and returned in even better in the early hours of the following morning, on Sunday, and who had been murdered sometime that day.

The invitation was to somewhere in Grunewald, and the host was a Mrs Frankewitz. A lady, probably, some kind of matron or dowager, if he was any judge of the type of people still living there in what was – or what used to be, he corrected himself, sardonically – a very well-heeled part of town, an oasis of sylvan calm and tranquillity. Not quite the sort of address one would expect a man who lived in a place such as Zuleger's to have, or to be invited to.

He put a call through to one of the police stations in Grunewald, to the one he thought closest to the address he had found at Zuleger's. While he waited to be connected to the duty officer, he took a closer look at Zuleger's *Wehrpass*. An air force officer, as the building's witnesses had said. A Lieutenant. In a fighter squadron designated IV./JG56. He frowned at the numbers, before digging Noell's file out of his desk, and flipping open the photo album. To the group photograph, the one of pilots posing in front of a regimental shield, and to another, a photograph of Noell in front of the tail of an aircraft.

The same designation.

IV./JG56.

He dug through the other photos, finding the group shot, but he could not spot Zuleger. He might have been staring back at Reinhardt, but the faces would not coalesce for him.

The Grunewald station's duty officer's voice distracted him a moment. He gave the man Mrs Frankewitz's address and asked for a patrol to be sent to check it tomorrow morning. The duty officer's voice was terse and no-nonsense as he acknowledged the request, and Reinhardt hung up, distracted, thinking of Zuleger's uniform, glancing at the pamphlets, wondering if it had all been for some kind of event. Possible, but unlikely, he thought almost straight away. The wearing of uniforms was forbidden. If there had been any gathering at which uniforms had been worn, it would have been one hell of a risk. In any of Berlin's occupied sectors. No, he thought, the uniform was probably some form of reminiscence.

It was late, the daylight flushed from the sky, and Reinhardt was exhausted. His leg ached fiercely, and he found he was light-headed with hunger. With his head on his hands as he closed his eyes a moment, he realised he had had nothing to eat since leaving the house. He put Zuleger's papers aside, and flipped through the newspapers the secretaries had found, selecting the one with the article that seemed most comprehensive, and folded it into the pocket of his coat. Flipping his hat onto his head, he headed downstairs and out into the evening chill in search of something to eat. As he pushed through the doors he fancied he heard someone calling his name back upstairs, but he ignored it, too interested in finding food, and finding it in one of the little beer halls that catered to the police trade in the roads around and behind Gothaerstrasse.

He followed two uniformed officers down a couple of steps into a darkened restaurant, the air damp and fugged with cigarette smoke and the smell of beer, bare brick walls glossed with condensation, and tables made from a variety of flat wooden surfaces, most of which seemed to have been doors. It was all but empty, though, which suited Reinhardt just fine as he pulled out a tall stool at a table near a window. He hung his coat over the back of a chair, and put his cigarettes, matches, and his baton on the table.

'Hey there, darling,' one of the uniformed officers greeted the waitress with a lazy reach of his arm. 'I'm so hungry I could eat a rat.'

'You've come to the right place, then,' the waitress shot back. The two policemen guffawed, and even Reinhardt's mouth twitched. 'There's potato soup and black bread,' she said to all three of them.

'A couple of beers to go with it,' the officers said. They glanced at Reinhardt a moment, then turned away, leaving him alone, and Reinhardt put them out of his mind, smoking and waiting until his soup and beer came, and then unfolding the newspaper, and the mystery of a man who had drowned on dry land. The body of Emil Haber had been found at his house on the fifth of January, dead in his living room. The body bore the signs of having been beaten, and police were baffled at considerable traces of water in Haber's lungs. Haber was described as a valued member of the community, a pharmacist, and there was only a small mention of his wartime service as – and Reinhardt paused with his spoon halfway to his mouth – an air force researcher.

'Hey, darling,' the same officer called, 'I think there's a cockroach in my soup.'

'So, what do you want,' the barman called back, 'a funeral?'

Reinhardt stayed in the beer hall after he had finished his soup, smoking another cigarette slowly and nursing his beer. He looked out through the moisture on the window at the darkened lines of the city, looking without seeing at the dart and rush of droplets as they pearled down the glass, and he was looking through it…

... through the glass of a train compartment as it idled at a platform in a small Belgian town. Outside, out on the edges of the night, the pitch of the sky bent and fractured to a rhythm that jumped and flickered and danced across the horizon. The compartment was dense with the breath and stench of men cast where exhaustion had discarded them, but he watched that far-off bombardment, mesmerised. They had warned him about the Western Front, and he watched as if the welds to a world beyond had warped, jagged fissures that offered staccato glimpses into furnace brightness, like the pulse of creation. Like the fires of a new world, lying just beyond this one.

The sound of the door opening behind him did not make him move, but the sight of the barman momentarily stopping what he was doing caught his attention, and he turned to look over his shoulder to see Fischer standing in the doorway.

'Them coppers messed up my place, roughed up my wife, had me down the cells half the day. What for?'

'I don't know, Fischer. I told you.' A quick glance showed him the other police officers were gone. The bar was empty.

'No trouble, gents,' the barman called. 'If it's trouble you want, take it outside, now.'

Neither of them paid him any attention.

'Embarrassing my wife. Smacking me around. Making me out to be some murderer.'

'I told them you weren't a killer. Are you going to prove me wrong now?'

'I'll just have to do your legs,' Fischer said, as he pulled an iron bar out of his coat, 'Just like the old days, seeing as you brought them back and all.' Reinhardt jerked his chair in front of him, and flicked his baton out. Fischer smiled. 'Been a long time since I seen one of them. Be sure you know how to use it, now.'

The door opened again, and Markworth stepped inside.

'*A problem, Reinhardt?*' he asked. In English. He looked very calm, eyes firmly on Fischer.

'No problem,' answered Reinhardt, in the same language, surprised his voice was steady. 'Mr Fischer here was just leaving,' he said, switching back to German.

'I fucking wasn't,' Fischer growled, but he had backed away.

'Yes, you are,' smiled Markworth, stepping aside from the door, his left leg dragging. 'Out. Otherwise it'll get nasty in here. I think you're in enough trouble as it is without adding assaulting an Allied officer to your list of woes.'

'You cozying up to the Allies, now, Reinhardt?' Fischer snarled, but Reinhardt knew it was just bluster.

'Take your friends where you can find them, I say,' quipped Markworth, a steady glint in his eyes as he stared at Fischer.

'Another time, Reinhardt,' Fischer said, as he angled himself past Markworth, then out into the dark. The Englishman peered out into the night a moment before coming back inside and closing the door.

'Well, well… playing rough, are we?' he asked, a little smile on his face.

'What are you doing here?' Reinhardt asked, collapsing his baton.

'Following you. What is that you've got there?'

'An old police baton. Why are you following me?'

'To talk.' The compact man stepped slowly into the bar, his eyes scanning left and right as he limped over to Reinhardt's table. 'About Carlsen's investigation. I called you back at the station as you were leaving, but I don't think you heard me. They told me this was the only place likely to be open, so here I am. Lucky for you, eh? May I see it? The baton?'

'Why do you want to talk to me about Carlsen's investigation?'

'Because I've the funniest notion you're the only one in Gothaerstrasse, in fact in this whole bloody excuse for a police force, with a brain.' Markworth flicked the baton out, slashed it through the air, watching its bend and flex. 'Would you like another drink?'

'No, thank you. Who says I'm the best brain?'

'Would you like a *proper* drink?'

'No. Thank you.'

'Come on! Come and have a *molle*. I know somewhere not too far away where they still brew a good one. Almost prewar quality, if you can believe it.'

'Another time.'

'All right.' Markworth gave him back the baton, raised his hands in acquiescence, the light slick on the scars on his right hand. 'Just talk to me then.'

'I can't. I don't know much about Carlsen's investigation, because I'm not on it,' he said, to Markworth's raised eyebrows.

'Their best brain, and you're not on the main inquiry?' Markworth's face had flattened, though his voice was still light. 'What are you on?'

'I'm on Noell's. Who says I'm the best brain?' Reinhardt asked, again.

'Noell? They've got you on *Noell*?'

'Someone has to be. Who have you been talking to, Mr Markworth?'

'Well, yes, but…' Markworth tailed off, the light of his eyes very dark. 'Talking to? Collingridge,' he said, distantly and dismissively.

'If that's all, I should get going.' Reinhardt gathered up his things, shrugged back into his coat.

'Yes. Yes, of course,' said Markworth, coming back to life. 'I'll walk with you part of the way. If you don't mind. Maybe your friend will show up again.'

Out in the dark and the chill, there was almost no light, just enough from the moon to pull the street's cobbles from the dark, and the sound of their footsteps seemed to fall away. Reinhardt looked around but it was hard to see very far. Fischer could have been feet away, or streets away, it was impossible to tell, and for a moment he felt absurdly comforted by Markworth's presence. The man exuded calm, a kind of rocklike stability, like some of the men Reinhardt had known in the Feldjäegers. Even his limp seemed inconsequential.

'So you know nothing about the Carlsen investigation?' Markworth asked.

'I know they found the prostitute, and questioned her. And they've been bringing suspects in all day.'

'Any closer to finding the man she described?'

'Yes, I believe so, but I'd rather you spoke with Tanneberger or Ganz. They're the ones leading the investigation.'

'Wouldn't you rather be on the Carlsen case?' Markworth asked, a plaintive note in his voice, as if he sincerely could not understand why he was not. 'Want me to have a word?'

'That's your prerogative, Mr Markworth,' Reinhardt said, equivocating, and uncomfortable discussing internal issues with an outsider. 'I'm going that way,' he said. 'So I wish you a pleasant evening.'

But even then, it was not over. As Markworth walked away back towards the police station, as Reinhardt made his way to the tram stop, a small voice came out of the dark.

'Hey. Bull.'

Reinhardt peered into the shadows where a wall had tumbled in on itself. 'Leena?'

'Yes,' said the orphan girl. He could hardly see her. 'You said to come to you if anything happened.'

'What's the matter?'

'Someone came to the building today. Someone we hadn't seen in a long time. Someone called Kausch. He used to live there. He used to live where Noell lived.'

'You mean Kessel?'

'No. Kausch. We're sure. We've seen him before, and we don't like him. We don't like the look of him. Or his friends. We never did. They chased us. They caught one of the boys, once, and beat him bad.' Reinhardt stayed quiet, listening to the girl's voice as it came low and steady out of the dark. 'This Kausch, he had a word with Ochs. Him and one of his friends. They roughed him up. Scared him half to death. We listened. And we followed them when they left. They went to Plantagenstrasse, up in Wedding in the French Sector. They went into a building half in ruins. We watched it for a bit. Other men went in and out. And there was a man watching the street from the rooftop. We thought you'd want to know.'

'Thank you, Leena. That was very brave of you.'

'It's nothing. We never liked him. He reminds us of the bad old days.'

'What do you mean?'

'He should be wearing black, bull. That's what it means.'

16

Tuesday

Reinhardt's phone call to Hamburg went through at nine o'clock, on the dot. He did not know how Dommes had arranged it, but there it was, a miracle of organisation and determination. He sat in the exchange in a small booth with the receiver pressed to his ear, listening to the hustle and bustle of a distant office. There was a clatter, a heave of breath, and then a voice came on the line.

'This is Lassen.'

'Inspector Lassen, good morning, my name is Gregor Reinhardt. I'm a detective with Kripo in Berlin.'

'Good to speak with you. You want to talk about Haber, right?' The man had a thick Hamburg accent.

'Yes, that's right.'

'Why, may I ask?'

'First, may I ask you a couple of questions? To make sure I'm on the right track?'

'Fine, go ahead.'

'Thank you. Can you tell me, what was the condition of Haber's body when you found him?'

'Pretty nasty, yes. I remember. He'd been dead about, oh, three or four days.'

'He was found in his living room?'

'Yes.'

'Did anything strike you about the way the body had been left?'

'No, not really. Not that I can remember.'

'There was an autopsy?'

'Yes. It determined death by asphyxiation. There was water poured down his throat. Whoever killed him incapacitated him first, and then the water literally drowned him.'

'Water? You're sure?'

There was a silence on the line. *'Pretty sure. He drowned. At least that was the coroner's findings.'*

'How was he incapacitated?'

'A severe blow to the sternum, as I recall. And he was tied down. The autopsy was a bit of a mess, as the body was pretty far gone when we found it.'

'Did anyone ever come forward as a witness?'

'No. Never. He lived alone, worked in a pharmacy. Kept himself to himself, mostly. I remember, he had a dog. He was often seen walking it. It was the dog barking that led to the body being found.'

'Did you ever arrest anyone, or suspect someone?'

'No. No one. The case was a complete mystery. No evidence at the crime scene. No suspicious individuals. No threats. No problems at work. No money problems. Nothing. No leads at all.'

'What about his service history?'

'What about it?'

'Haber was former air force.'

'Yes. He was a medical doctor.'

'Any leads there?'

There was a silence on the line. *'No,'* Lassen said, finally. *'I can't say we followed up with that.'*

'Do you know where he served?'

'I don't. Look, your turn. What's going on?'

'I've found two bodies in Berlin. They were killed in similar ways to Haber.'

'Jesus. Go on. What links them?'

'Both bodies showed signs of having been severely beaten. Incapacitating blows to the sternum. Ligature marks indicating they had been tied down. Both men were former air force.'

'Jesus,' Lassen said, again.

'There's a slight difference, though. One of my victims drowned, like Haber. The other had sand forced down his throat.' Reinhardt was sure of Noell, although Endres had not yet confirmed it on Zuleger.

'Sand? Jesus.'

'Lassen, I'm following up several leads here, but one of them has to be the air force connection. Have you something to write with? The first victim's name was Andreas Noell. The second was Conrad Zuleger.' He spelled both names out. 'I think Noell served in a squadron called IV./JG56. Got that? IV./JG56.' He held Zuleger's *Wehrpass* open with his fingers. 'Zuleger served in the same squadron until he was transferred to another one…' He checked the booklet. 'In April 1943.'

'Where to?'

'Err… III./NJG64. Sorry, I don't know what it means.'

'Neither do I, if it helps.'

Reinhardt turned the *Wehrpass* in his hands. Every able-bodied man had been given one on demobilisation and was required to keep it until retirement. Reinhardt had one himself. It contained a man's service history, but he stared at it with sudden suspicion, remembering the evidence that had been hidden in plain sight in the *soldbuchs* of the soldiers whose murders he had investigated in Sarajevo. What secrets might this *Wehrpass* hold that he just could not see, that might be staring him in the face…?

'Reinhardt? You still there?'

'Yes. Sorry. Did you find a *Wehrpass* at Haber's residence? Yes? Perhaps you could have a look at it for the same entries. One last thing. Perhaps you could reopen your inquiries into Haber's service history. If all three of them were in the same squadron, and at the same time, we might have a link. Or at least a way to understand what's happening.'

'Consider it done, Reinhardt.' Lassen's voice had a ring of enthusiasm to it. *'I shall call you. Say at the same time, in two days?'*

'Thank you, Lassen. I look forward to it.'

They said their good-byes and Reinhardt hung up the phone with a warm feeling of satisfaction in the pit of his belly. The satisfaction lasted as long as it took him to walk up to the squad room to pick up his hat and coat. Ganz and Weber were both waiting by his desk, the younger detective's face dark with some suppressed anger.

'Reinhardt,' Ganz said peremptorily. 'You're going to Zuleger's workplace?' Reinhardt nodded cautiously. 'Good. You'll take Weber with you.'

'Fine.'

Both Ganz and Weber looked taken aback at Reinhardt's acquiescence. But really, Reinhardt thought to himself, what was he going to do? Ganz frowned, as if he had some explaining to do.

'You and I may have our differences, Reinhardt, but you are a good detective. Maybe,' he said, a flat glower thrown at Weber, 'you'll be able to teach this one some of your better habits. Such as not losing track of your prime suspect in a murder. Or nearly starting a riot in a police station. Or losing your star witness.'

'You lost the woman?' Reinhardt snapped. Weber went red, and even Ganz had the grace to look sheepish momentarily. 'After what happened here, you didn't bother to watch over her?'

'What's done is done, Reinhardt,' Ganz snapped.

'And you've lost your main suspect? Stresemann?'

'Enough, Reinhardt.'

'He's probably killed her, you know.'

'I said *enough*, Reinhardt. Weber's off the Carlsen inquiry, until further notice. He'll work with you.'

'So this is a punishment detail, is it? Fine, whatever you want,' said Reinhardt, short of temper and time, but already regretting his waspish remark. It would do him no good, but the warm glow that had followed his call to Hamburg was gone. 'I'm going now,' he said to Weber. 'Get your things.'

'And if there's two of us,' he said to Ganz, 'how about a car? It's a long way.'

Ganz just looked at him, turned away, but then he paused. 'Reinhardt, have you spoken to Markworth?'

'Last night. I bumped into him on the way out of here,' he said shortly, not wanting to get into the specifics of what had happened.

'He ask you about the Carlsen investigation?'

'I'll spare you the time, Ganz,' Reinhardt said. 'He was surprised I wasn't on it, and asked if I wanted to be.'

Both Ganz and Weber stood still, looking at him. 'And?' Ganz prompted.

'I told him to talk to you.' Reinhardt hesitated. 'Why?'

'Tanneberger's been asked why you're not working the case.'

'By whom?'

'By Bliemeister, and by Margraff. So? Do you want to be on your case, or on Carlsen's?'

'You still seem to think they're different, Ganz,' was all Reinhardt said as he headed out. Weber followed him after a moment, and a terse nod from Ganz.

Mercifully, the trains seemed to be working that morning, and they caught an S-Bahn from Potsdam Station heading to Charlottenburg-Nord, in the west of the city. The trains were old stock, literally rolled out of retirement. The Soviets had taken advantage of their unrivalled mastery of Berlin in the two months before the Western Allies arrived to uproot miles of track and send it, and every train they could find, east as reparations, and the Allies had worked hard to put the network back together, pulling old trains out from the dust of their hangars. The two of them stood pressed close by passengers, shoulders shoved together, but worlds apart. Reinhardt looked out the windows at the roll of the city, the train sometimes clanking high across streets on iron bridges over the eviscerated remains of buildings, sometimes deep down in slab-sided cuttings in the city, with walls of scarred brick and stone looming up above it. At times like that, Reinhardt could only picture the train as a rat, scurrying along below the notice of the masters of the house.

They rode the train out into a sprawling area of industrial

workshops and factories, clattering past the leaden flow of the Spree, past the Westhafen docks, past Plötzensee prison. Beneath a low, white sky they walked down roads and past factories where the bomb damage was heavy, but not quite as bad as that in the centre. Most of the factories were shut, it seemed, and the air was still as they headed to the address of Zuleger's workplace, not far from Siemensstadt borough and its Weimar-era workers' housing.

'Turns out you were right,' Weber said, breaking the silence.

'About what?'

'About the prostitute being a camp survivor. We talked to a friend of hers.'

'When did she disappear?'

'Last night. After we dropped her off home. Stresemann, he was also…' Weber paused, his lips tight as he looked at the ground. 'He was a camp guard. Somewhere called Sachsenhausen. We found that out this morning, as well.'

'Been a busy morning. How did you find that out?'

'When we got to his place, we found all kinds of stuff. Including his SS pay book. And… other things.'

'But not him?' Reinhardt shook his head, simultaneously frustrated and uncaring, and not liking the way that made him feel.

'Don't be getting all high and mighty on me, Reinhardt,' Weber snarled. The cold did nothing for him, starring his face with blotches of red against the pale of his skin.

Reinhardt ignored him, stopping outside a big iron gate. There was a sign outside, Vollmer Altmettal in big black letters. The factory was alive and well, judging from the noise of machinery and the heavy clangs of metal they could hear from out on the street. The gate was open, leading into a long, narrow courtyard that fronted a stained and dirty expanse of dark red brick wall, pierced with tall windows of glass so filthy and old it had to be all but opaque. There was a small guard post just inside the gate, with an elderly man sitting inside reading a newspaper. His mouth fell open at the sight of their police warrant discs and request to see the owner. He hopped out of his little shack and led them at an anxious pace across the courtyard and into the building, eventually handing them over to a secretary in a starched white shirt sitting behind a vast expanse of desk.

'Inspectors Reinhardt and Weber, Berlin Kripo,' Reinhardt introduced them. 'We'd like to see the director or owner about one of his employees, please. A Conrad Zuleger. I'm afraid he's been murdered.'

The woman blinked her eyes very quickly at the news, but she came quickly to her feet. 'Conrad Zuleger, you said? One moment, please, let me speak with the owner.' She glided away, knocking softly on a big door of dark, varnished wood, then slipping inside.

'Weber, listen carefully,' Reinhardt said, turning swiftly to face the younger detective. 'You leave the questioning to me. Ganz put you with me to clip your wings, for sure, but this needn't be the punishment he wants it to be, or you think it is. Just, please, don't mess things up for me, all right?'

'What're you afraid of, Reinhardt?'

Reinhardt sighed. 'That's what's called a leading question, Weber. I'm afraid of a lot of things, a lot of which you don't want to hear. So don't ask a question if you've not got a pretty good idea of the answer, or are ready for it to be an answer you don't like.' He heard voices from within the office, and pushed on, quickly. 'Frankly, you're known to be rather free with your fists and your tongue.'

'What're you talking about?'

'You left your calling card on the barman's face. You remember? The bar where Carlsen was supposedly last seen.' Weber flushed. 'Fists and lip, Weber. There's a time and place for them. And neither will get you very far, especially not here, so you leave them out and leave things to me.'

'Fine, Reinhardt,' sighed Weber, his face twisting, perhaps attempting something of a withering put-down. Reinhardt blinked at him, for a moment recalling the way Friedrich, his son, would look when Reinhardt tried to speak sense or reason to him. The feeling was startling, disconcerting, even, interrupted by the secretary coming back out.

'Mr von Vollmer will see you now, gentlemen.'

17

The owner's office was long, quite well lit, the floor covered in a smooth expanse of carpet. It was not opulent, but the windows were all intact and clear, the furnishings were of good quality, heavy wood and rich leather, and a chandelier of frosted white glass hung low over a varnished conference table. The walls were bare of ornamentation, but a sideboard behind the owner's chair was covered in a variety of photos, memorabilia, and plaques, including what looked like a photo of the manager himself in uniform.

The owner was already standing to the side of his desk, a tall man, well-dressed in a three-piece suit of dark wool and with his iron-grey hair brushed straight back from his forehead. A monocle hung from his neck, and a chain for a fob watch glittered across the slight swell of his stomach. Reinhardt pegged him immediately for some kind of aristocrat, a Prussian Junker, one of those eastern landowners who had supposedly been the backbone of Germany from time immemorial. As if attuned to it, he felt Weber stiffening beside him as if he, too, could feel it, as if any number of class or historical grievances had come churning up inside him.

'Gentlemen, good morning. I am Claus von Vollmer, the owner of this factory. I understand you have some news about an employee of mine?'

'I am Inspector Reinhardt, this is Inspector Weber. That is correct. One of your employees, a Mr Conrad Zuleger, was found yesterday. He had been murdered.'

'I am very sorry to hear it,' replied von Vollmer, nodding. 'I knew

Mr Zuleger. Not that well, so I have sent my secretary for his personnel file, and have asked Mr Bochmann, my managing director, to join us as well.' Reinhardt was right. The man was a Junker, from his eastern accent, to his tone of voice. Haughty, somewhat distant, proper with his courtesies to within an inch of what social decorum moved him.

Reinhardt and Weber were offered seats in front of von Vollmer's desk, where they sat rather like students awaiting the pleasure of a headmaster. Von Vollmer seated himself and offered each of them a distant smile before focusing on Reinhardt as the elder of the two.

'Tell me, then,' von Vollmer said, something of a let's-pass-the-time manner to his voice, 'how are things in the police these days?'

'We get by,' Reinhardt answered.

'What does this place do?' Weber demanded.

'Scrap metal recycling,' said von Vollmer with a tight smile. 'Rather successful, too.'

'No shortage of scrap,' said Weber. Reinhardt flicked a glance at him, but the other detective's face was straight.

'That's right,' said von Vollmer. His eyes flickered up and over Weber, and Reinhardt saw in the slight flare of his gaze that neither the Junker he would always be, nor the officer he suspected he had once been, liked what they saw. 'No reason to let any of it go to waste when it can be turned to both a profit and a source of renewal.'

'I notice the memorabilia behind you, sir,' said Reinhardt. He felt, more than saw, Weber's twitch at Reinhardt's use of *sir*.

'Yes,' said von Vollmer, looking over his shoulder. 'Mementos. Keepsakes from… different times.' There were a number of framed photos, including ones of von Vollmer with what looked like General Nares, the commander of the British Sector, and with Arthur Werner and Otto Ostrowski, the previous and current mayors. Von Vollmer cast a considering eye over Reinhardt, dismissing Weber again without even a glance. 'You served as well?'

'In the army. Yourself?'

'Air force.'

'Air force,' Reinhardt repeated, a sudden thickness in his mouth.

'Fighters,' said von Vollmer, a note of pride in his voice. He reached behind and picked up a plaque, a metal sigil, a bird of prey with lighting in its talons, mounted on a dark piece of wood.

'What type?'

'Night fighters.'

'Dangerous work,' observed Reinhardt.

'The most dangerous,' nodded von Vollmer, a glow of recollection in his eyes as he looked at the plaque. 'But,' he said, as he put it carefully back, 'necessary work. And at least, at night, we could say we ruled the dark. Not like the day, when the Americans would, quite literally, fill the skies. I participated in one or two daytime actions, you know,' he continued, warming to his memories and leaning back and onto one elbow, the leather of his chair creaking around him. 'It was almost as if I could have got out of my plane and walked, there were that many of the devils.'

'What squadron?'

'A good one. The Night Hawks.'

'I'm afraid I'm not familiar with it.'

'Of no moment,' said von Vollmer, loftily. 'Work such as ours, it often went unnoticed. It was the work that counted. Not the recognition that might have been due.'

'Oh, for…' Weber snorted, his eyes incredulous.

'What was its designation?' Reinhardt stepped in, with a firm glance at Weber. 'The squadron?'

'Group, Inspector. It is a Group designation. III./NJG64.'

Reinhardt sat straighter in his chair. Weber remained oblivious, too busy glowering at von Vollmer, not realising it just made him seem like the ill-formed adolescent that in many ways he still was.

'You'll have to forgive my ignorance,' said Reinhardt, 'but Luftwaffe designations mean nothing to me. Can you describe it?'

'Of course,' replied von Vollmer, warming to a subject obviously still close to him. 'The "N" is for *Nacht*. The "JG" means *Jagdgeschwader*. "Fighter wing." So "NJG" means "night-fighter wing". The "III" is the group designation within the wing. There were usually four groups to a wing. And "64" is the wing's number within the air force's strength.'

'And a group was made up of squadrons, is that correct?' Reinhardt asked.

'Correct,' said von Vollmer, an austere nod acknowledging Reinhardt's interest. 'Usually three squadrons to a group.'

'So, in order, wings had groups, and groups had squadrons.'

'Correct.'

'Very interesting,' Weber drawled.

There was a knock at the door, saving Reinhardt any potential embarrassment, and a tall, rather aesthetic-looking man with thinning hair stepped inside. Von Vollmer glanced up at him somewhat dismissively, and with a contemptuous flick of his eyes at Weber, handed them over to the newcomer.

'Bochmann, there's a good chap. See if you can't help out our police friends with their inquiries. Apparently one of our workers has met with a sticky end.'

Bochmann nodded between Reinhardt and Weber. He appeared flushed and flustered, as if he had rushed here, and he held a thin file in spidery fingers.

'Gentlemen,' he said, indicating the conference table. 'I am Heinrich Bochmann, the general manager here. I have Zuleger's file. How can I help you?'

'What can you tell me about Zuleger?'

Bochmann's mouth pursed, and he shook his head, slightly. 'There is not that much to say, I'm afraid. Zuleger was a good worker. There were no complaints against him. He was a good man. Quiet. Conscientious.'

'What did he do here?'

'He was a shift manager.'

'How long had Zuleger worked here?'

'Since December 1946,' said Bochmann, scanning the file.

'When was the last time he was seen?'

Bochmann shook his head and looked over at von Vollmer, behind his desk with pen in hand poised over a letter. 'I really wouldn't know,' Bochmann said. Von Vollmer nodded agreement. 'I would have to check with the records. I remember him here last week. On Friday. More than that… I'm sorry, I couldn't say.'

'What did he do during the war?'

'I'm sorry, how is that germane to this inquiry?'

'You let us worry about that,' snapped Weber.

'Please, just answer the question,' said Reinhardt.

'He was a pilot.'

At the end of what was a positive, but rather mundane, character reference, Reinhardt knew with some certainty they were hiding something.

'Sir,' he said, looking over at von Vollmer. The Junker raised his head from his papers. 'Is there anyone else from your old unit with you these days?'

'What do you mean?' frowned von Vollmer.

Reinhardt feigned surprise. 'I mean simply that a gentleman such as yourself would not knowingly leave old comrades out in the cold. And not always the metaphorical cold either.'

'Yes,' said von Vollmer, his brow clearing from whatever concern had creased it. 'Bochmann here, my managing director, used to be my Group's XO. Its executive officer.'

'That's all?'

'No. There are others.'

'Like Zuleger.'

'Zuleger,' nodded von Vollmer, learning forward on his elbows. 'Zuleger was an ex-comrade – former air force, like me, like Bochmann – and as such I would always like to think they would have an open door in one of my enterprises. I would consider it both a duty and honour to help such as him.'

'Did you serve with Zuleger?'

Von Vollmer gave a small shrug, looking at Bochmann, who paused before answering. 'I believe Zuleger did serve under the director.'

'Thank you, Bochmann.' Von Vollmer picked up the thread of

the explanation. 'Whether he served directly under me or not, he was an ex-comrade. I offered him a place and employment, as I would have done any man who served under me. I really did not know him all that well. So that you know, I only joined the Night Hawks in the last six months of the war. Prior to that, I was a staff officer in the air ministry.' Reinhardt could not fail to notice how von Vollmer's apparent pride in being the Night Hawks's commanding officer had suddenly become curtailed, but he focused on Bochmann. He had been the Group's executive officer, according to von Vollmer. It would have been him who actually ran things.

'Did you know Zuleger, Mr Bochmann?'

'I did.'

'Knew him how? Knew him well?'

'Well enough, Inspector,' replied Bochmann. His voice was quite soft, in keeping with his aesthetic appearance. 'He was a pilot. One of many who passed through the Group. Neither the best, nor the worst. Neither the brightest, nor the dumbest.' He had heavy, watery brown eyes, their colour muddied and silted with moisture, or as if something in the air bothered him or he were constantly on the verge of breaking out in tears. 'You served, I would wager. You would know, then, that after a while, one no longer notices those that come and go. They simply are, until they are not.'

Von Vollmer cleared his throat, a nervous rasp, as if he was embarrassed. 'Steady on, old chap,' he murmured solicitously to Bochmann. 'What you have, Reinhardt, is simply a case of solidarity between ex-soldiers. Heaven knows, there's little else for us to rely on these days.'

'Old-boy networks are still alive and well, then,' muttered Weber, his voice low and slurred, like a boy who could not help saying what he did and knowing it would do him no good. It did nothing to help the image von Vollmer had already made of him. Von Vollmer's face lengthened as he screwed his monocle into his eye, turning its flinty glitter on Weber.

'I say, young man, try not to sound like one of those dreadful Soviet propaganda films.'

'I am a detective in the Kripo "old man", Weber snapped into von Vollmer's carven expression. 'And looking around this place, I can see those films make a lot of sense. Not doing so badly are you, Mr von Vollmer?'

'I see no reason to eschew one's initiative and resourcefulness. Not when there is such opportunity and when needs are so great. There are those,' von Vollmer said, with a barely veiled look at Reinhardt, 'who understand the values of initiative and enterprise, of capitalism and free markets, and there are those who do not.'

'Be careful, Mr von Vollmer, those are political words,' Weber spat out. Reinhardt winced to hear them, they made the younger man sound so callow and petulant.

'Are they, young man?' von Vollmer said, smiling. 'I do believe that you are not the political police, and that in this new Germany of ours, such thoughts are not forbidden us.'

'Maybe what we need's a bit of political police, eh? Set things to rights a bit.' Weber's mouth curled shut, as if he wished the words back. 'But such thoughts were forbidden before, weren't they?' Weber bristled. 'And before that, on your eastern estates, did your peasants have to tug their forelocks and bite their tongues when you rode by? You and your Junker brethren, as you led Germany down its Fascist path.'

'My dear young man,' von Vollmer murmured, pityingly. 'Its "Fascist path"? Where *do* you get such ideas? From a Soviet commissar? Like the ones who confiscated my ancestral estates? Who hung a banner that read "The Junkers' lands in the peasants' hands" across the front of my manor? In any case, I will thank you not to speak out of turn, and when you speak to keep a civil tongue.'

'May I have a sheet of paper?' Reinhardt interrupted. 'Thank you,' he said to von Vollmer as the owner handed him one. He scribbled something on it and handed it to Weber. The detective looked at it a moment, then rose from his chair and left the room, Bochmann and von Vollmer watching him go.

'I do apologise for my younger colleague,' said Reinhardt, a little smile on his face as the door closed behind Weber. 'There is much he does not understand, or thinks he does and interprets wrongly. Such as the solidarity between ex-soldiers and servicemen. It is something natural.'

'*You* understand, of course,' said von Vollmer.

'I understand. It saved my life. After the first war.'

Von Vollmer nodded, looking at him with a different set in his eyes. 'For me as well.'

'But for my brothers in arms, I would have fallen by the wayside. It was nothing to be ashamed of then, and so *why*,' said Reinhardt, putting the faintest lash into his voice, 'did I have to drag it out of you?'

18

Von Vollmer and Bochmann were silent. 'You are correct to castigate us, Inspector,' von Vollmer said, after a moment. 'But the solidarity that exists now is… not what we knew, you and I, in 1918. It is a solidarity that cannot always call itself what it is. There are those out there who might take this place apart if they knew that veterans were working here.'

'Not just veterans,' said Reinhardt. 'Men who actually served together. Who else is here from your command?'

'Seven,' Bochmann answered, quietly. 'Six,' he said, correcting himself. 'I was thinking of… Zuleger.'

'Pilots?' asked Reinhardt?

'One,' Bochmann replied, after a moment. 'Zuleger was the second.'

'Names, please.' Bochmann paused, thinking, then wrote, handing the paper across to Reinhardt. He glanced at it, seeing Noell was not on it. 'I would like to interview all those from your former command, please, starting now if they're working today.'

Bochmann nodded. 'Inspector. You have not told us how Zuleger was murdered.'

'He was asphyxiated by sand being poured down his throat. Do either of you know why someone would do that to him? Kill him in that way?'

Neither of them had an answer, they just sat there looking blank, perhaps running over images in their mind of what had happened to Zuleger until the door opened, and Weber came back in with the piece of paper that he gave to Reinhardt. Von Vollmer and Bochmann looked at it with some interest, although Reinhardt said nothing about it, and then he realised why Bochmann looked familiar.

'Did either of you know a pilot named Andreas Noell?' Reinhardt asked, on a hunch. Von Vollmer shook his head, then Bochmann, but Reinhardt was sure there was the slightest hesitation in Bochmann's answer. Reinhardt looked at him, his eyes flat, and then Bochmann nodded, and corrected his answer to 'not sure'. Reinhardt laid down a photograph. It was the group photograph, the one from Noell's album. Von Vollmer rose from behind his desk and came round to look as well.

'There you are,' Reinhardt said, pointing out Bochmann, who craned his head around and smiled, the silt in his eyes clearing a moment. On the photo, Bochmann sat in the middle of the front row, seated, his legs and arms crossed. Bochmann's mouth tightened, as if around memories that were too much to handle, and he played a finger over the photo.

'That's Noell, I think. Yes, I think I remember him now.'

'Where's Zuleger?' Bochmann frowned at him. 'Zuleger served in IV./JG56. Is he on this photo?'

Bochmann's eyes scanned the picture. 'That's him, I think. It's hard to tell.'

'But that is not a picture of the Night Hawks?'

'No. That was IV./JG56.'

'So you changed units?'

'No, not quite. IV./JG56 was the original unit, but it was retrained and redesignated a night-fighter group in 1943.'

'It became another unit?'

'Yes. The personnel in it at the time mostly remained, as I recall. The pilots all went through extensive retraining. New fighters, new tactics. But not Noell. He had already transferred out. Sometime in early 1943, I think. I'm not sure exactly when, or where, but I think it was to test pilot status.'

'Test pilot?'

'Yes. I don't know anything about it. But this photo,' said

Bochmann, pointing out the group shot, 'was of the original flyers, the Group of 1940-41.' There was an element of pride in his voice. 'Most of them are dead now,' he mused. 'Dead or wounded. Or missing. Shot down. Taken prisoner. Gone. Like Colonel Elbers, there. Shot down over the Channel. We never heard what became of him.'

Von Vollmer harrumphed, as if to cut short any reference to the squadron before he joined it. 'And so just why, Inspector, are you asking about former pilots from the Night Hawks, or who we might have served with?'

'It's because someone's murdered two of them. Zuleger and Noell. And what links the pair of them is IV./JG56 and III./NJG64. So I ask again, does anything occur to you as to why, or what, would link those two men?' Again, they shook their heads. 'How about this, then? Would you have any idea what this is?' He spread the apparent manifesto and related documentation he had found in Zuleger's apartment. 'Any idea?'

'That's political, is what that is,' Weber said, a slight crow in his voice as if he had recognised something before anyone else. Von Vollmer and Bochmann lifted their heads from it, looking at Weber, then at each other. 'Political, *and* illegal,' said Weber unnecessarily, perhaps reading too much into von Vollmer's and Bochmann's silence.

'For once, your impetuous young colleague is right, Inspector. It's some kind of manifesto. I've seen similar.'

'You've seen such before?' gloated Weber, and there was a light of petty triumph in his eyes, of the kind Reinhardt had seen far too frequently these past few years. His temper frayed at Weber's vehemence, but he admitted it had its uses, watching the effect it had on the other two men. Von Vollmer straightened, and he had none of the disdain in his voice and face as he looked at Weber, then at Reinhardt.

'Such things circulate, you know. But I've never seen that.'

'Perhaps we should invite you to Linienstrasse to continue this conversation,' smiled Weber.

'Enough,' said Reinhardt, curtly. Weber flushed, and opened his mouth, but Reinhardt shook his head. 'Thank you both for your time,' he said to von Vollmer and Bochmann. 'One final question: did either of you know Zuleger in any capacity other than as a worker and as a former comrade?'

'I did not,' said Bochmann.

'No,' said von Vollmer curtly, the word neatly encapsulating the social distinctions that still ruled him. He might have seen it as his duty to provide for those who had relied on him or over whom he had had authority, and thus a sense of responsibility in the way his class might have defined it, but it almost certainly did not extend to mixing with them in social settings.

Bochmann showed Reinhardt and Weber out of the office to an adjacent room, where the six other factory employees who used to be in III./NJG64 were waiting. According to Bochmann's information, there was a pilot and five who were former ground staff. Zuleger was known to them, and they took his death with varying degrees of shock, exchanging wide-eyed looks among one another, but it was little more than the shock that would cross anyone's face and mind on hearing someone they knew had died.

'*How* did he die, again?' they asked.

'Drowned,' answered Weber quickly, a twist of scorn to his face as he looked at Reinhardt.

'Suffocated,' Reinhardt corrected him, watched the other men for a sign, any sign, but could see nothing, see no deeper than the seamed, tired lines of the faces of six ordinary-looking men of middle age.

'Please,' said Bochmann, looking across them, 'the owner and myself invite you to help the police in their inquiry.'

'Can you give Inspector Weber and myself some personal details? Anyone who knew Zuleger?'

'I knew him pretty well,' said a man who had a patch over one eye. 'Name's Dorner. We flew together. Same squadron. Until I lost this,' he said, pointing at the patch. 'There was nothing wrong with him, if that helps. He was his normal self last week.' The others nodded agreement.

'Anyone know if he had plans for the weekend? A party? Dinner?' Again, a round of negative answers, although Reinhardt sensed a certain shiftiness, and Weber seemed to sense it as well.

'Did anyone know a pilot named Andreas Noell?' One or two nodded, including Dorner. Reinhardt gestured for him to go on.

'I knew him. Not well. We were in the squadron about… about a year together.'

'And…?' shot Weber.

'And what?' Dorner shot back. 'He was just a normal bloke. I haven't seen or heard of him since nineteen forty bloody two, when I got this!' he spat, another jerk of his fingers at his eye patch. 'I mean, what do you think? That we all of us spend our free time drinking and reminiscing about the old days?'

'"All"?' Reinhardt asked. 'Just how many of you here in the factory are ex-air force?' Reinhardt asked Dorner. The question seemed to leave Dorner short of words, and he looked desperately to Bochmann. 'A large number of the staff has that honour. Von Vollmer takes seriously his duties towards not only his own former men, but those of the same service. He has strong principles of solidarity.'

'How many?' Weber pushed.

'The majority of the workforce,' Bochmann answered.

'We've got nowhere to go,' Dorner said. 'We can't work anywhere else. No union will have us.'

Weber's face seemed to lighten. 'How's this? Veterans congregating together? You know damn well that's illegal.'

'We stick together,' said another. 'We have to.'

The secretary poked her head into the room and beckoned to Bochmann. 'You have had a call from your headquarters, Inspector,' he said, glancing at a slip of paper the secretary had handed him. 'A Professor Endres has important information for you. He asks can you come to him as soon as possible?'

'Thank you, Mr Bochmann.' Reinhardt looked at Weber, then

back at Bochmann. 'I think we are finished, here, in any case.'

'Finished? Reinhardt, there is much more we can inquire into,' protested Weber.

'*Finished*, Weber,' said Reinhardt, firmly. The other men shuffled their feet, looking interested despite themselves in this show of division, and Reinhardt silently cursed this impetuous officer, this – *callow* – youth who could not seem to master himself, could not seem to understand the value of a united front.

19

In the cold outside, Reinhardt paused to light a cigarette. He offered one to Weber, but the detective only sneered at Reinhardt's Luckies and lit a cigarette of his own, shifting his weight from foot to foot in his excitement. Reinhardt cupped a hand around his match at a sudden swirl of wind through the factory's courtyard.

'What did you make of that, Weber?'

'I think we left a lot undone and unsaid,' Weber replied, as Reinhardt unfolded the piece of paper Weber had given him in von Vollmer's office. 'What is that, anyway? And don't say "it's an address" because I know it's an address.'

'Well, it's an address,' Reinhardt said with equanimity, unable to resist that little dig. 'I found an address at Zuleger's apartment, on an invitation. I wanted to compare it with von Vollmer's.'

'Why?'

'To eliminate possibilities, Weber. It's police work. Basic police work.'

'You hoped it would match.'

'I didn't "hope", Weber. That's not how this works.'

'There's more going on here, isn't there?' Weber's voice was excited.

'Like what?'

'Like... like political... stuff. That literature you found. That manifesto. There's ex-air force and ex-who-knows-who-else in there. They're not supposed to be gathering together.'

'They're working, Weber. Not plotting to bring back the Third Reich.'

'Says you.'

'The laws forbid the formation by veterans of any association or organisation with a military or militaristic character…'

'Like what we just saw in there?'

'… but they say nothing about who a businessman can hire or not.'

'Oh, *listen* to yourself, Reinhardt. You're a bloody apologist for them. It's true what they say, isn't it? You officer types all stick together and watch each other's backs. What do you do for fun? Reminisce about the bloody *Kaiser* and how to bring back yesterday's politics?'

'Why are you so excited about the politics? And what's that you mentioned about political police?' Weber gave an angry sigh as he pulled on his cigarette. 'Weber, what did I tell you about keeping your mouth shut in there?' Weber coloured, the red rising unpleasantly up his neck. 'Did you have to be so unpleasant?'

'I have to ask you, Reinhardt,' Weber said, his nose twisting as if at the scent of something unpleasant, 'where your loyalties lie? Unpleasant?' He seemed to swell up, all teenage anger with no clear outlet for whatever moved him except Reinhardt, and he stepped up close, poking a finger into his chest. '*Unpleasant*, you say? To men like *von Vollmer*? It was men like *him*,' he spat, poking Reinhardt again, 'that got us into the war.'

'Will you calm down, Weber?' Reinhardt said quietly, but it only seemed to infuriate Weber further. Instead of poking him, Weber closed a white-knuckled fist into Reinhardt's coat and pushed him step-by-grudging-step back against the wall. As he did so, Weber seemed to grow, as if through the shame that stung the back of Reinhardt's eyes at being manhandled thus, manhandled by a mere boy. Weber became more focused, a proclamation of the harm men could do – that a man could do – given the wrong means in the right circumstances. Reinhardt felt a shiver of fear, suppressing the instinct to slap Weber's hand away, but the humiliation was worse. Humiliation at being pushed around by someone like Weber, but aware – so aware – that the man in front of him was not just some young man, barely out of adolescence. Despite the sanction imposed upon him by Ganz, Weber was *someone*. Moreover, he was some*thing*. Reinhardt was honest enough to admit he was scared of Weber's callow strength, and through him of Ganz, and of his blatant opportunism. And through Ganz… behind Ganz there was the communist-dominated hierarchy of Berlin's police, and Reinhardt was aware, painfully aware, of his place in that. Unbidden, his tongue began to stroke the gap in his teeth.

'These are new times, Reinhardt,' Weber hissed, his breath acid with bad tobacco.

'What colour are you, Weber?' Reinhardt cast it out as if to throw Weber offtrack, unbalance him, but Weber frowned, his face untwisting itself. 'Are you brown? The Nazis were brown. Are you red? Are you old enough to understand what that means? Are you one of those who changes his colours? There are plenty of them around. You'd be in good company.'

'Fuck off, Reinhardt.'

'And where are you from? I can't place your accent. You're not from Berlin. And you're not from Saxony. There's a lot of Saxons sitting in the Soviet Sector, starting with Ulbricht at the top. Are you one of them? Are you one of those who came back with the Red Army?'

'*Listen*, Captain Crow,' Weber snarled, both fists coming up to grip Reinhardt's coat, thrusting hard against him. 'You need to watch your mouth. Never mind my history. What about yours? I'll bet there are parts of yours that might not stand up to scrutiny either.'

'"Either"?' repeated Reinhardt. Weber went white, then red, a flush that subsumed the splotched archipelago of his face into a wash of blood. His hands tightened on Reinhardt, twisting. Without thinking, Reinhardt lifted his hands to cover Weber's fists, clenched his thumbs hard against the ends of the other man's little fingers where they curled into his palms. Weber frowned a moment, then his face creased with pain and he tried to pull himself back, but

Reinhardt held him tight, held him tighter until, just for a moment, he felt something deep inside, a sudden serpentlike coiling. As if something old and hoary had turned over, giving him a glimpse of a darker nature, mud-smeared and with the mad rolling eye of an animal gone wild. Reinhardt squeezed tighter still, frightened as always by that glimpse inside himself, of how he imagined and internalised what he could do as something awful rising from ruined ground, then released the pressure. Weber pulled his hands away as if burned, stumbling back.

'We're finished here. I'm going to go back to the morgue to see Professor Endres. You can come with me. But if not, you can visit this place,' Reinhardt said, holding out the invitation he had found at Zuleger's apartment. His eyes were flat, as if daring Weber to come back at him, and effectively ignoring the other man's display of aggression.

Weber blinked, flexing his hands against his pain, looked down at the paper. His face twitched, and he shook his head. 'You bloody go. I'm going back in there for a look around.'

'Suit yourself,' Reinhardt said, dropping his cigarette butt on the ground. 'Get some dates. Squadron postings. Times those pilots were all together. Something factual,' he finished, walking away, feeling Weber's furrowed astonishment as he did so, but he had neither the time nor the patience for him, and right then he could not have cared less for Ganz's inevitable anger at his having left Weber behind. Weber was a big boy. He could look after himself.

Reinhardt walked quickly out of the factory, pain stabbing his knee with every step as if it could feel his intention to try and outpace his own frustration and was warning him against it. He waited for what seemed like a long time for a train, smoking, cursing Ganz for not giving him a vehicle. When one finally came, he squeezed himself into it, worming through the press of people until he found a corner to wedge himself into and take the weight off his leg, letting his mind go blank, feeling it as the only way he could calm himself down.

His mind stilled, but it was a viscous stillness, torpid, heavy with introspection, thoughts adrift and lost somewhere between here and there, between now and then. Between the Berlin he had known, and the one that stumbled before him through the clouded glass of the train's windows. Between the man he had been, and the man he was now. Always, he thought, always this seemed to come back to haunt him. The fact he could not be the man he wanted to be. Time and circumstance never seemed to permit it, and he never seemed to find a way to fit himself into where and when he was.

The war was over, but it would not leave him alone. He was not the only one feeling that, he knew, and he felt no temptation to self-pity, but he could not help a mounting fury and frustration at how he, an individual, was being subsumed into the mass of those men who had fought the war so badly, so awfully, so criminally. Thinking of reflections again, thinking of the times as a policeman when he had held up the truth of a suspect's actions only for that person to reject it, he knew men could not be prodded to truth. They had to come to it themselves, and he could not see truth in the eyes of the people all around him.

He had once thought of reflections. On a mountainside in Bosnia, listening to Partisans as they sang the night in and watched the sun set across a horizon of knuckled mountains, he had thought of reflections, the truths they could sometimes give back. He had thought back then there would be a reckoning when the war ended. Every man would have to stand face-to-face with judgment of some kind, and often the hardest judgment came from the face you saw reflected back at you every day. A face you saw reflected everywhere, in mirrors and windows, in metal and water, sharp-edged or sunken, chopped or blurred. The splintered facets of yourself that stared back at you from a thousand pairs of eyes. A face you saw reflected within you.

Reflections were everywhere, he had thought then, but he knew better now. Berlin was closed to him, shattered in on itself, and its walls gaped blind. Its people were closed to him, and to themselves. They reflected nothing, except the stunned labour of living. The city reflected nothing except the damage men had done it.

20

He stayed like that, like a wheel running itself down, until something, a flicker of light, perhaps, a word spoken that slipped out of the crowd into his ear, made him lift his head and realise he could swing past the address that Leena had given him for Kausch before going to the morgue. He switched trains at Putlitzerstrasse, catching another one towards Wedding Station in the French Sector, where he made his way by memory and directions from passersby to Plantagenstrasse, which ran along what used to be, he remembered, an elegant, shaded cemetery.

His memory of the layout of the place served, but of the cemetery not much remained except a swath of ground rutted by the tilt of shattered tombstones and the stumps of trees. Remembering what Leena had said, he watched the street from the far side of the cemetery, behind the chipped façade of an old tomb, listening to the quiet. There were three buildings on the street, all apartment blocks, all with façades scored and scorched by fire. A few windows reflected the sky, but most were covered with wood or cardboard. He scanned along the rooftops, but could not see any movement, although there were enough dark holes in the tiled roofs where roofs still existed, or enough hiding places in the saw-backed jumble of ruins where there were none, to hide an army of spotters.

'It's the middle one.'

Reinhardt jumped, turning to see two boys crouching down behind a grave. They grinned at him, clean flashes of teeth amid the grime of their faces, clearly pleased at having snuck up on him.

'You'll give someone a heart attack doing that,' Reinhardt

grunted, lightening his words with a rueful shake of his head and smile.

'Leena said to watch for you,' one of them said. He pointed. 'The middle one. And there's someone watching the road from the roof, up there.'

Reinhardt nodded. He shook out a few Luckies and left them on the tomb. There was no door at the entrance to Kausch's block and no superintendent. Although the rooms for one were there, they were abandoned, the angles of floors, walls, and corners softened with rubbish. There were letterboxes by the stairs, but Kausch's name was not on them. Nor was there a Kessel. The whole building felt abandoned, no sounds, no smells beyond a cold scent of waste and neglect. But at the first floor, an old lady answered his knock and gestured at him with two fingers pointing upward when he asked for Kausch. She said nothing, but her rheumy eyes blinked quickly at him as she shut the door.

On the second floor, only one apartment had a door. He knocked, waited, knocked again, calling 'police'. He leaned close to the door, listening to the kind of silence that wrapped itself around those who wished not to move. The silence that accompanied a policeman's knock at the door. He knocked again, louder, calling again, hearing finally a shuffle of feet from inside. The door cracked open to a man's face, clean-shaven, with heavy-lidded eyes.

'I'm looking for a Mr Kessel.'

The man shook his head. 'He's not here.'

'How about Kausch?' The man blinked. 'Are you Mr Kausch? I am Inspector Reinhardt, with the Kripo. May I come in?'

The man moved his mouth, as if around a dry tongue. 'Why?' he managed, after a moment. 'What is the matter?'

'May I come in, please? It would be easier to talk. Are you Mr Kausch?'

The man nodded after a moment. 'Yes. But I'm sick, can't you see?' Kausch said, rucking the blanket he wore higher up around his shoulders. The man's fingers were long, the fingernails filed and clean, and his hair was streaked with grey about his ears. 'What do you want?'

'Do you know a man named Andreas Noell?'

Kausch coughed, hunching further into the blanket. A cold wind feathered the hair on Reinhardt's head, blowing from within Kausch's apartment, bringing with it the musty odour of damp, of unwashed clothes, of badly cooked food. But from Kausch came a faint, but distinct, odour of soap.

'I did, yes,' Kausch coughed again.

'You did? You knew him from where?'

'I knew him from before.'

'From before…?' Reinhardt said, beneath a smooth brow, keeping his eyes level on Kausch.

'Before. We were in the same apartment before.'

'You? Or Mr Kessel?'

'Yes.'

'Yes?'

'Me.'

'Kausch, then. So is there a Kessel?'

'No. Yes.'

'But he's not here. So you said. Where did you know Noell from then?'

'In Neukölln.'

'You lived in the same apartment?'

'Yes. No. I lived there. He needed a place. After the war. We discussed it, I left him the apartment to come here.'

'Why? Why would you do that for Noell? Did you know him well?'

'Not very well, no.'

'Have you heard from him lately?'

'No.'

'When was the last time you heard from him?'

Kausch shrugged. 'A few months ago, perhaps.'

'You weren't friends?' Kausch shook his head, a slight twist to his mouth.

'So why the arrangement with the other apartment? So far as I can see, unpleasant as it was, this is worse.' Reinhardt put levity into his voice he did not feel, all the while watching Kausch's eyes, and listening as hard as he could for sound.

'My mother, Inspector. She was ill, and I needed to look after her.'

'What was wrong with her?'

Kausch ducked his mouth in the blanket to cough. In the hallway behind Kausch, Reinhardt saw several pairs of shoes. He looked at them, then back at Kausch, eyebrows raised for Kausch's answer.

'Tuberculosis.'

'Is she here?'

'My mother? No.'

'And now?'

'Now what?' There was a sudden parade-ground snap to Kausch's voice.

'Your mother? How is she?'

'Oh. I am afraid she passed away. Over the winter.'

'I am sorry to hear it. It wasn't anything to do with Poles?'

'With what?'

'Poles. You weren't worried about Poles?'

'I have no idea what you're talking about, Inspector.'

'When did you last see Noell, did you say?'

'I didn't. But it was months ago.'

'You weren't close?' Kausch shook his head. 'Weren't friends? May I come in?' Reinhardt asked, again.

Kausch's mouth moved, and he turned his head to dry cough, dragging it up and out of his mouth. There were small flecks of white in the fold beneath his ear.

Kausch coughed. 'Inspector. I am very ill, and I have answered your questions. If there is nothing else…?' He made to shut the door, but Reinhardt put a hand against it.

'You haven't asked me.'

'Asked you what?'

'Why I'm asking about Noell.' Kausch blinked. 'But maybe Ochs told you he'd been murdered when you went to see him yesterday.' Kausch blinked again. 'Why did you go? Had you heard something?'

'I don't know what you are talking about, Inspector.'

'Did you serve in Poland?' Reinhardt watched Kausch closely, but saw nothing in the man's eyes, or in his face. 'This place smells like a barracks. Damp towels, soup, and socks. Not a smell I care to remember. I really don't care who is living in there with you, or what kind of scam you may be playing. Ration cards? Benefits? Something more serious, given the man you have up on the roof? So long as it and you and they had nothing to do with Noell's murder, I am not interested. But I will be back, Mr Kausch.'

21

'I have finished the autopsy of Zuleger,' Endres said, handing over a typed sheet of paper in his office at the morgue. 'Without a doubt, he was killed by the same man who killed Noell and this other man, this Carlsen. Or a man trained to deliver blows in the same way. The time of death was sometime on Friday, I would say. Late on Friday.'

'Can you confirm what was left in the mouth?'

'Yes. Traces of sand, and more in the throat. In the oesophagus, to be precise. But, more importantly, I have something else for you.' The Professor's hands played with a rough-edged folder of poor quality. It had a smeared stamp on the front and a series of handwritten notations. 'It is, in my opinion, a loose approximation of a medical report, but…' He paused, his lips bunching as he considered what lay in front of him. 'But I think the facts of this victim's death correspond closely enough to those of Zuleger's, and perhaps of Noell's. You will tell me what you think,' he finished, handing over the file to a suddenly energised Reinhardt.

'An autopsy report?' Reinhardt passed over his packet of Luckies and his matches, settling back into the chair to view the file.

'If you call what they did an autopsy,' cavilled Endres, absorbed in the glowing tip of his cigarette.

The 'loose approximation of a report' Endres had found were the autopsy records of the body of a man discovered in a ruined building in early 1946. The autopsy had determined the cause of death to be a crushed sternum because of rubble found on and around the body. Dust had been found in the mouth, he read, wondering if it had been misidentified, and if it had been sand... the body had been found in one of the Western Zones – the American one, again.

'You will have to see what sort of an investigation there was,' Endres said, as Reinhardt finished reading. 'The evidence in there could easily be classed as circumstantial. I don't think there were what we would term investigations at that time. I believe the authorities would have had other things on their minds. And the evidence therein is not conclusive of murder. Before you get carried away,' he said, tapping his cigarette into an ashtray, 'you should remember Berlin was an unsafe city at that time, and young men – like that one had been – had a particular set of dangers to be endured or avoided, and not all of those dangers had been wearing Red Army uniforms,' he finished around a smooth drift of smoke, the slightest twist of irony in his voice.

'Your points are well taken, Professor, thank you,' said Reinhardt. 'May I borrow the file? I will need to cross-check the references with what we have.'

'By all means.' He shifted in his seat as Reinhardt rose to leave. The smallest and slightest of gestures, a slide of his hand across his desk, but it was unaccustomed, outside of the ambit of Endres's habitual control, and it made Reinhardt pause and take his seat again. Endres's mouth moved, as if around something unexplained. 'You will recall that photograph you showed me. The one you found at Noell's apartment.'

'The one of him in air force uniform?'

'Precisely. I have found... someone. Someone who knows what it might be. This person would be willing to meet you. If you would find that interesting.'

Reinhardt kept his face blank as he stared back at the Professor, considering what it was that unsettled a man as imperturbable as Endres. 'I would be pleased to meet him, of course,' he said, eventually.

'It is settled, then,' said Endres, looking relieved as he reclined back into his chair. 'I shall try to have you meet him soon.'

'I shall make the effort, Professor,' Reinhardt said, but his mind was already gone, questing ahead along this new path.

From the morgue he went to police HQ. When last Reinhardt had served in Berlin's police, the headquarters had been at Alexanderplatz. The Alex, as it had colloquially been known, was a ruin now, bombed out, fought over and through during the Soviet assault back in May 1945. Everything still in the building had gone up in smoke – offices, records, files, archives, documents, forensics laboratories, morgue facilities, the telephone exchange, barracks, and dormitories, everything. The Alex's shattered frontage now looked across the pitted expanse of the square at other buildings equally damaged, a crescent of smashed and blackened façades that hid the tangles of devastation the war had wrought inside them. Although cleared of wreckage now, the surface of the platz still showed the scars of the fighting that had raged across it, the surface scarred and scorched where vehicles and fires had burned themselves out. In his mind, Reinhardt still remembered it as a place of light and movement, with windows lit and shops open, the flow of crowds and the dart and buzz of cars, one of Berlin's arteries with the U-Bahn and trains sliding in and out of the stations day and night.

Berlin's main police HQ had moved to a building on Linienstrasse that had previously belonged to the DAF, the German Labour Front. It was in the borough of Mitte, and, as buildings went, it was not a patch on the Alex, not in accommodation, not in location, and not in cachet. The Alex had had presence. It had been one of Berlin's landmarks. One of the city's fulcrums. No one knew how long the police would be in Linienstrasse. As long as the Soviets insisted it stay there, Reinhardt imagined, but perhaps it would be long enough for it to forge its own identity, but Reinhardt thought not, as he entered the building. Its new masters would not give Berlin's police any more authority than what they allowed. Or, as Reinhardt sometimes preferred to put it, just enough rope to hang themselves with if need be.

In Linienstrasse, he looked up the case file with the help of a surly records clerk, confirming that the body had indeed been found in the American Sector, in July 1946, but the man – Josef Stucker – had lived in the Soviet Sector, in Friedrichshain. Moreover, he read, his heart picking up just a little, Stucker had had a family, and had been listed as ex-military because of a *Wehrpass* found on his body. The investigating officers had conducted little to no investigation, it not being obvious then that Stucker had been murdered, and his death had been put down as accidental. A finding, Reinhardt saw, that Stucker's wife had rejected. He read her statement, noting her insistence that her husband had been concerned and increasingly worried, but unable to say to the detectives' satisfaction what it was he had been worried about.

Stucker's address was in an apartment that backed onto the Volkspark in Friedrichshain. The park used to be a lovely spot, one of the city's older green spaces, with a beautiful cemetery to the south. The area had been shredded and raked by the war, and then by Berliners' need for fuel to survive the bitter winters of 1945 and 1946. In the middle of the park, the colossal bulk of the Friedrichshain flak tower squatted like a wounded titan. The fortress had been split in two, the halves leaning away from each other, and millions of tons of rubble from ruins elsewhere in the city were being piled around its massive walls. The tower seemed to be drowning in the debris that now fringed it, the whole becoming a new landmark to the city's postwar façade. Grass would grow there eventually, Reinhardt knew, trees as well, and a future generation of Berliners would have little to no idea what lay beneath the green hill they lay or walked on.

The widow's apartment had once been in a fine building, now very run-down, reeking of damp, dust, bricks, and bad cooking. An old optician in a tiny shop with bells over the door that tinkled a discreet little chime directed him to a small laundry close by, where he found her. Reinhardt showed his warrant disc to the laundry's owner, a pinched-looking woman with a hatchet for a nose and darting, suspicious eyes. The owner admitted that Mrs Stucker worked here, and grudgingly allowed Reinhardt to speak with her.

Stucker was a tired-looking woman in her late thirties, hands reddened and raw from her work, blond hair pulled back under a cloth cap on her head. She seemed surprised, then wary at his visit when he said he wanted to ask her questions about her late husband. She flicked a glance at the owner, who had retreated behind a high desk with a huge ledger upon it, then asked if he had a cigarette. Her eyes lit up as she saw his Luckies, and she swirled a shawl onto her shoulders as they stepped outside and went a little way along the street. She took a deep pull on the cigarette, leaned back against the wall with her eyes closed at the sky, and nodded for him to ask his questions.

'Mrs Stucker, last year you mentioned in your statement that your husband was worried about something.' She nodded. 'Can you elaborate a little more?'

'Why? Why now? Why you? Back then, your colleagues weren't interested. They didn't listen.'

'I'm not them, Mrs Stucker. That's all I can say. And perhaps you can help in more ways than you know. So, please…?'

'Josef came back from the war in early 1946, from a prisoner-of-war camp. An Allied camp, thank God. Things were hard, but all right. He never talked of his war. Before he came home, I had not seen him in about a year. He had changed, but he wasn't unrecognisable. He managed to find work. We were getting by. Then, one day, he came home worried. The next day was worse. He was convinced someone was following him. He would not say who he thought it was, just that it was "something from the war".' She paused, her mouth and chin firming as she remembered. 'The next day,' she continued, around a long breath of smoke, 'he went to work, but never came back. The day after that, I reported him missing to the police station. A day or so later, they found his body.' Over her shoulder, the laundry's owner poked her head out, looking at Reinhardt with flat, beady eyes.

'He said nothing about any trouble?' She shook her head. 'Black marketeers? The Allies? The Russians? His war service?'

'I've no idea. He said nothing, except that one time. That whatever was bothering him, it was something from the war. That's all.'

'He had his *Fragebogen*?'

'Yes. Denazified and Persil white,' she said, shortly. 'Got the certificate to prove it.'

'Who was the last person to see him alive?'

'His boss. Emil Krey,' she said, confirming the information in the police file. 'He ran a little electricians', but he's dead now. Pneumonia, over the winter. But his business is still going. I'm not even sure the police checked with him,' she finished, with a bitter twist of her mouth as she flicked the stub of her cigarette out across the street. The laundry owner peered out again, and this time hissed her displeasure beneath her breath at one of her employees idling in the street.

'What did he do during the war?'

'Air force pilot. Why?' Stucker asked, seeing Reinhardt tense up.

'Do you know what squadron? Or where?'

'He was a fighter pilot. He was posted pretty much everywhere.'

'The name of the squadron? Or the number?'

'I don't know. But I have his *Wehrpass* at home.'

'I would like to see it, please.' The owner stepped out of the laundry, hands on hips, and Reinhardt snapped his warrant disc out at her. 'This is police business, woman!' he said brusquely. 'Kindly stop bothering me, and mind your own bloody affairs.'

'It's all right,' Stucker murmured, tightening her shoulders beneath the shawl. 'It does not… pay… to annoy her. She has connections in the administration.'

Reinhardt felt immediately contrite, angry as always at himself for losing his temper. He hated doing it, the consequences were invariably unpredictable. 'I'm sorry,' he murmured. 'I hope…'

'Forget it,' Stucker interrupted him. 'The apartment is not far, if you want to come now?'

'Lead on, then, thank you.'

He followed her back to her block of flats, waiting in the hallway of her apartment, as she vanished into one of the further rooms. He stared at a little corner of the living room that resembled a coloured sanctuary of pillows, books, and toys, where a rag doll slumped across the arms of a little chair, and a furry bear lay face down across a mismatched china tea set. The sight froze him, and he did not realise it had taken up so much of his attention until Stucker was standing in front of him, her husband's *Wehrpass* held out in one hand and her head cocked quizzically.

'I'm sorry. I apologise,' he managed, fumbling the book from her hand.

'It's… nothing,' she said, the smallest of frowns creasing her brow.

'It's only, I haven't…' He swallowed, feeling foolish, feeling a need to explain. 'I haven't seen… haven't seen colour, a child's colours, in a long time. Your daughter?' Stucker nodded, and Reinhardt felt desperately uncomfortable, even voyeurish, and he fixed his gaze instead on the *Wehrpass*, freezing as he read out Josef Stucker's squadron.

III./NJG64. And before that in IV./JG56.

How could it have been anything else? he wondered.

'Mrs Stucker, may I take this for my inquiries? I will bring it back.'

'Take it, take it, for all the bloody good it does me,' she said bitterly. 'No benefits, no pension, nothing for Josef's career, nothing for his family but what I can eke out.' She tightened herself, giving a small, sharp shake of her head. 'My turn to apologise,' she said, from under lowered eyes.

'I understand, Mrs Stucker. I, too…' but the words all of a sudden stuck in his mouth, like something dry, mealy. 'I, too, was a member of the armed forces.'

'What's done is done,' she said, and the words fell meaninglessly between them, just sounds, the type two people make when they no longer know what to say to each other, or about anything.

Reinhardt took a long breath in, and made to leave. A last glance around the apartment, and he noted something that a quick check of the *Wehrpass* confirmed. 'This was where you were living before the war?'

'Oh, yes!' she laughed, and for a moment there was a glimpse of the handsome woman she had been as she raised one hand to brush a stray wisp of hair back over her ear, darting her eyes around as if looking for something misplaced, then pointed out the window at the hulk of the buried flak tower. 'You wouldn't believe the noise when that thing was in operation during an air raid, but we were quite safe here. Almost no bombs landed anywhere. And when the Ivans were coming through, well, we took shelter in the tower with half the neighbourhood.' She stopped, her fingers kneading themselves white, then she gave a quick smile. 'When I think of the luck!' she finished brightly, but there was a brittle cast to her voice.

A rap at the door announced a little boy with a message from the laundry owner that Ms Stucker was to return at once. Reinhardt encouraged her to go, not wanting to get her into any more trouble. As they walked out the front door, as Stucker draped her shawl around her shoulders, she turned to him, an earnest look to her, but trepidation lurked there in the corners of her eyes.

'Look, don't take this the wrong way, but…' Reinhardt frowned at her as she visibly firmed herself up. 'When you talked of… of my daughter's things… do you have anyone? I mean, are you with someone?'

Reinhardt blushed furiously as he realised what she was asking, although it was not the first time he had been propositioned in this way. There were simply too few men, or so he had been told.

'You seem like a nice man, and you're not unpleasant on the eye.' She twitched a smile. 'And you're here. There's too many men that aren't. I just thought… the times, you know. It makes things different. So, if you wanted someone, I could maybe… it's just me and the little one, but she doesn't make any trouble, and I could take good care of you.'

'It's not that I'm not flattered, Mrs Stucker…'

'… and I'm clean. I mean, they got me too. The Ivans. Not more than once or twice. Oh,' she replied, as Reinhardt's words caught up with her, and a slight blush rose into her cheeks. 'Flattery's got nothing to do with it. It's not that kind of world, is it? But there, I asked.'

'Thank you. I appreciate what it must have taken to do so.' He felt terribly prim as he said it, wishing the words back but she seemed not to have noticed. At the entrance of the building she paused.

'Is… is it true? Is it true what I thought? Was he murdered?'

Reinhardt nodded, slowly. 'I think so, Mrs Stucker. I can't be sure, but I think so. And I think whoever did it is still killing.'

'Well… ' She hesitated, then firmed her mouth. 'Good luck. Finding him. And thank you.'

'For what?'

'For believing me,' she said. There was a slight moistness in her eyes, probably a memory, and then she was gone. Reinhardt watched her go, a woman alone raising a child in a city like this.

22

There still being time and light, Reinhardt decided to go to the address where Stucker's body was found. He had to go back across town, all the way to Rüdesheimer Platz on the A line as it arrowed out into the southwest of the city, and reminded himself, again, to ask for a driver. To go over Ganz's head if he had to. The transportation around the city was not what it used to be, although he mentally tipped his hand to the engineers like Uthmann who, somehow, were keeping it all running through, around, under, and over the ruins. But he could not take the walking anymore, despite the thrill in his step as he felt facts and theories beginning to coalesce into a shape, a form. There was more out there, much more.

The address in Wilmersdorf where Stucker's body was found – *not*, Reinhardt mentally reminded himself, necessarily where he was murdered – was a bombed-out apartment building in a street lined with them, the whole neighbourhood a sagged ruin, the site of fierce street fighting during the Soviet assault. Telephone poles leaned haphazardly down the length of the street, wires looped and skeined like tangles of wool. Moss and weeds grew thickly across the slides of rubble, and the smell of human waste was strong. Tin cans or scraps of fabric hung from bent and rusted poles thrust into the rubble, makeshift markers that bodies or unexploded ordnance lay below, but it was not enough to discourage the life that still managed to exist, even in such conditions. Here and there, metal chimneys poked up out of the debris, signs that some people eked out a troglodyte existence down below the ruins.

Reinhardt picked his careful way into the rubble, consulting the police report so as to find the exact spot. He found it, his knee a taut line of pain as he went gingerly down a mounded glacis of rubble that fanned down into the basement from the street. Amid heaps of detritus, pressed in by a stench of damp and the pulverised remains of stone and concrete, he wondered what could have brought Stucker down here. He stood where the roof had collapsed, looking all the way up the interior of the building through a haze of dust that spiralled the cavity, tracing the mazed lines of water, gas, and electricity pipes and wires, all the way up, over the pastiche of colours and fabrics that marked the walls where different rooms had once stood on different floors, and traced the lines down again, all the way down, seeing without realising at first that down in the basement with him was a junction box. All the wires led into it.

All the electric wires.

Reinhardt felt cold, as if something had reached out and touched him, realising that Stucker had not been dragged or forced here, but had come of his own free will. For a job, most likely, or some kind of consultation. Stucker had been an electrician. Someone got him out here for an electrician's job, down here and out of the way. Stucker would have had no fears, no apprehensions. No stealthy midnight meetings. No running from some nameless figure seeking shelter down here. Something had indeed spooked him in the last days of his life, but it was not that fear that had driven him here. It was something much more mundane.

An appointment.

An appointment with his own murderer, Reinhardt thought, shivering again and wondering at the patience, calm, and confidence of this killer.

He was consumed by what he thought he had found, hence the crack of rubble against rubble did not at first register, but when it came again, when there was the rasp of leather across stone, he looked up and around.

Fischer and another man were slipping down into the basement, iron bars in their hands.

Reinhardt moved fast, pushing himself past the snarl of pain from his knee as he whipped his baton out. Fischer and the other man were both still coming down the slide of wreckage, their footing unsure. Fischer tried to back up against the rake of debris, but his footing lurched away, and Reinhardt slashed the baton into his ankle. Fischer yelped in pain, and his feet slid further back, down towards Reinhardt, who slashed the baton across his knees and thighs. The other man tried to jump down the slope, his feet scattering detritus as he heaved himself up, but he only succeeded in losing his footing completely, and the bar he carried clanged away into the basement's gloom. Reinhardt hit him across his knees and ankles, blows that would incapacitate rather than maim, or kill. The man cried out, folding up and over the pain in his legs, and Reinhardt crashed his batoned fist onto the back of his neck, turning back to Fischer as the man foundered to stillness.

Fischer was climbing to his feet, one hand on the rubble. Reinhardt hit that wrist with the baton, flicking it out like a whip so that the ball on its tip flayed into Fischer's hand. Fischer crashed back down, his other hand raised up.

'Enough! *Enough!*'

'What the hell are you doing, Fischer?' Reinhardt yelled. He clamped his voice shut, feeling the edge of his words beginning to quaver with his stress, not wanting to give Fischer any way back at him.

'Hoping to give you a bloody good seeing-to, what's it look like?' Fischer's face creased up around the pain of his hand as he hugged it to his chest, folded into his other fist.

'Why, for God's sake?'

'I told you, you shouldn't have brought them coppers to my door.'

'I *didn't*.'

'Can't believe anything a copper says, Reinhardt,' growled Fischer, rubbing his good palm over his fist. ''sides, you were marked out for us.'

'Marked out? Marked out by whom? What are you talking about?'

'Just some bloke, said he was nicked for the same things they brought me in for. Says you were behind it.'

Reinhardt shook his head, standing back. 'Fischer, I don't know what you're talking about, I really don't. Who was this man? Who was he?'

Fischer shook his head up at Reinhardt, a pitying gesture, as if he heard the strained crack to Reinhardt's words, the stress that weighed them down.

'I'll tell you. You won't know him, though. Poor bastard's just one of dozens you coppers roughed up in the cells. But he knows you. Knows you very well. He knew the coppers'd never have found him if it weren't for you. They're all piss and no bull in the Kripo these days. Not like in our day, right? You're the brains of that outfit now, I'll give you that, Reinhardt. But what's it feel like? What's it feel like to know you're watched, without knowing it? Oh, he's a smart one, Reinhardt. He hides it well, but he's a smart little bugger, got your number, told us where to look for you…'

Maybe it was what Fischer was not saying, as much as the stream of verbiage. Maybe it was the stress. God knew, in times past, stress and danger had given Reinhardt a heightened sense of his surroundings because the chink of rubble somewhere up behind him sounded like the ringing of a china cup when a spoon tapped it. Something in the way he stood must have been obvious to Fischer, something must have told him that his game was up, because his words trailed off, and he grinned. He had time to blink before Reinhardt tightened his grip on the baton and smashed his fist into Fischer's jaw, a short jab, swinging hard from his hips. Fischer slumped back onto the rubble, and Reinhardt was climbing past him, as quickly as he could go, back up the shattered glacis of broken bricks. He slipped, banged his knees, gritted his teeth against the pain, and his baton clattered away back down the slope. He heard the scrabble of feet behind him, a frustrated shout, and then he was up and on the street, and he was running, the pain in his knee something distant, as if it belonged to someone else.

23

Reinhardt struggled home on the trains, a slow and lurching journey on the S-Bahn from Schmargendorf to Templehof, and the U-Bahn one stop north to Paradestrasse. The illuminated airport was visible to his right as he went north, a wide arc that parcelled the huge crescent of the landing apron into splintered islands of light. When he came up out of the U-Bahn, he could hear the hum and drone of an aircraft in the darkness somewhere behind him as he paced out his long, hesitant walk through streets lit and lined by a furtive sliver of moon, each step paced out to the slow burn of his knee. The power was out in the district, and there were only drifts of light from window frames, ripples from candles and open flames. It was very cold, and he was so caught up in measuring his steps, in the slow roll of the day through his mind, that he saw the car parked outside his house too late.

He hesitated when he saw it, and he stopped when he saw the Red Army plates. The doors opened and men slipped out. He felt a gelid stab of fear, thought to step backwards, froze again at the whisper of a footstep behind him. A man was there, a man he had not seen or heard. His face was blank, the low brim of a cap tracing a flowing line of shadow across his brows.

'*Ti, idi siuda.*' The words were Russian, the voice lazy, as if it knew no circumstance under which it might be disobeyed. All German men knew what those words meant, and what it might mean to disobey them, and so Reinhardt walked slowly over to the car where two men waited for him, removing his hat as he went. It felt right to do it, but it felt wrong, and he squirmed around a momentary hitch of loathing, but whether of himself or these men he did not know. He refused himself the opportunity to wonder. He needed to concentrate.

'Rukhi verkh,' one of them ordered, and Reinhardt raised his hands and was frisked by the man behind him, feeling the man's breath intimate on his neck, fetid with the stench of *makhorka*, that tobacco the Russians all seemed to smoke and, for just a second, the faintest scrape of an unshaven chin across his nape. It jolted him, then froze him still. Only his eyes could move, and so he ran them over what he could see, trying to make himself think.

The men wore dark uniforms, dull gleams of metal on epaulettes and collars. Belts slanted across their chests, big pistols were holstered at their hips, their tunics flared out over the tops of their wide trousers, which were tucked into knee-high boots. Rules and regulations tumbled through Reinhardt's mind, were swept away, but he knew any member of the Allied Occupation forces had access to any sector at any time, so long as they were in uniform. As these men were.

The man searching him found his warrant disc and handed it to one of the others who looked at it with vague disinterest. The man turned the disk in his hands, showed it to the other who shrugged.

'Nu ladno,' the man behind him said.

The man who had his disk pointed at the house.

'Zaxhodi,' he said. 'Inside,' he repeated, in German. 'Go inside.'

Reinhardt felt the chill as soon as he stepped inside the house. The man prodded him in the back, and he walked forward through the muffled quiet into the kitchen. It was empty, but there were cups and a pot of honey on the table, and a uniform cap, lying upside down. A stir of wind pointed to the door to the garden. It was ajar, but suddenly washed open in a ripple of reflected light. Mrs Meissner walked straight-backed into the kitchen, followed by another Soviet, an officer with a major's insignia on his epaulettes.

'It is wonderful work, the way you have sheltered them from the winter,' the officer was saying, as he shut the door. 'My grandmother would keep her bees by…' He stopped as he saw Reinhardt.

The soldier behind Reinhardt put a heavy hand on his shoulder, stopping him, then he leaned past and placed Reinhardt's warrant disc on the table. He spoke briefly, a few words in Russian. The officer nodded, the faintest movement of his head, then gestured the man out with his eyes.

Under the buttery glow of the lantern that hung over the table, Mrs Meissner sat very still and stiff in her chair. The officer was not a young man. He had a face creased and lined with wrinkles, webs of them to either side of his eyes, deep channels that grooved both sides of his nose, down to the corners of his lips. One side of his mouth was ridged by scars, as if he had been wounded and never properly healed, and the skin seemed to sag inward, just a little. From the look of the pale lines across his high forehead, he frowned often, and his hair was little more than a grey fringe around his ears and round the back of his head. He spun Reinhardt's disc around with one finger, looking at it, then his mouth firmed and he lifted his head. He looked at Reinhardt a moment, then smiled, but a smile that spread no further than a tautening of his lips. He turned courteously to Meissner. He was not a tall man, at least a head shorter than Reinhardt, but he had a deep breadth of chest.

'Mrs Meissner, thank you for the tea. And for the honey. It was delicious. It reminds me of the honey my grandmother would serve from the hives she kept.' Meissner inclined her head, graciously. 'I congratulate you for keeping your bees alive through this terrible winter. I wonder, though, if you would be so kind as to give me and the captain some privacy.'

She nodded, the light rippling over the silver of her hair, and she took the hand he offered her to rise stiffly to her feet. Reinhardt watched her go, saw the blankness in her expression as she fixed him momentarily with her eyes when she passed behind the officer. Then she was gone, her steps slow and halting up the wooden stairs, and in the silence she left behind, Reinhardt suddenly heard the clock in the front room ticking heavily.

The officer watched Meissner leave, and then smiled at Reinhardt, a stretch of his lips with no glimpse of his teeth, but it changed his face, as if a younger man had parted the lines and creases life had left on it to peer out. 'You have to admire people like her. Ladies of a certain generation and class. You would think nothing could ruffle them or cause them to break stride. They take what life gives them, and adapt. I had a look outside, in her garden. She is remarkably self-sufficient. Some vegetables. Which I see you have protected like a World War One trench! Beehives. Herbs. The mint tea is particularly good,' he said, lifting his mug and taking a sip. 'Truly, she reminds me of my own grandmother. Nothing ever stopped her.

'She told me she used to be a director at the Decorative Arts. An amazing place. I preferred the Pergamon, myself. Or the Tell Halaf! It made me want to be an archaeologist and go running off to Syria to dig through the sands.' The officer's voice was low, quite deep, and his German was smooth, almost unaccented, and somehow archaic, as if he had learned it a long time ago, in a different time and place.

'You are probably wondering what's going on, Captain. Let me put you at ease, first. I am not here to take you away. My name is Skokov. I am a major with the Soviet MGB. You are, of course, familiar with the MGB.'

'Soviet intelligence,' Reinhardt said around a dry tongue.

'"State security", rather,' corrected Skokov, with another tight smile. Reinhardt said nothing as the major enjoyed another sip of his mint tea, but he could not help but note the man's manners. Somewhat anachronistic in what he knew of Soviet political policemen, and either a show or real, but in both cases, disconcerting.

'Tell me, Captain, why did you go to Friedrichshain today?'

Reinhardt blinked, swallowed. 'It was part of a murder investigation.'

Skokov smiled, sipped from his tea, the scars shining along his lips. 'I have heard about your investigation, but I want to hear it from you too. It always sounds better coming from one closely involved, and I never tire of hearing a good story.' His eyes glittered, and they seemed to be saying 'don't bother hiding anything; I'll know.'

'I think… I think that the man I am pursuing has been killing for some time. One of his victims may have been a man who lived in the Soviet Sector.'

'This "Stucker", correct? A former air force pilot.'

'Yes,' said Reinhardt, shaken at how fast information had percolated up to this man. 'That is why I was there today.'

'The others? All pilots as well? All from the same squadron?'

'The same Group,' Reinhardt corrected him. Skokov's eyebrows rose, guttering the skin across his forehead, and Reinhardt cursed himself, covering his fear up with an air of perplexity. 'I am confused, Major. What would a Soviet state security officer want with a murder investigation?'

Skokov did not immediately answer, instead lifting a small leather satchel onto the table, and taking from it a package wrapped in greaseproof paper and a bottle of clear fluid. 'A good story requires good food. And good food requires good drink. Do you have two glasses, Captain?' Reinhardt brought two mismatched glasses to the table, as Skokov unwrapped the paper exposing a length of sausage, and half a loaf of black bread. 'You pour, please,' he said, as he began to slice the sausage, and then two slices of the bread. Reinhardt twisted the cork out of the bottle, and then poured two measures into the glasses. It was vodka, he smelled. Skokov lifted his glass.

'To our meeting and our mutual understanding. *Za vstrechu i vzaimnoye ponimaniye.*' Skokov inclined his head, a light of expectation in his eyes beneath the furrows across his brows.

'*Na zdorovie,*' managed Reinhardt.

Skokov nodded, smiling. He breathed out to one side, and knocked his drink back.

Very good vodka, Reinhardt realised as he took a drink, feeling the alcohol swell through his mouth and then chase itself down his throat.

'*Pozhaluysta.* Please,' said Skokov, taking a piece of bread and sniffing it. 'You were saying you are confused, Captain,' he continued, popping a slice of sausage almost delicately into his mouth. Reinhardt's eyes were hooked by a sudden glimpse of a row of silver teeth in Skokov's mouth along the side that seemed sunken in, before he concentrated on his own food. The sausage was very good, some kind of smoked beef, he thought, better and stronger than anything he had had in a long time. 'That would be because you are being left in the dark by your English and American friends. And so tell me. Tell me your story of this investigation.'

'I have two pilots – Noell and Zuleger – who have been murdered in similar ways, within days of each other. Noell was murdered after attending some kind of event, or function. Zuleger was murdered before Noell, and maybe before going to the same function. I found an invitation at his apartment, to an address in Grunewald.'

Reinhardt paused. There had been a note at the station, from one of the secretaries. The police in Grunewald had gone to the address as he asked and found an abandoned property. A dead end, maybe, but Reinhardt knew he would eventually have to go himself and check. He had never liked leaving aspects of his inquiries to others, and he liked it less now, in this environment, with this police force.

'I have a third pilot – Stucker – murdered last year. All three of them were in the same fighter Group, IV./JG56. At least two of them – Zuleger and Stucker – were in the same unit when it was redesignated as a night-fighter group, III./NJG64. The Night Hawks. There is a link between them and a man called Carlsen. I found him dead at the same address as Noell. All four of them were murdered in the same fashion.'

'This business of sand and water, correct?'

Reinhardt blinked his surprise back, covering it with a sip of vodka. 'Yes. There is a matter of water found in Noell's mouth, and sand in Zuleger's.'

'Stucker's autopsy report said nothing of the kind?'

'It was inconclusive. And there is also the precision of the blows that all but killed them.'

'Go on,' Skokov encouraged him, slicing off more sausage.

'There is a potential fifth victim in Hamburg. This man – Haber – had also served in the air force.'

'But not in either of these squadrons,' said Skokov.

It was terrifying how much this man knew. 'Groups. Not squadrons. No, we don't know that, yet. But the body was found in a similar state to the ones we found here. Only his murderer forced him to ingest water.'

'Water? Like Noell? How interesting. A toast, Captain!'

'You're longer dead than you are alive.'

Skokov laughed, a glitter of teeth along one side of his mouth. He huffed his breath out and they drank. He poured again, sniffed his bread and ate it, reflectively, then sharpened his eyes on Reinhardt. 'There are other names. Tell me of Gieb and Stresemann. Tell me of Markworth and Whelan. Tell me,' he grinned, a wet metal glisten, 'of Collingridge.'

24

'Gieb was a prostitute who claimed to have been with Carlsen the night he was killed. She said he was killed by a man named Stresemann. Both of them have vanished. Markworth and Whelan are British agents…'

'Whelan is on the Public Security Committee, yes.'

'I think they were colleagues of Carlsen's…'

'Yes. He was a legal adviser to the British member of the committee. Colonel Stewart.'

'Thank you,' said Reinhardt, confused by Skokov's apparent knowledge. 'And Collingridge…'

'… is your American benefactor,' Skokov said, when Reinhardt's voice ran to a stop. 'It is all right, Captain. There is nothing wrong with a benefactor. There is no shame. He brought you back to Berlin, didn't he? Back into the police. He does not ask for much, just a little information from time to time. Am I wrong?' Reinhardt said nothing, and Skokov smiled again, but there was no mockery in it, reaching across the table to pour vodka into Reinhardt's glass. 'A toast, Captain. Give me another toast.'

'To the best. For the best is the cheapest thing to buy.'

Skokov blinked at him, then guffawed, clashing his glass against Reinhardt's. '*Captain!* You are full of surprises! Say rather, a useless thing is dear at any price,' he laughed, huffing out and knocking his vodka back. He tore a piece of bread in half. 'Here. Eat. Eat! Ah, Captain,' sighed Skokov, brushing a finger at the corner of one eye. 'You are no storyteller. You have no soul for it,' he said, shaking his head as he poured more vodka for them both. 'No embellishment.

No *drama!* A Russian would know how to put drama into even the dreariest of stories. Look at what you have,' he enthused, waving his glass in one hand, 'a story involving a conquered but still proud people, a swirling mix of politics, obstructionism from within, interest from without, dead pilots – cavaliers of the air! – a dead British agent, and yourself. An ex-policeman and an ex-officer in the Fascist armed forces. Men who are despised, mistrusted, robbed of nearly all self-respect. I saw your *Fragebogen*. The one you filled out for employment with the police. Quite a war you had. Would it interest you to know that the Soviet representative to the Public Security Committee was not happy having you back on the force? The Americans wanted you to work with Bliemeister, the assistant chief of their sector. You know he is allowed three advisers: one each from the detectives, uniformed police, and administration. You would have been the detective, but you were assessed as too independent. But the Americans insisted on another position for you, and fair is fair, I suppose. They have their men, we have our men. Everyone has their men. Still,' he mused, holding his vodka up to the light, the sunken side of his mouth a gentle, shadowed dip, 'despite your best efforts to tell it otherwise, it is quite an interesting story.'

'Perhaps one you could finish,' Reinhardt dared, conscious suddenly that he had held Kausch's name back, reeling from what Skokov seemed to know about him.

Reinhardt's temerity seemed to delight Skokov. He smiled, a full flash of his metal teeth, and he lifted his glass. '*Za vstrechoo!*' he toasted. 'To our meeting, for a good meeting always fills the heart, Captain.'

'Why do you keep calling me that?' Reinhardt managed around the vodka's scald. His head was spinning, and he felt adrift. He wedged his feet uncomfortably between the legs of his chair and pressed them into the wood, feeling a slow burn in his knee under the strain.

'I feel it defines you more than "inspector". Perhaps I am wrong?'

'It is what I was,' Reinhardt said. 'Not what I am.'

'So, I shall resume. This Carlsen is the first victim you find, but not the first victim of this killer. Nearby, you find Noell. The British tell you Carlsen is one of theirs and demand the German police investigate his murder as a priority, leaving you on your own to follow up on Noell. You are on your own because you disagree with the Allies' orders, and because you are something of a pariah. You will forgive me,' Skokov said, his hand opening around his vodka glass in a gesture of conciliation, 'it is not an opinion I share, merely an observation I proffer. You continue your investigation, uncovering more bodies, a worrying trail that goes back years. Meanwhile, despite all the evidence you lay out for them that there is only one killer, your poor colleagues are bumbling along dragging in half of Berlin's underworld, and in doing so, they manage to mislay this prostitute, their prime witness and as well their prime suspect. When were you going to tell me about Fischer?'

Reinhardt pressed his feet harder against the chair. Skokov smiled at him, cocking his head slightly to one side, his brow furrowed into lines of query. Reinhardt bit back the first question, the 'How did you know about that?' and instead forged ahead. 'I did not see the relevance,' he managed. 'I thought it was an old score being settled. Nothing to do with the investigation.'

Skokov's mouth pursed, the lines on his forehead smoothing themselves out. 'I'm not sure I believe you, Captain. That upsets me, somehow. You would think, of course, that a man in my profession is used to lies, and to obfuscation. I expect it even. I did not, I shall be honest, expect it from you. Somehow, it offends me. If offends my sense of this house, and that grand lady who runs it.'

'Fischer said that… he said that some of the men in the cells who were rounded up got to talking. Some of them knew me, so they thought maybe I was behind some of the arrests.'

'No mention of an individual in particular?' Reinhardt said nothing, his mouth opening. 'No? Well, it may comfort you to know Fischer could not say who it was put him on that particular path.

He heard it from someone, who heard it from someone… you know how it goes.'

'You spoke with Fischer?'

'He spoke to one of my men, who then spoke to me.'

'Where is he?'

'In a cell somewhere, I should imagine. Or perhaps on the street. We've no further use for him. What shall you do next?' Skokov asked, changing tack again.

'I need access to official records. The kind the Allies have.'

'You mean the Berlin Document Center?'

'No. That material is related to the Nazis, not the armed forces. Four of the five victims were ex-military. I need Wehrmacht records. I need to get into the WASt.'

'Ah, yes, the WASt, the Wehrmacht Information Office for War Losses and POWs. A treasure trove of information, from the mundane to the munificent. Under the control of our French friends. When shall you go?'

'One does not… someone like me does not just walk into it. I shall ask my chief to try and obtain access for me.'

'You shall have it,' Skokov said, with an air of confident dismissal. 'About your story. I would like to keep hearing of it. What you find out. What you hear.'

'You want me to report to you?'

'You can say that. Don't worry, Captain,' Skokov said, as he sliced off a piece of sausage, 'I don't need you to come to Karlshorst or anything like that.'

'That is… a relief.' Karlshorst was known colloquially in Berlin as the Little Kremlin. It did not pay for Germans to go in there. Karlshorst triggered a sudden thought of Kausch and Poles, and Reinhardt realised he had said nothing about either of them.

'I would imagine so,' Skokov grinned, a tight clench of his lips that pulled the sunken side of his mouth down. 'Although remember, the devil is never so black as he is painted. No. Whatever you find out that touches upon these murders, or whatever you hear from your

Allied friends, be sure that I will be interested to hear of it.'

'That's it? Nothing in particular?'

'I will tell you something for nothing, Reinhardt. Or rather, I will tell you something for the excellent welcome your Mrs Meissner afforded me. Carlsen may not be your priority, but he is indeed interesting. He was a particular type of British agent. He was an Anglo-German who fought for the British in the war.'

'Anglo-German?' Reinhardt repeated.

'Even so,' Skokov said, as he began wrapping up the sausage and bread. 'You should look into them if you have the time. Churchill's Germans! That old imperial fox! There were quite a few of them. Children of two peoples who fought for the Allies – for the West, and for us – instead of the Germans. You can imagine their use, now, in occupied Germany.'

'How do you know this?' Skokov smiled, said nothing. 'What more can you tell me?'

Skokov smiled and shook his head, putting the package to one side. 'You have an expression in German, I believe. "The listener never hears any good of himself". I should not need to remind you, Captain, that the flow of information in this relationship needs to be from you to me.'

'Why would I do that?' Reinhardt asked, skating along the awkward impression Skokov gave him, of erudition and eloquence and yet a man with a mouthful of metal teeth. However Reinhardt had judged him, whether the vodka had eroded any sense of caution, he knew it was a risk and a danger in talking so to a Soviet officer, but Skokov only smiled again, as he put another tightly wrapped packet on the table.

'You will find it is in your interest. And if you doubt – after all, it is only human to doubt – I remind you that Berlin is but an island in a sea. An island cannot survive alone. It must trade. Goods and people must come in. And out. And that the sea around this particular island is red. This,' he said, rising to his feet and pointing at the packets, 'I leave for you to give to Mrs Meissner. There is butter and cheese, and the rest of the bread and sausage. There is sugar here. Tell her, she should give some of it to her bees. And we shall drink a last toast to her, and to women like her. To the lady of the house! *Za hazyaiku etovo doma!*'

Reinhardt stood as well, untangling his feet from the chair legs, and washing the last of the vodka down and back.

'And with that, Captain, I wish you a pleasant evening.'

Reinhardt sat at the table after Skokov left, listening, waiting. He heard voices, doors slam shut, and the car drive away into the night, and then he waited a little more. His head was buzzing from the vodka and he sat breathing deeply, trying to still and centre himself. After a while, he rose and poured a glass of water, still listening to the night as he drank it down, and poured and drank another. When he was sure there was nothing and no one around, he went quietly up the stairs to his room and pushed open the door.

Brauer was lying on the floor in the corner. His eyes twinkled back at Reinhardt as the light lit them.

'How much of that did you hear?' Reinhardt asked.

'Most of it,' Brauer replied, sitting up, moving stiffly beneath his blankets.

'What have you got there?'

'What?'

'Rudi,' Reinhardt growled.

'Oh, this old thing,' Brauer said, pulling out a Bergmann submachine gun, a First World War relic.

'Ah, Christ. Rudi. Do you *still* have that? That "old thing" is, I'm sure, in perfect working order and it'll get you in more trouble than it's worth. If that Soviet had found you with it…'

'Don't worry about things that haven't happened.'

'There's vodka downstairs. Come and have a drink.'

Down in the kitchen, Reinhardt poured two small measures, Brauer's eyes following his every movement. They were sunk deep beneath the troubled line of his brow. Brauer seemed to have been whittled back to the blunt edges of his body, his face harshly planed beneath the obtrusion of his cheeks. His hands, where they played with the vodka glass, turning and turning it slowly with his fingers, were corded with tendons splayed between knobbed joints that looked like pebbles.

'What have you got yourself into?' Brauer asked, elbows on the table.

Reinhardt knew someone had talked. It could have been anyone. He suspected Ganz or Weber, but it did not really matter.

'I need help, Brauer. Will you watch my back for me?'

'Of course I would. Of course… but… I'm not. I'm not…'

'You know, during the war, there was a captain in the secret field police. His name was Thallberg. I met him in Sarajevo during that investigation I told you about. The one into the murder of that journalist. Well, he knew all about you. About us. He asked after you. After the infamous Inspector Brauer.'

'Really?' asked Brauer, straightening.

'I told him you were in the army, probably terrifying new recruits.'

'Not far off,' murmured Brauer. He sniffed at his glass, took a swig. 'Christ, that's not very nought-eight-fifteen,' he wheezed, the old trenches slang for the *common* and *commonplace*. 'That's good stuff.'

'He said he fancied the pair of us for the secret field police. Imagine the trouble we'd have caused, you and I.'

Brauer grinned, took another swig, nodding to himself. 'Look… if you want me to help… of course, I'll do it. You know I will.'

Reinhardt nodded, a small, tight smile. He had wanted to shake Brauer out of his despondency, perhaps bring him back to himself, but Reinhardt felt himself draining away, all of a sudden. The end of a long, long day, and Reinhardt began to sink back into himself, retreating, remembering Sarajevo, remembering what he had accomplished there, the people left behind. Remembering Suzana Vukić, remembering the last time he had seen her with her grey-blonde hair pulled back behind her neck, walking away from her under the chill light of a spring morning.

Those thoughts stayed with him as they went to bed, Brauer curling himself up into his corner. Reinhardt lay awake, desperately tired, but he could not drift off, thoughts plucking at him at random, and so he was awake to hear the sound of steps on the street, awake to hear them pause, and he knew they were outside the house. He sat up in bed as he heard steps on the pathway that led up to the door, pause again, then move around the side of the house.

He stole downstairs, pulled on his shoes and opened the door onto the garden silently. His feet soughed through wet grass as he scampered to the corner of the house, pushing himself into the shadows, waiting. He heard steps, the scuff of a shoe, the sudden gasp as fabric and skin hooked on the wire Reinhardt had laid. The detective slid around the corner. There was a man hopping on one leg, the faintest edge of moonlight lining his head and shoulders. Reinhardt stepped quietly up to him, squeezing the man's head into an armlock and pushing a knee into his back. The man gave a startled cry, lurching backwards into Reinhardt, fabric tearing as he came off the wire.

'*Quiet!*' hissed Reinhardt. 'What the hell are you doing?' He released the pressure, enough to allow the man to speak. 'Who are you?'

The man twisted, hacked a breath.

'*Father!*'

Reinhardt froze, with a fist in the man's collar, he turned him, tilting his face up enough into the moonlight.

It was Friedrich.

25

Reinhardt watched Friedrich while the water boiled. His son sat at the table, his hands clasped together, very still, and his eyes downcast. Reinhardt poured the water over two cups of mint and brought them to the table with some of Mrs Meissner's honey. Even sitting opposite him, Friedrich seemed unable or unwilling to meet his father's eyes. His son was gaunt, drawn long and tight against the angles of his bones. His eyes held a shadow that was more than the dim light in the room could cast, and he held himself as if he sullied the air around him, as if he were something dirty, something unclean.

'You know,' said Reinhardt quietly, as he stirred honey into his tea, 'the last time I saw you I was having tea.'

Friedrich went even more still, rigid even, until his eyes came slowly into focus and he looked at Reinhardt, for almost the first time. There was a distance in them, as if Friedrich held himself in and away from the world, and something else, although Reinhardt could not see what it was. Friedrich blinked once, twice. 'The morning Mother died.' The memory of it was suddenly there, clouding the grey of his eyes like a rumour of sorrow, or regret.

'You were with that friend of yours. What was his name…?'

'Hans Kalter,' Friedrich breathed.

'Kalter,' said Reinhardt. He remembered the name. He wondered only if Friedrich had. 'What became of him?'

Friedrich shrugged. 'Dead, I think.'

There was silence, only the chime of spoons against china. Reinhardt lifted his teacup in his fingers, letting the steam writhe up over his eyes. 'That day...' Friedrich began, placing his hands flat on the table on either side of his cup, 'that last day we saw each other. You made tea in Mother's blue pot. Somehow, I can't forget it. I can't forget that teapot. I keep going back to where we used to live, thinking I could look for it.'

Reinhardt stared at his son, wondering, Could it have been him he had sensed those times he had felt someone else there? Someone watching him. His instincts, already bruised and ragged from the day, twitched, and he forced down the feeling, the feeling that made him doubt his son. That made him feel he was being played. 'What has happened to you, Friedrich? Where have you been?' he asked, his fingers restive on his spoon.

'Where do you think?'

'In a POW camp?' Friedrich nodded. 'Tell me.'

'There's nothing to tell, Father,' Friedrich retorted. He turned in and away, just a little, as if he were embarrassed, or unclean. As if measuring out the rhythm of his unease, Friedrich's fingers began to move on the table, the tips brushing softly, back and forth, over the wood.

'It was difficult?' Friedrich snorted, but there was nothing in it, no vigour to give offence. Just something habitual, a reflex, like the slow movement of his fingers. 'Why did they let you out?'

'What do you mean? "Why?"'

Reinhardt winced inwardly, cringing away from conflict, from confrontation. It would have been so easy to have fallen back into their old patterns, of cut-and-thrust, of parry-riposte. 'Just that, Friedrich. We hear so many rumours of the camps. About what the Soviets are doing to our prisoners.'

'Ah,' Friedrich said, seemingly mollified. He closed his fingers around his cup, sipped from his tea and spooned more honey in. 'Rumours. Most of them are true, I suppose. They put us in a transit camp in Gronenfelder, up near Frankfurt-on-the-Oder. That was pretty bad. But the camps in Russia were... awful. There were times I didn't think I'd make it. Many of us... most of us they got after Stalingrad... didn't.'

'How did you survive?' Reinhardt asked.

Friedrich shrugged, eyes on the slow pulse of his fingers. 'Isn't it always luck? Towards the end of the battle, I was wounded, couldn't walk much, so a friend arranged to get me onto the field marshal's staff. We were down in the basement of this huge department store. It was warmer. Food was a bit better. So when the end came, I was that bit better off. And the Ivans weren't so bad to the field marshal's staff. The march to the camps was...' Friedrich stopped, and Reinhardt shook his head, bemusement and understanding vying for place. His son lifted his eyes, and there was that depth and distance in them, a shadow that would not lift. 'Well, it was bad. The months went by. The years... you... made your accommodations, right? You made your peace with yourself, and with your comrades, because you never thought you'd make it out. And then... it ended. The war ended. And I suppose even the Ivans can't keep everyone they've got. I suppose I wasn't much use to them. I don't know, and they didn't tell, and you don't question the orders that put you on a train home.'

'No,' Reinhardt agreed. 'Of course not. And what are you doing now?'

'Not much, I'm afraid,' Friedrich said, and there was the sudden ghost of a smile on his face, something ironic. 'Seems things turned out the way you predicted, Father. You always said I'd come to nothing with that lot, with the Nazis, and you were right. No, it's fine,' he said, raising his hand, forestalling the protest that had risen to Reinhardt's lips. 'It's fine. Things just... turned out... the way they did.'

'I'm very sorry for that, Friedrich. And I'm sorry... I'm sorry we weren't... that I wasn't...'

'Father, it's fine. It's fine. It's past.'

'Yes. Yes, but,' and Reinhardt felt the words damn up inside, swelling up into his eyes and he blinked back a hot sting of sudden tears. 'But they're years we'll never get back.'

The words hung between them, and the mood was uneasy.

Tentative. There was too much bad history between them for it to be anything else. Or it could be nothing else so soon.

'Where are you now?'

'I'm in a halfway house run by an old comrades' association. It's in Rummelsburg,' he said, naming a part of the city to the southwest in the Soviet Sector, 'not far from Ostkreuz station.'

'You could move here,' Reinhardt offered.

'This is your Colonel's old house, isn't it? I don't think so, Father, but it's kind. I… we need to start again. I need to find my own way, as well. The comrades help, I suppose. Although, sometimes, I can't bear to look at them. They carry such memories. I carry them, too…' His words made sense, but the clench of his posture said something else entirely. *Unclean*, it said. *Outcast*, it cried.

Reinhardt nodded, hands twisting his mug. 'I remember, after the first war, the same thing. I was in hospital. I could not stand to look at the others. But I don't know how I would have survived without my friends. Without those who had known what it was all like. How did you find me?'

He would have bitten back the question if he could have. He would have bitten his own tongue to have it back. It slipped out without him realising, the type of question he would have posed to a suspect in an interrogation but, to his relief, Friedrich seemed not to have noticed, his fingers still measuring out their rhythm and reach across the tabletop.

'I cannot stay away from where we used to live, and I saw you there. I followed you.' Friedrich shrugged, sipped from his tea. 'Nothing fancy to it, really,' he finished, a smile pulling down one side of his mouth.

'Why did you come?'

'I don't have one answer, Father. But I think I was compelled. I was visiting the ruins where we used to live. I went once. I kept going. Then I saw you. And I thought, I wondered, Did you feel the same things as me? Some connection back to that time we were all together. It wasn't always bad, was it?'

'No,' agreed Reinhardt, but it had been. It had been bad. Friedrich had never been an easy child, and he grew more difficult the older he became and the more the Nazis pulled him into their orbit. Into their vision of how a child should behave, and what duties it owed.

'Look, I have to go,' Friedrich said, suddenly. His eyes had gone murky again, openings into some inner darkness, and he held himself as if he had seen or heard of some risk to him, some rumour of trouble. 'I shouldn't… I'm sorry to have done this. Done this like this.'

'It's fine,' Reinhardt assured him.

Friedrich seemed to clench in on himself again, bracing his shoulders on the table like a strangler's on his victim. His face, already gaunt, grew longer.

'No. I should go. But can I come again?'

Reinhardt nodded. 'Yes, of course.'

Friedrich's mouth twitched, some semblance of a smile flitting across his lips. 'Until then, then,' he said.

'Until then.'

Reinhardt walked him to the door. They paused on the step, neither sure what to do, until Friedrich seemed to come to some decision, and he darted his head up at Reinhardt. 'Did you ever look for me? Did you… did you think I was alive?'

The question froze Reinhardt where he stood, cored him right to where a priest might have said a man's soul would be. He could not move or offer any answer, only look at his son, his tongue probing the gap in his teeth. Friedrich's eyes changed, darkened, as if some memory, some thought rode his gaze like a plague ship. He gave a tight nod, as if Reinhardt's reaction were normal, as if Friedrich himself were something to be shunned. He drew himself in around the arc of his shoulders and backed away down the path that led to the street, and then he was gone. Reinhardt watched him away, watching until he lost him in the night, until, almost involuntarily, he lifted his eyes to the sky, at the bright shoals of stars that hung overhead, and let the gulf above him draw his feelings up and out.

He was stunned. That was the least of it. He would be stunned in any case, but after the day, after the length and stress of it, he felt himself wavering. As much as he was relieved to see his son – the son he had almost given up hope of ever seeing, the son he had consigned to the dead – he was honest enough to know he was not happy to see him. Not happy in the way books and films showed you could be happy. How you were *supposed* to be happy. The father he was – had suddenly become again – feared for his son. The policeman he was feared there was far more to Friedrich's story. Although many had returned home, Reinhardt knew the Soviets were suspected of holding many more. Those who had returned had brought with them tales, of pain and suffering and neglect. Many had been invalids, of no use to the Soviets as labour, and many – too many – were suspected of having turned, become collaborators. Like Margraff, the chief of police.

Also captured at Stalingrad.

Reinhardt looked at the stars, and feared the worst about and for his son.

The Tiergarten was quiet, the daytime crowds gone. The Sunday fathers, the ice-cream salesmen, the bands, the people strewn across the grass and benches. The uniforms, the flags, the marching and parades, the new swastikas everywhere, leering and lurking crookedly from every arm and banner.

'See, Friedrich, see how bright they are.'

Reinhardt had one arm on Friedrich's shoulder, spread the other at the sky. The lights of the city were muted, distant behind the park's trees, and stars studded the night in abyssal profusions, in glittering spreads and swirls. Friedrich gazed up solemnly. Dutifully, Reinhardt thought a moment, crushing out the spite in his mind as soon as the idea sprouted. His son. His boy. A teenager, now, with an adolescent's growing gawkiness to his movements and thoughts.

'Remember when we used to try to count them?' Friedrich nodded. 'Remember what you said when I asked you how long it would take you?'

'Pappaaa,' Friedrich protested.

'Come on! You remember. It wasn't so long ago.'

Friedrich sighed. '"A long, longer time," I said.'

'"How long a long, longer time?"' Reinhardt replied, goading Friedrich to recall those memories.

Friedrich considered, his eyes roaming and flickering up at the stars as much as around his memories. 'As long as it took us to see the statue of Roland.'

Reinhardt smiled. The huge walrus had been a popular attraction. After his death, the zoo had sculpted a life-size likeness of Roland, and half of Berlin had turned out to see the statue when it was finished.

'You remember that, do you?'

Friedrich smiled, and they walked on in silence.

'Orion's bright tonight. And the Bear.'

'The big bear,' growled Friedrich in a baby voice, fingers hooked at the sky.

Reinhardt smiled again, ruffling Friedrich's hair.

'Remember that time we came when you were little, and we picked a star for you? Can you find it again? Remember how?'

Friedrich's eyes narrowed as he began to hunt. Reinhardt turned slowly with him. Reinhardt loved the night sky over the city, loved watching it, loving the way more and more of it would emerge the longer he looked. Sometimes, he felt if he watched long enough, a pattern would make itself known, just for him, one only he would understand.

'There it is,' Friedrich said, firmly, pointing to a bright star that hung above the steeple of the Kaiser Wilhelm Church.

'That's it, well done. What about the one you chose for me? And for Mummy?'

'Who is there?'

The voice came out of the darkness, a pair of patrolmen with a lantern, their eyes lost beneath the peaks of their shakos. Reinhardt stood in front of Friedrich, made to fish out his warrant disc, but his son stepped straight out from behind. He stood straight and as tall as he could, facing the policemen, drawing himself up as his right arm licked out ramrod straight.

'Heil Hitler,' he piped.

Part Three

The Only Blessing Wickedness Possesses

26

Wednesday

Reinhardt woke again after too little sleep, feeling as if his blood had congealed within him. He had to force himself up and out of bed, joining Brauer and Mrs Meissner downstairs for breakfast. She had laid out the supplies Skokov left, making no comment about them, and indicating to Reinhardt no hard feelings about the way her house had been all but taken over by Soviet soldiers. Skokov was right about one thing, Reinhardt mused as he ate black bread with butter and honey, thinking he had rarely had anything as good, and watching Mrs Meissner boil sugar water for her bees; she was imperturbable.

But at the station, as Reinhardt settled in for a day of checking records, of searching for other deaths with similar circumstances to those he was investigating, Tanneberger summoned him to his office, where Ganz was waiting for him as well.

'Explain that, Reinhardt,' Ganz said, handing him a sheet of paper.

It was an authorisation from the Soviet Commandatura allowing Reinhardt into the WASt. It bore General Kotikov's signature.

'I received the visit of a Soviet MGB agent last night.' Tanneberger and Ganz said nothing. 'He was interested in my inquiries, and expressed… a wish… to help.'

'Your inquiries? Into the murders of these pilots? Not Carlsen?' Reinhardt nodded at Tanneberger. 'How did this Soviet find you?'

'I went into the Soviet Sector yesterday following a lead. They noticed me then. At least, that's what he said, but he knew too much.'

'Meaning...?' asked Ganz.

'Meaning someone's talking.'

'What are you saying?' asked Tanneberger, a worried tremor to the light in his eyes.

'Conspiracy theories, sir,' said Ganz. 'The product of an excess of imagination. Reinhardt's always had that tendency, haven't you Gregor?'

Reinhardt tried to bite down the anger that snarled up the back of his throat, thrusting his tongue into the gap in his teeth. Feeling giddy – tiredness, frustration, the feeling of being on the scent of something again – Reinhardt could not help the words that billowed up. 'Look on the bright side, sir. It's not as if I used my so-called contacts and asked the Americans for help. The Soviets came through. Even Margraff can't object to that,' he said, brusquely, seeing, as he hoped, Tanneberger flush with embarrassment and anger at the reference to Berlin's chief of police, a man so deeply under Soviet influence there may as well have been a Red Army general in his chair.

'Watch yourself, Reinhardt,' Ganz snapped. 'Remember just who and where you are.'

'Is there anything else, sir?' Reinhardt asked.

Tanneberger dry-washed his hands, glanced at Ganz.

'You are going now? Take Weber with you.'

'No.' Reinhardt shook his head at Ganz.

'You left Weber at the factory,' said Ganz. 'I told you to keep him with you.'

'I'm not a babysitter, Ganz,' Reinhardt's voice was level, but his emotions were anything but. 'He chose to stay and dick around with politics out at the factory. I'm not having him with me. What's it matter, anyway? Is he someone particular that we've got to take special care of him?'

'It's not a request, Reinhardt.'

'I don't care what it is, Ganz. He was a prick at the factory. And if he'd have come farther along with me, he might have been some use. I found Kessel. The man Noell's superintendent claims Noell was subletting from. Except his name is Kausch. I found him in Wedding. He would not let me in to see him, claimed he was ill, but he was entirely too well-groomed for someone who claimed to be suffering, and he had a manner. A parade-ground manner. I wouldn't be surprised to find that he's ex-military…'

'… like most men in Germany, Reinhardt,' Ganz interjected.

'Present company excluded, of course,' Reinhardt smiled, then continued, giving Ganz no chance to come back at him. An *excess of imagination, indeed*, he bristled. 'Ex-military or ex-air force, given the preponderance of ex-air force officials in this case. And he's not living there alone. He's definitely worth following up on. Send Weber. Maybe the boy can kick his way in. In any case, that authorisation for the WASt only mentions me, so, if there's nothing else?'

Reinhardt threaded his arms into his coat in a muted atmosphere. The station was calm and quiet, detectives and patrolmen like men after a hard night's drinking, coming to terms with their excesses and starting to pay for them. Gieb was still missing, Stresemann was nowhere to be found, and Weber was still, apparently, in the doghouse. Reinhardt passed him on the way out, suggested again he check addresses – the one they had found at Zuleger's apartment that the Grunewald police said was abandoned, the one they had got at the factory for von Vollmer, Kausch's address in Wedding – but Weber only stared back at him sullenly, and Reinhardt walked away without another word.

Reinhardt picked up the U-Bahn at Bayerischer Platz and rode it north then east up the B line to Hallesches Tor. Jostled in the scrum of people, all changing trains, he squirmed through the crowd and took the B line back two stops, past the destroyed station at Möckernbrücke to Gleisdreieck. He came up out of the station and found a small café, where he took a table in the back and waited until a man stepped inside, a hat pulled down low over his eyes. He spotted Reinhardt and joined him at his table. Reinhardt leaned past his shoulder and held up two fingers at the waiter for coffees.

'I got your message, Gregor,' Collingridge said, in German, hunching around so his back was to the window. His jaw clenched around his chewing gum. 'It's all a bit of a rush. Did we have to meet here?'

'It's as good a place as any,' Reinhardt replied, hoping he did not come out as too disingenuous. Collingridge flicked a glance at him, nodded, turning the movement into a slow glance over his shoulder. 'Are you worried about something?'

'I'm always worried about something,' the American quipped. 'Anyway, I took my precautions.' Reinhardt grinned at him. He could not help it, Collingridge was so childish sometimes. The American's eyes narrowed. 'What? What the hell's so funny?'

'I'm sorry, David. It's just, you can't expect to walk around Berlin chewing gum, wearing a coat of that quality, and not have people spot you for an Ami straight away. Besides,' he said, smiling to take the sting out of his words, 'maybe whoever you think's following you is following me.'

Quick to anger, quicker to calm down, Collingridge nodded, ruefully. 'That Russki you mentioned? Skokov? We got some things on him.' Reinhardt said nothing about Kausch, and Collingridge went quiet and leaned back from the table as the waiter put two mugs of coffee down, then leaned back in. 'He's a big cheese in their state security apparatus. Speaks fluent German, used to be in the embassy here back before the war, apparently. He's something of a Germanophile, been in and out of the country countless times since the 1920s. We think he was initially trained by you Germans back in the mid-'20s, when you guys were secretly using the USSR as a training range for illegal military activities. Remember all that?' Reinhardt nodded. 'Then Skokov turns up again in all that… *hunky-dorey stuff*,' he said, stumbling into English a moment, 'between the Nazis and Commies, before everything went sour with the war.'

Reinhardt nodded. The *hunky-dorey stuff* Collingridge referred to had been part of the Molotov-Ribbentrop Pact between Nazi Germany and the Communist USSR. The Soviets had provided the Nazis with commodities – hundreds of thousands of tons of cereal, grain, and minerals – and got advanced industrial and military supplies and technology in return. The Nazis had used all that material to rearm and re-equip, while Stalin had continued to believe Hitler would never invade him. Reinhardt had heard that the Soviets had continued to send grain shipments by train right up until Operation Barbarossa, the grain literally coming west as the Germans were going east.

'Not too much more is known about Skokov. He keeps his head down, he doesn't show up much in the Control Commissions, he's only been spotted once or twice out at the Kammergericht. At first we thought he was involved with these rumours out of the Soviet Zone that they were setting up some kind of new political police. We've heard talk from Saxony about something called Kommissariat V. K5. You heard of it? Some of those Germans that came back from Moscow with the Red Army are heading it up. But now we think Skokov's involved in some kind of Soviet operation to gather up technical knowledge and specialists from the Third Reich. Everything, from… coffee roasters,' he said, pointing at his mug, 'to power stations. The Soviets feel they've got a lot of catching up to do, and they figure you guys have all the skills to help them do it.'

'The race for whatever glitters in the rubble.'

'That's one way of putting it.'

'You're talking about the hunt for Nazi scientists, equipment, and resources.' Collingridge nodded. 'That's what the Allies are doing too.'

'It's true. We are. Except we can guarantee a nice job somewhere in the good old US-of-A and we'll throw in the family as well, whereas the Soviets'll promise you house arrest in Siberia for the rest of your natural life as you slave away for them.'

'That's one way of looking at it,' Reinhardt said noncommittally. Skokov and pilots. Reinhardt's murder victims were all pilots. From a night-fighter squadron. What would Skokov want with night-fighter pilots?

Collingridge shrugged, tapping a cigarette out of a packet. 'You got skills the Reds want, they'll take you off the street. Literally. You remember in October last year. They did that after they lost the elections. Cordoned off whole neighbourhoods, went house to house, door to door, with lists. Everyone they wanted, carted off east.'

Reinhardt lit a cigarette. 'A Soviet state security officer, around since the 1920s… he's seen it all come and go. Factions, wars, purges,' Reinhardt murmured. 'The man's a survivor.' And knowledgeable, he remembered, looking at Collingridge and thinking over what Skokov had said about himself.

'The man's a survivor,' Collingridge affirmed. 'He has to be, with his background, to be his rank and in the crowd he runs with…' Collingridge shrugged, tapping ash onto the floor. He sipped from his coffee, and winced. '*Jesus H. Christ. That's like the inside of my shoes.*'

Reinhardt thought about Skokov's German. Its fluency. Its precision. What he had said about Mrs Meissner. A lady of class and quality. The old museums, the Decorative Arts, the Pergamon, the Tell Halaf. 'I'd guess he was bourgeoisie at birth. Maybe even an aristocrat. Maybe his family were White Russians, exiled after the Civil War. His German's too good. He learned it somewhere special. Probably here. In good schools and company. And I'm guessing he became a revolutionary as a young man, and he probably picked that up here too… back in the '20s…' Reinhardt tailed off, remembering Berlin after the first war, the riotous mood of the capital, the clash of left and right, the teetering slide of politics.

'And somehow, he keeps surviving…' pondered Collingridge. Maybe not, Reinhardt thought to himself. He remembered Skokov's metal teeth, the scars around his mouth. Something went wrong at some time. 'In any case, don't underestimate him.'

Reinhardt nodded. 'And the two Brits? Whelan and Markworth?'

'Whelan's a British rep on one of the Kammergericht's commissions, the one on war crimes, criminal law reform. Markworth's a bit shadier. He's based out of Bad Oeynhausen,' he said referring to the spa town in central Germany where the British had set up their Occupation headquarters. 'He comes to Berlin from time to time, but he works on something relatively secret. Some British project. It's nothing to do with CROWCASS,' Collingridge said, referring to the American unit running the hunt for Nazi criminals, 'or I would have heard of it.'

'And Carlsen?'

'A lawyer. He worked with Whelan. I think I met him once or twice. Quiet guy, but pretty intense. We had eyes on him from time to time. He spent quite a bit of time in East Berlin. We suspected he was talking to the Reds.'

'About what?'

'Who knows? The guy was a lawyer. He had eyes on all kinds of things.'

'But the Kammergericht commissions are all quadripartite, right? What one side sees, the other three sides see as well.'

'Except the confidential materials. The briefings and background notes. Like when General Clay's got to go head-to-head with Kotikov, he's got to be prepared. Take police reform. You should see the paperwork that generated in notes and assessments and political analysis. It's valuable stuff. Embarrassing stuff, if taken out of context or put in the wrong hands.'

Reinhardt thought a moment. 'Skokov seemed to know a bit about Carlsen. That he was a German who'd fought for the British. Other things.'

Collingridge shrugged. 'Maybe Carlsen was talking. A lot of these German exiles have a thing for East Berlin, for all the old German Commies the Nazis banged up or who went to ground during the Reich. The heart of resistance against the Nazis, they say. If there's one thing an intellectual likes, it's talk, right? Maybe they prefer all that talk about a new society to actually getting out and building one.'

Reinhardt breathed out slowly, his eyes on the sludge in his cup. 'The Soviets take all that "talk" seriously, David. Art, culture, theatre. Germans do, too. There's a place for that.'

'Yeah? Well, I guess we all have our priorities. We want buildings rebuilt, people fed, and a clean government in place. They have no compunction about stripping their Zone bare, dumping millions of refugees on us, and then demanding food and coal and God knows what else, but hey, at least the theatres are all open.'

Reinhardt twisted his cup from one side to another. 'Perhaps you should try living in a basement with a foot of stagnant water in it, or try living on the rations you allow us, David. Try putting your nose in a cooking pot, any cooking pot, in any house in this city. And then talk to me about what's important. Or about what can take your mind off the hole in your belly,' he said, raising his eyes, feeling cautious and embarrassed but wanting, needing, to make Collingridge think again, think more, think *complicated.*

'Well, however you put it, Gregor, you're better off with us than them.'

'I don't know what it's like in the Soviet Zone, David. I hear things, that's all. But I know of whole families here in Berlin sharing rooms, not because their own homes are wrecked, but because they were evicted to make room for officers' wives and families from the States, or from France, or from the UK.'

'What's your point?'

Reinhardt shook his head as he stubbed out his cigarette. 'Every man's misery is his own, David. And every man's misery can only be taken and understood in the here and now.'

'So you're saying things were better with Hitler in charge?'

'I'm sure you'll hear a lot of that, and if that's what you're looking for, you'll find it. But think of it this way. A family may have been starving on five potatoes before, but they're starving on two now. Were they better off before, or after?'

'Oh, *really*, Reinhardt. You can't reduce before and now to a matter of potatoes on a plate.'

'You absolutely can. That is absolutely the point for many people, but it's not my point at all.' Reinhardt's face screwed up a moment, a grimace of confusion and frustration. 'I'm sorry, David. I'm not making much sense. My wife… she would always tell me I kept too much to myself and so made little sense when I actually opened my mouth. All… all I am saying is, you look at us, at us Germans, and you see one block. One great whole, and you look and you find the whole is riven with cracks, and through those cracks runs Nazism. But you confuse cause and effect, and you ask the wrong questions. You cannot expect any of us to draw lessons from our hunger about good and bad. You cannot expect a mother to draw a lesson from her child dying of tuberculosis about Nazism and democracy and Communism. They will not see justice in that, they will see injustice. They will see those who should have helped them doing anything but. They will not look beyond the immediate, and so the past will loom so much larger for them. A past when their needs, however imperfectly, were met.'

'You know I think you're wrong. Look at the elections. Social Democrats defeated the Communists just about everywhere. Especially here.'

'They did. That's a fact. As an exercise in democracy, they were an undoubted success. What does it tell you?'

'I have a feeling you're about to tell me,' quipped Collingridge.

'It tells me there is one thing greater than hunger, and that's fear.'

The two of them stared at each other.

'Christ, how did we get onto this? You can't go back, and there's only two ways forward. Ours, and the Reds'. You need to work out what you'd like, Gregor,' said Collingridge, a dark line of annoyance running across his brows.

'I'd like to die in bed aged one hundred, shot by a jealous husband.'

'Sorry. Was that you being funny? Only I'm not used to levity from you.'

'It happens from time to time,' Reinhardt murmured.

Collingridge shook his head as he stubbed out his cigarette. '"*You pays your money, you takes your chances*",' he said, in English. He looked at Reinhardt, his lips moving against his teeth. 'So, when're you due in the WASt?'

'Next hour or so,' said Reinhardt, checking his watch. 'If Markworth's based in Bad Oeynhausen, what's he doing in Berlin?'

'No idea. Ask him. And happy hunting,' said Collingridge. He slipped a few packets of Luckies across the table. 'For you. And if you need to grease a few palms.'

From Gleisdreieck, Reinhardt took the U-Bahn east to Kottbusser Tor, then a northbound D line. At the big interchange at Alexanderplatz, he was almost sucked off by people exiting, then washed back into the train by people pressing themselves on. He watched the crowds, remembering all the times he would get off at this station and take the stairs up to the square and over to the Alex to police headquarters. The train pushed on up the stops, languishing along the tunnels, moving slowly, finally emerging in fits and jerks to Gesundbrunnen and the D line terminus. The Wehrmacht Information Office for War Losses and POWs – the WASt – was a tram ride from Gesundbrunnen in Reinickendorf, in the French Sector, and there was a streetcar waiting outside the station for once.

He alighted at Eichborndamm Strasse, down the street from the WASt. It was a huge building of red brick, occupying an entire city block. Long-sided, low-walled, towers and turrets at each corner. Reinhardt could smell the archives the moment he stepped into the building. It was almost overpowering, a musty scent of paper and cardboard that flowed over and through him. A French soldier escorted him to a waiting room filled with dusty, red leather armchairs and left him there. He did not wait very long before a young officer scurried into the room, a lieutenant with two yellow bars on his epaulettes. The Frenchman skidded to a halt, almost stumbling in his tracks, and straightened a pair of rimless spectacles on his nose as he looked at Reinhardt.

'You are the policeman?' he asked. 'I am Lieutenant Armand De Massigny. Come with me. We see my chief. Then we see the papers.'

Reinhardt followed him into an office where a French colonel sat like a beached whale behind an acre of desk. The colonel had Reinhardt's access papers in front of him and, from what Reinhardt's rusty French could make out, he wanted some reason to refuse him, so Reinhardt stayed silent and let the game play out without him. The colonel was some kind of throwback to a bygone age, a vast man stuffed like a quilt into his uniform, a splendid moustache spiking each side of his mouth, and aristocratic disdain in the way he looked at the pair of them, down the length of his nose. The skin of his cheeks was an archipelago of burst veins and purple skin. But for all his blimp-like size, his foul temper, apparent dislike of Reinhardt, and peremptory manner with his young subordinate, the colonel wore a Croix de Guerre on his tunic. Reinhardt glanced at it, thought of his own Iron Cross that he was no longer allowed to wear, and wondered if he and the colonel might ever have come at each other across the trenches.

Eventually, the colonel scrawled a signature across the papers, stamped them, and flicked them back at the two of them. The young lieutenant scooped them up with an air of barely repressed enthusiasm, snapped a salute and spun away. Reinhardt paused a moment, waiting until he had the colonel's eye, then inclined his head.

'Merci beaucoup,' he said. The Colonel blinked, his breath huffing like a walrus's, then he nodded and went back to his paperwork.

'You must excuse the colonel,' De Massigny enthused, as he led Reinhardt through a maze of corridors at a brisk clip. 'He is a cross man. They bring him from retirement for this. He is, how do you say it…? The old warhorse?' Reinhardt nodded. 'He is not for the administration. He hates it,' De Massigny chuckled, his French accent layered thick across his German. 'And, I am sorry to say, he hates the Germans too.'

'What about you?'

'I don't hate the Germans,' De Massigny protested, his smooth face creasing in a frown. 'I mean, you were not very nice in France.

But I don't blame the Germans for that. I blame the soldiers that were there.'

'No, I meant what do you do? In the army?'

'Ah, *excusez-moi.* I am sorry,' De Massigny said. 'I am not a soldier. I am an archivist. I work in the state archives in Paris. They make me a lieutenant for a time, while I do this work,' he said, as he opened a door for Reinhardt. The room they had entered was ballroom-sized and filled, wall to ceiling, and in serried rows across the expanse of parquet floor, with filing cabinets and shelves of all shapes and sizes. Another soldier was on duty behind a desk by the door, and De Massigny handed him the access paper with an absent gesture, his attention fixed on the cabinets where pairs of French soldiers were dotted around the room, examining files and making notations.

'The heart of the WASt, it is here,' he said, a light of ardour in his eyes. 'This is the alphabetical registry. There are millions of names, here. *Des millions!*' he breathed, a keen edge to his voice. 'We have made a good start, but so much needs to be done. But still, what a treasure! You Germans,' he chuckled. 'Always with the papers and records, but I thank you for it. This is a dream, for me!'

Reinhardt smiled, shook his head at the young man's fervour.

'So, *Inspecteur*, we are already looking for the names you sent. Haber. Noell. Stucker. Zuleger. Correct? *Très bien.*' He pointed to a stack of small card files, exchanged a few words in French with the soldier at the desk. 'There you have the personnel cards of Noell, Stucker, and Zuleger. We are still searching for Haber's.' The cards were standardised forms, noting basic biographical details and the men's units. 'We have to hope these cards were somehow kept up to date, but towards the end of the war, it was a bit the chaos,' De Massigny said. 'But we have some help. This is Mr Semrau,' he said, indicating a middle-aged man in civilian clothing. 'He is one of our German assistants. He worked in the archives before, and has been helping us since. So, tell us, exactly what it is you want.'

'You understand I am conducting a murder investigation? These four men have been murdered. I am looking for all the details we can find on them,' Reinhardt said, as he shook hands with Semrau, 'and the records of their service history in fighter group III./NJG64, known as the Night Hawks. Before that, the same unit carried the designation IV./JG56. I am looking for details of those four men in particular, but as well, all the men who would have served at the same time in this unit. So I can cross-check them and try to find a link between them, and possibly come to a motive for the killer. That is perhaps the most important thing.'

'So, for that you will need as well the unit's logbooks,' added Semrau. He had watery blue eyes that were almost lost behind a permanent squint, as if he had spent too much of his life looking at paper and writing.

'That too,' agreed Reinhardt.

'The air force sections are a bit better organised than the army's,' Semrau said. 'Do you know where this group surrendered?'

'Not exactly. But their former commander mentioned fighting the RAF.'

'So, Western Front. That's good. The records of units that surrendered to the British or Americans are in generally much better shape than those that surrendered to the Soviets.' Semrau's voice was soft, with a pedantic ring to it. 'So, these file cards will lead us to personnel files. Those files should give us more information on their deployments.'

'I would also like details on another man. Kausch. I do not know what he was. Army, air force, I have no idea.'

'Shall we start, then?' grinned De Massigny.

27

The search took most of the rest of the day, and the enduring memories for Reinhardt were of dust, and the overwhelming scent of paper in various forms of conservation, and of a humbling sense of the sheer scale of the war. He, who had fought in part of it, who had had an idea of the mass of it, found in the archives an expression of its breadth that seemed to brook no argument, a monument that hulked high and wide, inscribed with the records of men. Millions of them. Records of the living, the dead, and the missing. Records of prisoners, German as well as Allied. Records of the army, air force, and navy. Records of the Nazis' various military and paramilitary organisations.

His own were in here somewhere too.

So were Friedrich's.

But it was not really the scale of what he saw in front of him and the scale of what it represented in lives. It was what each of those lives had done in turn. The millions of files in here had belonged to millions of men who had taken the war to other lands, other nations, and he had been one of them. Millions more lives had been affected. Lost. Destroyed. Erased. And he had taken some of them. Each of the lives represented in here had rippled outward, the ripples of what they had done rippling farther still. It terrified him more and more as the day went on. It began to wear him down, until he was moving listlessly, his mind stunned to a virtual standstill, as much by the stultifying weight and odour of paper as by what the paper represented.

De Massigny signed them into the air force section, a cavelike complex of long storage rooms, and left them to it. Relatively quickly, Semrau found the logbooks, along with the rest of the Group's administrative records, including its pay list, which was a real treasure trove. The pay list allowed them to view the Group's personnel. Pilots, gunners, fitters, armourers, mechanics, medics. Reinhardt felt a tingle of anticipation at each name found. Together, he and Semrau began matching the names they had with the lists, and found three of them – Noell, Stucker and Zuleger – but not Haber. Haber seemed not to have served with III./NJG64, so was something of an anomaly, like Carlsen.

The pay lists also gave Reinhardt the squadron the pilots had served in together. This was the Group's second squadron. That finding narrowed the search a little more, and Semrau and Reinhardt found more names of pilots, several dozen, who had also served during the war in that same squadron. His heart lifted a little more with each name, until Semrau doused it with water when he asked whether Reinhardt was sure he was only looking for pilots. There were dozens more names – ground crew, technical specialists, mechanics and engineers, staff officers… Reinhardt's mind spluttered, fragmenting a little under the weight of all the paper and the thought of having to dig, dig, dig through it. He paused, then shook his head.

'Pilots,' he said, more firmly than he felt.

'Pilots it is,' nodded Semrau.

'You were air force?' Reinhardt guessed.

Semrau paused, his eyes widening slightly. He nodded, after a moment. 'Air Ministry staff,' he said. 'I was never more than an administrator,' he finished, a defensive twist in his pedantic voice. 'Don't worry, the French know.'

'I wasn't worried,' Reinhardt replied. 'I just noted how fast you brought us to where we need to be.'

The archivist left to hunt down the personnel files of the individuals they had identified, leaving Reinhardt with the Group's logs. He found a table and chair, and sat down to begin going through them, tracking quickly through the unit's deployments, from its initial establishment in the late 1930s at Ritterfeld air base, to France, the Netherlands, the Battle of Britain, to North Africa, to Italy, and finally back to Germany in the last two years of the war. He read over it more slowly, trying to find some pattern, but knowing full well he did not really know what he was looking for, his eyes running over terse accounts of battles, postings, victories, and losses. The only pattern he could see, as he read, was ever fewer victories as the years went by, and far more losses.

The transfer of IV./JG56 to night-fighter duties came in mid-1943, he saw, confirming what Bochmann had said. In May 1943, the unit was pulled out of North Africa, evacuated along with what was left of the Afrika Korps and retrained on night-fighter tactics, finishing the war based in western Germany, in Bremen.

Semrau returned with armfuls of personnel files. Each one contained a variety of information, from fitness reports to disciplinary hearings to authorisations for compassionate leave. Most of them contained a *soldbuch*, each book noting in detail the individual's military experience, but a couple contained a *Wehrpass*, meaning the *soldbuch* had never been returned for one reason or another. Reinhardt picked up Noell's *soldbuch*, for the first time getting a look at the man's service history.

'Very well,' he sighed. 'Let's start with what we know. Noell, Stucker, and Zuleger. Let's match their service history first, and then see what we can find out about the others.'

What linked them was North Africa, they realised after combing through the *soldbuchs*. Noell and Zuleger had been in the air force from before the war. Stucker joined IV./JG56 in 1941, and his first operational posting was to North Africa. Stucker and Zuleger had stayed on when IV./JG56 became III./NJG64, but Noell had left. There was something strange in Noell's *soldbuch*, though, and Reinhardt pointed it out to Semrau.

'Here,' Reinhardt said, 'Noell joins IV./JG56 in September 1938 as a lieutenant. When the war starts, he's a first lieutenant. In April

1943, he leaves the Group, and he's promoted to captain. Nine months later, in January 1944, he joins another unit. He joins what…? A search unit…?'

'Long-range reconnaissance,' said Semrau. 'In Bergen, in Norway.'

'He's a fighter pilot, and he ends up in a reconnaissance unit in *Norway*? What did he do, piss someone off?'

'It's a fair assumption.' But Semrau's pedantic manner had been ruffled.

'Between April 1943 and January 1944, where was he? The entry in his *soldbuch* has been redacted,' said Reinhardt, pointing at a thick black line that hid whatever had been noted beneath it. 'Where was he for nine months between leaving IV./JG56 and turning up in Bergen? Wounded?'

'No. That would not show up as a break in service,' replied Semrau. His manner had definitely changed. 'The *soldbuch* would record it as convalescence. There's a code, there. By the redacted entry…'

Reinhardt gave him a moment before asking. 'You know what it means?'

'Of course,' said Semrau quickly, as if offended. He seemed to catch himself, continued more slowly. 'It is the code for a file section on… secret or unorthodox units or training methods.'

Reinhardt looked at him, then hunted through the files for Haber's, flicking it open. Haber's photograph showed a bookish-looking man of indeterminate age, a chemist by training, recruited into the air force from university before the war. He had spent the first few years of the war working in air force research centres, on what, it was not clear, but Semrau identified the locations and knew that at least one of them was working on specialised food supplies for aircrews. But in mid-1943, Haber had been transferred, and his *soldbuch* had also been redacted. Reinhardt pointed it out to Semrau. The archivist's mouth worked dryly.

An hour later, using the *soldbuchs* and the personnel lists, they had compiled a rough list of nine pilots – Albrecht, Fenski, Gareis, Hauck, Jurgen, Meurer, Osterkamp, Prellberg, and Thurner – whose service history paralleled that of Noell, Stucker, and Zuleger. All of them had served in North Africa at the same time. All of them had served in the Group's second squadron. All of them, with the exception of Noell, Prellberg, and Gareis, had gone on to serve in the Night Hawks, and Prellberg had the same redacted notation in his *soldbuch* as in Noell's and Haber's, and Gareis had one in his *Wehrpass*, there being no *soldbuch* for him because he was noted as being killed in action over the Eastern Front in early 1945. Twelve names overall, to which he added Bochmann as the Group's executive officer. Thirteen names. Other names he had come across that he recognised – like Dorner, the one-eyed pilot from von Vollmer's factory – he put to one side if they had not served in North Africa. Then he removed Albrecht, Gareis, and Meurer, because they had all later been killed in action.

That left him with nine names – Noell, Stucker, and Zuleger, plus Hauck, Jürgen, Osterkamp, Prellberg, Thurner, and Bochmann – of which he knew three had been murdered. While he kept making notes on them, Semrau went looking for information on the gaps in Noell's, Prellberg's, and Gareis's service records, and returned some time later looking blank.

'There was only a notation in the records that the files were transferred to the Berlin Document Center.' Semrau paused, his narrow eyes narrowing further. 'Meaning, whatever it was, it was something related to the Nazi regime itself. The only thing left was this record in the file that the materials had been transferred.' Semrau handed him a sheet of paper with rows of typed and handwritten notations. 'You can look at it, but I'll have to take it back.'

It was as Semrau had said: an official notification that the records of said file had been transferred to the Berlin Document Center in February 1946, while the WASt had still been under US control. Below that, a signed list of names of people who had requested the file. There were only three.

One of them was a name of someone he had never heard of, called Boalt, in July last year.

The second was Skokov, at the end of last year.

The third was Carlsen. Just two weeks ago.

Semrau said he remembered Carlsen as an Englishman, and vaguely remembered Boalt. 'Nothing special. But he was one of us.'

'A German?'

'Yes. But working for the Allies. He would not say on what. But I'm not the only archivist. And sometimes, visitors don't need or want help. We'll have to add our names to this form,' Semrau said, with the worried look of a grocer who wanted to close up shop. His body language spoke his distress louder than his soft, pedantic voice could. In a way, Reinhardt could understand him. Secret files and missing documents. If Semrau had worked in the archives as long as he said he had, he must have seen it all come and go, must have dealt with the schizophrenic paranoia of the Nazis that their mania for secrecy and meticulous bureaucracy had engendered.

'What about the Russian? Skokov. Remember him?'

Semrau said he did not, so Reinhardt sent him looking for records of Noell's Norwegian posting. He himself went back to IV./JG56's logbook, poring over the North Africa entries more closely, worrying that it was only instinct and sketchy evidence that had him focusing on this period, failing to find anything that stood out, except for one thing: the squadron leader. Prellberg had been removed from command. In Prellberg's personnel file, Reinhardt found the demotion, a reprimand for failure to obey orders, citing a mission that should have been flown in one place, but was not. Whatever Prellberg had done, or not done, had happened in late October 1942. And two weeks later, Prellberg and Gareis, the squadron's second-in-command, had been hospitalised for injuries sustained in a fight. A soldier called Leyser had been involved, but although it caught Reinhardt's interest, there were no details beyond cursory ones. Not in the squadron's log, nor in any files he found. He kept thinking about it as he read further, remembering the evidence of the crippled veteran at Zuleger's apartment. That he had met a man who used army slang on the stairs the night Zuleger had been murdered.

Something was bothering him, but he did not know what it was. He stretched his leg, walking to a high window and looking up at the ashen light that pushed its way through the clouded panes of glass, and all of a sudden he found himself remembering North Africa, the heat, the blinding shimmer of the desert, the sea like hammered metal. The joy at capturing tinned British food. The dust that got into everything. The flies, most of all.

The building oppressed him. The weight of all these records, it was pushing in on him, as if he were something malleable being moulded and shaped to a template he could not imagine. He stared up at the light, stared through it, and it was the vast bowl of the sky over the desert that he saw, the scrawled line of the Bosnian mountains as they ran along the horizon, the swirled contours of forests and hills, and he felt a prickling on his neck, as if he were being watched. He swallowed, steadfastly refused to look around, but the feeling grew until he turned, and his breath caught in his throat at the sight of the records chamber sunk in pallid gloom. He stared across rows of cabinets, shelves of binders and papers, and the records seemed to ripple, once, shivering like the surface of water, as if, somewhere deep within them, something had beaten, or been struck, as if the records had a heart, and it had thumped, just once.

He blinked furiously to clear his eyes, his breathing coming high and fast. What was he imagining, he thought, a flair of desperation to the whirl of his mind? When the door to the room cracked open, he felt his heart had stilled, but it was De Massigny with a thermos of coffee and a tray of sandwiches. If the Frenchman noticed anything in Reinhardt's behaviour, he said nothing, inquiring gaily into how they were getting on. Reinhardt was grateful for the break, but he could not shake off the feeling of being watched, could not shake off a rising fear that the heart of the records would beat again.

De Massigny offered to help, so Reinhardt had him begin copying out particulars from the *soldbuchs*, especially addresses of wives or next of kin and dates of service. But something kept nagging at him, and he knew it was something he had read that day. Semrau returned with the logbook of Noell's Norwegian unit, but there was nothing in it. It had been a long-range reconnaissance outfit, flying surveillance out over the North Sea and Arctic Ocean, hunting for the British convoys to the USSR. Reinhardt went back to Noell's personnel file, searching through the records for the times that would have coincided with his stint in Norway, and found a report by the Group's medical officer. Noell, the report said, was on the verge of a nervous breakdown. Another report, from his commanding officer, noted his flying as exemplary, but also noted burnout. Noell volunteered all the time, as if he had a death wish. No one wanted to fly with him.

The light in the room sank, a rising crepuscular grey. De Massigny turned on the lights, the electric glare carving the room into lines and blocks of shadows, and somehow lifting the oppression Reinhardt felt in this place. When Semrau came back with a file on several *Kauschs*, none of which resembled the man Reinhardt had found in Wedding, he knew he had come to the end of what he could usefully do in here. It was indeed a trove he had found. He looked over the sheaves of notes he had made, the lists De Massigny had drawn up for him, and it was enough, he thought. He did not know if he would be able to come back, and that thought was the only note of dissatisfaction he had, a feeling of something undone or overlooked.

De Massigny escorted them back out of the air force section, and as he was signing the registry, on impulse he began searching back through it. The guard made to stop him, but De Massigny calmed him. Reinhardt checked the dates that the missing file had been consulted, flicking back through the air force registry, back to the same periods, and found them.

Boalt and Carlsen. But no Skokov.

Whoever Boalt was, Reinhardt saw he had been into this section of the WASt several times. The name was strange, like nothing else he had seen or heard of, but the man must have been working for the Allies to have the access he had. Reinhardt noted the dates, seeing there were two entries: the first was in July 1946, not long after the WASt had relocated to Berlin from Fürstenhagen in the US Zone, and reopened, the second time about five months ago.

'Were you here at that time?' Reinhardt asked De Massigny.

The Frenchman shook his head '*Non.* I do not think anyone working now from the French administration was here at the time. Semrau, maybe?'

But Semrau shook his head. 'Like I said to the inspector, I recall him, but only vaguely.'

'What of Carlsen?'

'A quiet man. An Englishman, so with full access. He knew what he was looking for and asked for no help.'

'Can we do anything else for you, Inspector?'

'Thank you, Lieutenant. If you could, please look up the records for this soldier. Leyser. He was serving in Africa in 1942. That's all I have.'

And a *Reinhardt, Friedrich.* The name was right there on the tip of Reinhardt's tongue, but he swallowed it back.

'Just a name?' Semrau asked. 'We'll see what we can do.'

'Of what interest is this name, Inspector?' De Massigny asked.

'The commander of the squadron was demoted for something to do with a failed mission. A short while later, he and two other pilots were involved in a fight with that soldier. One of those pilots was Noell. Could be nothing. Could be something. It's just a lead.'

'We shall do our best, *n'est-ce pas*, Semrau?' De Massigny said jovially.

Reinhardt shook hands with Semrau, thanking the archivist for his help, and stood on the steps of the WASt with De Massigny. He offered him a Lucky and lit them both up. The day was almost gone, he saw to his surprise. He felt disoriented, and he breathed deeply, feeling lightened and light-headed. De Massigny glanced at him, his cigarette held elegantly at the height of his chest.

'It is quite something, is it not?' he asked, seeming to understand a little of what Reinhardt had felt and was feeling.

Reinhardt nodded. 'Somewhere in there are my records. And those of my friends.' My son. 'Just… pieces… in a structure.' He glanced back over his shoulder at the red brick walls, down the long length of the street. 'It is humbling. And I don't fully understand what it all means.'

'For me, it is the perspective.' De Massigny blew smoke at the sky, straightening his glasses. 'And the permanence. The mark we leave behind. Or the mark we choose to leave behind. It is not always the same thing. Searching for order in that, searching between the official for the unofficial. Searching for the small truths, or finding them by accident. For me, it is a great pleasure,' De Massigny said, an undertone of satisfaction to his words.

'I wish you luck with it,' Reinhardt smiled, extending his hand. 'Should I need to get in touch with you again…?'

'Of course! *N'hésitez pas!*' De Massigny exclaimed. '*Tenez.* My card.'

'And mine,' said Reinhardt. 'You may reach me on that extension, or leave a message.'

A final handshake, and Reinhardt left him on the steps of the archive, feeling the bulk of it looming above him much larger than the building. He felt that if he turned around, he would see… *something…* rearing up and out. Something harrowed and clenched, rigid with the sorrow it bore. Reinhardt felt his back go clammy with sweat, and there was a hitched rhythm to his breath, like a child scared of the dark, or of the water. He clutched his papers to his chest and scurried down the street, ignoring the pain of his leg, walking until distance and the lowering light of the evening had put enough between him and the building that he could afford to slow, to look back, and see nothing.

At Gesundbrunnen he fairly flung himself through the U-Bahn station's turnstiles onto the platform, anything to get away from the oppressive weight of the archive. He began to calm down, waiting with dozens of others, eyes fixed on the gunmetal gleam of the tracks until, on a wash of dirty air and squeal of brakes, a train crashed into the station.

28

It was not until the doors shut and the train had closed the darkness of the tunnel around itself that he relaxed. He sat on a bench and watched his reflection, watched how lights flashing by outside would sharpen its haggard draw, watching how it collapsed back into watery focus. Back and forth. Back and forth.

He felt very lost.

A man in the flat cap of a labourer, his clothes and face seamed with a lifetime of toil, sat near him reading a newspaper. He held the paper close and high, as if nearsighted, his face screwed up in concentration, tongue protruding past the yellowed gaps of his teeth. Or perhaps in disbelief, thought Reinhardt, seeing the man's head come up suddenly, blinking at the carriage around him as if not crediting what he saw and what he read.

At Alexanderplatz, Reinhardt waited until the train's doors were closing, then slipped off the train, making his way to the A line platforms. At Stadtmitte, he changed to a southbound C line that would take him back to Paradestrasse, but he left the train at Hallesches Tor, three stops early. He walked slowly down the platform, head lost in thought until, with a quick sidestep, he slipped back into the train as the doors were closing. He did not think anyone had followed him, and he saw no swift repeated movement, but still. It paid to be safe. He got off again at Flughafen, one stop before his normal station, climbing heavily up out of the underground, feeling as if his muscles had turned to ash within him. Night had come down over the city. The streets were dark, only a few cars moving with their headlamps sweeping the darkness in fans of yellow light. He stopped at a small bar and ordered a beer, waiting. He tried to stay alert, but his mind drifted, again, lost in the overwhelming weight of the archives. He rubbed his forehead with his fingers, rubbing hard, as if the stamp of the archives had left a mark on him for everyone to see.

'You look like a shower of shit.'

He started, looking up as Brauer sat down next to him. 'I don't think anyone's followed you, but there were a few people who lurked outside the WASt most of the day. I think you were in there so long, though, they got bored.' He focused his eyes on Reinhardt. 'And you came out so fast, I barely kept up with you. You all right?'

Reinhardt nodded. The weight of the archives had pulped the fear he had had initially, of being followed and so asking Brauer to watch his back for anyone watching him. The police, the Soviets, the Americans, his son. It all felt trite, after the archives…

'Can you describe those men you saw at the WASt?'

'Pretty much nought-eight-fifteen. Run of the mill, ordinary. One was short, blocky. Dark hair cut close to his head. Nondescript clothes. Flat cap. He had a little barrow, full of bits and pieces. He sat on a bench across from the WASt until about four o'clock in the afternoon, smoking and drinking from a bottle in a paper bag. There was another, young bloke, blond hair, just sort of lurked along the street, not doing much. He didn't stay long. Boredom, I'd have said. No staying power. The third was definitely a Russian. I asked them all for smokes, tried to exchange a few words. The one on the bench was German. A Berliner, I would have said. Said he came often because his son had been killed in the war, and he felt a connection with the records inside. He talked of how one day he would know what his son had done, but until then, he said he had to hold faith that his son had done well.' Brauer paused, seeing how Reinhardt's face had clenched in on itself, but he could not know how close that other man's vigil came to Reinhardt's own worries of what Friedrich had seen and done in the east. 'The second bloke told me to get lost. Didn't say enough for me to get a sense of his accent. But the last one had a Russian accent so thick I could have fluffed it up and called it a pillow.'

Reinhardt nodded. The description of the third man sounded like a Soviet agent sent to watch him. The second man, who knew? One of Kausch's, perhaps? The first man could have been anyone. A father on some sort of pilgrimage for a lost son…

'Friedrich's alive,' he blurted. Brauer frowned at him. 'Friedrich's alive.'

'I heard you. I just… what do you mean, he's alive?'

'He's back. From a camp. He came to see me the other night. The same night that Soviet officer came.'

'Friedrich's back from the east?' Brauer took a long swig from his beer, caught Reinhardt's eyes, and looked away.

'Say it.'

Brauer's mouth twisted. 'Why's he home so early?'

'Why's he home at all, you mean,' Reinhardt said, a snarl lying along the base of his words.

Brauer heard it, but his friend had seen and heard it all with Reinhardt, and he said nothing, only twisting his mouth again and sipping from his beer. 'He'll have some stories, I would imagine. I've got a story. The one you've been wanting to hear.'

'It's all right, Rudi.'

'I know, Gregor. Now's the time. I killed a boy. That Hitler Youth kid they put in charge of our Volkssturm squad. He was all fired up. Rabid. He had us on a street corner, and the… the Ivans were coming up the street. Right up the middle of Sonnenallee. Fucking T34s. Machine guns. Artillery. Mortars. Shooting up everything. Every door. Every window. There were Katyushas firing somewhere. Glass breaking. Someone was screaming. It was like nothing I had ever…'

Brauer lifted his beer, but seemed to forget he had done so. 'The kid's wet himself with excitement. He wants us to knock out the first T34. I tell him he's mad. There's infantry advancing down both sides of the street. We stick our heads out, they'll get blown off. He pulls a gun on one of the men, tells him to fire his grenade. The man said no. The kid killed him. He aims at me. I snatched it off him and hit him on the head with it. He goes down. Blood everywhere. The others are looking at me. I tell them they can stay if they want, but I've already got an Iron Cross and I'm off. We all run. I looked back once and the kid's lying there, and then the corner is blown to pieces, and a T34 comes round…' Brauer remembered his beer, drank deeply. 'A kid. He was just a kid.'

They sat, the two of them lost in memories, until Brauer shook his head, firming his elbows on the table, and Reinhardt knew he was ready to talk.

'Friedrich said he's in a halfway house out in Rummelsburg. Can you… can you do me a favour…?' Reinhardt could not go on.

'You want me to have a look? Of course. You want him to see me?'

'No! No. Just…'

'Just tell you. I understand.'

Reinhardt felt the weight of Brauer's story, another one to add to the weight of the day, but he knew Brauer did not want pity and so he said nothing. There would be a time, but not now. They left their beers half-drunk, too tepid and flat to finish, then Brauer proceeded them out into the night, back to Meissner's house. Brauer left him there, continuing on alone. Reinhardt never knew where he went, and Brauer never said. Brauer had opened a crack into the core of what troubled him, but the crack offered little, and it could close again. Reinhardt did not have the right words to unlock Brauer's intransigence, his self-imposed rigidity, the control, and right then he had no energy to try.

There was electricity on Meissner's street, and he opened the front door to a waft of steam from the kitchen, and to find Mrs Meissner mashing potatoes in a bowl. A huge sack of potatoes stood in a corner, and a can of oil upon the work surface.

'What good fortune is this?' Reinhardt asked.

Meissner smiled at him. 'It's you, isn't it?'

'Me what?'

She frowned at him as she slid chopped herbs from her garden into the mash. Rosemary, thyme, a sprinkle of salt. 'Didn't you send these?'

'I did not.' He felt a creeping unease. 'You must have an admirer.'

'A bit young for me,' she smiled, but unease gathered in the fine net of wrinkles at the corner of her eyes. A policeman's wife, a conspirator's spouse, Meissner recognised danger when she sensed it.

'Who was it?'

'A man came to the door with the sack, a can of oil, and a packet of salt. He said they were from you.'

'Can you describe him?'

'Of middle age, I would guess. Softly spoken. Polite. He wore a worker's clothes, with a flat cap. He had a little handcart that he used to carry the sack. His hair was greying. He was clean-shaven, but for a little moustache. Of medium height, but… broad. Solid.'

'He came in? You talked?'

'A little. I gave him tea and honey. He seemed to know you, Gregor.'

'What did he say?'

'It's not what he said, but the way he said it.' She served up a dish, and laid it in front of him. 'There was a level of familiarity. But it was respectful. As if from a man you might have served with. He remarked on your dedication, and on your fatigue.' They looked at each other in silence. 'Who was he?' she asked, finally.

'I do not know.' But he did, and he wondered at the man's daring and his close knowledge of him. *Dedication and fatigue?* Was the man *challenging* him? Putting him in shape for the hunt ahead…? Reinhardt looked down at the mashed potatoes, his nostrils full with the scent of the crushed and warmed herbs. Meissner sat opposite him, and closed one hand about the other, waiting. 'I think… I think it might be the man I am chasing. What else did you notice?'

'The man was a Berliner. But there was something in his voice. In his accent. Something else. Some other influence. I could be wrong.'

'You're a Berliner born and bred, Mrs Meissner. You would know.'

'*You* sound different, Gregor,' she answered. 'Seven years elsewhere, I can hear other places in your voice, now. But then,' she said, smiling softly to take any sting out of her words, 'you never were much of a Berliner. Far too polite. You should eat.'

'What about you?'

'Later,' Meissner replied, toying with the pages of a newspaper.

'More artwork?' Reinhardt asked, trying to change the subject.

Meissner smoothed the pages out, nodding. 'A Belgian commission arrived today,' she replied, but she was distracted and went up to bed shortly afterwards. Reinhardt washed up the dishes, cleaning down the surfaces, then sat under the yellow glow of the bulb, his notes and papers from the WASt spread around him, and Skokov's bottle of vodka and a glass. He looked at the bottle, hesitating, eyes flicking back and forth from the vodka and the papers. Mrs Meissner showed little, gave less away, but she was upset. She had never talked of it, but Reinhardt knew she had had to go into hiding after Tomas's arrest. Men watching, intrusions into her world, there would have been too many memories from the war.

He took a long breath, then began going through the notes he had made, trying to put things together, to find a pattern in the information. He listed the pilots of IV./JG56, then those who had gone on to serve in III./NJG64. He listed those who had been killed during the war, eliminated them from the investigation. He drew up deployment dates, double-checking who had been where at the same time. He noted addresses he had taken from *soldbuchs* of wives, of next of kin, drawing up contact lists for Mrs Dommes and her ladies to begin tracking down pilots living elsewhere. He stumbled on through the night, blinking back tiredness, feeling a headache rising up his back, seizing his neck and shoulders. He was not sure this was the best use of his time or the information he had, but he had no other way to analyse things, and when he was finished he had four lists, complete with a range of ancillary information.

He had Haber, Noell, Stucker, and Zuleger, the victims of the killer. Two killed by water, two by sand. He had their prewar addresses, as noted in their *soldbuchs* and personnel files. In a second list he had Noell, again, and his mysterious break in service, resurfacing in Bergen, but he also had Prellberg and Gareis. They, too, had gone somewhere, and that destination had been redacted, and the chances were they and Noell had gone somewhere together. In the third list, he had the other pilots from the second squadron, and their addresses across Germany. And in the fourth list he had Haber, and the limited information he had secured from what was in the WASt that indicated he had done work for the Nazis. After thinking a moment, he added Prellberg's, Noell's, and Gareis's names to that list as well. Thinking a little more, he added Leyser's name to the mix. Maybe something. Maybe nothing, he thought, going back to the sergeant's telling him about the man he had bumped into at Zuleger's building. An ex-soldier, with a veteran's slang. A man who wore a flat cap, like the man who had come here, to Mrs Meissner's house.

He looked at it all through eyes that stung and swam from tiredness, and thought it was not much, but then thought it was far more than he had mere days ago. It was the third list that interested him most, the list of those other pilots across Germany. God only knew where they were now, and if they could be found, but it was something to hang onto, a hook to cast into the flow of events.

Reinhardt shuffled his papers back together, and put the bottle away without touching it, noting it down as a small victory over himself. He went out into the garden to the latrine in the wooden shed he had built when he arrived here, made his ablutions, then stood a while in the chill and smoked a cigarette, staring up at the star-studded sky. He thought of Mrs Meissner, of how she had survived the Red Army's sack of Berlin by making a small den inside the brambles that hedged the bottom of her garden. She had seen the end coming, and steadily filled a small hollow with preserved food and bottles of water. With the Soviets at the city's gates, she had broken open her own front door, smashed the ground floor windows, wrecked furniture and strewn the contents of the kitchen all over the floor and left a dozen bottles of the colonel's old French brandy in evidence before retreating to her hideaway. She had stayed in it for several weeks, listening to the sack of the city, creeping out at night if she had to, and only emerging once things had calmed down. She found a Soviet captain living in the wreckage of her house who spoke a little German, and she had cooked and cleaned for him until he left, and this part of Berlin was occupied by the Americans, and at that moment Reinhardt realised what had bothered him in the WASt. He knew it had been something he had read, and now he knew.

Noell's *soldbuch* had indicated he had finished the war a captain.

But the uniform at his apartment had been a colonel's.

A colonel with polio.

Reinhardt looked at the stars, wondering how he could have missed that, and then realised something else. None of the men murdered, with the exception of Stucker, had been living at their prewar addresses. Noell even seemed to have vanished from circulation. No identity, no ration cards. Nothing.

So how was the killer finding them? What linked them together?

He went back inside to look over his lists a last time, resting his head on his crossed arms in a vain effort to pull the tension from his shoulders and neck, the smell of paper still strong in his nose and on his skin.

He dreamed of a stone. A small stone, like a pebble. It began to roll downhill. Other pebbles, other stones, joined it, until it was a slide, an avalanche, down a pitted and crazed slope. The stones tumbled and rolled into a lake, like a tarn, a dark expanse of water that gave no reflection. In they tumbled, stone after stone, a frantic rush, and the water swallowed them all, only ripples fanning out across the surface, until the last stone fell in. The surface of the water humped and bulged, and something heaved itself up into the air, a golem of stones, water streaming from it, from the titan length of its grotesque limbs as it flailed for balance. It turned its head, its eyes like boulders, and they searched blindly across the darkness, across the crazed and pitted slope, searched, until the weight of their gaze fell upon the dreamer…

It was the pounding at the door that woke him, not the dream. He stumbled sleep-heavy from the table, seeing up on the landing the wavering light of a candle, and seeing Mrs Meissner in a white nightdress with her hair unbound and running silver about her shoulders. He waved her back to bed and opened the door, blinking out into the thinning night at a patrolman, and beyond him the dark lines of a car.

'Inspector Reinhardt? I've been ordered to fetch you, sir. There's been another murder.'

29

Thursday

'So, what's your plan for this investigation, Reinhardt?' Weber asked, a facetious edge to his voice. 'To wait until a body turns up in every building in Berlin?'

The hotel was the Am Zoo, a good establishment on the Kurfürstendamm in the British Sector. It was something of a miracle it was actually open, but Allied bombing and the Soviet assault had only damaged but not destroyed it. The hotel staff had finally opened the guest's room – a man called Jürgen from the state of North Rhine-Westphalia, created just last year by the British – after he had failed to keep an appointment and they went to the room to check on him. Jürgen, who Reinhardt now knew as one of IV./JG56's pilots, was laid out on his bed, dressed in a dark suit. Reinhardt knew, with Weber here, he need not worry about Ganz or Tanneberger bestirring themselves to actually be at a crime scene, let alone one so early in the morning, but his mind was at once too fugged to care, and too focused on what he saw in front of him.

From the look of the body, Jürgen had not been dead long. Certainly not more than a day or so, that was clear, meaning the killer was still killing, still moving around the city. The ex-pilot lay on his bed, face up and, unlike the other bodies, his arms were still tied to the head of the bed by lengths of rope, and the skin was raw and livid from where, it seemed, he had struggled against his attacker. A dark tie curled across the white of Jürgen's shirtfront, and his head and shoulders were covered in a dusting of grit. Sand, Reinhardt was sure, forced down the man's mouth. Jürgen's shirtfront was unbuttoned, and he carefully separated it to reveal a massive bruise across his chest.

'The same killer?' Weber asked. Reinhardt nodded. Weber pursed his lips, nodding his head, as if it affirmed something for him, but when Reinhardt glanced at him from the corner of his eye, the young detective was chewing his lip, his attention focused on something elsewhere, and there was a trace of amusement in the angle of his mouth. Probably picturing Reinhardt in Margraff's office explaining the city's rising body count, he imagined, not liking the self-pity that tinged his thoughts. Taking a deep breath, Reinhardt gently prised open Jürgen's jaw, a trickle of wet sand flickering from the corner of the body's mouth. Reinhardt opened Jürgen's mouth wider, saw within the packed outline of sand. Bruising around Jürgen's mouth and nose indicated the killer had clamped his nose and mouth shut as the man asphyxiated.

'May I see his documents, please?'

Weber handed over an identity card from Cologne, in the British Occupation Zone. Jürgen's face stared up blandly from the card, older by nearly ten years from the photograph in his *soldbuch* that Reinhardt had seen hours earlier.

'What else did you find?' Reinhardt directed his question at Weber, and at an elderly uniformed officer, a lieutenant, who stood by the door, a shambles of a man in an unkempt uniform who looked like he wished he was elsewhere.

'It's not that easy, Reinhardt. You don't expect us to do your job for you now, do you?' Weber snapped. He glared proprietorially around the room, nodding to himself. 'They just called me 'cos I'm on the fucking graveyard shift, thanks to you.' Weber bit each word as if he were chewing it before uttering it, glaring at Reinhardt as if the other officer were not there.

'Misplaced anger is a characteristic of youth, Weber,' Reinhardt said, his eyes suddenly seeing nothing but his son, 'but it's still misplaced anger. You can stay. There's work enough for both of us.'

Weber's mouth worked, his cheeks stained red with his anger. 'Do your own work, Reinhardt. Ganz will want you to report to him before midmorning,' he cast over his shoulder as he left.

Reinhardt and the uniformed officer exchanged a blank gaze, then the officer shook his head. 'Look, I don't have much for you. My lads were called when the hotel opened the door. They called us. We came, took a look, and called Kripo. Your man Weber showed up, took a look for himself, unbuttoned the shirt, and then called you.'

'Have you talked to the hotel management?'

'The manager's downstairs waiting.'

'Any witnesses?'

The officer gave a tired nod. 'Rooms either side are unoccupied. The one opposite, the guest said he saw Jürgen two days ago. At breakfast. And he remembers him on Sunday morning looking somewhat the worse for wear.'

'Meaning?'

'Meaning he looked like he'd been out on the town,' the officer said, flicking a couple of pages in a notebook back and forth. 'The receptionist, or concierge, or whatever they call them in fancy places like this. The man on the front desk. He thinks he might've talked with our killer. They're all downstairs.'

'Anyone know where he was between Sunday morning and now?'

'The front desk saw him Monday. But they left him alone until last night. There was a note,' said the officer, handing over a slip of paper embossed with the hotel's emblem, and upon which someone penned a message in an elegant handwritten script. 'That was under the door. He'd written – someone had written – that he was feeling indisposed, and asked not to be disturbed until further notice.'

'Convenient…' Reinhardt muttered. And simple. And clever.

Alone, he noted the key in the lock, and that the door and doorjamb were undamaged. The killer was not forcing his way in. On a low table by a cupboard, a suitcase was folded open, and there were papers spread across a desk. A fountain pen, its cap half-off, lay at an angle atop them as if it had been laid down only momentarily.

Like at Zuleger's, Reinhardt thought, Jürgen had been disturbed, or stopped in what he was doing.

A knock at the door. Faint. Unobtrusive. Perhaps a voice. A reassuring tone. He opened it…

The cupboard held clothes, an overcoat, another dark suit, two shirts and ties, changes of socks and underwear. All of good quality. French labels. In the bottom of the cupboard was a large, square suitcase, of the kind a doctor might use. Reinhardt went to pull it out and frowned at its weight, heaving it back and onto the floor and hearing the dull clank of metal from inside. He opened the suitcase, folding open the top flaps. With his gloved hand, he fingered through the contents. Metal samples, technical journals, and what looked like a variety of correspondence in a cardboard folder. Flipping open the folder, he paused, frowned, fingered through the sheets of correspondence. Letters exchanged between Jürgen and a factory owner about the possibilities of entering into business together.

The factory was Vollmer Altmettal.

Von Vollmer's factory.

Reinhardt went back through Jürgen's identification, fingering the pockets of his suit, his wallet, the clothes in the cupboard, the suitcase, the wastepaper basket, the small bathroom. He ran his eyes over and around the room. Jürgen's tie made a curlicue across the white of the body's shirt. He frowned at it, back at the cupboard, his arms parting coats and suits, and pulling out a dark jacket with a satin lapel. A dinner jacket, with a bow tie folded into a pocket.

He looked around the room. It was a good room, in a good hotel. Clean. Comfortable. Jürgen's clothes were good quality. A travelling businessman. With a dinner jacket. He was here for something more than selling metal. Reinhardt pulled out his notebook, unfolding from within it the invitation he had found at Zuleger's apartment, the address belonging to a Mrs Frankewitz at whose home a party was to have been held, the address the Grunewald police had said was abandoned, and wondered that there was none of the literature

Reinhardt had found at the other locations, at Noell's and Zuleger's. No manifestos, no lists of grievances.

When he was finished in the room, he found the hotel's manager downstairs, along with the concierge. The manager was a fussy-looking man who seemed more worried about the hotel's reputation than the fact that a man had been murdered in one of its rooms. But the concierge seemed a more grounded man, who had seen a lot of people come and go in front of him, leaving him unfazed by human nature. The manager fielded most of the questions, painting a picture of an unobtrusive guest in a hotel that prided itself on being able to offer more than the basics to those who stayed with them. The guest who had seen Jürgen at breakfast could add no more information than what he had told the police earlier, that on Sunday morning Jürgen had looked like a man who had hit the bottle in a big way the night before.

'There were no disturbances?' Reinhardt asked. 'No arguments? Did he have visitors? Did he seem distracted?' A *no* to everything. 'Any women?'

'Detective!' gushed the manager. 'This is a respectable establishment.'

'I've no doubt, sir. When did he arrive?'

'Friday last, sir,' the concierge answered, consulting the hotel's register. 'By train from Cologne.'

'How long was he to stay?'

'He was booked to leave Friday. A week's stay.'

'When was the last time you saw him?'

'Monday afternoon, sir. He had appointments in town that day. The maid cleaned his room. I recall him returning to the hotel and going up to his room. At around four o'clock in the afternoon.'

'The maid found this…?' Reinhardt asked, raising the card.

'On Tuesday morning, sir, as she was doing her normal rounds. She left Mr Jürgen in peace, as requested.'

'Tell me again why the hotel opened the door last night.'

'We became concerned for him, that he might have fallen very ill, so we opened the door.'

'You told the sergeant you might have seen someone?' Reinhardt asked the concierge.

'Yes, sir. It was on the Monday evening. Mr Jürgen had returned to the hotel, and a man came asking for him.'

'Describe him, please.'

'Very… unremarkable, sir,' was all the concierge managed. 'Very normal. Well-spoken. Polite. Not at all pushy. He wore a hat and coat. He had spectacles with thick frames. He was clean-shaven. He asked simply if he could leave a letter for Mr Jurgen. He said he did not want to disturb him.'

'He was German?'

'Yes, sir.'

'How do you know?'

The concierge stared at him, then shrugged with his lips. 'His accent. It was Berlin. Upper class. He seemed like a man who had seen better days. His clothes were prewar quality.'

'Do you have that letter?'

The concierge took down a long envelope from a row of little pigeonholes that stretched behind the front desk. It was bright red paper. Reinhardt held it by the corners, flexed it from side to side, then tossed it on the counter. The concierge and the manager frowned at it, then him.

'What is the meaning of it, Inspector?' the manager asked.

'I presume you don't give out guest's room numbers to strangers? That was the killer's way to see in which room Jurgen was staying. The envelope's empty. He would have marked into which pigeonhole the concierge put it. He would have watched, either from the street,' he turned, pointing at the windows, 'or seen it when he came back later. He probably waited until your concierge went off duty so his replacement would not recognise him.' The two men looked at each other wordlessly. 'By any chance, on Saturday, did Jurgen have an appointment?'

'Yes, sir. A gala function, I believe, judging by what I overheard and the way in which he was dressed. Dinner jacket and tie.'

'Any idea where he was going?'

'Yes, sir. We ordered him a taxi. I have the address,' the concierge said. He looked pale as he flipped through a ledger, and then pointed out an entry. 'One does not forget addresses in that part of town very easily.'

That same address. Mrs Frankewitz.

30

The destination had stuck in the staff's mind, as it should have. Grunewald was still a good part of Berlin. It always would be, Reinhardt knew, no matter what happened to the city, no matter what its new masters made of it.

Out on the city's western edge, Grunewald was one of Berlin's more aristocratic suburbs, a part of the city that seemed to have escaped the worst of the fighting and bombing. The streets were clear and wide, the greenery was not shredded or splintered and, where they stood, trees still showed their age. Even denuded of their spring colours, they still seemed to spread themselves like benedictions over the wide avenues. The tangled tracery of their branches was like ironwork against the dull sheen of the sky as the taxi the hotel had been good enough to procure for Reinhardt drifted along the streets. It was a veritable antique, all upright angles and wheels that looked barely thick enough to support its own weight. With its battered coachwork showing the wear and tear of life on Berlin's streets, it coasted to a stop in a reek of charcoal like a piece of flotsam that had washed up on a pristine shore, the driver craning his head out of his window to check the address.

'This is it, mate,' he said, laying an arm across his seat as he twisted around to look at Reinhardt. His eyes gave a quick flicker up and down, from Reinhardt's dusty shoes, the frayed edge of his coat, the shine of his trousers at his knees. 'You sure this is the one you want?'

'Sure,' said Reinhardt, fishing in his pocket for the fare.

'Want me to wait?'

'Have a bit more faith,' Reinhardt muttered.

'As you say, mate,' the driver said, taking his fare. 'You're the one that fits here like a fist in the eye.'

The neighbourhood was like a vestige of prewar times, Reinhardt thought, standing on the street in the quiet after the taxi had gone, belching smoke from the boiler bolted underneath it. It was like something that should have seemed out of place in this postwar Berlin. Clean. Wide streets. White walls, although the war had still made itself felt here. Trees had scars of white flecked across their bark, holes had been chewed in bushes, walls had been chipped of stone and plasterwork, but compared to elsewhere – to Mitte, to Schöneburg, to Neukölln – it was as if nothing had ever happened here. He looked around, listening to the quiet, and could not help but think about what these walls hid.

They had always hidden power, he knew. And he knew that, far from the beer halls and the streets and the raucous blare of the workmen's meetinghouses, these white walls and manicured lawns and gabled roofs had done as much – if not more – to engender and incubate support for Nazism. It was behind such walls and under such roofs that those lived who thought they could control and channel the energies of a man like Hitler and a movement like the Nazis. And still did. He looked at the well-kept houses, at a governess in a strict black dress pushing a baby pram, and thought about the people who still lived here, people who had done nothing to stop the rise of the Nazis, who had in fact profited from it, and who now seemed to be profiting from the rubble of the war.

Reinhardt stood in front of a gate of wrought iron in a wall of old red bricks. The wall was taller than he was, the top frilled with ravels of bare ivy waiting for its spring greenery. The gate was heavy iron, rust sitting in the curls and curves of its decorative work, and the hinges looked swollen shut, but there was a new padlock on the gate holding together a short piece of bright metal chain. Through the bars of the gate, Reinhardt could see the house at the end of a gravel-strewn carriage circle, in the middle of which stood a dry ornamental fountain. The house itself was elegant enough, but the windows were all dark, and grass and weeds grew tall along the base of its walls.

Reinhardt checked the address against the tarnished brass of the plaque by the gate: 169 Albrechtsrasse – Frankewitz. This was the place. He looked up and down the street. Opposite was a small park, to either side were more blank walls. Gripping the bars with his hands, and putting his foot on a crosspiece, he hauled himself up the gate, throwing a leg over when he was high enough, and letting himself down on the far side of the gate the same way he had come up.

He hopped on to the gravel, rubbing his knee, and then walked up the side of the driveway, feeling very self-conscious, even voyeurish, expecting at any moment the door or a window to open, and an accusatory face to emerge, but the house, when he reached it, gave every impression of having been closed up for a long time. He walked all around it, tracing a path along the overgrown scrub on its walls, and his feet crunched once on some broken glass. It was not a very large house, wider than it was deep, although it had two floors above the ground floor, and dormers in the high pitch of its roof. The back was like the front, but as he stood away from the walls, looking up and around, he noted what looked like a path through the grass, leading away from the house and back into a high growth of bush and shrubbery.

He stood to one side, looking at the path with cocked head, before following it through the damp clasp of the greenery. The path turned to one side, and another, before it opened out into another garden, much wider and deeper, most of which was given over to vegetable patches. Another house stood there, much bigger, an altogether grander affair with a turret and ornamented gables, and unmistakably inhabited. Smoke drifted up from chimneys, curtains hung in windows, a conservatory glittered against one wall with a tracery of plants visible behind the glass.

Reinhardt took a cautious line around the edge of the vegetable patches, up the side of the house and to the front door. A big car was parked in a carriage circle, similar to the one at the other house. It was in fairly good condition, and a driver in shirtsleeves was polishing its metal work. The man straightened slowly, suspiciously as Reinhardt came around the corner of the house.

'*Hey!*' the driver called out.

Reinhardt ignored him, and the front door was opened to his ring by an elderly man in what seemed to be a butler's old-fashioned livery. Reinhardt gave his identification and asked to see the owner of the house, turning to see the driver standing not far from him. The man was big, built solid, and the set in his eyes and shoulders was not friendly.

The butler was courteous enough for both of them, however, asking him to wait in the hallway, a tall space with a fretwork of dark, heavy beams holding up the high ceiling. A whisper of voices and the light fall of steps presaged the butler's return, accompanied by an elderly lady in an elegant suit of blue wool, the upright image of a dowager, with civil, old-fashioned manners, who identified herself as Margarit Frankewitz. She seemed confused as to what Reinhardt wanted, her eyes glittering within the lattice of wrinkles that seamed the porcelain of her skin.

'Officer,' she said, holding up a hand. 'I'm afraid I haven't any idea what you're talking about.'

'Madame,' Reinhardt said, again, 'your address has come up several times in a murder inquiry…'

'*Murder* inquiry?' She frowned imperiously. Her fingers were long and thin, the nails perfectly manicured, each finger with a ring. But the knuckles were swollen with age, each length of each finger slightly off true. 'Heavens. How common. I think you should speak to my nephew. He'll know what's to be done. I shall call him to come, and I'm sure we can resolve this to everyone's satisfaction. If you would care to wait…?' Although she phrased it as a question, it was not meant as such, and she was already turning away to the butler, telling him to put Reinhardt in the conservatory – he would surely appreciate the light, Mrs Frankewitz said in an aside – and to summon Claus.

She was gone before he could protest, and he followed the invitation of the butler's arm with resignation, but when he entered the conservatory, he found it a place of warmth and light, with wicker seats in among the nodding arms of plants and flowers. It was still relatively early, and after the night of broken sleep he had had, he knew that if he sat, he would start to drift off, so he stood looking out at the garden, facing the light that shone in soft-edged streams through the windows. A door banged shut, there was a clatter of voices, and he turned, frowning at the edge of familiarity the voices carried, standing and turning as a man came into the room, tall and bluff, three-piece suit, watch chain stretching taut across a swell of stomach.

'Mr von Vollmer,' Reinhardt said.

Von Vollmer blinked at him. 'Inspector… Reinhardt?' His lips moved, as if discarding word after word.

'Somehow, I am not surprised by this.'

'By the house? Yes, remarkable isn't it. We're so lucky to be in the British Sector, otherwise this house would have been requisitioned.'

'They're accommodating a dozen families in a place like this elsewhere in the city,' Reinhardt said, a deliberate stab at provocation in his words.

Von Vollmer looked aghast. 'Dear God, no. Think again, Inspector. Places like this, to the victor the spoils. Some Russian officer would have taken it, then kept food in the toilet and shat in the sinks,' he said, the vulgarity riding easily along his accent. He cocked his head over his shoulder to tell the butler to bring coffee. 'Won't you sit down? I mean, *honestly*, Inspector. Will the Allies permit the proletarianisation of me and my class? What will that do to their hopes for a *democracy*,' he continued, pronouncing the word with particular precision, as though trying out something new, 'if people like me – Germany's eternal backbone – are impoverished to an extent our energies are consumed with survival instead of thought? Think. Just think how much more I could have contributed did I still have my estates. If they had not bee…'

'You lied to me.'

Von Vollmer coloured. 'I am not accustom –'

'You lied to me,' Reinhardt interrupted him. 'At the factory. When I asked you if you had known Zuleger outside the workplace.'

Von Vollmer's colour fell, but his lips still moved as if biting off words he chose to discard. 'I am not sure that I did know him, Inspector. Perhaps you would be so kind as to explain yourself.'

'Zuleger had an invitation to an event organised for Saturday night. Except it's not this address. It's the address of that other house. The one at the end of the garden.'

'This used to be one property. The other house was the guesthouse. We don't use it anymore.' Von Vollmer's mouth chewed its own words back for a moment, his eyes glancing up at Reinhardt. 'It was a small event I organised for some among the workforce. It was just over a year since the factory reopened. I thought it worth celebrating.

'Inspector, I believe I told you that I see it as my stern duty to provide for my workers, especially for my ex-comrades, to those who carry the values of "*soldierdom*".' He used this word with a tone full of gravitas, looking hard at Reinhardt to see if he understood the measure of it.

'Those values you might imbue to that concept are all but outlawed in modern Germany, sir. There are many who would say that those values – honour, sacrifice, duty – were the same ones that carried the Nazi cause out into the world.'

Von Vollmer's colour rose again. 'Values…? Who would say…? *You*, Inspector? *You* would say such a thing?' he blustered. 'Say rather that the Nazis misused traditional German military values, that…'

'I'm not here for a political lecture, Mr von Vollmer. I want to know what Zuleger was doing with an invitation to this place last Saturday.'

Von Vollmer's mouth firmed, and he nodded, finally. 'I admit, Inspector, I did not tell you the whole truth that first time you came to the factory. But the explanation really is quite simple. As a factory owner, as a man who employs many men who served under me during the war, I have a strong sense of duty – both as an aristocrat and as a former officer – to take care of my workers and former comrades. I believe as well that regular events help to inculcate a sense of teamwork and spirit in the workplace, as well as improving productivity. And isn't that,' he asked, with no little irony, 'an end much prized by our new Allied overlords?' Von Vollmer glanced outside at the garden. 'I organised a gathering but, because of the Allies' Occupation laws that forbid the gatherings of veterans, or what might seem like one, I was obliged to organise it under my aunt's name, here, at her house, to help escape suspicion.'

The butler brought in a silver tray of coffee, and von Vollmer paused as the elderly servant poured and left. Von Vollmer indicated milk and sugar, taking a cup of black coffee for himself. He sighed, his fingers playing with the chain of his watch, 'I know that in our Germany of today, such gatherings of ex-servicemen are viewed with suspicion. A man in my position, I could not afford to have any problems. So I used the address of the guesthouse. But I assure you, there was no ulterior motive, and I cannot guess why or if Zuleger's murder was related to our organisation.'

'"Organisation"?' Reinhardt queried.

'Of the events. Organisation of the events.'

'Did your organisation have a name?'

'I told you, Inspector, there was no org –'

'Ritterfeld.'

Von Vollmer blinked, and his chin went tight. 'What?'

Reinhardt unfolded the manifesto from his pocket. '"Ritterfeld Association". Ritterfeld was the name of the air base where the Group was initially formed.'

'I know what Ritterfeld is,' snapped von Vollmer. 'But I've never seen that.'

'I don't believe you. And I don't care that you organised a gathering of war veterans. And I don't really care why…' he said, raising a hand to forestall von Vollmer's protest. 'Just please, stop lying or hiding things.'

Von Vollmer shook his head. 'I insist, Inspector, that the meeting was not political, but simply a gathering that promoted comradeship and teamwork. All principles that lead to greater productivity in the factory. And productivity,' von Vollmer intoned, resolutely, 'is a capitalist virtue, thus not something the Allies could possibly criticise.'

'You said that already.'

'*What?*'

'I would like to know who was at that gathering.'

'Why?'

'Did it involve anyone other than veterans from the Night Hawks?'

'What are you asking me? To incriminate people?'

'Was anyone there other than people who work for you? Was a man named Kausch, there?'

'No.'

'Does a man named Kausch work at your factory?'

'Honestly, Inspector, how would I know that? But, no, I don't think so. It was a private gathering, Inspector. All I will tell you is it involved those with whom I work.'

'If that is the case, why was Noell invited?'

'Who?'

'Andreas Noell. I mentioned him when I came to your office. Also a former pilot of your command, although before your time, I believe. But he was murdered as well, early on Monday morning after attending some kind of party, and I find it hard to believe you would organise a gathering of men who served with you and he would not be here.'

'I believe this meeting is over, Inspector,' von Vollmer said, heavily.

'Was Noell here?'

'Inspector, I must warn you now. I have been patient. I have been collegial. I have spoken to you as one former comrade to another. But if this harassment keeps up, there will be legal implications. I am not without friends and influence who believe, as do I, that Germany must not be allowed to come to naught as she has done in the past.' Von Vollmer clamped his mouth shut, as if he realised he had said too much.

'Are you threatening me, Mr von Vollmer?'

'And I have good reason to believe that should I so request it, you will be removed from this case.'

'A lawyer is perfectly within your rights, Mr von Vollmer. Should you wish one to be present, I would be happy to wait. Or he can join us at Gothaerstrasse. Or perhaps at HQ on Linienstrasse.'

'Thank you, Inspector,' said von Vollmer, rising to his feet.

'You have not even asked me why I am here.' Von Vollmer blinked. 'You have not stopped talking about your gathering. I do not wish to veer into arguments over reasons and ethics. I want simply to know why I have four dead bodies connected to your Group.'

'Four?' said von Vollmer. 'At the factory, you mentioned three.'

'The body of Mr Jürgen was found this morning in a hotel room.' Von Vollmer straightened up, the blood draining from his face. 'You and he have been corresponding, on business matters, for some time. But I think he came to Berlin for your gathering, meaning more people than just those who work with you were here on Saturday. He was probably killed sometime on Monday.'

'I met with him at the factory…' Von Vollmer seemed genuinely shocked. On Monday morning. The day before you came. We talked about… about business. He has a factory… of his own…' Von Vollmer tailed off. '*Jürgen?* You are *sure*?'

Reinhardt nodded. 'I think you know more than you are telling me. Someone is killing people who are all connected, and the connection is your Group. So I ask you,' he said, leaning forward in his chair, 'what linked these men to each other that someone is killing them, other than that they had served together?'

'I don't *know*, Inspector. So, if there is nothing more…?'

'Yes. How about a lift?'

31

They came for him later, as the day was drawing to a close, as he was finishing drawing up a list of people for Mrs Dommes and her assistants to start trying to contact, using the information he had gleaned from his day in the WASt. Like with the call to Lassen in the Hamburg Kripo, Reinhardt found the endeavour daunting in the extreme. Trying to track down individual men across postwar Germany made looking for a needle in a haystack easy, but Dommes shrugged off the difficulties.

'Four names, then, Inspector. Hauck, Osterkamp, Prellberg, and Thurner. In Aachen, Stuttgart, Braunschweig, and Stettin. That last one will be hardest, Inspector,' she said, with a firm slant to her mouth. 'All the other locations are in Western Germany, in the Allied Occupation Zones. But Stettin is in Poland now. I don't know how we'll find out any information on Mr Thurner there. If he indeed survived the war, it's unlikely he would have returned. He could be anywhere.'

Reinhardt nodded, going back over his notes. 'Their fighter squadron surrendered at Bremen. Perhaps we could make inquiries there. In any case, do what you can, Mrs Dommes, perhaps starting with the others first. I will see if I can find some other way to locate him.'

'Very well,' she said, looking at the page of handwritten notes as if she expected the answers to leap off the page at her. 'I shall proceed as we discussed. Calls to the central police registries in those cities with requests for information on these ex-pilots, and for checks to be made on them. Follow-up calls as necessary.'

She paused, and he glanced at her, but she was not looking at him. Ganz was standing in the door, his face grim. He pointed a finger at Reinhardt, then crooked it.

'You. Come with me.'

Dommes gasped at Ganz's display of manners, or the lack thereof, but Reinhardt laid a gentle hand on her arm. 'Thank you, Mrs Dommes, you have been most helpful as usual. Let me know what you find out.'

'But of course, Inspector,' she said, directing a withering glare at Ganz.

Reinhardt followed Ganz into Neumann's office. Tanneberger, Whelan, and Markworth were waiting there, with their translator sitting all prim and proper, and the atmosphere was thick. Collingridge was not there, but Bliemeister was, the assistant chief for the American Sector in a chair to one side of Neumann's desk. Reinhardt was not offered a seat, and he flushed a moment at the image he suddenly had of a schoolboy hauled in front of the headmaster. Ganz handed him a photograph. It was a shot of a man with the back of his skull caved in. Ganz handed him other photos like a card dealer in a game, one after the other. All shots of the same man, shots of the injuries he had sustained, what looked like welts on his arms, thighs, and across his back.

'Who is that?' Reinhardt asked.

'That's Stresemann.' The translator's words floated softly behind Ganz's.

'He looks dead.'

'He is. He was found in Neukölln.'

'Stresemann was beaten to death.' It was Markworth who spoke. Reinhardt said nothing, knowing the value of silence in such situations. 'Sometime on Tuesday, we think. He was beaten to death with a long, narrow object.' He waited, but still Reinhardt said nothing. 'He was beaten to death with something like a police truncheon.' Markworth held Reinhardt's eyes. 'Like a baton.'

'Where were you on Tuesday night?'

'At home.' Reinhardt replied to Ganz. He looked at the others. At Whelan, at Markworth, at Neumann and Tanneberger. Whelan and Neumann looked uncomfortable, like men out of their depth. Markworth looked imperturbable, inscrutable even. Sitting quietly in his corner, Bliemeister said nothing.

'Witnesses?'

'My landlady.' Ganz raised his eyebrows. 'And an officer of Soviet state security. He came to the house.'

'You have such a baton, do you not, Reinhardt?' Markworth asked.

'I lost it.'

Markworth said nothing. No one said anything, only the translator's voice fluttering gently, then fading away.

'When did you lose it?' Ganz asked.

'Two days ago.'

'Two days ago?'

Reinhardt clenched his teeth, holding his lips tight against them. 'When I went into the Soviet Sector the other day, I was attacked by Fischer. I lost it then.'

'I see,' said Ganz, as if he saw anything but. 'And were there any witnesses?' Reinhardt shook his head. 'Did you report the baton lost?' Reinhardt only shook his head, again.

'A trip into the Soviet Sector. An alleged attack. A contact from a known member of Soviet state security.' Markworth's voice was low and level, but each word struck home as if aimed.

'Given current relations, and given what we told you of Carlsen's work on the Control Council, we find this very concerning,' said Whelan.

'Given Soviet infiltration of the police and the overwhelming Communist sympathies of its officers, we find it more concerning still,' said Markworth bluntly. Reinhardt watched Whelan as he said it. It was clear that the old Englishman had a rather different sense of how to deliver unpleasant news, but he made no effort to cushion Markworth's words. If they were not playing 'good cop, bad cop', Reinhardt did not know what their game was.

'Gentlemen, please,' said Neumann, a worried slant to his words and a glance at Bliemeister. 'All this talk of influence and infiltration is unnecessary.'

'I think not' was Markworth's candid response, almost an interruption. 'Police command is in Mitte, in the Soviet Sector. The Chief is a Soviet creature to his fingernails, or do I wrong him? Police officers in the Soviet Sector cannot travel to the Western ones and must report any contact with their colleagues here or with Allied officers. Police officers have done little to protect the meetings or premises of non-Communist political parties across the city, especially in East Berlin. Police officers have, conversely, provided protection to Socialist Unity Party meetings,' Markworth continued, referring to the new party the Soviets had created from a merger between the Communists and Social Democrats. 'Police officers are overwhelmingly represented in the Party-dominated trade union. Soldiers of the Western Allied nations have at times been harassed by Berlin police officers. Please, correct me if I am wrong? No? Then perhaps you will understand our *concern* that a Soviet state security officer has taken it upon himself to show an interest into a murder investigation involving a British agent.'

None of what Markworth said was wrong, Reinhardt knew, but it was more the *way* he said it. His words had an awful weight to them, like a stone rolling downhill, and for a second he shivered as he remembered his dream, that nightmare of a figure of stones broaching the eldritch waters of a blackened lake…

'Moreover,' Whelan continued, 'you will understand our concern that, having asked for efficiency and a measure of discretion, what we get is expediency and a shambles of an investigation in which the main suspect is dead and the main witness is missing.'

'What did this Soviet officer want, Reinhardt?' asked Tanneberger.

'He wanted to know about my investigation into the murder of Noell.'

'And what did you tell him?'

'What I told you and the councillor. Just the facts.'

'This Russian asked about *Noell*?' asked Whelan. The big Englishman leaned forward, but Markworth stayed quite still. 'He was more interested in *Noell*?'

'Yes. Does that surprise you?'

'Reinhardt!' snapped Tanneberger, as Neumann's face tightened up.

'He told me Carlsen was half-German.' The Germans in the room stirred and stilled. 'That he was a particular kind of agent.' The translator's voice hesitated, and she looked to the Englishmen as if for guidance, but if guidance she sought, there was none forthcoming.

'Anything else you would like to tell us?' Markworth's eyes were stone.

'He told me our relationship is a one-way affair.'

'You will appreciate that this puts you in a difficult position, Reinhardt,' Whelan said, his words laboured, as if he regretted being the bearer of bad news, or bad news so plainly spoken. The English, Reinhardt thought. They so loved their equivocations…

'No. I don't see that,' Reinhardt said, his words short and sharp. 'What evidence connects me, the baton I lost, and that body?'

'The wounds on Stresemann's body are particular,' said Markworth. 'Not just strike wounds from a baton-type object. There are characteristics to the wounds. Characteristics that would indicate he was struck by an extendable baton. Like yours.'

'That's supposition. And I didn't have the only extendable baton in Berlin.'

'They're rare enough. And you were in Neukölln on Monday, weren't you?' Markworth asked. The room went chill again. Reinhardt said nothing. 'And let's not forget the Russian,' Markworth said, behind a slow blink of those marble eyes.

'Any member of the occupying forces may contact a member of the police, Mr Markworth,' Neumann said, primly. 'Like now. Should that contact become an occasion to pass on instructions, or become coercive, that would, of course, change the nature of the contact and become a cause for concern.' Markworth swivelled his dead eyes on Neumann, and the Chief seemed to clam up.

'Has Professor Endres done an autopsy of Stresemann, sir?' Reinhardt asked Ganz, strangely impelled to take the pressure off Neumann. 'Has Berthold seen the body?'

'No,' Ganz answered. 'Nothing connects you definitively, Reinhardt. For now. But you will appreciate if we pay a little closer attention to what you are doing. Starting with a daily report, to me.'

'It means your wings are being clipped, Reinhardt.' Markworth's smile was tight, and there was a tinge to it. A rueful quality, perhaps…? Reinhardt could not be sure he had seen it at all.

'Especially as we've received a complaint against you.' This from Whelan. The Englishman's face was taut. 'It seems you have been making unsubstantiated accusations against certain individuals.'

'Can you tell us who made such a complaint?' Bliemeister asked, suddenly and solicitously.

'I'm afraid I cannot,' Whelan replied ponderously, shaking his head enough to set his heavy jowls waggling. 'Confidentiality. You know how it is.'

Markworth held Reinhardt's eyes, and he fancied something glittered in them. A challenge perhaps. A call to provocation.

'Mr von Vollmer, from whom I believe this complaint has come, is exaggerating certain things,' Reinhardt said. 'Nevertheless, I maintain that he and his business have come up several times in my investigation, and will remain part of it for as long as I am permitted to carry it out,' finished Reinhardt, looking first to Bliemeister, then to Neumann, and, finally, back to Markworth. Challenge accepted, he thought.

'Von Vollmer's in trouble with the Soviets,' said Markworth, the slightest of mocking twists to his lips, but whether the gesture was meant for Reinhardt or Whelan was not clear. 'One of his shipments was stopped in the Soviet Zone on its way west. It's been "lost". He's upset. He thinks he's being hassled because of you.'

'I would like the Inspector removed from the Carlsen case,' said Whelan.

'He's not *on* the Carlsen case,' said Ganz. Whelan blinked furiously, like a bull brought to bay by some unforeseen obstacle. 'Are you saying the two cases *are* connected?' Ganz tilted his head to one side, and for the first time since he had known him, Reinhardt felt a surge of gratitude for the detective.

'I believe my colleague misspoke,' said Markworth.

'That's quite a misstatement to make, Mr Markworth.' Neumann frowned at Ganz, as if surprised to hear such a challenging note.

'I still would like him off the case. Of all the cases that touch upon our affairs,' said Whelan. He sounded stuck, as if mired in something. Neumann looked at Ganz, as if for help, but if help he found, it was not quite what he was looking for. Ganz gave nothing away, sitting heavily in his chair.

'What about you, Assistant Chief?' Markworth asked, looking at Bliemeister. Reinhardt wondered if they were playing a game with Bliemeister, if they had brought him along to add weight to their demands. He was, after all, an appointee of the Allies. He was 'theirs', as Skokov would have said.

'I understand your concerns, gentlemen,' Bliemeister said, finally. 'However, as you know, my position does not allow me to interfere in operational matters. Concerning the inquiries into the murders of Noell and Zuleger, and matters pertaining thereto, I cannot in good conscience advise Chief Neumann to withdraw one of his officers from an investigation, given the resources at his disposal.' Reinhardt listened with a grudging measure of respect as Bliemeister droned on. Prevaricating. Tying things up with process and qualifications.

'With all due respect for our working relations and the priority we accord your needs,' Bliemeister continued, somewhat torturously, 'I feel that Inspector Reinhardt is qualified to remain in the lead on the inquiries into the deaths of Noell and Zuleger, under the close supervision of Chief Inspector Ganz. I take the breach in protocol that led to his not reporting a contact by a Soviet state security officer seriously, and should new elements come to light regarding his conduct in this case, I shall have no hesitation in suggesting to

Chief Neumann, and to Police President Margraff, to review his status as an investigating officer, and indeed, as a member of this police force.' Bliemeister spoke hesitantly, as if testing the ground beneath each word, and he seemed relieved to have reached the end of what he wanted to say without being interrupted.

'Very well,' said Whelan. 'However, rest assured that the British authorities will be paying close attention to this as well from now on. I must express our disappointment into the current state of affairs into the inquiries into Carlsen's murder.'

'Your concern is noted, Mr Whelan,' Bliemeister said smoothly, as if on firmer ground. He flicked a glance at Ganz, nodding, as if to hand the conversation back.

'I should like for our services to have a look at Stresemann's body, so as to complete our inquiries,' said Ganz.

'Of course. See to it, James,' Whelan said, in an aside to Markworth, who gave little sign he had heard him.

The meeting broke up, the British taking their leave and Tanneberger escorting them out. Markworth's eyes lingered on Reinhardt, their flat, marble sheen giving little away. Ganz indicated to Reinhardt he could leave as well, and he returned weak-kneed to his desk, unsure what had just happened. He poured himself a cup of coffee from the urn, drinking it in a patch of sunlight, before realising he was not alone, and that a silence had fallen over the squad room.

'Deftly played, Reinhardt,' Markworth congratulated him. The British officer was standing by his desk. It took a moment for Reinhardt to realise Markworth had spoken to him in English, as if on purpose, as if he sought to widen the wedge that already existed between Reinhardt and the other officers. In a corner, Weber sat with Schmidt and Frohnau, watching closely. Reinhardt felt a twist of anger, a sudden uncoiling that came from within, and he knew that the darker side of him had turned over, like something shifting uneasily in its rest, deep inside.

'You seem to think I'm someone I'm not.'

'And what's that?'

'A player of games. I'm nothing like that.'

'Everyone plays, Reinhardt.'

'Tell me about Carlsen. Tell me more about him than he was just your friend.'

'That's not enough?'

'Tell me what he was doing in the WASt.'

Markworth blinked, shook his head. 'What are you talking about?'

'I found his name in the WASt's records.'

'You were in the WASt?'

'Skokov arranged it.'

Markworth's face suddenly cracked into a smile. It changed him, made him suddenly someone else. 'Bravo, Reinhardt, bravo!' he said. 'But I still don't understand about Carlsen.'

'He was looking at the same things I was. He was making links with Noell and the other murders. Are you still insisting Carlsen's death was not linked to the others?'

'I… I have no idea what you are talking about.'

Markworth seemed surprised, and Reinhardt found the man's surprise perturbing. Markworth had seemed implacable, a solid presence. He reminded Reinhardt so much of some of the Feldjäegers he had served with. To see him rattled was somehow wrong.

'Was it true what the Russian told me? He was a German?'

Markworth nodded.

'Why would someone want him dead?'

The Englishman's eyes went flat. But after a moment, life seemed to flow up from somewhere within them, their marble glaze taking on a sheen of warmth. 'Just being someone's friend can sometimes mean a great deal, Reinhardt. I'm guessing someone like you should know that. Let's just say, he and I went through a lot together. But we differed on one thing. He had hope for Germany. He had hope for Germans. I did not. And I still don't.'

32

Despite having spent the previous day in the WASt and despite having attended a third crime scene that morning, Reinhardt did not see either Tanneberger or Ganz for the rest of that day, for which he was glad. He felt he had come to a stop and was not sure which way to go, but he knew he would have fought any direction suggested or imposed on him by them.

He waited, the time turning into an hour, then more, and still neither of them came. What was he to do then? What was he to do in a city where the police served four masters, but one of them above the other three? What was he to do when all the signs he had pointed to there being one murderer on the loose? A murderer who knew the city, who could blend into a tenement or into the foyer of an upmarket hotel, who could come into the house where Reinhardt lived. What was he to do when he knew Carlsen had himself been investigating Noell, or at least whatever it was Noell did during that time when his service record had been redacted? What connection was there between a Luftwaffe pilot and a half-German British agent? And what linked them to a Soviet officer who had also gone looking in the same place for the same information?

He did not know how long he might have sat there if he had not received a call from Endres, asking him to come to the morgue. That was enough to trigger him into motion. Shrugging into his coat and flipping his hat on, he left the squad room through the usual gamut of inquisitive eyes, one or two derogatory calls, and the now habitual cawing of a crow.

Outside in the streets, the sun had begun its fall toward late afternoon. Despite the burnished timbre of the sun's light that gave brightness and depth, it was cold, as if the sun could not warm through or beyond the surfaces of the city, be they concrete or flesh. The station at Bayerischer Platz was shut for maintenance, so he decided to walk up Potsdamer Strasse to Bülowstrasse station, making himself walk quickly through the burden of his knee, as if he could somehow outpace his difficulties. There were people everywhere – men, women, the elderly, children who flitted and flashed as they chased each other over the ruins, a worker in a flat cap who pushed a handcart loaded with bricks down the street behind him – but he felt very alone.

He passed a block of flats that had once formed a square, but the side that had overlooked the street was gone, blown out and away. At the ends of the two wings that would once have joined the missing one there was only a ground-to-rooftop crosshatch of the remains of apartments, their cavities spilling pipes and wallpaper that flapped in the wind and radiators that clung to the walls like limpets. As he passed, though, he saw into the square within the wings. Against a backdrop of fire-scarred masonry, of windows boarded up with cardboard and wood, of electrical wires that crazed the gap between the buildings, was a small playground. A group of toddlers tumbled in a sandpit, and two boys, all bone-white flesh and scraped knees, were putting the finishing touches to a fort made from bricks and rubble. Mothers rocked prams, a pair of elderly gentlemen played chess, a man with a cigarette in his mouth and a faraway expression on his face pushed a little girl in a swing.

As he approached Bülowstrasse, he began to come up on the outskirts of the market around Potsdamer Platz. Spivs and touts, and dozens of children – some of them in rags for shoes – wound through the crowds with practised ease. Allied soldiers bartered among the jumbled collections of wares for oil paintings, porcelain tea sets, silver cutlery, carpets, military medals and decorations, cameras, gramophones, and the piles of books their owners had not yet burned for warmth. While the soldiers sought souvenirs,

Germans sought the more prosaic things in life: cigarettes and tobacco, butter and fat, meat and milk, medicines and drugs, and fuel. Fuel above all, coal or wood to heat freezing homes and cook the meagre rations most families lived on. Women sauntered through the crowds or stood by the entrances to buildings and watched the men, especially the soldiers, and sometimes him, with hungry eyes. Although it had calmed down in the last months from its peak as one of the fulcrums of the black market in Berlin, Potsdamer Platz – along with Alexanderplatz further to the northeast in the Soviet Sector – was still thriving.

An organ grinder with one leg and one arm leaned heavily against his machine, cranking a well-known Berlin tune. It was an old tune, but the words most Berliners knew were those which dated from the time of King Friedrich Wilhelm III and the wars against the French, and Reinhardt hummed them to himself as he walked past the cripple, laying a couple of cigarettes atop the casing.

When my legs were shaved off me
In the war that has just passed
Then my king, as though for payment,
Slapped a medal on my breast.
And he uttered, 'Dearest Fritz,
So that you may live in ease,
We now further here reward you:
Let you crank songs in the streets.'

The cripple nodded his thanks to him, something in his eyes, veteran to veteran, but Reinhardt walked on, not wanting any contact. There was something wrong with him, he thought, as he turned aside for the station. Something wrong with him that he could not look at his city, at his people, without seeing them through a patina of suspicion, or worse, that he could not seem to see past a veneer of distrust. That he was surprised when he broke down the human tapestry around him into discrete parts – a face, a smile, the sound of laughter, the play of light on a woman's hair – and found humanity there. Even at the worst of times during the war, even during the very worst of times in the first war, in the trenches, he had found humanity, or he had found the strength in himself to look for it.

Now he could not find it. He did not have the energy to look for it. It was as if he could not let himself go again and just become one of them. A person. A Berliner. A German. He wanted to believe what he had done during the war lifted him up and above. He wanted to believe he did not bear what he saw as their stain, when he knew he looked and walked and sounded no different from them. Just a tall, shabbily dressed man with a face drawn through tiredness and hunger, and his hair streaked with grey. When he knew the surest path to a place of loneliness and ostracism was to think that he was better than those around him, these people who swayed from side to side with the U-Bahn's motion, shoved together on the carriage's benches or hanging from its leather straps.

Markworth looked at Germans and saw no hope. More and more, Reinhardt believed that. What, he asked himself, not for the first time, was he doing back here…?

'You always did have a soft spot, Gregor.' Brauer had appeared beside him, all rumpled clothes and stubbled cheeks. 'That organ grinder, wasn't he there before the war?'

'Who gave you that shiner?' Reinhardt asked, pointing at a bruise that purpled Brauer's temple.

'Eastern Front veterans with chips on their shoulders. Forget it. I've got news about Friedrich.'

'That was quick.' Reinhardt nodded Brauer to go on, his guts notching themselves tight.

'Bad news isn't hard to find, Gregor. Friedrich's not a popular man. It was asking about him that got me into trouble. No one who's come back wants to remember the east, and none of them wants anything to do with the Ivans. Friedrich's not living in that halfway house, he works there. Word is, Friedrich's a snitch for the

Ivans. That he keeps an eye on what veterans are up to, and an ear to what they're saying.'

'Go on.'

'No one knows for sure, right, but they say he was turned during the war. That he couldn't handle the POW camps. There's a whole bloody value system and pecking order among the survivors from the Eastern Front, particularly among the officers and the SS, and Friedrich and those like him are at the bottom.'

'Is my son in danger?'

'More because of what he's doing rather than what he might have done.'

'Like what?' Reinhardt asked, regretting the snap in his voice but it seemed to roll off Brauer, or else his old friend understood the stress he was under.

'He strikes up conversations, they say. Like he was testing the waters. He passes out Socialist Unity Party literature. Encourages veterans to attend Party meetings. He's close to a couple of Party councillors, both of whom were prisoners, and both of whom came back with the Soviets and who were put into power right after the fall of the city.'

'Enough,' Reinhardt said, raising a hand. 'Enough,' he repeated, weakly.

'Look, Gregor… Friedrich's not doing anything wrong. It's not like he's breaking any laws, or hurting anyone. It's just… I mean…'

'It's not very nought-eight-fifteen, you might say.'

'I might say that, indeed. Look, keep your ears stiff, all right?' Reinhardt nodded. 'I'll keep an eye on him a bit longer. But nothing will come up, I'm sure. He'll be round the house again, soon enough, and you can talk this out with him.'

Reinhardt made himself stop outside the morgue and smoke another cigarette, calming himself and trying to lighten his mood. Endres, for all his professionalism, was no bundle of laughs, and Reinhardt needed time to try and sort out what Brauer had told him about

Friedrich's situation. He waited in the Professor's office while Endres finished an autopsy of a woman. He joined Reinhardt a short time later, bringing with him a touch of the morgue, of solvents and chemicals, of human rot.

Snap out of it, Reinhardt swore to himself. He blinked, as if to clear his mind and sight of the sludge of his thoughts. For a moment it seemed as if Endres had caught a glimpse of something, perhaps something that fled into the corner of Reinhardt's eyes, perhaps some straightening of the rigour that tautened his face. The Professor's eyes considered, but he said nothing.

'Thank you for coming, Reinhardt,' Endres said. Reinhardt blinked. This was not how conversations with the Professor usually started. 'You will recall our conversation about that photograph you showed me? Yes? Well, that person is willing to meet with you. Now, if you agree.'

'Right now?' asked a surprised Reinhardt. Endres nodded. 'Very well, yes, then. I was expecting something else.'

'News of the autopsy of that body that was brought in earlier? Stresemann? I have something for you, yes. Shall we go?'

Reinhardt blinked back further surprise, but followed Endres's tall, angular frame out of the morgue, and then had to keep up a smart pace to stay abreast of the Professor, who seemed to devour the corridors of the hospital with his long strides.

'Stresemann first,' said Endres, tipping his hat to the guard at the hospital gate, who ducked behind his post and re-emerged with a pair of bicycles. 'We'll take these. We've not that far to go, but it'll be faster this way. It's all rather bizarre,' continued Endres, as he began pedalling. 'I checked the bruising on the body and, I'm afraid to say, the strike marks are characteristic of an extendable baton, the type,' he said, glancing over at Reinhardt, 'I am told you carried. An old SiPo model, correct? Indeed, the bruising shows the evidence of the individual segments of the baton as they struck the flesh. So instead of one long strike mark, the mark is broken in two or, in some cases, three. There is also another characteristic, which is that the baton was also flexible, and would "wrap" around the body,' Endres said, demonstrating with one hand in the air before him before snatching it back to his handlebars when his front wheel wobbled precariously, ignoring the startled look a pair of pedestrians gave him. Reinhardt smiled, then grimaced as his knee began to hurt from the pedalling. 'The baton also had a weighted tip at the end, and there are distinctive signs of that injury as well.'

They cycled past the Charité hospital complex and crossed the Spree at Kronprinzen Bridge. Over the bridge, Endres angled right across Königsplatz, with the blackened hulk of the Reichstag off to their left and just beyond it, absurdly pristine amid the drear expanse of the remains of the Tiergarten, the Soviet war memorial glittered white and gold.

'Reinhardt, are you listening?'

'My apologies, Professor. Please continue.'

'You were not listening. Otherwise you would have heard me say that none of the wounds he sustained from the beating killed this Stresemann.' Reinhardt's pedalling slowed, and Endres's balance teetered in front of him. 'Keep up,' he chivvied Reinhardt. 'I am quite surprised at you for not seeing it yourself. A detective of your experience, you should have seen the clue in the photographs. Especially the one of the back of the skull, the apparently fatal wound.'

'It had not bled,' Reinhardt blurted out. Of course, he should have seen it.

'It had not bled,' Endres repeated. 'All of the strike wounds were received postmortem. Whoever did it struck at areas primarily showing high degrees of lividity. He obviously thought striking there, where the blood had pooled after death, would leave more traces and cause more damage. In both assumptions, he was right.'

Endres led him down paths and roads that paralleled the flow of the Spree to their right. 'So what killed him, Professor?'

'A knife wound. Very precisely delivered to the back of the neck. Up under the skull. A very sharp, thin knife. Death would have been instantaneous, and there would have been minimal bleeding. Furthermore, the exact entry point of the wound would have been obscured by the later blows that split the skull. In essence, I believe the killer was quite literally covering his tracks.'

'The time of death?'

'Sometime between Monday and Tuesday I would say. Lastly, there were ligature marks on wrists, ankles, and knees. Stresemann was tied up and also gagged. And now, please, I should save my breath.'

They pedalled on, a fairly easy pace, but still Reinhardt's knee began to throb at the unaccustomed strain. They passed through the Tiergarten, stripped almost bare of its trees and foliage, and much of its area given over to vegetable allotments. Once hidden by hedges and decorative shrubbery, statues and memorials poked up incongruously across the churned expanse of the park. And yet, in the middle of it, the Victory Column still stood, blackened and scarred but upright, which was more than could be said for most of the rest of Berlin, and Golden Lizzy – the name Berliners had given to the angel at the summit – still watched over the city. Off to the west, another flak tower hulked out of the wrecked remnants of the Zoo. Endres led them up Altonaer Strasse, finally bringing the bicycles to a breathless halt in front of a big block of a building on Lessinger Strasse. 'Here we are,' he said, panting over his short breath.

'And here is?' wheezed Reinhardt, rubbing his knee and then fumbling for a cigarette.

'The Luftwaffe-Lazarett.' Endres breathed deeply, frowning disapprovingly at Reinhardt's cigarette. 'The air force hospital.'

33

The man would give no name, but he reminded Reinhardt of someone he had met in Sarajevo, in the 999th Balkan Field Punishment Battalion. Kreuz had been a convict in the battalion he was investigating, a man with a loaded past, a live wire, a man constantly in need of being grounded.

This man wore the white coat of a medical officer, and had a faintly cadaverous air about him, with a sharply receding hairline and a chipped line of yellow teeth. He would say nothing about whether he was a doctor or a nurse or neither but that, and the way in which the man's heavy black eyes remained fixed on a point just out of sight, told Reinhardt he, too, had a heavy past.

'Before you ask,' the man said, 'I've been denazified. All right? The Professor here's seen my certificate, so we're above board on that. I'm not giving you my name… because… I don't want any part of a police investigation. All right? My name goes nowhere. It stays with me.'

'That's fine,' said Reinhardt quietly. They were sitting in an abandoned office that reeked of something chemical. The building echoed with noise, and smells and scents tangled across Reinhardt's nose. He hated hospitals, and this place was redolent with the smell of old blood, of misuse and disuse, of men's misery. He pushed a packet of Luckies onto the table, and then the photograph of Noell, kneeling with another man over something in what looked like a tank of water. 'What can you tell me about that?'

The man recoiled from the photograph, lit a cigarette, inhaled deeply, then picked up the photo in both hands. The cigarette smoked gently over one corner of the photo as he looked at it. Then he nodded to himself, his nose crinkling. He took another long drag of the cigarette and began to jiggle his legs, tapping his heels against the floor.

'All right. I know what this is. I saw it. I didn't have any part in it though.' The man's heavy eyes swung across the space between Endres and Reinhardt without ever quite focusing on either of them, as if searching for the contradiction in what he had just said. Reinhardt said nothing, waiting. 'What do you know about the various experiments the Nazis conducted, using human beings as the test subjects?'

It was not a rhetorical question. The man waited, going very still, until Reinhardt's mouth moved around words he did not want to speak. 'I'm not sure I know that much. I heard rumours when I was a POW. That some of the camps did… things. Before the war, there was the euthanasia programme. My wife's cousin was…' He tailed off, but it seemed to be enough for the man as he juddered back to life, jiggling his legs up and down, up and down with his heels.

'Well, whatever you heard, however far-fetched, they were all true. All right? All the rumours. Everyone was involved in some way. The civilian administration, the navy, the air force, the SS – *everyone* – was involved in some way. Everyone wanted something. All right? Everyone had some idea that needed to be tested, some cure that needed support. Illnesses. Battlefield trauma. Eugenics. Sterilisation. Curing homosexuality. Testing racial theories and vaccines and blood coagulation. You name it, everyone had a need or a project, and there was a never-ending pool of subjects to try them on.' He went still, again.

'Prisoners of war,' said Reinhardt.

'Millions of them. We took Christ knows how many millions of prisoners in the USSR, right? Hundreds of thousands of Poles. And not just prisoners. Jews. Homosexuals. Political dissidents. The elderly. Women. Children.' The man's hands shook and he trembled to a stop. Reinhardt's mouth was dry, as if he had been talking a long time. All three of them pulled on their cigarettes at the same time, letting the smoke fill the silence, until the man quivered again and resumed talking.

'All right,' he said, stabbing the photograph where it lay with his cigarette jutting at right angles from between his fingers. 'Judging from the people in it, their ranks, what I can see of what's happening, this particular photograph was probably taken at Dachau concentration camp, sometime in 1943. There was a Luftwaffe facility there that conducted experiments on human beings. These experiments were under the direct authority of Erich Hippke, the Luftwaffe's general surgeon. Its chief medical officer. There was a variety of projects, particularly those linked to the impact of pressure and of survival in extreme conditions. All right? So, one of the two men in the photograph is Dr Sigmund Rascher. Him, there,' the man said, pointing at the man next to Noell, with his face down looking at whatever they were doing. 'He led the experiments. Rascher was a doctor. He was an ardent Nazi. He was an arch self-promoter. But he may as well have been insane.'

The man drew another long, shuddering breath, then drew deeply on his cigarette. 'What you are looking at is an experiment in survival times of a human being in water chilled to Arctic temperatures. All right? Various iterations were run. With the subject naked. Clothed. Or in a flight suit. Or clothed in different versions of specially designed survival gear. Like that one is wearing. It's a survival suit. The man inside it is probably a Polish prisoner. It's doubtful he survived, but there was a recovery element to the tests. After a certain amount of time, subjects would be removed from the water and immersed in warm water, or water at body temperature, or water that was slowly warmed up, or wrapped in various kinds of blankets or other materials. Sometimes they'd get a couple of women prisoners, strip them naked, and make them lie on either side of the test subject to see if that would help. Or not. It didn't.' He tailed off again, drew on his cigarette, his feverish quivering winding to a stop.

'Go on,' Reinhardt said.

The man nodded, lighting another cigarette from the stub of his first. 'Rascher worked on that stuff for about a year. All right? He also worked on special tests that aimed at establishing the effects of pressure on human beings. Pressure like that experienced at high altitude. Consider,' the man said, seeing Reinhardt's frown of incomprehension, 'a pilot bailing out of an aircraft at great altitude, the body will experience extremes of pressure, from low to high, as it falls. What effect does this have? Are the effects permanent? Long lasting? Short term? There were also experiments to determine the effects of a sudden loss of pressure in a pressurised environment. They called it "explosive decompression". The results were… unpleasant,' the man finished, clamping his mouth around his cigarette.

'What did all this work lead to?'

'I don't know. There was an element of the research that took the results of the experiments and trialled various products with actual pilots, in proper conditions. But I was not familiar with that.'

Reinhardt frowned again, parts of the mystery beginning to coalesce around him. 'You're saying there was a, a flight unit attached to this? That would have made it a sort of test unit?' The man nodded.

'Yes,' the man said. 'For example, one of the demands was to increase the survival rates of pilots shot down on operations over the North Sea and the Arctic. Survival times for airmen shot down over water were very low, and attrition was high.'

Reinhardt toyed with the cigarette packet, thinking of that gap in Noell's *soldbuch*. 'Would that unit have been secret?'

'Probably. Everything was secret. Everything was secret from everything. The air force from the army. The army from the navy. Everyone from the SS. Everything was broken down. Compartmentalised. Feudal. No one had the whole picture.'

'You did, apparently.'

The man's face twisted inward, as if he wanted to swallow himself, swallow his shame, but then he stilled himself with a visible effort, smoothing his hands across the tabletop in front of him. 'I had a good part of it. All right? I made myself useful. And when you make yourself useful, you hear things. You learn things.'

'I'm sorry,' Reinhardt hesitated. 'I understand you don't want to give your name. But how can I trust you? How do I know you know what you're talking about?'

'All right. All right,' the man jiggled in his seat, lighting another cigarette. 'I was there. Yes. At Dachau. But I didn't have much choice. I was a lab technician before the war. I worked for the air force's medical research centre. I got sent up to Dachau in '39.' He paused, jiggled his knees again, then made a sign against his chest with one finger. 'Pink triangle. All right?' Reinhardt nodded. The man was a homosexual. 'Dachau was… it was fucking awful. All right? You had to survive. Any way you could. All right? I managed to catch the eye of one of the SS guards. I managed to get into the hospital wing. I made myself useful. All right? Useful. I made myself useful to them,' he finished, pointing at the photo. 'To anyone who would keep me alive another day.' His legs thudded furiously under the desk. 'Then, when Rascher turned up and began experimenting, I got myself transferred. As I was ex-air force, it wasn't too hard. I just had to stay alive.'

'And now?'

'And now I'm here,' the man said, raising his hands around him. 'Lab technician, again. But a nurse most of the time. People need nurses, and no one asks questions.'

'This place is an air force hospital.'

'It was,' said Endres, the first thing he had said. Even seated, Professor Endres seemed ramrod straight, as if clenched tight around the strictures of his self-possession. 'It's just a hospital, now.'

Reinhardt felt soiled. 'What happened to Rascher?'

'He's dead. He was executed at Dachau. He went too far with something or other. His Nazism was only equalled by his ego and desire for self-aggrandisement. Well, that was a dangerous game to play with our leaders. You played, you won. You played, you lost. All right? He lost. I don't know what he did, but whatever it was, they put him up against a wall and shot him.'

'You're sure?'

The man nodded. 'I was still at Dachau when they did it. May 1945.'

'What about the other one in the photo?'

'That's Colonel Noell. He was more on the operations side. He was based somewhere else. Up north, I think. I don't know where. He would take Rascher's experimental results and operationalise them.'

'"Colonel" Noell? You're sure? Not "Captain"?'

'Colonel,' the man said, nodding. 'The other brother was the captain.'

34

Noell had a brother.

Reinhardt cycled the darkened streets, his mind as mazed as the ruins.

Noell had a brother. A twin brother.

Ochs and Uthmann and the others at the apartment had remarked on Noell's mood changes. On his behaviour. It was because there were two of them.

A captain and a colonel.

Andreas Noell, the pilot. Theodor Noell, the doctor.

And one a cripple, unfit for duty.

God, why had he not seen it sooner…?

It explained the gaps in Noell's *soldbuch*. The man at the hospital had confirmed that Andreas had flown for a test unit. A unit that tested what Theodor developed. It meant Theodor had pulled his brother out of front-line service. It meant the other pilots, Prellberg and Gareis, had gone with him when he left IV./JG56, before it became a night-fighter unit.

The light fell further, the streets sinking into gloom as Berlin's ruins etched a serrated line across a sky tangled with clouds, limbed and lined with the furnace glow of the setting sun, as if a new world were being cast up above them. Reinhardt switched on his flashlight, holding it balanced across the handlebars as he pedalled on. It wobbled a vague patch of light along the road ahead and he fixed his mind on it, ignoring the pain in his knee.

The technician had talked and talked, a sewage spill of memories and names. One of the names was known to Reinhardt. Haber. The man who had 'drowned' in Hamburg. The technician had seen him several times with Theodor Noell running experiments in Dachau. Another name was Lütjens. A doctor. There had been someone called Cohausz, another researcher. Other men he remembered, but no names.

The gates of the house were open when he arrived. He managed the last few feet before coming to an unsteady stop, crouching over the bicycle's frame and breathing hard and heavy, feeling sweat cooling all over him. He leaned the bicycle against the wall by the door and rang the bell. He pulled himself together, wanting a cigarette very badly.

'I hope you have a good explanation for this,' von Vollmer said, as he opened the door, his face drawn with disdain as he stared down at Reinhardt. 'Otherwise I can assure you, your career is as good as finished.'

'Is he here?' There was no reply, only a tautening of the disdainful lines on von Vollmer's face, and so Reinhardt stepped into the house. As he did, another shape angled out of the light and a heavy hand came to rest on Reinhardt's shoulder.

'Mr von Vollmer, while you may feel yourself sufficiently well-protected to try and brush me off, I can assure you that your driver is not.' Reinhardt looked into the driver's face. The man was big enough, heavy around the shoulders, but the mood Reinhardt was in, he knew that if something started now, he would not be able to control himself. 'Therefore, I advise you to tell him to get his hand off me before I break it, and to leave us alone, and for you and me and Mr Bochmann to have that discussion.'

Von Vollmer grunted something at the driver. 'Follow me,' he snapped at Reinhardt. He followed von Vollmer to another room in the large house where Bochmann stood before a marble fireplace. The room was decorated with damascened wallpaper, and old leather tomes filled shelves of highly varnished wood. Lamps with opaque glass shades shaped like seashells or waves stood on small tables. It was surreal, the echoes of a former world, as if the building reverberated gently to its own past. The two of them – von Vollmer and Bochmann – stood side by side, falling effortlessly into their roles of commander and executive officer.

'Now, Inspector, you will explain…'

'Jürgen,' Reinhardt interrupted von Vollmer. 'He was probably murdered on Monday night. He was not part of your factory, or your workforce, but he was a veteran of the Night Hawks, and of IV./JG56 before that. He came all the way from Cologne for more than the possibility of a commercial deal.' The two of them had gone very still. 'Zuleger worked for you. He was killed on Friday night. He had an invitation for the Saturday to a gathering at your aunt's "lodge",' Reinhardt said, putting a little emphasis on the word. 'Noell did not work for you. But he was at the celebration on Saturday night. And I found materials – pamphlets, manifestos – at his apartment that were the same or similar to those I found at Zuleger's. Gentlemen, I reiterate: I am not interested in the politics of what you are doing. But I do need to know *what* you are doing. No more obfuscation.'

The butler chose that moment to enter the room. Perhaps the old man felt the atmosphere, perhaps not. He poured three tumblers of whisky, handing them to each man with a white-gloved hand. Bochmann was the one who finally began to speak, once the butler had left them, the door closing on the room with a murmur and click of wood.

'You know, Inspector, of the situation of veterans of the German armed forces. Devoid of any purpose, bereft of any support, denied all rights… they are desperate, downtrodden, the scapegoats of all that went wrong. Living embodiments of the Führer's failure, or the walking proof of their inability to kill or remove him.

'The war has ended, and much has changed, and yet much remains the same. People like Mr von Vollmer,' he said, indicating the Junker who stood stiffly next to him, expressionless, 'with resources and a position independent of his military service, found themselves in positions similar to those of the days of the aristocracy: dispensing protection and largesse. Veterans began to coalesce around him. For solidarity. For comfort. But above all, for their very survival, but their attempts to organise themselves were disrupted by the Allies. Laws and directives were issued that forbade the association of veterans.

'The situation of all these men was difficult, intolerable even. You must know this, Inspector. Depression and suicides are rife in the ranks of the demobilised. The situation is worse for the widows, the orphans, who are denied the pensions and disabilities their husbands and fathers so dearly won. Veterans from the first war, even, veterans who served between the wars, are also similarly bereft.'

'Indeed,' grated von Vollmer, and his eyes were splintered with his outrage. 'You must know this yourself, Inspector. Where, I ask you, is the justice in bereaving a man of his pension, whose only crime was to serve his country in the trenches? Of the rights of his children to their health and education?' Reinhardt said nothing. Von Vollmer spoke truly. Reinhardt's first war pension was gone, as was his right to wear his medals. He had never thought he would miss the presence of his Iron Cross on his left breast, but its absence had left behind… something. Something more like a mark, if it could be possible to mark something no longer there.

'Such is the situation bequeathed us by the Allies,' Bochmann said softly. 'And so, we began to organise ourselves. We decided to start bringing our former comrades together. It took some time, some months, but eventually I was able to track down everyone we could, and when finally we had found them, we decided to invite them to Berlin, to hold a gathering.'

'You used the one year anniversary of the factory as the excuse.'

'Yes,' Bochmann said.

'You called it the Ritterfeld Association.'

'Yes,' Bochmann said, again, a slight frown on his face at that knowledge of Reinhardt's. 'So they came. The pilots of III./NJG64 and IV./JG56, together again after nearly three years. Together in comradeship. Together in solidarity, renewing old bonds and forging new ones.'

Reinhardt shook his head slightly. 'Mr Bochmann, although I

can… see… why you did what you did, it nevertheless was and is illegal.' He stopped, looked from face to face, and felt something surge up inside of him. 'There is a reason veterans like ourselves maybe cannot or should not associate. I will tell you something of myself. I was with the Abwehr, with military intelligence, and then I was a military policeman, with the Feldjäegerkorps. I saw… terrible things. I did not stop them. Perhaps… I could not have. But I will never know because I tried my best not to be involved in them.

'Later, I gained the power, and the courage, to oppose what I could, where and when I could. But I learned one thing, above all. I learned that cooperation need not always spring fully formed from our breasts for it to be cooperation. Those who turn away, who stay silent, they, too, cooperate. We all, gentlemen,' he said, his eyes swinging from von Vollmer to Bochmann and back again, 'we all, willing or not, duped or not, were part of a terrible enterprise. And some suffering for that is inevitable.'

'Dear *God*. Next you'll be saying it may even be *beneficial*,' von Vollmer sneered.

'Maybe it is.' Reinhardt tilted his tumbler to the light, watching the gentle play of light through the facets of its crystal. 'Didn't the Nazis say that great suffering would be needed for victory? Weren't we all called upon to pay the highest price, if need be? So why should it be any different in defeat? We were willing enough to undergo pain in pursuit of victory. We should not be surprised at pain as payment for our failures.'

'You sound like a damned *Catholic*,' snorted von Vollmer.

'Well, I'm certainly one of the two things you accuse me of, sir,' Reinhardt replied. He put his glass down, untouched. 'But like I said, your politics do not interest me in so far as they do not connect to this case. I do not wish to veer into arguments over reasons and ethics. I want simply to know why I have four dead bodies connected to your Group. I think you know more than you are telling me about the Ritterfeld Association. I think that someone is killing members of it. And not just any members. There is something linking the victims beyond service in the same Group or squadron. So I ask you,' he said, laying out his notes from the night before with his lists, 'what linked these men to each other that someone is killing them, other than that they had served together?'

Bochmann and von Vollmer leaned forward, their eyes going over the names. They must have seen something, because they both straightened, looking up at him. 'Where did you get these names from?' von Vollmer breathed.

'From the WASt.'

'You've been in the WASt?' Von Vollmer sat back with a pert twist of his lips, shaking his head. Bochmann stayed longer, seeming to strain over the papers, but he, too, sat back, apparently defeated.

'I'm sorry, Inspector. I don't know. And I feel I should, I, who was with the Group almost the whole way through the war.' The silt of his eyes was watery with something. Regret, perhaps? Chagrin?

'Do either of you know anything of this?' Reinhardt asked, laying down the photograph he had found in Noell's apartment, what he now knew to be a human experiment. 'No guesses? What about a man named Carlsen? A man named Boalt?'

'Nothing, Inspector,' said von Vollmer. 'I am not sure what more use we can be to your inquiries.'

'I will let you know when I feel the same, sir,' Reinhardt said, a little more waspishly than he would otherwise have wanted, but his irritation at himself was softened when he saw a smile flitter across Bochmann's mouth and twinkle in the muddy darkness of his eyes.

'Need I remind you, Inspector, that I am…'

'Not without friends. Yes, you've told me, Mr von Vollmer. Feel free to pick up the telephone to General Nares at any time.'

'How? How do you…?'

'Know? I guessed.' Reinhardt threw a little caution to the winds, taking a sudden perverse pleasure in poking and prodding the Junker's archaic authority. 'There's a framed photograph behind your desk of yourself with the British commandant. I'm sure there's one of you and General Keating around somewhere as well. Perhaps one of

General Kotikov, too,' Reinhardt said, listing the commanders of the American and Soviet Sectors. 'Perhaps not General Ganeval, though. I don't imagine you and the French go down that well together.'

'You *impudent...*'

'Yes, I've been called that, too,' Reinhardt interrupted.

'Perhaps, Inspector, you and I could examine your names further,' Bochmann interjected, in a low voice.

'*Capital* idea!' said von Vollmer, clapping Bochmann on the shoulder, his face flushed. 'Stay here and work, by all means. I, for one, have an engagement. And perhaps some telephone calls,' he said, darkly, darting meaningful eyes at Reinhardt. 'The butler will look after you, so, by your leave, Inspector...?'

For the next hour or so, Bochmann and Reinhardt compared notes. Bochmann confirmed that all the men killed so far were in IV./JG56 together, but would not be drawn on whether they were all together at the same time. Pilots came and went, he said, transferred in and out, went on leave, were injured, were killed. It had been a long time since the war, longer still since he might have had any reason to remember which men flew in the squadron and when. On Reinhardt's reasoning – that the one thing in common the dead men had that he had found so far was service in North Africa – Bochmann would not be drawn.

To Reinhardt's eyes, though, Bochmann was clearly uneasy about something, but he would not reveal it, insisting he had to check things against his own lists.

But on one thing he was clear.

'Gareis is alive,' he said, pointing at the name. 'He was shot down during the war, and for a long time believed dead, but during our inquiries for the association, we discovered he was living in the Soviet Zone and not answering our messages. I myself went out to see him. He's living on a small farm, and told me he wanted nothing to do with the association.'

'How many of these men on my lists were invited to your association's meeting?'

'I would have to check, Inspector.' Bochmann's eyes quivered, clouding up. 'The association's list… well, you will understand it is private.'

'This is a murder investigation, Mr Bochmann. I will need to see that list.'

'Of course. Only, I would ask you to be discreet with it.'

'How did you put it together? I mean, it can't have been easy. It must have taken time.'

'It did. We started with those we knew of. Those for whom we had contacts. That is why Jürgen's death is… so shocking. He was one of the first we contacted. One of the first ones we found. He was still living at his old address. He put us in touch with another. We found others, they put us in contact with more. And so on.'

'So, how many did you find, in the end?'

'There were a few who were contacted by us, but who either never answered, were untraceable, or who had died during the war…' Bochmann paused, hesitated, as if finally realising something. 'Or who had passed away.' He showed a sudden moment of panic. It passed like a glimmer of light across the muddy glaze of his eyes, but he calmed himself quickly. 'We were never informed of any murders.'

'How about deaths? Were you informed of those?'

'Only one of them was what you might think suspicious,' Bochmann answered, a light of reminiscence in his eyes. 'From early 1946. A death in Bad Oeynhausen. You know it?'

'It's a spa town in western Germany. Better known for being the British Occupation Authority's headquarters,' said Reinhardt.

'Yes. Well, we only classed that one as suspicious because we received a letter from the pilot's son that hinted at some kind of scandal or cover-up.'

'And…?'

'That was all we ever knew. The son wanted nothing to do with us, and we had no means to search further into his accusations.'

'Who was it?'

'Prellberg.'

'The second squadron's commanding officer?' Bochmann nodded. 'He was demoted during the war. Do you remember? He was also transferred with Noell and Gareis.' Bochmann frowned, his head cocking slightly to one side, then he nodded, hesitantly. 'How did you find Noell?'

'He was in contact with another member of the Group, and we found him that way. He was one of the last ones we found. And one of the hardest. He was not very interested in any contact.'

'There is a question I have for you, Mr Bochmann. Do you know when Noell was promoted to colonel?'

Bochmann frowned, shook his head. 'Noell was a captain, Inspector.'

'At Noell's apartment, when I found his body, I also found a colonel's air force uniform.'

'That must have been his brother's.' Bochmann nodded. 'Noell had an elder brother. He was a senior officer in the air force's research division.'

Reinhardt had needed to ask. He had needed to double-check the medical technician's assertions of two brothers. Something seemed to snap inside. 'Mr Bochmann, *think*. Please. *Think* what links these men.'

'How can I *think*, Inspector?' Bochmann was flustered, angry, his eyes flashing, like choppy water, and his words rose into Reinhardt's like two tides surging against each other. 'I cannot be expected to remember *everything*. Do you? Do *you* remember every shot you fired? Every man who passed in front of you that you… that you *condemned*?' Reinhardt went cold, then felt a flush climb his back, seeing himself suddenly, seeing *himself* staring back at himself over a flat desk of chipped wood, a harsh light carving shadows down and away as he signed something. An order? a condemnation…? God knows, the last days of the war had seen enough of those as the Feldjäegers strove to maintain order behind a front line collapsing into chaos. 'Well? *Can* you? So why, why should I be expected to remember *everything* the Group did? Everything each squadron did? Every mission, every botched raid…' He stopped, a deathly pale swelling up over his face.

'Bochmann?' Reinhardt waited with bated breath.

Bochmann shook his head, his eyes far away. 'No, Reinhardt. No. I will not say any more. Just. Please, give me some time.'

'You have until tomorrow morning, Mr Bochmann. I expect you at the station on Gothaerstrasse at eight o'clock with your lists.' Bochmann nodded, distracted, but his eyes cleared suddenly at Reinhardt's next words. 'And you will tell me what the British have to do with the Ritterfeld Association.'

35

Reinhardt cycled to Uhlandstrasse, where he showed his warrant disc and persuaded the stationmaster to let him on the U-Bahn with his bicycle, unable to face the thought of riding all the way home. He settled onto a bench in the all-but-empty carriage, stretching his leg out, feeling the tension loosen in his knee. He leaned his head against the window, closing his eyes and slowing his breathing until a guard blew a whistle, and the train's doors slid shut and it jerked into movement. Reinhardt opened his eyes, reaching out to steady the bicycle, and saw Kausch's reflection in the glass of the carriage's interconnecting door.

Reinhardt twisted round. Kausch was sitting a few benches down, two other men with him. When he saw he had been seen, Kausch came and sat opposite Reinhardt. The man was tall, well-built, his hair brushed back from a stern countenance, like something one might see in marble or stone, or staring determinedly out from a propaganda poster, out over a glittering future of red and black.

Leena had been right, Reinhardt thought.

He did look like he should have been wearing black.

'I see you're looking much better, Mr Kausch. Or should I call you Kessel?'

'Inspector Reinhardt. I understand you are an old comrade. We wore the same uniform. We may speak man-to-man, soldier-to-soldier.'

'I don't think you were ever a soldier, Kausch,' said Reinhardt, missing his baton more than ever, 'and I'm certain we never wore the same uniform.'

'We took the same oath then. We are German patriots and members of its resistance. We have friends in many places. We have not forgotten our oaths – once taken, they may never be relinquished, save by him to whom they were given – and do not accept the occupation of our sacred country.'

'What you mean is you all have something to hide, and you've gone to ground and can't get out of Berlin because the Ivans'll have you up against a wall.'

Kausch let nothing show on his face, and only a suggestion of movement made Reinhardt realise one of the other two men was sitting right behind him. 'Inspector Reinhardt, there is someone who would like to speak to you. Be thankful that person has some weight in our considerations, because I have had men's tongues for less impertinence than you have shown me tonight.'

Kausch glanced at the second man, nodded, and the man walked up to the connecting door. He waved at something or someone and stood back to pull the door open. There was a clattering blast of air, and another man stepped into the carriage and, even though he knew, Reinhardt still felt a thrill of fear, of superstitious recognition, as if he had seen a ghost, or a revenant.

'Andreas Noell, I presume,' Reinhardt said, surprised to find his voice steady.

The train slowed and stopped for Wittenbergplatz. The men – there were five of them now, and one woman – gathered close around, sitting on the benches behind and on either side. They gave off an air of menace, and the one or two people who entered the carriage took seats far away from them.

'You are the man leading the investigation into my brother's murder, is that right? Tell me, then, who killed him?'

'I don't know yet. Why don't you tell me what happened that night? It might help me to understand.'

'Sturmbannführer, if you would be so kind as to give me and the inspector some privacy.'

'Of course, Captain,' Kausch replied, with his flat gaze, as he rose and moved over to one of the other benches. Reinhardt watched him go, imagining him all in black with a swastika around his arm. Sturmbannführer. An SS major.

'There were two Noells, Inspector,' Andreas Noell said, leaning forward into the space between them. Seemingly on the cusp of middle age, he was a small, dark man, wiry, with hair thinning on the top of his head. 'Twins. One was called Andreas, a pilot. He just wanted to fly. The other was a scientist, called Theodor. Very driven, to both his research and to the Nazis,' Noell said, a flick of his eyes at Kausch and the others. His voice lowered, and he spoke to Reinhardt from beneath his brows. 'The two brothers did not always see eye to eye, but they were brothers. They looked out for each other. During the war, when I needed him, Theodor took me away from front-line service and arranged a transfer to a test unit. Other pilots from other squadrons were there. We all had extensive experience flying and fighting over water and extreme conditions.'

'Like the desert,' Reinhardt said.

Noell nodded, his eyes coming up to play over Reinhardt's face a moment, then going back down. He glanced out as the train stopped at Nollendorfplatz, but this late at night the big interchange station was quiet. Nevertheless, several of Kausch's men took up positions near the doors until the train lurched off.

'You weren't the only one transferred.'

'No. There were two others. Prellberg and Gareis.'

'Why were you transferred?'

'Theodor thought he was doing me a favour, but when I found out what the test unit was all about – testing equipment that was itself tested on human beings – I went slightly mad. Enraged, I confronted my brother who, so caught up in his research and so committed to the Nazi cause, did not understand my qualms. I dismissed myself from the test unit; on my own request I was transferred to search and rescue, in Norway. I chose it… I chose it to try and atone in some way for what I had seen.

'When the war ended, Theodor and I found each other again,

here. I had made my way back. I had been captured by the British, then released. I had papers. Theodor had none. He was with these – like-minded – men. Men who had been together at the test unit. Men who had not laid down the flame of the Nazi cause, styling themselves "resistance" fighters, patriots, who claimed to be fighting to keep something back for Germany for when she would rise again.' Reinhardt had to strain to listen to him. With his voice low and his head down, Noell seemed to heave the words up from somewhere deep within himself. 'They were in the shadows, often on the move. They were trapped here in Berlin. They could not get out, or dared not. Most of them are wanted men,' Noell said, a nod of his head towards the others. 'The Ivans would shoot half of them on sight, and probably kidnap the rest to work in the USSR. The war never really ended for them. But we… Theodor and me, we were brothers. Even if Theodor dragged me into hiding with him. So, who, Inspector? Who killed my brother?'

Reinhardt waited as the train stopped at Gleisdreieck. 'I don't know yet. I believe it is someone from your past. I think it may be someone you knew in Africa. In 1942. Does that ring any bells?' Noell shook his head. 'Do you remember an incident with a soldier? A man called Leyser?' Noell shrugged, shook his head again. 'Try and think, Noell. Prellberg and Gareis were involved in an incident with this Leyser. In October.'

'I don't… I don't remember.' Noell's eyes turned even further inward, then he looked up. 'I think… maybe… It was something to do with the unit's pride. Some nonsense like that. Prellberg was the one… was the one who started it.' Noell rubbed his head, digging his fingertips into the hollows of his temples. To Reinhardt's eyes, he looked evasive, but Reinhardt had seen men who struggled to remember things after a war, and if half of what Noell was telling him was true, it was no wonder the pilot was trying to forget what he had seen and done. 'There was a hospital. I think they went to talk to someone. But things went bad. There was a fight. Yes, now I remember. This soldier – Leyser, you say? – he was injured, but he was saying bad things about us. Prellberg wanted to teach him a lesson. It went bad, and then we were evacuating the city because the British were approaching.'

Noell stared into the darkness beyond the windows, then spoke abruptly, with precision. 'Prellberg was an idiot. And he was a Nazi. So was Gareis. The pair of them were… well let's say they were good soldiers for the Reich. Efficient and ideological. I lost touch with them long ago. But I want an answer, Inspector. These men with me want an answer. Theodor was close with them. They thought alike in all things. In all things…' Noell's hands tightened against each other. 'Someone has killed one of their own, and that person must be made to pay. There is no happenstance in their lives. Only malice and conspiracy.'

'Who are they?'

Noell's eyes twitched, but he did not look into the carriage. 'SS, Reinhardt. "Cream of the black". Guards, mostly. Administrators. The ones who ran the camps and the facilities. Kausch was in charge of the prisoners they sent to Güstrow for the tests. Before that he was… busy… out east. I think the Poles would like to talk to him. As they take him to pieces. Kausch and his men think Theodor was murdered because of them. Because of who they are, and what they have. To get to them. But he wasn't, was he?'

'I don't know. Truly. Tell me of the association.'

'Ritterfeld? Dreams of the past, Inspector. Plans for the future. A gathering of old comrades. All of that, and none. Or more. I don't know what it was, other than a chance to be… someone else. To be with others who thought like you. Who had known what you had known.'

'How did the association find you?'

'Through a friend. Another pilot. I met him at an old bar we used to go to before the war. Veterans go there. To reminisce. You know how it is.'

Reinhardt did not. He had never 'reminisced' with veterans. With anyone, except Brauer. The train slowed as it passed through the ruined station at Möckernbrücke, then picked up a little speed. Reinhardt craned his neck around, looking for Kausch. 'I need to change at the next station. What happened on the weekend? On Saturday night?'

'I went to a gathering of the Ritterfeld Association. The first one.'

'What happened there? Anything?'

'Speeches and toasts. To absent friends. To new friends. We drank. We sang. We ate.'

'What new friends did you toast?' Noell frowned at him, and Reinhardt felt a burst of impatience as the train began slowing for Hallesches Tor. 'You mentioned new friends.'

'Von Vollmer talked of "benefactors". Friends in high places. People who knew better than to keep Germany down. People who would not make the same mistakes as at Versailles. The sort of stuff Kausch and his ilk love to hear about. And then, at the end of the party, when von Vollmer had drunk rather a lot, I heard him talking to Bochmann about their English friends.'

'Kausch,' Reinhardt called quietly. 'I need to change here. You should change with me. But you should split up a little. A group of men, and one with a bicycle, will be remembered.'

At Hallesches Tor, Reinhardt wheeled the bicycle off, Noell walking with him, and Kausch just behind. The others split up and drifted away, moving ahead of them and behind them down the tunnels. Noell seemed not to notice very much, staring ahead of him with flat eyes.

'Who were these English friends?'

'I don't know. There were no Englishmen there.'

Conversation ceased as Reinhardt hauled the bicycle upstairs and then down, the wheels and frame clattering, drawing the stares of curious passersby and pithy comments from a few of them. Reinhardt spotted one of Kausch's men on the platform of the southbound C line train when he wheeled the bicycle out of the pedestrian tunnel, but a whistle and shout turned him around the other way.

'All right then, what the *bloody* hell's all this?' an irate platform attendant came stalking towards Reinhardt, his eyes fixed on Reinhardt's bicycle. 'You must be missing a few planks from your fence to bring a bloody *bike* into the U-Bahn. How'd you get that thing down here?'

Kausch had vanished, and Noell stood close to Reinhardt as he pulled out his warrant disc and calmed the irascible attendant.

'I've seen it *all* now,' the man muttered, stalking away as a train pulled into the station. 'Say what you like about *bloody* Adolf, you'd not have seen coppers with *bikes* in the *bloody* U-Bahn…'

'Keep talking about the party,' Reinhardt said as they sat down in a carriage. 'About friends in high places.'

'I don't know, Inspector. It just sounded like talk.'

'All right, then. After the party. What happened?'

'I didn't come home until early on Sunday morning, and then I slept most of the day. Theodor was not there. We sometimes tried to alternate being in and out, so it would not seem there were two of us. And, lately… we had been arguing more and more, and he had taken to spending more time with Kausch,' Noell said, looking up. Reinhardt followed his eyes, seeing that Kausch and some of his men had reappeared from seemingly out of nowhere. The train stopped at Mehringdamm. Flughafen was the next stop. Paradestrasse the one after that. There was not much more time, unless Noell planned to accompany him home.

'Go on,' Reinhardt prompted him, as the train pulled out.

'Theodor asked me to leave the apartment on Sunday evening. He said he had to meet someone. I thought it was another one of his contacts from the war. We argued again. Our last words were sour words, Inspector.' Noell's eyes went deader still. 'And when I came back, I found… I found Theodor dead.'

'Was there another body in the apartment?'

'Yes.'

'Had you seen that person before?'

'Yes. Just once. He was at the party, but only briefly. He came for a short while. It was…' Noell paused, lifting his eyes. 'Now I remember, it was after he left that von Vollmer began talking about his English benefactors. But that man wasn't English. He was as German as you and I.'

'You talked to him?'

'Just the once. It was a strange conversation. Only a few words. But it seemed as if… as if he knew me.'

'He thought he did. But it was your brother he knew.'

'But how did he know about my brother in the first place?'

'His name was Carlsen. A British war crimes investigator.'

Noell's face tightened up, his eyes flicking out to search for Kausch. 'He gave me a photograph. At the party…'

'Carlsen?' Noell nodded. Reinhardt remembered a photograph, crumpled up down the back of the sofa in the Noells' apartment. 'Of your brother?'

Noell nodded again. 'Dachau,' he whispered. 'I showed it to him when I got back. I was drunk, and tired. That's what made us argue. I told him… I told him I was so ashamed of him. I told him…' He screwed his eyes shut, his head swivelling down onto his chest.

'Noell. You said Kausch and his men are concerned they will be hunted for who they are, but also for what they have. What do they have?'

'All the records and equipment they could salvage from the test site,' Noell said, his eyes lost somewhere outside the train's window. 'Towards the end, Theodor and some others thought they could use it all as bargaining chips. Against a future when we would all join forces against the Soviets. They stored it safely, but then that area fell to the Red Army, not the Americans or the British, and then they saw there really would be little accommodation with the occupiers. They went into hiding, and then I suppose one day led to the next, and they never made their deal.'

'Where, Noell? Where was the test site?'

'Güstrow. Near Rostock. On the Baltic. They needed to be near the sea. For the experiments…'

Outside Paradestrasse, the night was cold and clear, and the angled lines of the neighbourhood's rooftops marched against the glow from Tempelhof.

'I will need to speak with you again,' Reinhardt said to Noell. 'How will I find you?'

'We will find you,' said Kausch.

'I'm not interested in you, Kausch,' Reinhardt said. He looked at Noell, but the pilot was silent, seemingly folded in on himself.

'That is quite irrelevant. We take our leave of you now, but we will be in touch soon enough. Heil Hitler, Captain.'

Reinhardt stared, then snorted, a quick burst of disbelieving laughter.

'What is so funny?'

'I just remembered a joke. You must've heard it. Hitler and his driver are in his car, when a pig runs in front of it. The driver hits the pig. Kills it. "Go and find the owners, make reparation," the Führer says. The driver gets out. Hitler waits, and waits, and waits some more, until finally the driver comes back, stinking drunk. "What the hell happened to you, man?" the Führer demands. "What on earth did you tell that farmer?" The driver shrugs. "Nothing. I just said, 'Heil Hitler, the swine is dead'".'

'Come. A word, please.' The former SS man took Reinhardt's arm in a light but firm grip and turned him out towards the street. 'It is important we understand each other. At Uhlandstrasse, there was a Soviet agent who tried to follow you into the station. We arranged that he missed the train, so our conversation was peaceful and not interrupted. It is important you know that, so you know our reach. What we can do. Then, there is this.' The blow to his ribs was an agonising shock. He felt his arm twisted up behind him, higher, and he bent over from the pain, bent further, planting his legs wide to keep from falling, and someone kicked him in the groin. It felt like the blow had climbed up into his sternum, and he collapsed as if something inside him had been cut, but fingers wormed into his hair and ground his head against the cobbles.

'I warned you of respect, did I not?' Kausch whispered down at him from out of a haze of pain. 'Remember this, Inspector. Captain Reinhardt. Your oath to the Führer was never rescinded. I hold claim to it. You will keep me informed of your inquiries, Captain Reinhardt. When I need you, I will call. If you do not come, I will find you. I will find you, and that woman you live with. That woman Meissner. A traitor's wife. And that man who haunts your steps. Brauer, isn't it? I will find them. And I will find your *son*, Captain Reinhardt. I will find Friedrich Reinhardt. Him, most of all. We know what he is, though he tries to hide it, worming his way into the confidence of men like us who never abandoned what we were. Men like him do not deserve to live, so I prefer to think of him as a boil. A festering little boil. Inconvenient, but tolerable. And we know where he is. So should you fail me, Captain Reinhardt, should you give me cause to regret letting you live, I will take your son to pieces before your very eyes. Do you doubt me, Captain Reinhardt? Do you doubt I will do these things as I have said them?'

Reinhardt did not doubt him, but could not have answered if his life depended upon it. At some point he realised he was alone, that they had gone, and he shambled onto his hands and knees. He lurched up to one knee, standing heavily against the wall. The world spun, and he vomited weakly, hearing and feeling it patter around his feet. His throat burned, his groin burned worse, his hand left grit across his mouth as he wiped his face.

'Filthy fucking drunk,' someone snarled from out of the dark. He heard the sound of quick footsteps, and then the scuffle of feet, as if two people struggled. Someone shouted something, a curse flung away into the night. Footsteps came closer, and someone stooped over him. Despite himself, he covered his head with his arm, but someone took his hand in theirs, and lifted him haltingly to his feet. He turned, and looked into Friedrich's face.

36

'I wasn't drinking. I wasn't,' Reinhardt whispered. He felt aghast at the way he must look, pinned almost immobile with shame, and the fear of what Friedrich might think. Like someone had run a needle through his mind, Reinhardt felt old memories tauten and quiver, threaded up out of the past. Old arguments with his son, the spiral into drunkenness to escape the insanity of those days, to avoid the creature Friedrich was becoming.

'I know,' Friedrich said. He steadied Reinhardt on his feet, brushing down his coat. 'I saw it.'

'You saw it?'

Friedrich nodded, and before Reinhardt's eyes he seemed to slump in on himself, as if he held himself crooked and bent, as if he held himself sideways from the world. *Unclean*, his stance cried. *Outcast*, it shrieked.

'You heard it as well?' Reinhardt said, his voice quivering. Friedrich nodded again. Reinhardt straightened up around the sickening pain in his groin, feeling the chill night air grate agonisingly over his sweat-drenched skin. 'What are you doing here, Friedrich?'

'I was waiting. I was hoping you might come this way.'

'If you heard it, then you can tell me. Kausch. Who is he? And how does he know your… how does he know my son's name?'

'I don't know how he knows my name. But I know what he is, and he knows what I am.'

'And what are you, Friedrich?'

'I am a traitor, Father.'

Reinhardt leaned back against the wall. His head was awhirl at the currents swirling round him. The murderer and his motivations, the Allies, the Soviets, these German 'patriots'… he was struggling before to make sense of this, and now it was worse. Perhaps because he was in so much pain and he was tired, and he was far more than rattled by what had just happened, he looked at Friedrich.

'Are you spying on me for these Nazis?' Friedrich shook his head. 'Are you spying on me for Skokov?' Friedrich made to shake his head again, but he stopped. 'Well, at least you don't deny knowing who he is.'

'I know who he is.'

'Kausch told me he wants me to help him find who is killing their friends. He told me to keep him informed, otherwise he said they'd kill you.' Reinhardt took a long breath, clenching his teeth to slice the cold night air between them. He kept back what Brauer had told him earlier that day, although it seemed an age ago now. 'What would you like to tell me, Friedrich?'

'I would tell you I was once like them, Father. You knew me. You saw me.'

'And now you're different.'

Reinhardt had not meant to sound so harsh, and he would have called his words back if he could. Friedrich seemed to turn even more sideways. *Outcast, unclean,* his being seemed to cry. Friedrich knelt to pick up the bicycle.

'Now I'm different. Two years on the Eastern Front and three in a prisoner-of-war camp will change a man, Father. Even the most obtuse, even the most bellicose. Even,' Friedrich sighed, 'the most misguided.'

'Oh, God, Friedrich.' The air seemed to go out of Reinhardt, as if it had been sucked out, leaving him empty, a husk, leaving him anchored only by the pain in his ribs and groin.

'Shall we walk? When I was captured at Stalingrad, during my interrogation, I was identified as a potential collaborator. I was questioned by a number of men, all of them very civilised. Not at all the image of the subhuman Slav we were told to expect. The last man to interrogate me… well, I began to see things in a different light. I came to understand it is not such a leap as I would have imagined, between Nazism and Communism.' Reinhardt walked slowly, one hand on the bicycle as Friedrich pushed it, and talked quietly, but inside he wanted to protest. It *was* a leap, he knew. Or at least, he wanted to believe. The two were not the same – could not be – even if it was sometimes easy to make that comparison, given the architecture of repression they had both built around themselves. Besides which, when Reinhardt thought about it, those to whom he had cleaved during the war when he had sought himself and the man he used to be – the Partisans Begović and Simo, even the ruthless Perić and Suzana Vukić – had all been Communist. Carolin, his wife, had been one. He himself never had been, favouring what he had preferred to think of as a pragmatic disinterest more properly suited to a life of service. But he viewed that belief now with the appropriate scorn of one who knows that much of what had happened these last years happened because people like him had preferred disinterest to engagement, self-important isolation to activism.

'At first, it was about survival,' Friedrich continued, 'but then I came to believe in this new cause. I joined a group called the League of German Officers. I found a sense of familiarity. There was a sense of brotherhood, German officers fighting together against a regime that had misused them. We conducted anti-Nazi propaganda and other things. We were despised, of course. Most prisoners would have nothing to do with us. The Nazis were strong in the camps. They kept their own form of discipline. Traitors or turncoats were often murdered.

'When the war ended, I came back to Germany with the Red Army. My tasks were to work with returning veterans. To see what they were thinking. To plant ideas. To monitor and report. But seeing what the Soviets were doing in East Berlin, and across the Germany they occupy – the rape, the plunder, the oppression – I found myself falling back into disillusion, and now I do not know where I stand anymore.

'Several days ago, I was summoned to Karlshorst. I thought... I thought my time had come. But I met an MGB agent.'

'Skokov.'

'Skokov. Somehow he had put two and two together and connected us. He knew of me. He knew what I had done in Russia. He knew... many things. He knew of my... pilgrimages to our old house. He told me to observe you. To keep an eye on you. But I do not believe he has any motivation beyond moving me as a piece on the board.'

'And in moving you, he moves me,' Reinhardt said, a bitter tinge to his words. 'He has a hold on me.'

'Father, how to say this? I'm trapped. I want to come home, but I no longer know where home is. So yes, I'm being used against you. It is the price to pay for being set free by the Ivans. If I try to leave them, they will either catch me again, or they will ensure my collaborationist past and... and other... and other things will be revealed.'

The father in Reinhardt reeled at what his son was telling him. *He knew what I had done in Russia.* The father in him yearned to comfort and succour Friedrich, but the policeman in him would not let the father be. *Other things...* the policeman in him heard the words, and searched beneath them for deeper, hidden meanings. The policeman in him heard Friedrich and heard a confession. He heard self-justification, even obfuscation, and when the car pulled up next to him, he was not surprised to see a window go down and for Skokov's teeth to glint up at him from the shadowed interior.

'Captain. Please join me.' Reinhardt looked to Skokov, back to his son, indecision engraved in his stance. 'Do not worry about your son, Captain. Please. Join me.' The driver stepped out, holding the door open.

'This is a nice setup, Major,' Reinhardt said. The inside of the car was warm, fragrant with a smell of oiled leather.

'This? You like this? It's a Mercedes.'

'Using my son against me.'

'A good workman will use whatever tools he has to hand, Captain.

Now,' Skokov said, casting a glance at Friedrich standing forlorn outside, like a beggar at a crossroads, 'tell me about the WASt. What did you find out?'

'I found out you've been in there, looking for the same things as me.'

'Of course you did,' Skokov said dismissively. 'I would have been surprised if you had not. Except you came to that same mysterious file by a different route than me, and I had given up that file as a lost cause until recently. Until someone began killing people connected to it.'

'What is so important to you in that file?'

'That's no concern of yours. Just tell me what you've found out.'

'That file concerns some kind of test unit. It was working on secret experiments for the air force.'

'I know that, Captain, but how is it that you do?' Skokov said, and there was a steel slither to his voice.

'I learned this today from someone who worked on issues related to it. I learned Noell was transferred to it in April 1943, together with another officer called Gareis and an officer called Prellberg.'

'And where are these two now?'

'Gareis was killed in action.' Reinhardt was not sure why he said it when he knew it was not true, but the words were spoken before he could call them back. He continued, faster than he would have liked. 'And it seems Prellberg might be dead, too. He died after the war.'

'Murdered?' Skokov looked askance at Reinhardt, that sunken side of his mouth a darker patch on his face, as if he had heard something in his voice.

'I don't know. I'm trying to find out.'

Skokov grunted, his lips moving against his teeth. Reinhardt watched him carefully, knowing he had held back everything he had just learned from Noell, not least that Noell was still alive. And he had kept back what he had learned from the lab technician in the Luftwaffe-Lazarett. But, as Skokov did not seem interested in what exactly the secret unit had done, he assumed Skokov already knew.

'Where did this Prellberg die?'

'Bad Oeynhausen.'

Skokov grunted again, staring out of the window. With the tip of one finger, he stroked the rippled scar tissue around his mouth. 'There were other pilots who went to this unit?'

'None from the same squadron as Noell, Prellberg, and Gareis. The British admitted Carlsen was half-German, and did special work for them. As you said. He was also looking for some kind of information in the WASt. He examined the same file as you did about two weeks ago.'

Every line of Skokov's body went taut as he turned back to look at Reinhardt. Skokov's eyes gleamed as he seemed to take Reinhardt's measure. 'Very well. Keep at it, Captain. Keep me informed.' He rapped on the window, and the driver opened Reinhardt's door.

'My son, Major.' That was all Reinhardt could manage.

'Your son's fate rests on the outcome of this investigation, Captain.' Skokov glanced past him to where Friedrich stood. 'To be honest, he is something of a disappointment. We had high hopes for him, but he holds none for himself. As a tool, he has few uses now.'

'I want him back.'

'The future is a gift that never quite arrives, Captain.' Skokov pursed his mouth. 'You can have him, should I have a satisfactory conclusion to your inquiries.'

'What exactly do you want, Major? What did this secret unit do?'

'That would be for me to know and you to find out. Get out now, and send your son in, please.'

Reinhardt and Friedrich faced each other a moment on the street beneath the flat gaze of the Soviet soldier. He raised a hand hesitantly, wanting to touch his son, to reassure him in some small way, and Friedrich seemed to see it, pushing the bicycle at him so he was forced to take it. He made to sidle past, but Reinhardt reached out.

Friedrich's body arched away. *Outcast*, he seemed to cry. *Unclean*. Reinhardt caught his arm and pulled him tight.

'I don't know what's happened. But I will do what I have to, to make you safe. I promise.'

'Make no promises, Father,' Friedrich whispered. 'Sometimes you have to keep them.' And with that, he was gone into the car, sucked down into its gloom with the door slamming shut. Reinhardt's reflection quivered before him in the windowpane, steadied, stilled, then was shaken apart again as the driver started the engine and drove away. Reinhardt watched it go, watched the flare of its brake lights as it paused at a corner, turned, and was gone.

37

Saturday

It rained overnight. The rain had the benefit of keeping the dust down, but it made the atmosphere heavy and muggy, the air cut and lined with the stench of sewage and waste. The sky was a luminous, milky grey, a flat sheet with nothing to hang one's eyes on, and the streets were blotted gunmetal grey with water that puddled in darkened pools or seeped foully out from under the ruins.

Reinhardt arrived later than he would have wanted at the station the next morning, a Saturday. He had slept badly, curled around his pain, arriving to find Bochmann already at the police station and ensconced with Mrs Dommes. If there was a silver lining to anything, it was finding that the two of them had already gone through Bochmann's lists and the list of names she was to call. Dommes had obviously found something of a kindred spirit in Bochmann, who looked decidedly worried as he clutched a cardboard folder to his chest with spidery fingers.

'Mr Bochmann has made my life a great deal easier, Inspector,' Mrs Dommes said, bright as a button, and bestowed a positively warm glance upon Bochmann. 'I understand Prellberg is dead. Thurner was never found. Remember his prewar address was in Stettin, and that's now in Poland. That only leaves Hauck and Osterkamp, and according to Mr Bochmann they seem to have passed away. So there's not much left to do it seems, Inspector.' Dommes finished, frowning at him. 'Are you well, Gregor?'

Reinhardt blinked at her use of his first name. He had not even realised that she knew it. 'Quite well, Mrs Dommes, thank you. Mr Bochmann. Perhaps you will come with me?'

He took Bochmann out of the station and through the little park, the ground wet and heavy from the rain and from the blocked drains that flooded half of it, over to a small café behind the Magistrates' Court. Reinhardt sat Bochmann down, ordered two coffees, then pinned him with his eyes, and if his voice was a little harsher than usual, he felt the situation merited it. 'Out with it, Bochmann.'

'I went over the registry again last night. After we finished.' Bochmann's eyes were muddy with apparent distress. 'Both Hauck and Osterkamp… I believe they may… they may have been murdered.' Reinhardt said nothing, only waited for him to go on, not dropping his eyes, not even when the waiter brought their two mugs. 'For Hauck, I see my records show he died in April 1946.' He fiddled with papers. 'See. Here. There's a letter from a neighbour. Hauck was killed when his house collapsed. The house had been damaged during the war. And there had been any number of Americans or whoever billeted in it. It was a mess.' Reinhardt looked at him, saying nothing, waiting. 'Osterkamp. He died in July. See. Another letter. From his wife. He died… he died… see. There.' Bochmann seemed manic as he stabbed at the paper with his finger.

'He died in a suspected fall down an embankment.'

'His wife writes that he was carrying home a heavy sack of potatoes. They said it was a heart attack. Too much effort. They found him on a stretch of road. They thought he must have fallen down into the ditch.'

Reinhardt looked at Bochmann, looked through him. He thought of the man who had come to his house with a sack of potatoes. Who had ingratiated himself into Mrs Meissner's house with offers of food. He thought of a man who might have lured someone out with promises of sustenance. Who might have lured him out at night, who might have finished him off on some road. Rolled the body into a ditch. He thought of Hauck and Stucker, just two more bodies found on ruins. Who paid any attention to men killed on bomb sites, killed by falling rubble?

'Prellberg,' said Reinhardt, his mouth a grim line.

'Yes. Prellberg. He *was* murdered. That we know because his son wrote to us. He was murdered at Bad Oeynhausen in February 1946. There was something of a scandal apparently. I have his letter. Here,' Bochmann said, thrusting a paper at Reinhardt, which fluttered in the air between them from his trembling hand.

Reinhardt read it slowly, the son's prose terse and factual. Prellberg had been captured by the British at the end of the war, and interned, but before year's end he was out of the camp and helping them track down certain military and Nazi Party personnel, but for what, the son could not say. Prellberg was accommodated in Bad Oeynhausen when he was not at home, and that was where he was found dead along with another man, a Dr Lütjens. Prellberg's son did not say much about his father, only that he was one of those men from the war whom the Allies had taken an interest in. The son did not know why, but Reinhardt could guess. What was it he had said to Collingridge? 'A race for what glitters in the rubble.' Both Prellberg and Lütjens had been beaten to death, the son saying the British had not classed the affair as murder, rather as some kind of settling of accounts. The son also described a British administration that, in his opinion, was more interested in covering up the deaths than actually investigating them.

'Did they find the person who did it? Any leads, or suspicions?' Bochmann shook his head, then dipped his face into his coffee cup. Reinhardt's gaze went back and forth between the lists, his and Bochmann's. 'Right, we're going to do this methodically. I've got fourteen names, all men who were serving in IV./JG56's second squadron in North Africa at the same time. We're going to check them off your lists, starting with those killed in action during the war. Albrecht, Kastel, and Meurer.' Bochmann nodded. 'Then we have Jürgen, Noell, and Zuleger, murdered in the last few days. We have yourself. Group executive officer. Very much alive. Thurner. Vanished. No contact with him ever. And we have Hauck, Osterkamp, Prellberg, and Stucker, all killed in 1946. That leaves

Gareis, who you say is living in the Soviet Zone, and… Fenski?'

'Yes. Umm. He was supposed to have come to the gathering, but he did not. We've not heard from him, and we didn't get any RSVP from him, either.'

'Oh, for Christ's sake, Bochmann.' Reinhardt shook his head, lit a cigarette, and took a long pull of his coffee. 'Did it occur to *none* of you what might have been going on?'

'Safety in numbers, Inspector,' Bochmann snapped back. He waved his lists at Reinhardt. 'There's over a *hundred* names here. Men who served with IV./JG56 during nearly *six years of war.* So no, the deaths of a few of them did not register with us.'

'You're right. I'm sorry. I'm being unfair.'

Bochmann's eyes clouded over suddenly. 'That means… that means it's just me and Gareis left. From North Africa.'

'No. I may as well come clean, as well. Noell's alive. I've spoken with him.' He nodded at Bochmann's surprise. 'The body we found was his brother. Theodor Noell.'

'I think Noell talked of him, but I never met him.'

'There's something else. All the men you have listed as dead – Hauck, Osterkamp, Prellberg, and Stucker – died or were killed in the places they lived in before the war. My information from the WASt has the same addresses.'

'So?'

'So the killer was able to find them through their prewar addresses. It means he had access to them.' It almost certainly meant he had access to them through the WASt. Reinhardt could think of no other source that might have contained that information. 'All of them were killed between February and July 1946. Prellberg was the first, along with this Lütjens. Then Hauck. Then Stucker and Osterkamp. Then there's a gap. Then someone called Haber, in January, in Hamburg. Not one of your pilots, probably linked to whatever group Lütjens is from, which means the killer is after two sets of people with some kind of common link. Then there's Fenski who was, according to your lists, living in Kempfen, although he was from a town near Augsburg. He was alive until recently?'

'We had a letter from him in January.'

'Zuleger, Noell, and Jürgen. How was he able to find them?' Bochmann shook his head, his chin bunching. Reinhardt looked over the association's list, then his own, and it leaped out at him. Or rather, it revealed itself from where it had been hiding in plain sight. 'What do they have in common, those four? No? No guesses? None of them were living in their prewar addresses. Therefore, the killer couldn't find them. Your list,' he said, pointing at it, 'your *association*... was all the killer needed to find his last victims, with the last three all murdered here. In Berlin. And all in the space of a couple of days.'

'You cannot suspect us?'

'No. I want to talk to your British backers.' Reinhardt threw the words into the conversation, darting them at Bochmann. 'Don't try to lie. I know there is a connection. There must be. You would not try to form a veterans' association without some form of backing, and the only backing that counts nowadays is Allied. Von Vollmer has gone to the British to complain about me. And I know nothing would bring men so far afield as Kempfen for Fenski, and...' he fumed, feeling anger suddenly rising in him, 'and *Cologne* for Jürgen, to Berlin, to *occupied* Berlin, for a simple veterans' reunion. And I know Carlsen was at your event on the weekend. Noell saw him there. So don't treat me as if I'm as dumb as a loaf of bread, and start talking.'

But Bochmann did not talk. He stubbornly refused to do so, his face firming even as his eyes silted up, becoming watery and unfocused leaving Reinhardt, a short while later, back in Mrs Dommes's office with an update for her lists and a clogged sense of frustration in his throat.

'Fenski, address in Kempfen. He's missing. Can you contact the local police and see what they might have? Then the same for Hauck and Osterkamp. Police reports, doctors' reports, anything they might have on those deaths. Keep looking for Thurner. Anything you can think of. Then a call to the police in Bad Oeynhausen with a request for information, and if there was an investigating officer or anyone with knowledge, could they call me? Then can you ask your ladies to kindly go back through the papers for me? I'm looking for news of a death – it may have been reported as a murder – in Bad Oeynhausen in February 1946. There may or may not have been Allied involvement.' Dommes arched her eyebrows at him, but nodded, pen poised over her writing pad. 'Lastly, can you have a call placed to this number, please?' he finished, handing over a business card.

Reinhardt returned to his desk where he seethed, quietly, smoking cigarette after cigarette until he sat in a sluggish swirl of smoke. He stared straight ahead, and for once he was left alone. Perhaps it was the image he gave off, of distant but furious concentration, or the way his chin bunched as he stroked the gap in his teeth with his tongue. When the telephone rang on his desk, he looked at it as he ground out his cigarette before lifting the receiver.

''alloo? *Inspecteur* Reinhardt?'

'Lieutenant De Massigny. Thank you for taking my call.'

'Not at all, *Inspecteur.* I have some news for you.' Reinhardt heard the rustle of papers. '*Alors.* For this Kausch person, I have nothing. No record. He was in the Wehrmacht, this person? He was armed forces?'

'No. SS. I recently found out.'

'Ah, *alors*, he is not here. You might look for him in the Document Center. They have all the Nazi files. But for Leyser, I have something, and nothing. I think you should come to the WASt.'

38

Reinhardt had to wait at the entrance to the WASt. A pair of vehicles with French army plates and starred pennants were parked in front of the building when he arrived, and the soldiers on duty kept him back. He waited on the street, smoking, until a flurry of activity at the entrance turned into a coterie of staff officers who scurried down the steps to the cars, opening doors and gesticulating at one another. One of them, a lieutenant, saw him. He stalked over to Reinhardt, looking him up and down, then pointed at Reinhardt's hat.

'Enlevez-moi ça, sale Boche,' he snarled, and with a snap of his arm he knocked Reinhardt's hat off his head. The lieutenant curled himself back as he did, as if awaiting or even afraid of a reaction, but somehow sure of his rights to humiliate another man in this fashion. Reinhardt blinked, taken aback by the ferocity in the man's tone, too surprised to feel any embarrassment. The lieutenant turned and left as a general came out of the WASt. Reinhardt recognised General Ganeval, the commander of the French Sector. If the General noticed anything of what had happened, he gave no sign. In his wake came De Massigny, who exchanged a rapid flurry of what sounded like mutually accusatory sentences with the lieutenant, before coming over to Reinhardt as he picked his hat up.

'I do apologise. Please come. Come.'

Reinhardt felt that oppressive weight as he entered the building, following De Massigny down echoing halls into a small room that had been converted into an office.

'Now, *Inspecteur.* I will tell you of my searches for this Leyser.

I looked for his file, and there was no record. No *soldbuch*. No *Wehrpass* either. But I found this strange. The name was in the files you found, so he must have existed. I checked with names spelled in a similar way. Nothing. I did some cross-checking of the army units in North Africa at the time of IV./JG56, and still found nothing. I checked with the navy. Nothing. I checked even with the air force. I checked the pay lists. I checked the ration lists. Nothing! *Ça alors*, I think to myself. *Un mystère*. I was hooked, as you say. This man, I was determined to find him. And I did.

'I am thinking, where can I look else for this man. I am stuck. A dead end. *Un cul-de-sac*, as we French call it. I think it is time for help, so I ask Semrau. He is our most experienced archivist. I tell him my problem, and he asks me if I checked the prisoner returns for the Afrika Korps. I check them. They were filed when they evacuated North Africa. But still, there I do not find this Leyser. Then Semrau, he says to look in the section on prisoner exchanges. These are the lists exchanged between the Allies and the Germans of prisoners who are deemed appropriate to give back. *Par exemple*, because they are wounded and not able anymore to fight.'

Reinhardt nodded at De Massigny to continue, the Frenchman visibly excited.

'And *there*, I find Leyser. He was on a list from the armed forces high command that was exchanged through the Red Cross to the British forces in Cairo. But he was not given back. The British kept him. But I have his name, at last. His name was Marius Christian Leyser. He was born in Potsdam, in 1911. He was taken prisoner by the British at Tobruk, in November 1942. That is all the personal information I could find. *Voilà!* What do you say to that?'

'I say that's rather impressive detective work, Lieutenant.'

'N'est ce pas?' De Massigny agreed.

'Somebody removed his records, then?'

'*Oui!* Somebody, how do you say…?'

'Redacted the records.'

'"Redacted"? A new word for me.' De Massigny sounded happy,

and Reinhardt's mouth twitched in a grin despite his mood. 'I think someone redacted the records. To erase the traces of him. *Intéressant, non?*'

'Yes, very *intéressant*. Who could manage such a thing?'

'It would have to be someone with complete access to the records. And time. And knowledge. The person would have to know where to look. And not to have been disturbed. A member of the occupying forces, *par exemple*?'

'Or someone in the WASt.' There was silence in the room.

'I am not surprised to hear you say that, *Inspecteur*. I am thinking, it makes some sense. How could we find out?' Reinhardt had his idea but he shook his head, waiting for the Frenchman to say his piece. De Massigny seemed very serious as he nodded and turned to look at the door. '*Entrez!*' he called.

The door opened, and Semrau stepped inside.

'Sit down, *Monsieur* Semrau, and tell the *inspecteur* what we talked about.'

Semrau looked abashed, like a boy brought before his schoolmasters. He sat, placing his hands folded one within the other on the table, then lifted his eyes to Reinhardt. 'I may not have been completely open with you, Inspector. I met a man in here, about a year ago, maybe a little more. He was searching for information similar to yours. Information on air force units and postings. He said he worked for the British authorities, but the man was a German.'

'You are sure of that?' Reinhardt interjected.

'Positive, sir. He was a Berliner. He was polite enough for one, in any case,' Semrau said, daring a little smile at Reinhardt, but it fell back and away when he saw nothing reciprocated. 'This would have been in July 1946, I think. It was after the WASt had moved back to Berlin from Fürstenhagen, after the Americans had handed it over to the French in June.' Reinhardt nodded at him to go on. 'I received a request to help someone do some research. The man introduced himself as Marius Leyser.'

Reinhardt went cold, tensing up inside. 'Describe him.'

Semrau shook his head. 'It is difficult, Inspector. The man was… the man was the very definition of nondescript. Can you understand that? He was of medium height and medium build. He had short, dark hair. Dark eyes. He wore a little moustache. I remarked on that with him, you see. During the day, as we worked together. I asked him why would any German want to wear a little, dark moustache, and he laughed, and said his British masters often affected one, particularly the officer class, and so he did too. Then he said something strange, about aping one's betters, wanting to fit in more, and he looked at me queerly. As if he knew something I did not. Or as if he knew something about me.' Reinhardt laid his cigarettes and matches on the table. Semrau shook his head at the offer of one, and Reinhardt indicated he should carry on.

'It turned out, it was the latter, Inspector. Leyser knew something about me, and he dropped hints about it both times he came. They were subtle, but they were there, and he couched them inside little remarks about himself. About what he had done and why he found himself doing what he did. Working for our new masters. Perhaps… perhaps I will have that cigarette. Thank you, Inspector.'

Semrau's voice had begun to quiver, trembling round the edges of something he still kept inside. Reinhardt said nothing, only pushed the packet of Luckies towards him. De Massigny lit one of his Gauloises, and the light from outside was suddenly sectioned and pillared through a veritable fogbank of smoke.

'What did Leyser say he was after?'

'He said he was doing research on air force units. The one you came looking for. He did research on the unit, on the pilots, and he left.' Semrau drew on his cigarette, blowing smoke across his knuckles, and he nodded slightly, as if giving himself permission. 'He came back. A second time, at the end of last year, looking for something else. Some kind of test unit. It was a secret unit. There was nothing here about it, and the only time he showed any emotion was when we came across the information the records had been transferred to the Document Center. He seemed to… he seemed to become all still, like he was frozen. He made me do what research we could in here about the unit, following up ideas, other avenues of research, but there was nothing. The Americans must have moved it all to the center before handing over the WASt to the French.' He tilted his head to draw on his cigarette, blowing out a long stream of contemplative smoke.

'Go on,' Reinhardt murmured.

Semrau started, blinking. 'Leyser changed tack late in the day. By that time, I was uncomfortable with him. He said, all of a sudden, he wanted to find his own records. For fun. So we did. We found his *soldbuch* and then, without so much as a… as a by your leave, he took it out. The whole file.' For a moment, the bureaucrat in Semrau peeped his head up, the outrage of a man who lived in the angular confines of rules and regulations and records and who saw those certainties questioned, those angles filed off just a little. 'He said to me it was our secret. I asked him, of course, to put it back, and why should I keep such a secret for him. He said it was because he knew a secret of mine, and mine was worse than his.' Semrau stopped, breathing lightly but rapidly.

'*Allez, mon vieux,*' De Massigny murmured. 'Just tell it like you told me.'

'You see, Inspector, I denounced some of my co-workers to the Gestapo. I had not wanted to. I never thought I would… ever have to do anything like that. But I did. There were two archivists. They were half-Jewish, both of them, and I… denounced them. I don't know why I did it. It seemed everyone was.' Semrau said it all calmly, but his fingers, where he held the cigarette over the ashtray, shook.

'You do know why,' Reinhardt said suddenly. It was not the banality of what Semrau had said that convinced him. There was more. There had to be, otherwise Leyser would not have used it against him.

Semrau's mouth moved, and then he nodded. 'You're like him,' he said. 'I don't say that in a bad way. You both see… things. No.

I denounced a friend. I regretted it. Of course I did. Why did I do it? It was a desire for conformity. I wanted to be like all those others, all those self-confident others, instead of a mousy little archivist with no life. And it was love, Inspector. I loved his wife. I never understood, or recovered, from her choosing him over me. I kept it inside, always. I never said anything. I thought I had got over it. And then… and then the chance came. Just like that. The opportunity was there. Everyone was doing it, or something like it. You were even encouraged to do it. And that… that little kernel inside yourself, the part that never got over the rejection, the part that never got over being rejected for a *Jew*,' Semrau hissed, 'it comes out, and the words… the words are out before you know it. And he was gone.'

'And she was left alone,' Reinhardt said. 'You looked after her. You are close now. But she does not know the truth.'

Semrau smiled, shaking his head as he tipped another cigarette out. 'Just like him, Inspector. You deduced it from my story. I do not know how he knew it, but knew it he did. He said he would tell her. Bring my world down, unless I made him vanish. Those were the words he used. He wanted to vanish. Leave his past behind. I guessed… I presumed he had things to hide, but he said no, he only wanted to erase what he had been. That Leyser no longer existed. I was to make him vanish.'

'So you did it. You redacted him.'

'So I did it, but I could not go all the way. The… historian in me would not let me. Apart from the mention you found when you came, in the squadron's logbook where we didn't look, I left just one reference, one obscure reference, for someone who really wanted him found. And the lieutenant did,' Semrau said, nodding at De Massigny. 'And then I noticed, after he had gone, I noticed he never signed his name anywhere. He signed himself as "Boalt". Always Boalt.'

'Perhaps, it is the name he has taken now,' De Massigny offered.

'Perhaps,' Reinhardt agreed, his eyes on Semrau. 'Beyond the threat against this woman, he never threatened you?'

'Never. What he had over me was enough, Inspector. It would have brought my world down. It still might. But he said his quarrel was not with me.'

'Who did he say it was with?'

'With those of us who carried Germany down into ruin, Inspector.'

39

Leyser. Boalt. Disguises and infiltration. A man who penetrated the WASt. A man who passed as an ex-soldier at Zuleger's. A man who came to Mrs Meissner's doorstep and inveigled his way into her house. A man who walked into the foyer of a fine hotel to murder Jürgen.

A chameleon.

And the British. Leyser's captors. The British were in all that, somewhere, somehow, Reinhardt thought as he stared up at the imperial façade of the Kammergericht, past the olive matte curve of the helmets of the American soldiers on duty.

Collingridge's name got Reinhardt past the outer checkpoints, past a pair of Negro soldiers, and inside. He climbed with a laconic American MP up through the echoing cavern of the giant building, past soldiers and diplomats and lawyers from all four of the occupying powers, and a dozen more countries besides. This was the heart of the Allied Occupation. The Allied Control Council met here, the font of all laws, directives, and regulations in conquered Germany, although rumours and more had reached the population of deep divisions within it, of the wartime alliance beginning to fracture along very different visions of the peace that would be required.

He waited in a corridor that squeaked and groaned along the length of its parquet floor at the men who strode it, looking out over the ragged expanse of Kleist Park. It took him a while to realise what it was that held his eyes, and he only understood it when a British MP with white belts and gaiters came to collect him. It was that the park, although poorly maintained, was still a park, and not a wasteland or not given over to growing vegetables.

'Inspector? I'm rather surprised to see you here.'

Whelan was dressed, seemingly *de rigueur*, in tweed suit and some kind of regimental or club tie. His office looked out over the narrow street to another building, so it was gloomy. His translator was with him, and the strange three-way conversation began, with both Whelan and Reinhardt clearly knowing enough of the other's language to understand each other fairly well.

'Thank you for arranging to meet me on such short notice, Mr Whelan. It's partly to apologise to you for the past. If my conduct was upsetting to you, I am sorry.' Whelan nodded graciously, and Reinhardt was glad to see the elderly Englishman seemed disinclined to make hay out of Reinhardt's apology. 'I am rather committed to my work, you see. I always have been. And so, I was hoping that in addition to making my excuses, perhaps I could ask you a few questions in the interests of furthering my inquiries.'

'Of course, Inspector,' replied a mollified Whelan. 'Please.'

'What can you tell me about Carlsen?'

Whelan frowned. 'I thought you weren't involved in that investigation.'

'I'm not, but his death has links to the murders I am investigating.'

'How so?'

'I found that Carlsen was investigating the men who have been murdered. I found that he had accessed the WASt in the last several weeks...'

'In the what?' interrupted Whelan.

'The WASt. The Wehrmacht Information Office for War Losses and POWs. It is the central repository for information on armed forces personnel. I was saying that Carlsen was looking at and for the same information as me. How is it that this could be? Supposedly, Carlsen's murder has nothing to do with Noell's. This is what you have been insisting on from the beginning. Especially Mr Markworth.'

Whelan seemed honestly perplexed. 'Listen, I don't quite know what to say, Inspector Reinhardt. I'm sure you must have your reasons, but...' He trailed off.

'So perhaps you could tell me more about Carlsen.'

'Well, he was a decent enough chap. You know.'

Reinhardt smiled, tilting his head slightly. 'I'm sorry. I don't.'

'Well,' Whelan said again, shifting a little in his chair. 'You know. Decent enough chap for a Jew. Nothing against Jews, you understand. Only they're not like us.'

'And he was a German, is that right?' Reinhardt asked. The translator looked desperately uncomfortable, staring at her knuckles where one hand lay folded over the other.

'Yes. Playing with a double handicap,' quipped Whelan. The translator stumbled over that one. Not over the words, but over the analogy. Reinhardt, who had understood Whelan's joke, let her find her way to explain it, giving away nothing of his command of English. Her halting explanation seemed to sober Whelan up a little, as if he realised his humour was misplaced. 'Still. Yes. Decent chap. Very decent. Did the right thing and all that. His parents were murdered by the Nazis. He got out, joined up in England.'

'I imagine he had to work doubly hard to be accepted. Being a German *and* a Jew.'

'Quite. He came back over with the rest of us and worked as a military lawyer here in the ACC with me. His only weakness was the bottle. He couldn't hold it. We tried to keep him out of trouble. Managed most of the time. Markworth was best at keeping him in line.'

'Yes, where is Mr Markworth?'

'Out and about, I should imagine. He usually is.'

'Is he also on the Allied Control Council?'

'No, no,' Whelan said. 'He's with the British Control Commission. The Occupation authority for the British Zone. He does his own thing, usually. He should be along shortly. I told him you were coming. Err... something to drink, perhaps?' Whelan pointed at a table with a bottle of whisky on it, around which a rank of tumblers paid court. He poured and handed Reinhardt a glass, leaving the translator empty-handed between them.

'Thank you. You never told me exactly what it is you do for the Control Council.'

'Oh, you know. Pushing papers and whatnot. I work for the section on war crimes. What is a war crime, what isn't. What the occupying powers can do in their own jurisdictions in terms of pursuing people for war crimes.'

'Delicate work.'

'Indeed. Since the Nuremberg trials, cooperation between the powers on war-crimes prosecutions has, shall we say, broken down.'

'Meaning?'

'Well,' said Whelan, warming to his topic, 'each of the powers now pursues its own interests. What it investigates. Whom it prosecutes. To whom it grants amnesties. Whom it keeps interned. Whom it re-employs. And so on and so forth.'

'I imagine the Soviets are rather unforgiving.'

'Oh, rather,' murmured Whelan. 'It's not that we aren't. You should see how the Americans went after the SS for the massacres of their GIs in Malmedy. We put the Bergen-Belsen guards through the wringer. And the French are tough enough in their Zone.'

'Yes. I read about it all in the papers. But, how shall I say this…? There is a sense that the appetite for justice is tailing off.'

'Hmm? No, it's just that we – that is, the Western Allies – take a rather, shall we say, more nuanced view. We're batting for a long innings, shall we say.'

'How so?' asked Reinhardt.

'Well, there's no use prolonging all this indefinitely. We'll have to draw a line under the past at some point. Otherwise it can go on forever, and Germany can't be kept down and out eternally. At some point she'll have to get back on her own two feet, and if we take too much fight out of her, she'll take that much longer.' Reinhardt nodded, encouraging him to continue, although he was a little perplexed at the Englishman's repeated use of sporting analogies. 'Think of denazification. Its goal is to remove National Socialists from positions of leadership in society and replace them with democrats, but there are millions of such people. Actual or suspected, some free, some incarcerated. But, we must ask ourselves whether continuing to discriminate against millions of people is in the interest of stabilising German society. Then, there's reparations. The French are a bit vindictive, and the Soviets seem to have stripped their part of Germany down to the bare bones. Understandable, I suppose, given what your lot did to them.' Both Reinhardt and the translator could not help a shared and quick exchange of eyes, both of them now used to the collective role assigned to them as Germans. Both of them, perhaps, seeking some kind of bizarre reassurance that, yes, both were tarred with that same brush. Perhaps Whelan sensed the sudden discomfort, as he sipped from his whisky, and changed tack. 'But for us, the British and the Americans, we're not out for our pound of flesh.' Reinhardt blinked at him. *Not out for...?* Perhaps he even believed it.

'What did Carlsen think of all that?' Whelan inclined his head questioningly. Reinhardt strung out his words, darts into the unknown, hoping to hit something. 'I understand he was committed to justice.'

'Ah. Yes. Well, it's often difficult for a man lost in theory to accommodate himself to the realities of the world.'

'That there is more grey in the world than black and white?'

'You could say that.' He sipped from his whisky. 'What news, then, of these investigations of yours?'

'Thank you. I can't tell you much about Carlsen's death. That investigation is being led by Chief Inspector Ganz. I am making some progress on my side. In fact, I was wondering if I might ask you a favour? Do you happen to know of two murders that occurred in Bad Oeynhausen in February last year?'

'Good Lord, Inspector! You don't ask much!' Whelan raised his glass and sipped. 'A year ago I imagine I was somewhere in England. I only came out here in summer last year. Why would you ask?'

'Carlsen had been looking at the same materials as me. Including, as I mentioned, into the backgrounds of at least one of those men murdered in Bad Oeynhausen. And… I hesitate to say this, Mr Whelan, but I am finding the British are appearing in my investigation.' Whelan frowned, leaning forward in his chair. 'Allow me to explain myself, sir. At the scene of the first murder, of Noell, I find Carlsen. A British agent. The second murder, of an ex-pilot called Zuleger, led me to Mr von Vollmer, who claims a relationship with you.' Whelan nodded sternly. 'I find now, though, that von Vollmer and some of his colleagues have formed an association of veterans. As you know, this is illegal under current law. No formation of former soldiers of any kind. But, once again – how to put this – I find British influence.'

There was a knock at the door, and Markworth stepped inside with his heavy limp. His face was blank as he came in, but it lightened when he saw Reinhardt. He nodded affably at Whelan as he shrugged out of his coat and took off his hat, scrubbing his hand through his close-cut cap of hair.

'Excuse the delay, Whelan, I was held up.'

'Not at all, old chap.' Whelan glowered at Reinhardt. 'The Inspector here was spinning the most fantastical yarn. About Carlsen, about British agents, about British involvement in all these murders, and about illegal veterans' associations, and whatever the devil have you.'

'Sounds fascinating,' said Markworth, with a tilt of his head at Reinhardt. 'Do go on, Inspector. I'll catch up.'

'Yes. Go on. Explain yourself, Inspector,' growled Whelan.

'Mr von Vollmer and his associates admitted to me that they only formed their grouping because they were encouraged to do so. My assumption is…' Reinhardt paused, hesitating, knowing he was overreaching himself, but he plunged on. 'My assumption is they were supported by someone, or some grouping, within the British occupation authorities.'

'"Encouraged"? "*Assumed*"? By God man, you don't assume

much, do you?' Whelan had gone florid with his anger. 'Did you… *inveigle*… your way in here to just spread your half-cocked theories?'

'Carlsen had dealings with the same group of men whose deaths I am investigating.' Reinhardt heard his voice rising, pitching higher, and hated it. 'Carlsen knew von Vollmer. He was seen at the gathering of this association. Von Vollmer's discourse, Mr Whelan, much resembled yours. No repeat of Versailles, Germany back on her feet, those within Allied circles who thought wisely and for the future. Lastly,' he raised a placatory hand at Whelan, 'the son of one of the victims of those two deaths in Bad Oeynhausen wrote a letter claiming his father, an ex-pilot with some kind of knowledge of experimental aviation techniques, was working for the British when he was murdered. And the man murdered with him was named Dr Lütjens. Does the name ring any bells?'

'None at all. Look here, just what are you implying, Inspector? I've a damn good mind to…'

'I would say the Inspector's only following the evidence as he sees it, Whelan,' Markworth interrupted quietly. He made a placatory gesture towards him, his eyes on Reinhardt. 'Let's hear him out.'

'Lütjens was a medical researcher, also specialised in something to do with flight technology. I found this out today in the WASt. His file is missing information. Someone had redacted the entries in it. I had had another name, Cohausz, and his file is redacted too. Three names, probably in the same unit, all information missing. Transferred to the Berlin Document Center. It means that whatever they were doing, it was linked to the Nazis, and it's got something to do with war crimes. That is a link to what you do, Mr Whelan, and what Carlsen did too. War crimes. Investigations.' Reinhardt paused, his mouth moving, and his tongue stole treacherously into the gap in his teeth. 'I wonder is this what I've heard called "the race for what glitters in the rubble".'

'Explain yourself,' Markworth said, his voice low.

'You. The Americans. The Allies. The Soviets. You all want what the Nazis had by way of technology. Science. Chemistry. Metallurgy.

You want it, and you're getting it. It's a race. And I think… Skokov is after something as well. He was looking at the same things Carlsen was, but *before* Carlsen did.'

'Are you saying the Soviets killed him?' frowned Whelan.

'I don't know who killed him. But I'm pretty sure he was not killed as a result of some barroom brawl or misunderstanding over a prostitute. It's the same killer. Whoever it is, he's murdering a particular set of pilots, and others.'

'Why?' Markworth asked.

'They were pilots with special skills. And they were researchers. Scientists. Men like Haber, and Lütjens, and probably Cohausz. Pilots and scientists. They worked together during the war in a secret unit, working on experiments into effects on humans of extreme flight conditions. There are some who want that information. Skokov wants it. There's a group of holdover Nazis that might not want the Allies getting hold of these people and what they know. But someone's killing for it. Or to stop someone else getting it. Or for a reason I haven't understood yet.'

'Well, whoever it is seems to have been most efficient,' sneered Whelan. 'There's just about no one left, is there?'

'How would you know that?' Reinhardt said nothing in the silence that followed. 'Who told you that? Was it von Vollmer? Was it Bochmann? Did he tell you there's just one of them still alive?'

'What are you talking about?' Markworth asked.

'There's still one more pilot alive. His name's Gareis. He's living in the Soviet Zone. I'll be going out to see him soon,' Reinhardt said. The words just seemed to rush up out of him. A truth that made itself, even as the words that defined it faded out of hearing.

'You realise, of course, if you go gallivanting off into the Soviet Zone, you'll be handing this Gareis chap over to them if you find him. This just makes things look worse for you. Makes you look more and more like a Soviet tool.'

'Whelan,' Markworth said shortly. There was a crackle of tension between the Englishmen. 'Just… let him speak.'

'Fine. Speak, Inspector. Say something. Keep digging yourself a hole, do!'

'Who is Boalt?' Reinhardt asked. Again, the words just seemed to rush up, spoken before he could even think of calling them back, or to order.

Both the Englishmen stared at him.

'I say what?' asked Whelan.

'Boalt. I found his name when I was searching through the WASt.'

'I'm afraid I do not know who Boalt is. Why would you think I do? Markworth, do you know?'

Markworth shook his head slowly. But slowly, like him, or quick with his words, like Whelan, Reinhardt was sure they were both lying.

'Who is Leyser?'

'I have no idea,' Markworth said. He glanced at Whelan, and the big Englishman shook his head.

'What is your relationship to von Vollmer?'

'Cordial,' rasped Whelan, red-faced as he crunched his tumbler down.

'Are you giving his association support of any kind?'

'No.'

'Are the British protecting one of their…'

'No,' said Markworth. The word dropped into a silence between the three of them, but it was a silence that crackled.

'Are the British involved in these…?'

'… you realise,' Markworth cut him off, 'these are the kinds of questions that will get you in trouble faster than you can imagine, Reinhardt. That is, if you were to ask them. Which,' he glanced at Whelan, 'you did not. Am I right?'

Whelan's jaw clenched, chin jutting like a bulldog's, but he shook his head after a moment. 'Leave, Reinhardt,' he grated. 'Before things get worse for you than they are now. But rest assured, you have not heard the last of this.'

40

'*Reinhardt! Wait.*'

Markworth caught up with him as Reinhardt walked shakily down the stairs. He was covered in a cold sweat, and he did not know what had just happened, nor really what he had tried to achieve.

'Listen, don't mind Whelan so much. He's a bit sensitive. He's a good enough sort, but he's not cut out for the rough and tumble.'

'And you are?' Reinhardt wished he could have called the words back, but Markworth seemed to pay them no offence.

'If you like. More so than him, in any case. Listen, I once asked if you wanted a drink. How about now?'

'I would like to,' Reinhardt sighed. He did. He needed one, and he liked Markworth, despite not wanting to. The Englishman felt solid. Dependable. 'I'm sorry, though, I've no time.'

'You do. You must. Just come with me. All right?'

He followed Markworth down and out, the Englishman taking the stairs and then the floor in even, decisive steps. Even as he limped heavily, it was as if nothing would stop him, as if no obstacle would hold him back or sidetrack him. Reinhardt followed him down the clear paths along the centres of a tangle of streets behind the Kammergericht, between slides of rubble to a building that had been cracked open like an egg. There was a door that led down to an underground cellar. Inside was a low-ceilinged bar, all brick arches and even a few prints and paintings hanging on the wall. A massive wooden slab, thickly varnished, stretched along one side. A barman nodded to Markworth, who raised two fingers, and then pointed

Reinhardt to a table under a narrow window crosshatched with metal bars.

They sat quietly, smoking, until their drinks arrived, two tall glasses of clear gold liquid beneath a tier of foam. The barman nodded cordially to Markworth, resting a hand on his shoulder a moment. The Englishman knocked his glass against Reinhardt's.

'Life. The only blessing wickedness possesses,' he said, and drank deeply. The toast seemed misplaced coming from him. It sounded more like something a Russian would say, Reinhardt thought, remembering Skokov, as he drank as well. It was Berliner Weisse, he found to his surprise, properly mixed with caraway schnapps. He had not had anything like this in years, memories flooding back as the drink swelled the contours of his mouth and flowed down his throat.

'I told you, didn't I?' Markworth smiled.

'A couple of Kassler's pork ribs to go with it, and it would be perfect,' Reinhardt said with appreciation.

'None of them to be had, I'm afraid. It is hard to believe this place survived, but there you are. You are welcome anytime, Reinhardt, but keep the place quiet. I do not want half the Berlin Kripo leaning their elbows on the bar. Listen, I owe you some answers,' Markworth continued quietly, his German slow and measured. 'About Carlsen. But first, a question. Something you said at the station before, when we saw each other last, and again just now in Whelan's office, does not make sense to me. You said Carlsen was looking at the same things as Skokov?'

'I found Carlsen had been in the WASt. Looking into information on the pilots being murdered. You didn't know?'

'I did not,' Markworth said, his face blank. He blinked his eyes, and his face cleared. 'It explains… it maybe helps to explain some things.'

'I hear that Carlsen spent time in East Berlin. Did you know that?' Markworth nodded. 'Do you know what he was doing there?'

'Intellectual diversion. That's the way he put it.'

'Do you know who he was talking to?'

Markworth shook his head, his mouth turning down. 'Not really. You think he met someone there involved in his death?'

'I don't know,' said Reinhardt, thinking about Skokov. 'I don't know enough about him.'

'You asked me, the first day we met, at the police station, how I knew about Carlsen. How I was on his trail so fast. I told you, he was my friend. You know he worked in the ACC with Whelan on military affairs. He was a specialist in what they're calling "international humanitarian law". It's all the rage now. They're busy signing treaties at this new United Nations, hoping new laws will stop wars like the one we just had ever happening again.'

'That's a worthy enough ambition, isn't it?' Reinhardt murmured, taking another long drink.

'Wishful thinking is what it is, Reinhardt. But Carlsen believed in it. I suppose he had to. Whelan told you Carlsen escaped to England, just before the war? His family were murdered in one of the camps. He could have let that define who he was, and who the Germans were, but he did not. He… he was able to get over and past it. He was fair and open. He took people for what they were. He…' Markworth paused, as if struggling for the right words. 'He condemned where condemnation was merited. He believed passionately in the law. He was a better man than me in that way, given what he had had to endure. Mistrust within the British ranks, something worse than death from the Germans if he was caught, but he persevered. He had to show the British that not all Germans were SS or brutes, and he had to show the Germans that their conquerors were men of honour, who would not act like barbarians once the war was won, who would apportion blame to the individual and not tar the race with the stain of the Nazis. In short, he was an honourable man. His honour was something precious, but it was dangerous. It left him defenceless against those with less honour than him, or against those for whom honour had no place anymore,' Markworth said, sadly.

'But he had two weaknesses, Reinhardt. Drink, and a need to

rescue people. From themselves. From their circumstances. He found Gieb some time ago. She had survived the camp where his parents were killed, I think. Or something like that. She was perfect for him. Someone to be saved, even if she didn't want saving. Or if people like Stresemann didn't get in his way.'

'Where did you and Carlsen meet?'

'Here. We became good friends. You wouldn't have thought it to see us. Me, I'm a bit of a thug, as you've no doubt guessed.' Markworth smiled to take the sting out of his own words. 'Carlsen was… a boy, really, despite what he had been through. He was… he always seemed a bit lost. Wide-eyed and blinking. He needed looking after, and more often than not I ended up doing it.'

'Did he fight in the war?'

'Holland and Germany.'

'You?'

'France. Then North Africa. Then up through Italy.'

'What service?'

'Take a look at me, Reinhardt,' Markworth grinned. 'Compact. Solid. Don't take up much space.'

'Tanks?'

Markworth lifted his glass. 'First Armoured.'

'The Rhinos, correct?' Reinhardt asked, lifted his glass back. Markworth grinned and nodded.

'That's where I got the hand,' Markworth said, holding up his right hand and pointing at the scars along the side and over the back of his fist. 'Too many hours spent next to an overheated cannon.'

'And the limp?'

'I tore the ligaments in my knee getting out of my tank after it was hit. End of my war, right there.'

'I have a bad knee too,' Reinhardt said suddenly. 'First war. British spade.' Why had he suddenly offered that up?

Markworth winced in sympathy. 'Here's to dodgy knees then, and the men they carry.'

They drank. 'Now what are you doing?'

'His Majesty's Service, Reinhardt.'

'Meaning…?'

'Does that not sound grand enough?' Markworth grinned again. 'I am a liaison officer between Bad Oeynhausen and the British staff in the Kammergericht and in Berlin. I make sure the uniforms and the civilians talk to each other.'

'Where are you from?'

Markworth raised his eyebrows over his beer as he drank. 'Place called Northwood. Near London.'

'Where'd your German come from?'

'Here and there. A few holidays when I was a boy. A few years at university reading German philosophy. A year in Heidelberg. What? *What?*'

'Sorry,' smiled Reinhardt. 'You just don't seem the philosophising type.'

'You know, I hear that a lot.'

'"Life, the only blessing wickedness possesses."'

'You studied the classics?'

'My father. He was partial to Schiller.'

'Your turn then.'

'I was in North Africa too.'

Markworth nodded as he drank. 'I know. Tell me something I don't. What kind of war did you have?'

There was something in Markworth's eyes, some challenge to the truth. If he knew about North Africa, he likely knew Reinhardt had been an Abwehr officer, and a Feldjäeger. That was not what the Englishman was pushing at. 'There was a time I didn't know what kind of war I was having. I only knew, it wasn't my war. I kept telling myself that. And I tried to do the least I could to get through it. It wasn't that war held secrets for me. I'd fought on the Eastern Front and been a stormtrooper in the first war. You didn't fight in that one?' Markworth shook his head 'That was a bad one. But it seemed… honest? Does that make sense? It doesn't always make sense to me. But this one… I'd never seen… never imagined… anything like it. I saw the camps around Munich. Christ, what we did, I'll never understand it as long as I live…' he whispered.

'And from what I know now, what I saw and heard was as nothing compared to what was going on in the East.' Markworth listened expressionlessly, but attentively. 'Come 1943, and after tours in Norway and France, and Yugoslavia and North Africa, I was on the edge of suicide, in complete despair at what my life had come to, when I was given a lifeline. I was back in Yugoslavia, in Sarajevo. A German officer and a journalist, a woman, had been murdered. I was asked to investigate.'

He talked on, of his redemption in his own eyes in a forest on a Bosnian mountain, his determination to make this war his. Reinhardt kept talking, and the years of frustration rolled by, until Sarajevo came back, and he heard rumours of Germans going missing and stumbled across a conspiracy to save something from the war's ruin. He talked of how he had dismantled an escape route for Ustaše and other German collaborators. He talked of Partisans, of the city of Sarajevo in the folds of its encircling hills, of his abiding love and respect for that benighted land of Yugoslavia. But the love he had found himself, the memory of Suzana Vukić's ash-blonde hair and the determined tilt to her eyes, he kept to himself.

'We call them "ratlines" now,' Markworth said, wiping a glitter of beer from his lip. 'You took apart a ratline… bloody well done, sir.'

A second round of molles arrived, and Reinhardt talked on. It felt liberating, somehow, to talk. To get so much out. He had talked with no one of the whole experience of the war since it ended. Collingridge knew some, Brauer knew more, Mrs Meissner knew a little. No one knew all of it, and it was not that Reinhardt was bearing his soul to Markworth, but he felt he had found someone to whom he could talk.

'The German resistance,' Markworth said, when the words tailed off, seemingly of their own accord, and Reinhardt found he felt good. Lighter, freer than he had in a long time. Markworth twisted his mouth into his beer. 'You have to wish and wonder why there weren't more of them.'

'People were scared, Markworth. It's lonely stepping out of line. The odds are terribly stacked against you. And there's that feeling, that question, that tomorrow, maybe the day after, things will get better.'

'Or someone else will take care of it. Whatever "it" is.'

'There's that too.'

'The famous German eleventh commandment,' Markworth murmured.

'"One must always take that view of a matter which the good Lord commands,"' Reinhardt quoted. He had not heard that one in a long time, but the good Lord had too often in German history been a king or some other despot.

They drank in silence.

'What happened to us, Reinhardt? What were we thinking to let things get so out of hand?'

'"Us", Markworth?' Reinhardt asked, wondering if he had misheard.

'"Us", Reinhardt. People. Germans and Englishmen. Americans and Frenchmen. Poles and Russians. The whole sorry damn lot of us. Human beings. Apes clothed in velvet. I'm led to believe we were and still are all in it together. At least, that's what Carlsen used to say. That's why he put such hopes in his laws and treaties and his United Nations.'

'I don't know what happened to us, Markworth. "Us" is too big a word, I think. I know what happened to me. I was afraid. And I kept hoping someone else would take care of things. And someone did, except it was not the right person.'

'And so here we all are…' Markworth said, peering into his glass as if for inspiration.

Reinhardt said nothing, reluctant even to move. He felt stilled with an unexpected shame, as if his very skin had shrunk around the taut lines of his bones.

'It bothers me, Reinhardt,' Markworth said, after a moment. 'That we may have pressured the police to look in the wrong places, and for the wrong people. When it seems to me we should have been supporting you.' Reinhardt stayed quiet. 'I was sure it was because of Stresemann. The man was a… *toe rag*,' Markworth spat, in English.

Reinhardt blinked. 'Markworth, how do you *know* all this?'

'I told you,' Markworth answered, an irritated toss to his head. 'Carlsen was my friend. I looked after him as well as I could. He came across Stresemann through Gieb. Are you *sure* the same man killed Carlsen and all these others? I want to believe it, if only because I want Carlsen's killer found.'

'It's the same man, I know it.'

'Not a group?'

Reinhardt thought of Kausch and his men, discarded the thought. They would not be so precise, those men, nor so consistent. Besides, they were trapped in Berlin. They could not have that reach, to leave bodies all across the length of Germany.

'You're sure… you're sure the same man is doing the killing?'

'They're being killed the same way. But I believe there's only one man. Murder is an intimate business. Killers hardly ever work together.'

'Except in wartime.'

Reinhardt lifted his glass in acknowledgment. 'Except in wartime.'

'And you seem to be saying there's a North African connection to these murders.'

'All the pilots murdered have, so far as I can tell, one thing in common. They served at the same time in North Africa. And several of them were involved in some kind of incident involving a soldier called Leyser.'

'That's it?'

'Not much, is it?'

'It's a damn sight more than your colleagues ever came up with following up on Stresemann,' Markworth muttered darkly. 'So how can I help, Reinhardt? I'm going to be honest. I'm concerned about these rumours of British involvement. I won't get in your way. I won't hide what I find, but I'll want to control that aspect. You understand? You want me to follow up in Bad Oeynhausen? Or with these veterans? The ones who seem to have started it in the first place? What do you think of their story? Someone, allegedly a Brit, convinces them to set up a veterans' association by harking back to past wrongdoings? Bit of a tall tale, isn't it?'

'There's just enough truth in it to be plausible. But listen,' Reinhardt said, sliding his beer glass to one side, sifting through the barrage of questions Markworth had fired at him. 'If you really want to help, you can do two things. You can indeed get in touch with Bad Oeynhausen and find out what you can there. And can you try to get into the Berlin Document Center? There's no way they'll let someone like me in. I pretty much know what that experimental unit was doing, but I need to know who was in it.'

'Why?'

'For starters, they may be in danger, Markworth.'

Markworth pursed his mouth into his beer and murmured something, some expletive in English. 'What's it to me, Reinhardt? Sounds like some of these men deserved what they got.'

'No one deserves what they got, Markworth. Being held down, and then asphyxiated?'

Markworth shrugged as he finished his beer. 'You remind me of Carlsen. We'd always argue about things like that.'

'Sounds like I would've liked him.'

Markworth smiled, a little lop-sided grin as a couple of elderly Germans came down into the cellar and sat at the bar. 'I'll see what I can do for the center, and I'll be up in Bad Oeynhausen directly. I'm due to rotate back in a couple of days anyway. What do you think about the murderer? This man Leyser?'

'I don't know it's him. He's just a name that's come up in the investigation. He was in North Africa at the same time as the pilots being murdered, mentioned in some kind of incident in Tobruk, fighting with several of the pilots. After that, nothing. But that's the thing. Nothing. He *vanishes*. Almost no trace of him in the WASt, but I know he survived the war. He was in the WASt not later than the beginning of last year.'

'So? What does that tell you?'

'That he's alive. That he's apparently working for the Allies. But how, I don't know.'

'What about Leyser the man?'

Reinhardt pushed his beer glass with one finger. 'He's quite something. From what I can tell he's… methodical. Patient. Clever. He's *efficient*. He plans ahead. He's manipulative. He's a chameleon. He can be anyone, anywhere.'

'Meaning?'

'So far, I've found him impersonating some kind of British liaison officer in the WASt, and I've found him in a high-end hotel, and in a working-class neighbourhood and, apparently, convincing von Vollmer to set up a veterans' association and – again, if it's him – he's been operating a long time across the breadth of Germany.' Of Leyser's visit to Meissner's house – because Reinhardt was convinced it had been him – he said nothing.

'Quite the character. What was he doing in the WASt?'

'Removing all trace of his existence.'

'Not all, obviously.' Reinhardt frowned. 'You still found his name.'

'In an obscure place. He coerced an archivist into redacting his records, but the man left one mention – in a list of prisoners for exchange between the British and the Germans – and there was another mention neither of them thought to look for in the logbook of the squadron in which all these pilots served.'

'What's next, then?'

'I go into the Soviet Zone to speak to this Gareis.'

Markworth's eyebrows lowered, and he tilted his head to one side. 'But why the Soviet Zone? Can't this archivist help? And what about von Vollmer and his crowd? They met this Leyser character.'

'Von Vollmer and Bochmann, his former executive officer, could describe him, but neither of them met Leyser during the war. The archivist could identify him, possibly, but there's no proof the man he might identify is Leyser. There's only Gareis, who actually met him during the war. Fought with him, actually. And I need to know what sparked this all off back then. Leyser is killing pilots, but I don't know why. Gareis could tell me.'

'Be careful, Reinhardt. It's not so bad as it used to be out there, but still bad enough. If anything goes wrong, you're on your own.'

'I'll be careful.'

'There's careful, and there's cautious, Reinhardt,' Markworth said as he shrugged into his coat. 'Be sure you know the difference when the time comes.'

It was darker outside on the street, the sky a luminous line up above the crazed scrawl of rooftops and walls. 'Don't worry about Whelan, all right? I'll smooth things over with him. He's a good man. He used to be a High Court judge, so he's a bit sensitive about his reputation. He probably feels you've slandered him or disrespected his authority.' Markworth took in a long breath, then held his hand out to Reinhardt. 'I'm sorry I doubted you. Or misjudged you.'

'It's all right, Markworth,' Reinhardt replied, taken aback. He could not quite figure this man out. Blunt, outspoken, quietly competent, solid, and reassuring. All that, but there was a streak of danger in him, a ruthless aspect of his character, and Reinhardt realised that, in many ways, Markworth reminded him of himself. Maybe not now, and Reinhardt was not sure he had ever given off that air of solidity, but he remembered how cold and clinical he had been about life after the first war. Was that what Reinhardt saw in Markworth? Was that what called out to him?

'You'll be in touch? Especially if you hear more about this infamous British connection?' Markworth asked, as an American staff car came to a stop, and an officer with a colonel's insignia stepped out onto the pavement, followed by a statuesque blonde. The officer looked the two of them up and down, as if expecting some kind of greeting or acknowledgment. The blonde and Reinhardt pegged each other for German immediately, and she studiously ignored him. Markworth and Reinhardt exchanged glances as they went past, down into the beer cellar.

'Fraternisation, eh?' Reinhardt mused.

'One rule for some, another for others,' Markworth said, and if he recognised the irony in the situation – that here, an American colonel had just taken a German woman into a bar while Carlsen had got himself killed trying to do his best for a broken-down prostitute – he said nothing.

Reinhardt nodded. 'Markworth,' he said. Markworth paused as he made to walk away. 'You said Carlsen felt compelled to rescue people from themselves.' Markworth nodded. 'Did he feel that with you? Was he compelled to rescue you from something?'

Markworth looked at him, then gave a tight smile and simply turned away, turning up the collar of his coat as he limped back up the road.

From the cellar, Reinhardt headed north, picking up Potsdamer Strasse and the U-Bahn station at Bulowstrasse. At Gleisdreieck he changed to the B line and rode the train to Hallesches Tor. He walked slowly through the ruined circle of Belle Allianz Platz, intending to head towards the place he used to live with Carolin, but his steps drew him more towards the Landwehr. He walked along its length, hearing it whisper quietly between its sculpted banks, the water backing and gurgling here and there where rock and stone had fallen down into it and disturbed the tranquillity of its flow. He smoked a cigarette, looking down into the canal. The water glistened past, a swirled invitation, but to what he did not know.

Reinhardt tossed the butt into the canal and walked the little way to the ruins of his apartment. He was not sure why he felt the need to come. Perhaps it was the sense, the risk, he might never be back. Markworth was right. The Soviet Zone was not a safe place for a German man, but he knew he needed to go. Either that, or bring Gareis here, to Berlin, but he did not know how much time that might take, or if it would be possible, or even if he wanted to leave the arrangements for that in Skokov's hands.

At the entrance to the building, he flicked on his flashlight, the light breaking and angling across the wreckage inside. He found his little spot and sat, rubbing his knee, emptying his mind, calming himself. He sat there a long while, just letting himself be. One or two people hurried down the street. In the darkness someone laughed, and a wheel crunched through patches of rubble and grit as a man pushed a small barrow.

He did not feel as calm as he had hoped, that sense of peace eluding him. It felt like it had those few times he had felt watched, those few times when he knew, now, that Friedrich had been there. He ran the flashlight's beam around, thinking perhaps that Leena or one of her children might have followed him here, but saw nothing.

Eventually he stirred himself, and made his careful way back to the street, skipping awkwardly over the rubble and hurting his knee, and heading back towards the U-Bahn. There was almost no light, and the city was quiet, only a soft crunch of wheels behind him. He glanced back, seeing a man pushing a barrow. He walked on a few more steps, and then felt a flood of cold come surging up and through him, drenching him with a sudden gush of perspiration.

He stopped dead in the street.

Behind him, the wheels ran, then stopped as well.

Reinhardt turned.

He could not make the man out, clearly. He wore a flat cap, what looked like a quilted jacket, ill-fitting trousers. Of the face, Reinhardt could make out nothing, but he could feel the eyes, staring hard at him out of the dark, and something more. A crackle of recognition.

The man straightened up. He seemed to change, become larger, and the street seemed to dim, the man's outline silhouetted in darkness. Reinhardt was suddenly very scared, his mouth dry as a bone, but he managed to work one word out of it as the man took a step towards him, his arms straight by his sides.

'Leyser?'

The man stopped. The pressure of those eyes increased.

Leyser – it had to be him, Reinhardt thought – took another step forward, another. He walked stiffly, as though he went through each movement with great care, Reinhardt noted, remembering the description the children had given him that very first night. Reinhardt felt rooted to the spot, pinned there by a will not his own. The man came closer and, remembering it suddenly, Reinhardt switched on his flashlight and aimed it at the man.

Leyser froze, one arm coming up to shield his face. Finding the strength somewhere deep inside, Reinhardt took one step towards him.

The man backed away.

Reinhardt managed another step, a third, and Brauer stepped out of the night behind the man. Leyser froze a moment, then swivelled his stance so he had both of them in his sight.

'Leyser?' Reinhardt croaked.

There was the echo of footsteps, and a laugh floated out of the dark. A couple walked into the street, arm in arm. Leyser turned and simply walked away, leaning into his stride, and the quilting on his jacket lengthening and folding into the night. Brauer took a step towards him, but Leyser suddenly shifted low, his weight skimming over the road, and he seemed to slide inside Brauer's sudden desperate attempt to ward him off. Leyser's shoulders curved, contracted, and Reinhardt saw Leyser's elbow scythe across Brauer's face, heard the second blow he struck into Brauer's chest. Reinhardt cried out as his friend cannoned backwards, sprawling legs and arms akimbo, and his head rattling on the street.

Reinhardt shouted again, pushed past the pain in his knee. Behind him, the woman laughed again, the sound incongruous in this street of ruins, cutting across the feral nature of this confrontation. Reinhardt shambled past Brauer's body, his eyes desperate for any sign he lived, and there was an abrupt dislocation as his mind wrenched up a memory…

.... of dashing across No-Man's Land, men falling left and right, but stopping for none of them. A friend ploughed into the ground ahead, arcing around the bow of his agony. His friend's face contorted into a bloodied wail as he clawed a hand across Reinhardt's leg but he shook him off, hurling himself on, always on, his body hunched into the storm of iron as if into a blast of wind and rain...

... but although he pushed himself as hard as he could, Leyser was just that little bit quicker. Reinhardt cursed himself, cursed his knee, but it availed him nothing, and when the man ghosted away up a slide of rubble and over the top, Reinhardt's light wavering behind him, Reinhardt knew he could not follow. He stayed down on the street, pushing his eyes into the darkness, but Leyser was gone.

Part Four

All Guilt Avenged

41

Tuesday

Two days later, and Reinhardt was on a train moving painfully out of Schlesischer Station in Friedrichshain. Reinhardt remembered Schlesischer as one of the more dangerous parts of Berlin for a policeman, firmly under the control of the city's organised crime. Even the Nazis had pretty much left it alone, trusting the criminal gangs to keep order, and essentially leaving them to make whatever profits they wanted, in whatever way they had wanted. Drinking, gambling, prostitution, drugs, racketeering… It had all gone on here, and if half the police had turned a blind eye, the other half had been on the take.

Reinhardt found a seat on a bench by a window and stared out as Berlin crumbled slowly away as the train moved east. It trundled through Köpenick, where Reinhardt had been born in 1898 and where he had grown up. It had been a small town then, on the outskirts of Berlin, but time and the city's expansion had seen it incorporated, and it was just one more stretch of gouged cityscape now, the houses perhaps a little quainter, a little older. Somewhere out there, he knew, as the train passed through the station without stopping, was his father's house. He had not been to Köpenick in years, in longer than he could remember, and he had no idea in what state that old house was in. He felt a pang of sudden nostalgia for his father's library, the smell of books and cigars, of long, genteel discussions with his father and his father's friends, professors and teachers all.

But the fondness was followed swiftly by bitterness at the memory of his father fading away in his library after he was sacked from the university, hounded out because he dared speak up about the ludicrousness of the laws this new Germany was passing, at the treatment of Jews among the students and professors. How quickly his father found himself alone, ridiculed and friendless, how fast a life of respect came to nothing, and how empty that library became. It killed him, eventually, Reinhardt knew, his father dying of a broken heart, and perhaps his son's parallel descent into loneliness and ostracisation had sped him on his way.

No, Reinhardt thought, as the train nosed on into the countryside beneath clouds smeared, like spilled milk, across the blue bowl of the sky, he no longer cared. That life he had had was so far gone, it may as well have been on the other side of the world. Instead, he filled his eyes with green as the train moved on. The countryside was copsed and wooded, trees cleared by the clean sweep of fields and meadows, but amid the seemingly pristine verdure, every small village bore its scars and ruins, its tumbled walls and its holed roofs with their patchwork braces of blackened timbers. He sat and watched a world that was not all shattered stone and rubble, and wondered that he had not thought to miss something as small as a stretch of meadow that was not given over to growing vegetables. Within the smashed confines of the city, he had lost track of time, of the passage of the seasons. He only knew when it got cold, when it got colder, when finally it warmed a little. There was nothing else to help pin the mind to the passage of time beyond Berlin.

He let his mind drift back instead to what he had done these past two days. Brauer had survived Leyser's attack, although he moved painfully, his sternum a huge, mottled bruise, swearing he had never been hit so hard in his life. He had not had a good look at Leyser either. Brauer only remembered the fixed glitter of Leyser's eyes, and a firm line of moustache amidst a riot of stubble. Brauer was also on the move, gone these past two days to Potsdam to follow up on the information that Leyser had been born there.

Reinhardt had hoped to have talked to him before his trip into the Soviet Zone, but there was no sign of him and he could only hope he had not come to grief. Reinhardt could have used the police there for his inquiries, but he knew anything he asked for would make it back to Skokov, and he had no wish to give the Russian more information than he had to. So Brauer had gone, armed with a carton of Lucky Strikes and an enthusiasm for a bit of investigative work. Reinhardt had rarely seen Brauer so happy in a long while, joking that if this jaunt – as he had put it – worked out, he might set himself up in private practice.

After an hour or so trundling through the countryside, the train stopped at a small village, a provincial station, with a stationmaster's house and a bullet-holed sign hanging from a chain. One or two other people climbed down with him, the platform becoming for a moment a swirl of people and baggage moving towards the exit from the station. Reinhardt paused to breathe deeply of the chill, fresh air, and was suddenly conscious of the city's dust on his trousers and shoes. He flapped it off, watching the people who had left the train bunch up at the exit. Reinhardt felt a quiver run through them as they filtered slowly out, a murmur, a susurration that raised the hairs on the back of his neck. Something was wrong, but he did not know what, nor did anyone else on the platform with him until it was his turn to pass out into the street.

A Soviet truck was parked across the road, a squad of soldiers in it and standing around it. And on the pavement, right outside the station, stood Skokov.

The Major smiled as Reinhardt walked out.

'Reinhardt!' he said jovially, the scarring about his mouth slipping across the taut line of his smile. 'Fancy meeting you here!'

Reinhardt said nothing, surprised, and yet not.

'What? Did you think your request for a pass would not reach me? Of course it would. But I do appreciate your attempt to be open and transparent, Captain. It does you credit, although all you had to do was ask me for help.'

'I was sure your contacts would be good enough, Major. I just did not expect to find you out here, yourself.'

'Indeed. Let me see the pass, please.'

Reinhardt handed it over, and Skokov passed it without looking to another officer, a lieutenant, if Reinhardt knew his Soviet ranks well enough. The lieutenant read the pass carefully, then handed it to two local policemen. Two militiamen, Reinhardt corrected himself, remembering how the Soviets had renamed the police in their Zone. The two men lowered their heads over the paper, looking up at him with heavy, hostile eyes, and then handed it back.

'Haracho,' the lieutenant said, nodding to Skokov.

'All is in order, it seems,' Skokov said. He tucked the pass into the pocket of his tunic. 'I shall look after this for you, if you don't mind.' If he noticed Reinhardt's eyes fasten on the pass as it disappeared into Skokov's pocket, as if yearning towards a last chance at salvation, he said nothing. 'Where are we going, Captain?'

'To a village called Bielwiese.'

Skokov snapped something at the lieutenant, who strode away to snap something at a sergeant. Orders and words were snapped, descending down a chain of command until they came back up, and the lieutenant leaned forward to murmur respectfully in Skokov's ear.

'Come, it is not so far, I am told,' the Major said. 'You can sit with me.'

Reinhardt followed him to a BMW with Red Army plates as the squad of soldiers climbed aboard their truck. The little convoy rattled through the streets of the village, then out across a ribbon of metalled road.

'So, tell me, Captain, what are we doing here? What have you learned since we saw each other last? Tell me of your new trips to the WASt and the Kammergericht. What did you find there, Captain?' he asked, with a smile that creased the scars at the corner of his mouth.

Reinhardt's tongue stole into the gap in his teeth, and he reminded himself, again, never to underestimate this man. 'I believe the man I am looking for is named Marius Leyser. He is a former soldier, possibly working for the British, or at least impersonating someone who is.'

'The British?' Skokov purred. 'Go on.'

'The archivists in the WASt had managed to identify him, but this Leyser had already been in the WASt and removed nearly all trace of his existence. We found one entry, hidden in obscure records, however. I confronted the British with this information and with other information that indicates British influence or presence in the murders.' Reinhardt talked on as the car drove through the countryside. He spoke of the pattern of the murders, the dead pilots' unit, and the veterans' association and the rumour of British involvement in it, to which Skokov reacted with suspicion. Again, the news the 'wrong' Noell had been killed, Reinhardt kept to himself. This was a big piece of the puzzle to hide from a man as dangerous and perceptive as Skokov, but Reinhardt found he was ready to take that risk.

'And so who is it you are going to see now?'

'A man called Gareis. He is the last survivor of this squadron. I do not know if the killer is aware of his existence as he was reported killed in action during the war.'

'Very good. You realise that you told me he was dead.'

'I found out the contrary from the veterans' association.'

'Precisely. And what else?'

'Nothing else for now, Major. Gareis may be able to give me information on what may have happened in North Africa.'

'There's a link, is there?'

'The only one I can find. I may be wrong.'

'We shall see soon enough,' Skokov said, settling into himself as if for a long voyage. He stared out the window. 'It is good country around here. Good for crops. For livestock,' Skokov said, staring out across undulating fields. To Reinhardt's eyes, despite the green that soothed and lulled, the countryside was flat and uninteresting. His mind, he found, still shaped the countryside around him to the folds and pitches of Bosnia's mountains, to its heights and depths, and what he found outside the window, he found wanting and a grim testament to the war. The burned hulk of a tank squatted in the middle of a field, half-overgrown with weeds, and Reinhardt spotted the crumbled remains of earthworks snaking across a rise.

'Does it remind you of home, Major?' Skokov nodded slowly. 'And where is that, if I may ask?'

Skokov turned his head slowly, looking at Reinhardt with blank, empty eyes that sparked, suddenly and finally, to life. 'Home would be not far from the Urals, Captain. Near Ekaterinburg.' Reinhardt nodded, gave a tight smile. He had been taken aback by Skokov's eyes, the distance and coldness in them. Perhaps, he thought, there was precious little time and space in the major's life for small talk about one's origins. Or perhaps origins were a source of weakness. To reveal them revealed something about you. Something that could be used against you by someone when the time came.

'Where your grandmother kept bees.'

Skokov smiled, relaxing slightly, and Reinhardt breathed a little easier, wondering if the major had seen through his ploy of steering the conversation back to safer ground. Out here, far from Berlin, Reinhardt felt very lonely and very alone. There would be no one to help him, if help was needed. Tanneberger and Ganz knew, but they could not help themselves within their own precinct, if push came to shove. Weber had grinned and wished him luck. Collingridge knew he was out here, but the American had shrugged when Reinhardt told him what he intended to do, quipped it was 'nice knowing you' and handed over a couple of packs of Luckies. 'Get-out-of-jail-free cards', Collingridge had called them, the cultural reference escaping Reinhardt. When he had met him again in the beer cellar, hunched over glasses of Berliner Weisse, Markworth had not trivialised what Reinhardt intended, running through the itinerary and plans and timing with military precision, but he, too, had ended the conversation with a shrug that anything could happen in the Soviet Zone, and the best-laid plans could come to naught.

Markworth had had little to say about his inquiries into the murders in Bad Oeynhausen. All he would say was that there was a Royal Military Police report he was trying to obtain, but he was clearly worried. The town of Bad Oeynhausen had been entirely taken over by the British. Apart from waiters and maids, and the odd technical expert, there were no Germans left living in it. It was fuel to Reinhardt's fire, Markworth said, that the killer was British or working for them.

'I cannot fathom such a distance,' Reinhardt said to Skokov, the words just popping into his mouth. 'From here to the Urals. Half a continent. Forgive me, though, but I must ask. Your German is very good. There is a touch of something old-fashioned in it. I wonder, have you spent time here before? Perhaps before the war?'

'You ask a lot of questions, Captain. Are you sure that's healthy?'

'It's answers that are bad for your health, I've found, Major.'

Skokov smiled, the scarring around his mouth shifting and tightening. He ran a finger across their glossy ripple, glanced at the flecked pink of the back of his driver's neck.

'Answers are often worse, Captain. Especially if they are the right ones. You are right. I learned my German at home, and then here, in the aftermath of the first war. My parents were White Russians. Landed gentry. They fled Lenin's Russia, the birth of the Soviet Union. I… I was an impressionable youth and, like most youths, I ran counter to the beliefs of my parents. I found Communism on the streets of Berlin, and I went back to Russia when I was old enough. I joined the Party. I did what was asked of me. I returned here in the mid '30s, working in the embassy in counterintelligence. I had connections. I was useful.' He stopped, looking out the window.

'Then the purges came,' Reinhardt prompted him.

Skokov shook his head. 'You call them purges. For us,' his mouth worked, and his finger stroked the scars, 'they were a paroxysm of growth. A necessary evil. A rejection of the weak and the burdensome.'

'Is that what you were?'

The Russian smiled. 'I am what the Party tells me I am. Useful, or useless. What am I, but a part of something greater? When I was called back to Moscow I suspected something. I was accused of… many things. Some of them were even true,' Skokov smiled. 'I had been warning about German rearmament. About Nazi intentions. How could I know such information went against the Party's objectives?'

'Against the pact?'

'Precisely. The Ribbentrop-Molotov Pact. Peace between our nations.'

'The deep breath before the plunge.'

'That too. But it gave us time. Precious years of peace.'

'We were talking of you, Skokov,' Reinhardt said gently.

'This *is* me, Reinhardt,' Skokov replied, as the car rocked over a section of bad road. 'It was part of me. I was part of it. So were you. Pieces of history. Moved by forces greater than us. Who are we to question how we are moved? What moved me was the historical impetus of class struggle, while what moved you was the warped ideology of racial superiority. But it was my past that did me in. My White Russian past. My *bourgeois* past. It was the camps for me. I thought I would end my days there, but one day they came looking for me. They needed someone with my skills.'

'You mean they'd seen the error of their ways?'

'All was forgiven. No system is infallible, you see? Any system can make mistakes, but not every system can admit as much.'

'You mean your system had suffered such casualties, it was no longer picky about who fought for it, nor where they found the people to fight.'

'As you say. You know our Marshal Rokossovsky? He, too, was in a camp. Did you know that? They released him and gave him an army, and what wonders he achieved with it! So, what system was it? One that imprisoned me, or men like me, wrongly? Or one that could admit its wrongs and release me?'

'Admit its wrongs when its needs were great enough, and release you to nothing but war. Is that where you got those scars? In a camp?'

Skokov stroked his mouth. 'One winter, things were so bad that some of the prisoners turned to cannibalism, and they didn't always wait for their victims to be dead. They came for me one night. One of them bit me in the mouth, tried to tear off my lips. The human mouth is one of the filthiest places on earth, Reinhardt, did you know that? I got rid of him, but he left a nasty infection behind that saw me lose most of my teeth and get a mouthful of silver in return. And so now that you have answers, are you happy with them?'

What Reinhardt was, was afraid. He had been a fool to ask questions like that, of a man like Skokov, in a place like this. The answers had put him in Skokov's power. Men like him rarely revealed anything, and when they did, it was either because they had something to gain, or nothing to lose. And if Skokov had nothing to lose, it meant he had little use for Reinhardt and no compunction in sharing such intimate information with him.

'And so here you are,' he said. It was all he could think of to say.

'No. Here *we* are, Reinhardt.'

42

The car had turned down a lane lined with boundary stones that had once been painted white. A track led to a large farmhouse, half of which had been burned down. The vehicles squealed to a halt in a cloud of dust, the soldiers leaping out to fan across a bare expanse of courtyard across which raced a startled brace of chickens. A man appeared in the doorway of the farmhouse. One of the soldiers levelled his weapon at him, then lowered it shamefaced at a snapped order from Skokov. Another order, and the soldiers fell back into a group, pulling away from the house. On the other side of the farmyard was what looked like a barracks, hastily constructed from planks and timber that was already warping from the weather. A couple of women came to its door, children peering out curiously from behind their skirts.

'Captain,' Skokov said, a tilt of his head. 'We are in your hands.'

The man in the door of the house stepped out, his eyes tracking narrow and worried across the soldiers, coming to rest upon Skokov and Reinhardt. He was of medium build, dressed in what looked like cast-off mechanic's overalls, a sleeveless sheepskin jacket around his torso.

'Are you Gareis?'

'I am.'

'Reinhardt. Berlin Kripo,' Reinhardt said, holding out his warrant disc. He said nothing about Skokov, lurking off to the side. 'I would like to ask you some questions about some people you knew during the war.'

'What people? I didn't do anything wrong.' Gareis's voice was low but insistent, and his eyes kept flickering to Skokov and to the two militiamen. 'I had nothing to with any of that. I was a pilot.'

'I know, Mr Gareis. That's why I'm here. It's about the pilots you knew during the war. When you served with IV./JG56.'

'Right,' Gareis breathed out, and Reinhardt saw tension flow out of him.

Gareis led Reinhardt into the heavy gloom of the farmhouse, into a kitchen filled with a mismatch of furniture, some of which looked like it had been rescued from a fire. An old lady sat in a corner, her head bent to a piece of fabric in her hand into which a needle and thread darted in and out. She blinked confusedly at Gareis and Reinhardt as they came in, then she started back in her chair with fear, and Reinhardt saw that Skokov had followed them in, quietly.

'Mother, it's fine, it's nothing. They've just come to see me. It's nothing.'

'What do they want?' the old lady stammered.

'They just want to talk to me. It's nothing,' Gareis soothed her as he led Reinhardt and Skokov to a big table. The old lady subsided, blinking round wet eyes at Reinhardt and Skokov from out of a face that seemed, on her left, to be shrunken in, as if the bone beneath was missing. 'I'm sorry,' Gareis said, as they sat. 'I've nothing to offer you.'

'Conrad, what do they want? Why are they here?' the old lady called.

'Nothing, mother. Nothing. It's all right.'

'That's all right, Mr Gareis. This should not take too long. Your mother is not well?'

'She had a rough time of it at the end of the war. You saw half the place burned down. She was here alone. And… well, you know what was happening to women then. Her age didn't spare her.'

'Do you know who did it?' Skokov asked. If he was being disingenuous, Reinhardt thought, he covered it up well.

Gareis stared at him, as if taking his measure or sharing the same thought as Reinhardt. 'Not Red Army, so far as I can make out. Could've been deserters. Or DPs. The countryside was awash with bands of them. But I think it was more probably the forced labourers. There were Poles on the farm, a couple of Frenchmen too. The government put them here to work the land during the war along with a… piece-of-shit overseer. When the neighbours got here, they were all gone, the place was half-gutted, the overseer was strung up in the courtyard, and my mother…' Gareis glanced over at her, where the old lady had gone back to her stitching and sewing, her face screwed up in concentration. 'That's the only thing that keeps her going now. Helps keep her mind off things. Anyway,' he sighed, folding big, callused hands on the table, 'you didn't come here to listen to all that. What do you want?'

'Mr Gareis, during the war, you flew with a squadron designated IV./JG56. You were posted in North Africa. Over the past year or so, all the members of the squadron within which you flew who survived the war have been murdered. Several of them have been murdered in the last few days in Berlin, after coming to the city to meet with other veterans in an association called "Ritterfeld".'

'After the Group's first aerodrome. Yes, I know of the association,' Gareis said. 'They contacted me, but I wanted no part of it. Those days are over. Let them go.'

'Can you shed any light at all on what might be happening?'

'List the men for me, please.'

'Prellberg, Hauck, Stucker, Osterkamp, Jurgen, Zuleger, Fenski, and Noell.'

Gareis was silent, and then he seemed to deflate slightly. 'It's funny, isn't it, how the past can sometimes catch up with you? You think it has a connection to North Africa? Well, you're right. When we were based in North Africa, we committed a war crime. No. Wait. It would be a war crime now. Back then, no one knew what it was all about. In any case,' he said, 'the squadron shot up a village of Arabs. A Berber encampment. Just a bunch of tents, camels, and a few people. There were rumours the Berber were working with the

British, but who really knew,' Gareis said. 'We were bored. Pissed off. Tired of retreating in the face of the British, so we shot the place up, killed everyone in it, and reported that we had been fired upon from the camp.

'Only we didn't know that it wasn't a Berber camp. Rather, it was, but with a difference. They were Germans, disguised as Berbers. They were Brandenburgers. You know about them?'

Reinhardt frowned. 'They were special troops. They used to belong to the Abwehr, to military intelligence.' Memories bobbed up, little more than generalities and rumours. Even within the Abwehr, the Brandenburgers had been a little-known organisation. Infiltration, he remembered. They were specially trained in infiltration. In disguises. In blending in, he thought, wondering how often Leyser had followed him through Berlin's streets wheeling his little cart.

'They were the equivalent of British Commandos. Masters at infiltration,' Gareis said, echoing Reinhardt's own thoughts, 'every man a weapons expert, multitalented. The squadron should have known,' said Gareis. 'At least, Prellberg should have known. We'd been briefed about a special mission, been told to stay away from a certain sector, but we had forgotten, or we'd got lost, or we'd been in a fight and barely got out if it alive. I can't remember. I only remember we were all pissed off, tired of always losing, itching for a scrap, and one of the pilots saw the encampment, and then someone remarked about how the Arabs are always spying, and you can't trust them further than you can throw them, and then someone else says "let's have some fun", and we did. We destroyed everything, especially when it turned out someone from the encampment *did* fire upon us. But it was friendly fire. The whole thing was a friendly fire incident. I remember… I remember chasing men across the desert, machine-gunning them as they tried to run, until there was nothing, only smoke and sand.'

Gareis brought a heavy pitcher of water back to the table and poured into three mismatched tumblers. He drank deeply, his eyes far away.

'A few days later, the word came in that a Brandenburger mission had been destroyed by enemy action, and we realised it was us who had done it. A few days more, and they brought in a survivor. He was badly wounded, almost delirious, but already rumours were spreading that the Brandenburgers might not have been destroyed by enemy action. We debated what to do. A couple of us decided to take matters into their own hands.'

'Who?' asked Reinhardt.

'Prellberg and someone else. I don't remember. Osterkamp, maybe. The squadron CO and his deputy. They went to the hospital in Tobruk and tried to kill the wounded man, but he defended himself. He was a Brandenburger, after all,' said Gareis. 'He almost killed them with his bare hands, almost killing himself in the process, and had to be restrained. The affair would have worsened were it not for the British. Their advance compelled us to pull out of Tobruk. The city was abandoned, the hospital and its patients with it, all falling into British hands. The squadron escaped any investigation and sanction, deployed to Italy, and… the war went on.'

'The name of the survivor?'

'His name was Leyser.'

'I, too, know of the Brandenburgers,' Skokov said, sipping from his water. 'They were elite soldiers. I heard that at the beginning of Operation Barbarossa, the invasion of the USSR, units of Brandenburgers sowed confusion in the Soviet ranks, passing themselves off as soldiers, or as security personnel, giving false orders, ambushing unsuspecting troops. Importantly,' he said, looking at Reinhardt, 'all Brandenburgers were multilingual.'

Reinhardt was looking at Gareis. His story did not tally with Noell's. 'Gareis, what role did you have in the squadron?'

'Pilot.'

'Apart from being a pilot.'

'That's it.'

'Gareis. I have been in the WASt. I have seen the records of all those who served in IV./JG56. You were not just a pilot. You were the squadron's second-in-command.'

'Very well. I was. So what?' Gareis answered with a lowered glance at Skokov.

'So, tell me again who went to see that Brandenburger? Prellberg and who? Remember, I've seen the squadron's logbook,' he said, still trying to keep Noell's existence out of the conversation.

Gareis sighed, nodding down at the table. 'I went as well. It is not a memory I'm particularly fond of. We left the man alive, at least.'

'From the sound of it, Leyser was the one did you the favour of leaving you alive.'

'It's true. The man was formidable. Even half-crazed, bed-ridden, drugged, he almost killed us.'

'Describe him, please.'

'There was not much to see, Inspector, and it was long ago. He was heavily bandaged because of the exposure to the sun. But he was of medium height, medium build. Dark hair, I think. Like I said, it was long ago, but I do remember one thing. The way he moved was… methodical. Injured as he was, he was terrifyingly efficient. I seem to remember he favoured his left leg. In any case, that leg was more bandaged than the other. I'm sorry, Inspector, but that's all I remember. I never saw him again, and I wouldn't recognise him if he were this Russian officer sitting next to you.'

Skokov smiled, that taut pull of the lips.

'So if you can't remember him, what makes you think this incident is the one that links all the murders?'

'It's the only one that makes any sense to me,' Gareis replied. 'Not long after that, we were pulled out of North Africa, and then the squadron was split up.'

'Very well, Mr Gareis, thank you.'

'Inspector Reinhardt, do you have further use for this man?' Skokov asked. His eyes had gone flat again.

Reinhardt's mouth opened, but no words came out. He frowned, a worried scratching suddenly grating the back of his mind. 'I don't know, Major. Possibly.'

'The man has told you what he remembered concerning your investigation. But there's more to your story, Gareis. After your squadron was broken up, where did you go?' Gareis went still, but his head began to shake. 'The Inspector knows, don't you, Inspector, but I'm not sure why he's held it back. But never mind. Tell me of the work you did, Gareis. The experimental work.'

'How… how did…?'

'I know it? It is my job in life to know things, Gareis.' Skokov's voice was deadly quiet. 'I knew of you, but I did not know you were alive. So? No words? I will tell you then. I know you transferred to a test unit. A very special test unit. One that tested high-altitude flight.'

'You told him!' Gareis glared accusatorily at Reinhardt as Skokov called out for his men. The lieutenant came into the kitchen, followed by the two militiamen. Gareis surged up from the table as his mother cried out in a quivering voice, her needlework folding to the floor.

'He told me nothing, Gareis. But your unique talents are required by the Soviet Union.' Soldiers closed in around a desperately furious Gareis. The former pilot's eyes were locked on Reinhardt, who felt as if he had somehow betrayed him.

'My mother! What of my mother?'

'This farm will be taken under new, collective management, Gareis, and farmed efficiently.' Skokov nodded to his men, and then rose to his feet. 'Your mother will be taken care of, especially if you do well for us. She may even accompany you, if you wish. Come, Inspector, it is time to go.'

'How can you do this, Skokov?' Reinhardt demanded as he followed the major back to his car. 'You used me.'

'I used you. Of course I used you. You used me. We all use each other. Think carefully on your next words, Captain,' he said, reverting back to the way he seemed to want to refer to Reinhardt when they were in private or away from others. 'I warned you that the flow of information needed to be from you to me. You have not done badly on that, but you could have done better.'

'How did you know about Gareis and the test unit?'

'I found his details in the Document Center after I learned they had been transferred there from the WASt. I thought he was dead, though, so for that I thank you.' From inside the house, they heard Gareis's voice suddenly raised, another man's rising with it, then the sound of something breaking. Skokov shook his head, tutting.

'There's someone else,' Reinhardt said in a rush, words cascading up. Something to say, anything to say, to divert attention away from what was going on, to maybe stop it. 'Boalt.' Skokov frowned at Reinhardt. 'Boalt. I found his name in the WASt too. Looking at the same things you were. Was he one of yours?'

'"Boalt"?' Skokov asked. He smiled. 'How droll. But then, you told me of the British involvement, it's true. Boalt is not a "he", Captain, but a "what". British Occupation Authority Liaison Taskforce. BOALT.'

'How…? Carlsen told you, didn't he?'

Skokov's smile tightened, and he gave Reinhardt a grudging nod. 'I only know it is an intelligence-gathering unit, with the peculiarity that its members can pass for Germans, so they can really listen and understand what is being said around them. Listening, observing, inquiring, and reporting back to the British on the mood of the country, the impact of Occupation policies. They could be anyone, anywhere,' Skokov said. 'An old man on a park bench, a foreman in a factory, a journalist, women queuing up for life's necessities.'

'Women queuing for bread? I hear that's where revolutions often start,' Reinhardt said bitterly, angry at finding himself in such deep currents of revelation.

There was another bellow of anger from the house, and the thud of something striking flesh. Skokov sighed.

'So what do you think Gareis can do for you?' Reinhardt asked.

'The test unit Gareis was assigned to was one testing high-altitude, long-range aircraft. They call them "strategic bombers",' the Major said, carefully, as if testing the word. 'The Americans have one, called a B29 Superfortress. It dropped the atomic bomb. It flies so high, nothing can reach it. Its cabin is 'pressurised.' Its armament is "remote-controlled". Do you understand these terms, Captain? I do not. I know the Germans had gone some way towards either developing one, or the elements of one. My function here is to find the research done on high-altitude flight, its effects on men, on survival techniques, and I want any information on long-range aircraft. It may not seem like much,' Skokov said, 'but every little bit helps in this topsy-turvy world we find ourselves in, where the Allies of yesterday are the enemies of tomorrow.'

'The race for what shines in the rubble,' Reinhardt muttered.

Skokov frowned, as if he had not quite understood. 'I am certain, Captain, that the Allies are undermining the Soviets in Germany. You discover pilots being murdered. You tell me of British involvement. I tell you of BOALT. I know that someone is also killing men who worked on air force research projects.' Almost, almost Reinhardt blurted out that he had found that link. That the wrong Noell had been murdered, but he held it back. 'How should that look to me, Captain? How should it look to me that people I am interested in finding have been murdered? And when those who have been murdered were all living in the Western Zones?'

'How do you know they have been murdered?'

'You yourself have told me of one. Lütjens. And I found news of others when I looked in the Document Center. Most of the researchers who worked in that test unit are dead, Captain.'

'If you look for a conspiracy, you'll find one.'

'The simplest explanation is usually the most likely one. You should know that.' Skokov snapped something at his lieutenant, who scurried to the car and came back with a leather briefcase. Skokov took from it a sheet of flimsy paper with a typed list of names and dates. 'Here. I will save you the trouble of checking for yourself. The senior researchers in the experimental unit known as XII./KG4. All dead. Or missing, which amounts to the same thing as far as I'm concerned.'

There were five names, including Lütjens – the man who had been found murdered in Bad Oeynhausen along with Prellberg – and Cohausz. All dead – or missing, as Skokov had sarcastically pointed out – between February and November 1946. Noell would be a sixth, murdered in 1947.

'How did you find this information out?'

'The Soviet Union is not without friends in the Western Zones, Captain' was all Skokov would say.

'Well, you should have a word with your friends. There is an error on your list,' Reinhardt said, echoing Bochmann's words to him about Gareis. Skokov cocked his head, waiting. 'You should include Theodor Noell.'

'What do you mean, Reinhardt?'

'We thought it was Andreas Noell we found murdered. It was not. It was his brother. Theodor. A colonel and scientist.'

'Reinhardt, Reinhardt,' Skokov shook his head, and the light in his eyes was very cold. 'When did you know this?'

'Only recently. Andreas Noell came forward. He told me he feared the murderer had misidentified him for his brother. But if I look at whom the murderer has been targeting, it has been a mixture of pilots and researchers. And the only link between them is this test unit, which took in three pilots from IV./JG56. Noell. Prellberg. And Gareis.'

'You are a wonder to me, Reinhardt. *Molodyets!*' exclaimed Skokov, recovering his good humour.

'What will become of Gareis, Major? I should know that, at least.'

'What happens to him in the Soviet Union is not my affair, but I meant what I said. If he does well for us, he will be treated well. If not, not.'

'Like my son.' The words just leaped out, faster than Reinhardt could block with his tongue in the gap in this teeth. Friedrich had come to see him each night, the second time with his face bruised from a beating, curled into his own sense of rejection, moving to the rhythm of his leper's bell – *outcast, unclean* – and yet drawn to the company of his father and, once, to Brauer. Friedrich could not say who had beaten him. Could not, or would not, Reinhardt had thought, remembering Kausch's words to him that his son was theirs whenever they wanted him. The three of them had finished off Skokov's vodka, the alcohol putting Friedrich into a state of weeping self-pity. Half-awake, he had mumbled names and imprecations into the crook of his arm, drooling on Meissner's table. The names were German, but they went on and on, becoming Russian, a long litany that had the air of being oft-repeated. Reinhardt and Brauer had stared at each other over Friedrich's slumped body, Brauer sporting a bruise across his face like the mark left by a whip from where Leyser had struck him, and with a hand laid lightly on his chest over the massive bruise there, before lifting him and putting him to sleep on a pallet in the colonel's study.

'When this is over, I will tell you of your son's war, Captain,' Skokov said, a glint of menace in his eyes that went with the weight of his words. 'But I'm not interested in Lieutenant Reinhardt's misdemeanours on the Eastern Front, although you might well be.'

'You find my son weak and untrustworthy. But he is my son. And remember what you told me of your own past. To still be alive today, have you really served the same masters? Or many? And what does that make you?' Reinhardt asked, pushing on into the wintry glare of Skokov's eyes. 'Does that make you weak or strong? Trustworthy or the opposite?'

Skokov was very still a long moment, and Reinhardt had enough time to wonder, again, at his foolishness. 'I salute your bravery, Captain,' he said, at last, 'in speaking in such a way to a Soviet officer inside the Soviet Zone. But I am not an unfair man, nor a vindictive one. You have helped me and so, I promise you, so long as you maintain your contact with me and keep me informed of the progress of your investigation, in particular, that you inform me of any British involvement, then I will let Friedrich go.'

'Do I have your word on that, Major?'

'I would warn you not to push your luck, but I think you are beyond that. So, yes, Captain. I will let your son come back to you when this is over. Remember, though, he has a past, and you are a policeman, and the truth is a vocation when it is not an obsession. Be careful, Captain, what your son's truth brings home.'

43

Collingridge was waiting on the street outside Schlesischer Station leaning against a Jeep and smoking. From the butts that peppered the street, he had been there some time. A pair of children squatted in the angled shadow of a doorway, eyeing the butts as Collingridge flicked them away. Collingridge wore his uniform, a pistol holstered at his waist. A couple of Red Army men were with him, sharing his cigarettes. They nodded a cordial good-bye as Reinhardt came up, and Collingridge gave them a bright smile and wave. With his easygoing demeanour, he was one of those men who made friends quickly and easily.

'This is the second time today I have had a reception committee,' Reinhardt said.

'Great.' Collingridge's eyes were tight, his easy smile fading away. 'You can tell me all about it. Let's get a beer,' he said, angling himself into the Jeep, and just then Markworth stepped out of the crowd.

'Good to see you're alive and well, Reinhardt,' he nodded.

Collingridge's face twitched its surprise as he stopped, half-in and half-out of the Jeep. He looked like a man who clearly thought three was more than company.

'Well, get in, the both of you. Reinhardt, sit up front with me.' Collingridge's last cigarette sparked to the ground, and the children were moving as the Jeep pulled away down Breslauer Strasse, then up Holtzmarkt.

'This isn't the best thing for me, David, to be seen with you. And in the Soviet Sector, as well.'

'Not to put too fine a point on it, Reinhardt, but tough shit.

You've got bigger problems than me. I hope you found what you were looking for out east, because all hell's broken loose here. Von Vollmer's dead, and Bochmann's missing.'

'What? What's happened?'

'Save it,' Collingridge said as he crossed the Spree at Janowitzbrucke. He swerved the Jeep around a huge shell hole in the road, then sped back up, taking Niederwallstrasse as it curved south of the heart of Mitte. 'It'll go down better over a drink.'

It was not that Reinhardt disliked Collingridge. The American had been good to him, in his way. It was just that he had no wish to drink with him. Drink, for Reinhardt, meant talk, and he could not talk to Collingridge as he had talked with Markworth. The two of them – the German and the Englishman – seemed kindred spirits, teasing truths out of each other, bridging the blunt frontages men often put up against each other. He would have liked to ask Markworth about BOALT.

Collingridge turned the Jeep down Leipziger Strasse, the shattered façades lit harshly by the setting sun ahead of them. High up, a long scrap of fabric waved from the ruptured frame of a window, as if Rapunzel had hopes of letting down her hair. Higher still, clouds streamed overhead, sunlight etching their contoured heights like fire along folds of paper. The whine of the Jeep's engine lifted and spread as Collingridge drove across Leipziger Platz, past the disinterested gaze of the Red Army sentries, and then they were in the British Sector. Collingridge manoeuvred them across Potsdamer Platz, around the ever-present black market, to the door of a bar that seemed to cater to GIs, given the cluster of them smoking on the steps and chatting with an equal number of German girls. The group broke up as Collingridge parked the Jeep, chaining the steering wheel to the vehicle's floor.

'As you were, boys,' he muttered, striding past them into the bar. Reinhardt and Markworth followed him into a low-lit room packed with GIs, a sprinkling of British and French, even a couple of Russians. The room was heavy with smoke and the jarring smell of a dozen types of perfume. A jazz quartet ran through its paces on a stage at the far end, a singer in a tight white dress crooning something Reinhardt did not recognise. He could not help but exchange a glance with Markworth, and hid a smile at the Englishman's raised eyebrow. It was not a patch on the place they had had their Weisses.

Collingridge found them a table at the far end of the bar from the band and ordered three Budweisers from a waitress dressed in someone's best guess of what a traditional German outfit would look like. Collingridge flashed her his best Hollywood grin as she took the order, then the grin slipped and was gone as fast as it came as he lit a cigarette and stared at Reinhardt, and began talking.

'Von Vollmer's factory burned down, and with him in it, by the looks of it. At least, the watchman says it's him. He confirmed von Vollmer came into work early, as usual, was the first one there. A few minutes later, he smelled smoke, and then the office block went up. They found a body in what was left of von Vollmer's office. They're working on dental records, but the watchman and others have identified him by his monocle and rings, apparently.'

'And Bochmann?'

'Vanished. No one's seen him since last night.'

'Bloody hell,' Reinhardt murmured. Collingridge's mouth firmed.

'That's putting it mildly. At least they aren't trying to pin this one on you, Reinhardt, like they had a mind to for Stresemann's death.'

'You are joking.'

'He's not, Reinhardt,' said Markworth. 'Whelan's hopping mad, and your own men are looking for someone to blame now. This one's gone as high as Margraff himself.'

The three of them leaned back as the waitress served the drinks. They lifted their glasses in a formulaic salute, and drank. The beer was wet and cold, and that was the best that could be said for it.

'By rights, I should be unhappy with you, Reinhardt,' Collingridge said. He glanced at Markworth, and seemed to make up his mind to speak it. 'All the good stuff, you seem to be giving to your Russki. Well, it's time you remembered your American friends, because I reckon we're the only ones you've got left. What did Gareis tell you?'

Reinhardt sighed. 'A lot and not a lot. He confirmed a fight during the war with a soldier called Leyser. Gareis's squadron destroyed Leyser's unit in a friendly fire incident. Leyser survived, and several of the pilots tried to kill him in hospital to cover up their mistake.'

'Go on,' Collingridge said.

'They didn't kill him. *He* all but killed *them*. Leyser was a Brandenburger. Unconventional forces.'

'Like British Commandos or American Rangers,' Markworth said in response to Collingridge's frown.

Reinhardt nodded his thanks. 'Leyser was left behind in Tobruk when the Afrika Korps evacuated, and the last anyone knew of him, he was taken prisoner by the British.'

'Huh,' grunted Collingridge, raising an eyebrow at Markworth. 'Hence the British connection to this case?'

'Possibly.' Reinhardt glanced over, but Markworth said nothing, only motioned for him to continue. 'Leyser survived the war, and he's out for revenge. He's killed every member of the squadron who shot up his unit. But... there's more. Not all of Leyser's victims have been pilots. Some of them have been researchers. Some of the pilots went on to an experimental unit during the war.'

'Leyser's killing both?' Markworth frowned.

'He's selectively killing both.' Reinhardt stared out across the bar, his eyes caught a moment by the shift and blur of the drummer's sticks. 'I think... I think Leyser must have discovered the link between the squadron and the test unit. Maybe it makes him think of justice. Of some kind of justice.'

'So Leyser's getting a two-for-the-price-of-one deal?' Collingridge muttered.

'I don't know what to think, David. It's barely coming together. It makes sense. There's some evidence to fit it, but it's just a theory.'

Collingridge twisted round in his seat. 'What about that experimental unit, then? Tell me more.'

'That's what Skokov's interested in. He's been looking into it for quite some time. He hadn't made the link between the pilots and the researchers until… well, until I came along. He's quite taken up with the British connection,' Reinhardt said, looking at Markworth. 'He's convinced you are going out of your way to deny him what he wants.'

'Typical Russki. Suspicious of everything,' said Collingridge, his face cast into sudden angled shadow as he lit a cigarette. 'What's he think this research unit'll give him?'

'It did experimental research on the effects of high-altitude flight. Tested equipment. Tested theories. Flew experimental models. Skokov mentioned the B29.'

Collingridge was silent, until a hissed *Fuck* squeezed between his lips. 'The Russkies are after German research on high-altitude flight?'

'Skokov is. Gareis was one of the test pilots. Skokov has him now.'

'Ahhh, *Jesus*! And you led him right to him!'

'I couldn't know!' Reinhardt protested.

The only response was the tip of Collingridge's cigarette that flared furiously to orange light. 'What now?' the American eventually asked.

'Give me a night to think about it, all right? I'm out of ideas, and I'm tired.'

'Sure. You want me to drive you home?'

'No. I need to think. But thanks.'

'Get some rest then,' said Collingridge as he flicked his cigarette into an ashtray. 'You're going to need it. Markworth, you want a ride? Five minutes, then. I gotta take a leak, and I'm guessing you two need a moment alone. I'm counting on that Allied cooperation for you to tell me what you've been talking about, Markworth,' he finished sourly. 'No secrets between Allies, right?'

Markworth unfolded a piece of paper from his coat when Collingridge had gone. 'Investigation by the British military police into the deaths of Prellberg and Lütjens in Bad Oeynhausen last year. They were found beaten to death behind some kind of barracks for German employees or specialists.'

'Suspects?'

'None.'

'Motive?'

'The MPs thought it might have been a personal disagreement or settling of accounts.'

'What made them think that?'

'It's what required the least thought.' Markworth had the grace to look sheepish. 'That is, if they thought at all. The two of them looked to have fought together.'

'Witnesses?'

'No one and nothing. No noise. Nothing untoward. But no sand, or water. What does that mean?'

Reinhardt glanced over the report. 'So far as I can tell, they were the first murders. Maybe... whatever significance sand and water has for Leyser, he had no opportunity to use it then. Maybe the significance came later. I don't know. Markworth, you realise it's almost a certainty Leyser is or was working for the British. There has to be some trace of him.'

'I'll find it. I'll be back in Bad Oeynhausen in a day or two.'

'Two Germans of interest to the British authorities die in suspicious circumstances inside an area controlled by the British. No suspect is found. The MPs probably knew it was someone inside, and they either didn't want to look, or were told not to.'

'I said, I'll find it.'

'Skokov told me about BOALT,' Reinhardt whispered. Markworth was hard to see against the light from the stage. 'You said you knew nothing about it, but that's not true, is it? Leyser's working for BOALT.'

'Reinhardt...' Markworth began, quietly. 'There are some things I can tell you and others I can't. I can't tell you of BOALT. It's secret. Or, it was supposed to be,' his voice taking a rueful tinge.

'What does it do?'

'It doesn't go around murdering people.' Markworth paused, his mouth moving, then he began talking, his German slow and precise. 'All right. You maybe don't know, but the Americans commissioned some reports last year about how they are viewed by the German population. They were horrified by what the reports found. GIs are considered louts, drunks, and ignoramuses. Americans are only interested in their comfort and getting rich on the black market. Americans are weak. American servicemen and policies abuse the civilian population. "An American is a Russian with his trousers pressed". According to the reports, three times more money is going back to the US than the Americans are putting into Berlin. Hardly surprising when a GI can buy a pack of cigarettes in the PX for fifty cents and sell it on the black market for a hundred dollars, or bring in a case of Mickey Mouse watches and sell them for a fortune apiece to a Russian soldier. The British saw the reports and determined that they would not want for information on the Occupation and German perceptions of it and where they stood. So BOALT was created. That is all I can tell you, and that is already too much.'

'Who controls it?'

'It works directly for the British governor in Bad Oeynhausen.'

'*That's* where you'll find Leyser. You said Carlsen was a German who fought for the British. Leyser was a German captured by the British, and I think he ended up fighting for them. A man like him, a Brandenburger, he'd be too good to waste.'

'Why would he do that? Change sides?'

'Change of heart? I don't know, Markworth. I've heard they happen. But both Carlsen and Leyser ended up here, and both of them were working for the British. There has to be a connection somewhere. Look. Please.'

'I will,' Markworth said. 'Look, Reinhardt. I said it before, but I'll say it again. I've been impressed by the way you've handled this investigation. To the extent I can, I'll make sure the British don't come down too hard on you over von Vollmer.' He paused. 'I wonder, though, if we ever find Leyser, will I want to shake his hand instead of clapping him in irons?'

'Do both. But the man's a murderer. Whoever he is, why he's doing what he does, let's not lose sight of that.'

'Be honest, weren't there times during the war you wanted to mete out a little justice?'

For a moment, Reinhardt was tempted to disagree, more for argument's sake than anything else, but he stopped, remembering his own actions during the war and the justice he meted out to the Ustaše. 'I did want that, Markworth,' he whispered. 'And I did do it. And it felt right then. But it wouldn't feel right now.'

'Why not?'

'Because there has to be something to come back to. There has to be a moment when we say "enough". Justice… justice has to mean something to the one being punished. Otherwise…'

Markworth shook his head. 'You sound like Carlsen. Otherwise what…?'

'Otherwise, I don't know. I'm no expert, Markworth. I'm just a man who's survived two wars. Survived them even when I had no right to. Survived them despite myself, or because of others.'

'You say those pilots don't remember what they did. But what they did changed Leyser's life. In an *instant*. How… how does that make someone feel who bears the consequences of an act long after… long after the one who did it has gone or forgotten it?' Markworth's eyes firmed up. 'Think of your son, Reinhardt. Think of all those sons on the Eastern Front. Think of all those instances, all those consequences. Think of all they've left behind.'

'I *do* think. Christ, don't you think I *don't*?' Reinhardt hissed. Friedrich's face flashed in front of him, his plague-ship eyes, and then Reinhardt's colossus, his golem of stones, lurching as it steadied its awful weight, as it searched for him. And it was as if the searchlight pressure of its eyes began to squeeze words out of him, words that began to tumble out, faster almost than he could form them. 'They haven't left it behind. None of us has. I never did. Not in the first war, not in this one. Both you and I have our "*instants*" and behind us, you and I, are a long stream of "*consequences*". Consequences we know about. Even more we don't. We're no different, you and I. We're surrounded by consequences. Every bloody man in this city who wore a uniform left a stream of consequences behind him. Every woman since its fall bears the consequences. I look east, and there's a million Poles and God knows how many million Russians, and they all bear *consequences*. I look west, and there's a million Frenchmen. I look south, and there's a million Yugoslavs and a million Czechs. I look around and I see no Jews. Consequences, Markworth. Every *fucking* place you look.'

Markworth leaned back, as if he cringed away from Reinhardt's ferocity, and a clinical part of Reinhardt's mind noted it was the first real reaction he had ever elicited from the man. But then Markworth leaned back in, pushing his way into the storm of Reinhardt's words.

'So, Reinhardt? What does it all mean?'

'I don't know, Markworth. I don't know. I'm a man with a lot of impressions, but precious few answers. I never was much good at those. And I never was much good at boiling the complicated down to the simple. I left that to the idiots in brown and black and the morons who stuck their hands in the air with all the others, and haven't I paid the price of *that* particular consequence since?' he asked, a whip within his own words. 'But the simple says "who sows the wind, reaps the whirlwind". Right? Something like that? But in that case, where and when does it ever end? Something happened to Leyser. But something happened to nearly everyone around us. Something happened to people everywhere we went. Imagine… imagine what would happen if everyone sought to act on that.'

'You mean it has to end?'

'It has to end. And I don't mean we have to draw a line under the past. Walk away and forget. Hang a few high, and let the rest hunker down low. I don't mean that at all. But the world fell into chaos for six years. What happened during those times…' Reinhardt shook his head, the words beginning to dry up. 'When I was in Sarajevo, at the end of the war, when I took apart that ratline, someone asked me what good it was. What good was it to act when it was only a small part of the whole you were acting against?'

'And?' Reinhardt did not realise he had stopped talking until Markworth prompted him.

'And I said that you could only act against what you saw. Well, now I see someone killing. For whatever reason. Maybe they're good ones. Maybe Leyser thinks he will never get justice if he does not serve it himself. But he needs to be stopped. Otherwise…'

'Otherwise, where does it end?' Markworth said quietly. Both of them spotted Collingridge making his way back through the crowd. 'I'm sorry, Reinhardt,' Markworth said. 'I didn't mean… didn't mean to get so personal. But sometimes I think I'd swap my suit and hat for a tank and just… ride over everything.'

'Look, it's fine.'

'No, it's not. I'm sorry. These things… God, we need another couple of molles to get anywhere near the truths we're looking for.'

'When this is over, I will take you up on that,' Reinhardt smiled.

'Now's the time, Markworth, my friend, if you want a lift,' Collingridge called out impatiently as he came back to the table, scooping up his matches and cigarettes. 'And Reinhardt.' Collingridge switched suddenly back to English. *'Take a page out of the Skokov playbook, why don't you? It's the page marked Keep Me Informed.'*

Reinhardt rode the U-Bahn home in silence. He kept his head down but his eyes open, giving his watchers – any of them – a chance to come out and speak with him, but no one did. He lingered in the damp fug of the platform at Hallesches Tor, but no one approached him, and no one approached him on the ride south, nor at Paradestrasse but, he found as he opened the door to Meissner's house, he need not have worried.

There was already a welcome committee waiting for him.

44

Brauer was there, together with Friedrich and Mrs Meissner. Heads rose as he came in. Friedrich smiled when he saw Reinhardt, and he allowed himself to be folded stiffly into his father's embrace.

'I was worried,' Friedrich said simply. Reinhardt said nothing and they stood by the kitchen table, his arm around his son's shoulders. Mrs Meissner put a cup of tea in front of him.

'This is quite the gathering,' Reinhardt said, looking around the faces. 'Is there an order to any news, or is it ladies first?' he asked, looking at Meissner.

She placed an envelope on the table in front of him. 'For you. It was delivered today by a Mrs Dommes. Quite a formidable woman.'

There was a single sheet of paper in the envelope, filled with writing in an elegant, cursive script. Reinhardt flipped the page over to read whom it was from, his eyes shooting up. 'It's from Bochmann!' He ran his gaze quickly over the letter, then put it aside. 'Rudi. Tell me how you got on.'

'Well, the first thing is, don't plan any weekend getaways in Potsdam. The place is a mess. Blown to pieces, most of it. And the municipal records with it. Sorry, Gregor. There's nothing left. But,' he said, with a flourish, 'be not downhearted, my friend. For your good friend, Rudolph Brauer, perseveres in the face of adversity. I sniffed around a bit, and thought to myself, if Leyser's from Potsdam where's a young lad like that going to go to school? There's only really the one. The Realgymnasium. The place where all the little royals went, right? So off I went, and managed to get directions to the former headmaster, who's a real old fossil, I can tell you. Still, a pack of Luckies'll go a long way, right? Right. We had a bit of a chat, and I ask him about the good old days and sure enough, I bring the conversation around to boys he knew, and did he remember little Marius Leyser?

'And would you believe, he did! Little Marius was there from 1921 to 1923. A nice boy, the head remembered. He excelled at sports. And at English. Apparently.'

'English?' Reinhardt repeated. Brauer nodded. 'No indication what the family was doing there?'

'Oh yes,' Brauer said. 'Didn't I say? The head told me the father was some sort of businessman. A very affluent one. Would've had to have been to have a place down there, even if the royals had fallen on hard times and Potsdam was no longer what it was. No, here's the clincher. The dad was a businessman, but the mother was English.'

'Leyser's mother was *English*?' Brandenburgers, Reinhardt thought. Skilled in languages. And here was Leyser with an English mother…

'Some kind of minor aristocrat or landed gentry. The headmaster couldn't remember. They married before the First World War, and she stayed by his side throughout.'

'Go on.'

'The family packs up and leaves Potsdam in 1923 for Berlin. The head thought they'd gone to Lichterfelde. I sniffed around a bit more in Potsdam, but there was nothing more to find. So off I go, back into the city, and into the American Sector. But it's pretty much the same story. Records are a mess in the Lichterfelde town hall. Bombed out, and what's not bombed and burned, the firemen doused. Anyway, long story short, and a pack of Luckies lighter, someone suggests I have a look at the municipal cadastre records. They weren't in the main building, so they might've survived, and they had. A few Luckies lighter, and I find that the Leysers bought themselves a place in Lichterfeld-East, on Sedanstrasse. Place looking over the park.'

'Christ, that's not all that far from Gothaerstrasse,' Reinhardt breathed.

'I know, right? You've been suspecting the Brits, but let's face it, this Leyser has been misbehaving quite a bit in the Amis' sector too. Anyway, I had a look. The place was bombed out. It's a wreck. But someone's spending time there. Most of the place is bashed up, and the roof's full of holes, but there are a couple of rooms inside that are locked, and one of the locks looks newish. I didn't touch anything, and I'm pretty sure the door with the new lock was rigged. Maybe not to blow, but rigged so someone'd know someone had been snooping. And round the back, on a rubble slide, I found rubbish. Bits and pieces. Tins, CARE packages, a stub of candle. Someone's there, I reckon.'

'This makes no sense,' Reinhardt muttered. 'If Leyser's working for the British, what's he doing… *lurking*… in his old family place in Lichterfelde and living off CARE packages?'

'Time can do funny things, Father,' Friedrich murmured. His head was down, his eyes on his hands where they moved against each other. He glanced up, and Reinhardt flinched to see his eyes had clouded up again, that plague-ship rumour ghosting behind them. 'It brought both of us back to where we lived with Mother.'

Reinhardt gave a tight smile, clasping his hand around the back of Friedrich's neck. He thought of the way Leyser had trailed him around Berlin – a tramp pushing a handcart – and realised Leyser was doing more than just haunting his old home. He was blending in, as he was supposed to. BOALT was supposed to surreptitiously observe German reactions to the Occupation. What better way to do it than as one of the occupied themselves, squatting in a ruin. Reinhardt glanced at Brauer, but his old friend shook his head.

'That's it from me, Gregor.'

'That's more than enough, Rudi. Thank you.' Reinhardt stroked his tongue through the gap in his teeth, a thrill of nervousness running through him. 'There's one more thing, Rudi. Now that I think of it. Do you think you could get back to Potsdam one more time? Here's what I'm thinking…'

Later, in the night, Reinhardt rolled from his bed where he had not slept. He sat there a while, his back curved as his head hung down, straining at his neck. He went downstairs quietly, sat at the kitchen table under the bleached glow of the light, and folded open the papers he had.

He reread Markworth's report, dry prose in English, into the unexplained deaths of Prellberg and Lütjens, found dead on a stretch of wasteland behind a barracks. They were never classed as murder, there being no evidence and the men seemed to have fought together. No one had been found for the deaths, much less fingered. The report did not mention the possibility of the deaths having been murder. That would have made the murders an inside job. But perhaps the absence of such an accusation spoke louder than inclusion would. The German police had been notified, Reinhardt knew. Mrs Dommes had inquired, and there had been no report of a murder, only of two deaths put down as accidental.

He flattened Bochmann's letter out on the table and read it again.

Inspector – if you are reading this, it means that the worst I feared is coming to pass. I have not been completely open or honest with you, but believe me when I say that my desire to protect our association from your intrusion was not the same as any attempt to cover up for the murders of my comrades even if, to you, it may seem one and the same.

One day last year, in late July, a man came to me. This man did not say who he was or whom he represented. Although he was fluent in German, he was with the Allies. With the British, we suspected, because of the way he talked, and what he said. The man sympathised with the plight of Germany, with Germans, with German soldiers. The man said they had to avoid the past, of a situation where Germany was left humiliated, beaten and downtrodden, left revanchist and embittered. The man said that Germans like us had friends among the Allies. That their friends needed to know the tenor of feeling in Germany, that they needed to know what was the mood and spirit among Germans, especially Germans of the calibre of the traditional soldier class.

The man identified himself as Leyser, and he said the Allies – meaning the Western Allies – would look away if von Vollmer and I decided to begin trying to organise things among veterans. He hinted, rather than said outright, that other agents like himself were working elsewhere. He talked to us of our war, the war in the air, in words guaranteed to stir our emotions. And what of the pilots now, Leyser asked? Those knights of the air, how are they adapting to life on the ground, their wings clipped? Summon them, Leyser said. Summon them quietly. Take their measure. Gather information. Bring them together, finally, and speak to them of the future, that it will not always be like this for them, that one day their sacrifices will be remembered, and they will have an honourable place in German society once more. Not only that, Leyser said, but our rights would be returned and, the most alluring of all, the day might still come when Germans would stand with the Western Allies against the Soviet threat.

Leyser was a persuasive man, of middle age. His hair and moustache were dark. He was small, intense, reclusive and secretive, but with charm. He gave von Vollmer and me suggestions, but left us to our own devices, and so the two of us began to work to find all those who had served together. We kept Leyser informed, meeting him from time to time, but more often posting messages to a particular address. If we needed him, which once we did, having run into trouble with the French authorities who had begun to suspect our activities, we could write to him at the same address. A day later, two at most, he would appear, and invariably our problems would disappear.

I now realise that Leyser was none other than the Brandenburger my squadron almost killed back in North Africa. I never met the man, and if I knew his name, I had forgotten it, but I remember the incident now. What you said triggered my memory. Leyser has, somehow, returned from the dead within whose ranks we assumed he stood.

You have a copy of the association's records. I beseech you to use it with care and tact. The men in it are guilty of nothing more than a desire for solidarity, and those who may have been guilty of something more, Leyser has taken care of in his own way. I include as well the address we used to contact Leyser at. I do not know how useful it will be, now, but it is the only way I know of getting in touch with him.

For myself, I must try to leave Berlin, and I ask you not to look for me. I have done nothing wrong, other than to try and help my fellow comrades.

Yours most sincerely,
Heinrich Bochmann

The address was none other than that of the house in Sedanstrasse that Brauer had found. Reinhardt sat there a long while at the table, thinking, remembering, playing words and conversations over and over in his mind. Impressions. Connections. New and old. Friedrich breathed heavily in the other room. Reinhardt's thoughts refined themselves as he listened to his son sleeping, paring themselves down, becoming options, avenues for action, choices that were hard, others that might be easier.

There was so much uncertainty left in this case, but he felt a narrowing of options and possibilities. There was a gamble to be played, a careful one. Because there were questions of right and wrong at stake, but there was something else.

Something deeper, more primal.

What a family should do for itself.

What a father owed to his son.

The sun was barely up as he left the house, just a banked fire across the eastern horizon that flushed the tops of the steepled clouds above Berlin. He made his way to Neukölln, to the apartment where it had all begun. The building was quiet, only a murmur of voices on the second floor as a mother hushed a crying child. Noell's apartment was as he had seen it last, only a few days ago. He walked through it, stopping in the kitchen to look at the sink and the one tap, as he remembered. The cloth was still there, caked dry where it was folded over the curve of the pipe.

He stood in the apartment some time. He felt lonely, and he felt absurd, and he felt scared. He left, walking back down, past Ochs's rooms and across the street into the ruins opposite. He found a piece of masonry to sit upon, laid a few cigarettes on what was left of a mantelpiece, and sat facing the corner, smoking, waiting. A soft scuffle announced them, a foot dragging across dust or rubble. Someone breathed not far away, another just behind him. Reinhardt's back prickled, the skin of his neck seeming to crinkle from the pressure of unseen eyes, but he forced himself to stay still, to not turn around from his corner. Then the breathing was gone, the shuffle of little feet, too, but he sensed he was not alone. He finished his cigarette, twisting the butt into a piled drift of litter.

'What d'you want, bull?'

'Hello, Leena. I want to thank you and your boys for what you did for me. It was very useful.'

There was silence. 'You're welcome,' Leena said, after a while.

'Can I ask for your help again, Leena?' Reinhardt took the silence for assent. 'I need to find that man. The one who should be wearing black. Can you find him for me again, do you think?'

'What d'you want with him?'

'I need to take care of him once and for all. So he can't hurt you anymore.'

The silence was longer this time, so long, he thought they had left. He strained his ears to hear something, anything, catching only the hollow scrape of the wind through the ruins until he felt her back, again.

'You promise to put him away?'

'I promise, Leena.'

'We know where he is, bull. We'll take you to him.'

There was no one in Ganz's office with him when Reinhardt knocked and went in, ostensibly to deliver his daily progress report. Ganz looked up from some paperwork, his pudgy face lit from beneath by a small table lamp. The long curve of his moustache glittered as he blinked, his eyes yellow and watery, and Reinhardt was reminded, again, of how old Ganz was.

'So, what do you have to say for yourself today, Reinhardt?' Ganz asked, his head already back down at what he was doing as Reinhardt walked across his narrow office.

'You and I have never liked each other, Ganz, that's no secret.' Ganz's eyes flickered up from his desk at Reinhardt's opening. 'Right from the beginning. I thought you were one of those heavy-handed old timers. You were free with your fists and stick when you were in Vice. Fingers in half the pies in Berlin, but you got your man more often than not, and then you turned into a heavy-hander for the Nazis before retiring.'

Ganz leaned back in his chair and gave a soft belch. 'Well, this conversation started on a light footing.'

'I need to tell you something about my investigation. I'm going out on a limb with you, but I think it's worth it. The Allies have their own games to play in our affairs. This investigation's no different. The other day, when Whelan and Markworth were hauling me over the coals after von Vollmer complained to them, I got the feeling you stood up for me. Or at least you stood up for some kind of integrity in what we're trying to do. That we can come out of this with some sense of achievement.'

'"We" as in "we Germans", Reinhardt?' Ganz seemed amused.

'If you wish.'

'I'm never quite sure if you *are* a German, Reinhardt, or if you even think you are one yourself. So what exactly is it you're trying to say?'

'I'm appealing to a sense of pride in you, Ganz.'

'I'd have thought you'd do better to appeal to my sense of opportunity.'

'That, too.' Reinhardt swallowed, tongue stroking the gap in his teeth. 'But you keep saying how frustrated you are with the police of today. And you've told me several times that' – Reinhardt stopped, always embarrassed to speak of himself – 'that I get my man, more often than not too.'

'I'm listening.'

'We both know we owe our positions here to the occupiers. The Americans put me back on the force. They found you here already, but you must be doing something right because they let you stay. I need to know, Ganz, what your relationship is to the Allies.'

'Why's that so important?'

'Was it you who told them about Carlsen? I've always wondered how it was they got hold of that information so fast.'

'Get to the point, Reinhardt.'

'I need to play them a tricky hand, Ganz. I want at least to take a stab at getting my man, and getting him in front of German justice instead of Allied expediency.'

'Perhaps I'm a man of integrity, Reinhardt. Or do you hold the conceit that you are the only such man left on the force? In Berlin, perhaps? Possibly in all of Germany?' Reinhardt said nothing. 'Did you know, when the Ivans took Berlin, they uprooted the force. Changed nearly every man. Thousands and thousands of new coppers. Half of them didn't know their arses from their elbows. And did you know that within a few months, before the Amis and the Brits arrived, most of those thousands had gone? Nearly twelve thousand cops out of a force of about fifteen thousand. Gone. Retired. Scarpered. Buggered off. What does that tell you about the force? What does that tell you about the state of the city and the way its occupiers treated it?'

If Ganz wanted an answer from Reinhardt, he gave no sign, only ploughing on. 'Now, what I thought when the Ivans came looking for me after they took the city, that's my business. Or maybe I went looking for them. Maybe I took a look at the state of the city and thought I ought to do something about it. Maybe I was just bored. You never liked me? Well, I never liked you either. You were always a crusader for something or other. No one in Vice liked you. But then, there weren't many of us in Vice who had much time for you lot in the murder squad. But I will say this for you, Reinhardt; you're a good policeman, and a better detective. Most of what I've got to work with now as cops are dumber than a basket of bread. You tell me you are closing in on your man, I believe it. You say you need my help, I say… you can trust me. As far as you can throw me.' Ganz leaned back in his chair, clasping his hands behind his head as if relaxing, but there was a challenge in his eyes. 'And I say if you want to pull the wool over the Allies' eyes, you'd better make it a good effort. Because if it goes wrong, you know that I'll feed you to them, a piece at a time, if it'll save me and assuage them. If I'm one thing, Reinhardt, I'm a survivor.'

'Noell had a brother?' Collingridge's face darkened, flattened, lightened in quick succession. 'A *brother?* Reinhardt. You… *you goddam sonofabitch!* You've been keeping secrets? From your friends? *You krafty Kraut, you!*'

'It seemed the right thing to do,' Reinhardt answered, relieved.

'So you really think this'll work, Reinhardt?' Collingridge asked, as he lit cigarettes for them both.

'It must. There's a mole in the police, feeding information to the Soviets…'

'A mole? Really? Throw a rock. In any direction. You'll hit one.'

'And we have to be careful with the British,' Reinhardt continued. 'Leyser is working for them. They're bound up in this. My guess is Leyser's identity will embarrass them. They're going to want to cover things up, or at least control what comes out, like BOALT.'

Collingridge grunted. 'BOALT. That Skokov's got some pretty good contacts. I didn't know anything about it.'

Collingridge fell silent, but as much as Reinhardt still liked him, he was not duped by Collingridge's offer of help. He knew the Americans would get something out of this.

'Ganz is one of yours, isn't he?'

The American said nothing, pinching a shred of tobacco off his lip. He nodded, eventually. 'Sort of. The Soviets dragged him out of retirement. We left him there. They don't seem to know that back before the war, after he retired he became a sort of private investigator. He had good contacts. He did some work for some American companies in the late 1930s. Good work, actually. He reached out to us when we arrived in Berlin.'

'To let you know he was willing to keep playing both sides. It's what he does best.'

Collingridge shrugged. 'To each his own, Reinhardt. I don't talk to him much, if that helps, and when he does talk, he talks to my boss. For all his… his… *hard-ass exterior*,' Collingridge said, stumbling into English when his German would not suffice, 'he's not that bad. He's got his own thing going, I don't deny it. We can't all be broken angels like you.'

Reinhardt's chin bunched as his tongue stole into the gap in his teeth. 'I suppose I deserved that. Thank you, in any case, for agreeing to help me.'

'This works, you're going to be even more unpopular than you are now.'

'After this, I think I'm finished in Berlin's police,' Reinhardt murmured. 'I'm all done, unless you find me somewhere else. Some cushy job in the American Zone, somewhere. No?' Reinhardt smiled to take the sting out of his mockery.

'God, Reinhardt, you can be a bit dreary at times. Just… don't get too far ahead of yourself, all right?'

'I need to be a father, again, David. I don't think I can do that here, and I don't think I can do it the right way. I can't… I need to trust my son. I need to trust that he'll learn to trust me. Otherwise… otherwise, he's just another suspect I've got to break down. But he's not a suspect,' he whispered, twisting out his cigarette. 'He's my son.'

45

Wednesday

Kausch and his men were in a tenement in Spandau, funnily enough just over the river from von Vollmer's factory. Two of Leena's boys emerged out of the dark to point at the building the men were occupying, then at a dim crosshatch of light, low at street level.

'Down there, bull,' one of the boys whispered. 'Little beer cellar.'

'You should ask to see the back room,' the other one said, his voice quivering across adolescence. 'Got some stuff in there from the old days. All red and black and brown, if you know what I mean.'

Reinhardt shook cigarettes into their little hands. Grubby fingers wrapped around them.

'We'll be watching, bull,' the adolescent whispered, moonlight glinting across a shock of blond hair, and then they were gone.

The cellar was crowded, bowed backs and shoulders arcing across the low-ceiled space. Only a few faces turned his way, but most of those were from a group that held tight together across the other side of the cellar. They watched him across the bar, turning, tracking, tilting up as he came to stand by their table. Kausch looked at him silently, then gestured at one of his men. The man rose, slipping through the crowd and outside. Another rose and, beneath the guise of welcoming him to the party, frisked him for weapons. Noell was there, the light shining on the top of his head through his thinning hair.

'I'm alone. And unarmed.'

'You will forgive me if I don't take your word for it,' Kausch replied. 'How did you find us?'

'I've found the man who murdered Noell's brother.'

'Where?' Noell demanded.

Kausch cut him off. 'I'd rather know how you found me, but well done.'

'You said you wanted to know.'

'I do. I didn't think you'd walk right in and spit it out.'

Reinhardt swallowed back his fear, pulling his tongue from the gap in his teeth. 'I want you to leave me alone. I want you to leave my son alone. If I give you this man, will you do that?'

'We might.' Kausch exchanged looks with his men. One or two of them nodded.

'We need to go now, then. The man is still at large, but the police are closing in around him. By tomorrow, they'll have him. If you want him, it's now.'

'We're not moving that fast, Reinhardt,' Kausch said. 'Sit. Tell us more. Who and where, for starters.'

'What does it matter?' Noell asked. Kausch raised a placatory hand, but his eyes never left Reinhardt.

'There's really no time,' Reinhardt said, an anxious tremor to his voice. 'It's in Lichterfelde. The man's staying in a ruined house there. His name's Leyser,' he said, looking at Noell. 'He was a Brandenburger. Your squadron destroyed his unit in the desert, in October 1942, and now he wants revenge.'

'Noell?' Kausch asked, looking at the ex-pilot.

'A *Brandenburger*?' one of Kausch's men breathed.

'I don't… I don't know… anything about it. I don't know…' But his eyes betrayed him, a shifting focus, inward, backward, and then a sudden flare of remembrance. Reinhardt saw it, the past being dragged up into the present. 'No,' Noell breathed. 'No.'

'What happened?' Kausch asked.

'It was a friendly fire incident,' Reinhardt answered. 'Noell's squadron destroyed Leyser's unit. He was the only survivor. Afterwards, they tried to kill him in hospital.'

'Shit, Noell,' one of Kausch's men muttered, slapping him on the shoulder. 'I'd never have thought you had that in you.'

'No!' Noell said again, louder. His eyes were fixed on Reinhardt. 'Are you telling me my brother was killed, taken for me, because of a bloody mistake we made years ago in the fucking *desert?*' The last word ended on a strangled croak as Kausch's men yanked him back into his seat from where he had arisen, his voice climbing. Heads turned, then turned back to their beers, their conversations. Kausch leaned close to several of his men and they left. He indicated to Reinhardt to sit, and they waited, in silence, until Kausch nodded. Then they walked out onto the street.

'Reinhardt, just so we are clear,' Kausch said, standing in the dark as his men gathered around him. 'We will follow you and seek some measure of justice for our comrade. But not all of us are here. We have not survived this long by being careless. Some of us will survive if anything goes wrong. But you will not. Do we understand each other?'

The house on Sedanstrasse showed no lights. There were few anywhere in the neighbourhood, and almost no noise. There was only a sickle of moon, but even that light was dim and dulled by a wash in the air, like a light covering of fog across the city.

The group stood in the shadows of the park. Reinhardt felt them straining like leashed dogs against the commands Kausch had put on them. Finally seeming to make up his mind, Kausch clamped his fist like a manacle around Reinhardt's arm, keeping him close, reminding him of his vulnerability.

'Reinhardt. Anything happens, I'll make sure you go first. Lead the way.'

There was a way into the building that Brauer had shown him. Down the side there was a low door for a coal chute. Brauer had told him he had left it ajar, and Reinhardt breathed silent thanks it still was. He risked a quick few seconds of light from his flashlight to show Kausch and his men, then he slipped inside and slithered down the chute on his backside.

The others came down one by one, and when all were gathered, he led the way across the basement, his flashlight fanning a clear path for them around the debris over to a door that was partly choked shut but left enough room to squeeze through.

'Upstairs into a servant's hall,' Reinhardt whispered. 'Then the servants' stairs up to the first floor. The stairs are stone, in good condition.'

They moved quietly, but even moving quietly, such a group could not move soundlessly. Breathing echoed up the stairs, the slide and scuff of feet, the chink of stone as someone kicked a piece of masonry, but they made it to the first floor without any disturbance.

'Through here, it gets more difficult. We need to cross into the main house now. It's badly damaged, but there's a gallery that's largely intact. It's of wood and will make noise, so we should cross carefully one by one. The room where Leyser is hiding is just on the other side.'

Reinhardt opened the door, moonlight spilling in as he did. The house here had been blown open, and the sky was visible through a checkerboard of roof beams, some broken and some whole. Sound seemed to lift and echo through the greater spaces that made up the front of the house. A double staircase spiralled up from the invisible floor below, arching dimly through the moonlight. Kausch motioned to Reinhardt, and he stepped out across the gallery. Reinhardt moved slowly, keeping to the edge of the gallery where it met the wall, Kausch's hand still banded around his arm. The wood creaked softly beneath their weight. About halfway across, a portion of the gallery had been destroyed, railing and floor chewed away, and they slid past the gap with their backs to the wall. Once across they moved farther into the darkness on the other side.

'We have to move back,' Reinhardt murmured. 'There's not room for all of us. We can wait through here.' He motioned to a room that seemed to mirror the one they had just crossed out of. Kausch pushed him forward, following him in.

There was a metallic click, and a voice came out of the dark.

'Don't move.'

Kausch's hand tightened on Reinhardt's arm. Reinhardt swung the flashlight round and switched it on. Kausch's face screwed up and away, and the light stayed on long enough for Reinhardt to see his head vanish as a hood came down over it. There was the muffled sound of a blow, something heavy and short. Kausch gave a strangled cry, and his grip on Reinhardt's arm was gone, but someone else had him. The collar of his coat was jerked back and down, and a hand clamped itself over his mouth. He panicked, a vision of the pilots and what must have been their terrified last moments as their chests heaved in search for air.

'Quiet!' someone hissed in his ear. The hand released its grip on his mouth, each finger lessening its pressure. 'Call them in,' his captor whispered, pushing him towards the door. 'Light the gallery for them.'

Reinhardt stood in the door and shone his flashlight back across, waving it over the floor where it had caved away.

'Come!' he called softly. 'One by one.'

They came across, one by one, Reinhardt standing back to let each one pass into the room. For each one, there was a sudden blow, the worse for being unexpected, muffled grunts, the drag of cloth. Reinhardt's fear rose and rose, gyring up within him, until there was only Noell left, and one more of Kausch's men. As they came up, Reinhardt angled himself so that Kausch's man passed into the room first. Noell heard the blow being struck, the slump of a body, and he tensed.

'What…?' was all he managed as Reinhardt hooked one of Noell's feet out from under him, shoving him to the floor. The breath whooshed out of the pilot as he fell, and Reinhardt ground his hand into Noell's neck.

'Keep still,' he hissed.

He waited, staring into the maw of the room. Light flared suddenly. Flashlights, sweeping round the room. The shapes of men lying across the floor, a man rolling slowly, a knee coming up. Someone groaned. A shape cut across the light, and a man came to stand in the doorway, staring down at Reinhardt. He looked up, and Reinhardt could not help the quick clench that grabbed his innards at the sight of the man. The height and breadth of him, clothes pulled taut across the tubular expanse of his limbs, a face dark as blackened wood staring down at him, and all Reinhardt could see of his eyes was a wet glitter, high up.

'*Don't be scaring the natives, Hillock,*' came a voice.

The huge man blinked, and the face split in a grin. '*No, sir, we wouldn't be wantin' that none.*'

The Negro – for Reinhardt saw the man was black – stepped aside, and Collingridge appeared from behind him. Collingridge grinned down at Reinhardt, then up at the Negro.

'You've met Hillock, then. That's not his real name, but he's big enough for one, ain't he? And the right kind of man for work in the dark! *Well done, Hillock. Go and help the others, please.*'

The huge man turned back inside, back into the quiver of light and a rising murmur of voices, and Reinhardt saw Ganz was there too. Collingridge knelt down next to Reinhardt. Noell squirmed on the floor, and Reinhardt released his hold on him. The ex-pilot scrabbled to his knees, poised as if to run, but another American soldier, another Negro, stepped out of the room and blocked his way back across the gallery. Someone protested in the room, and a blow was struck. Voices rose. 'Excuse me a moment, Reinhardt,' Collingridge said.

'Bloody hell, Reinhardt,' Ganz breathed. He did not seem to know which way to look. 'I don't know what to make of half of this.'

'Noell,' Reinhardt spoke softly into Noell's ear, ignoring Ganz. 'There's a way to make this easier. You need to tell me where those files are. Those files from the unit. The test unit. You told me of them. The *files*, Noell. Where are they?'

'What are you talking about?'

'The files, Noell. The *files*. You told me they were hidden at the end of the war. Where did you hide them?'

The noise in the room was rising, German and American voices clashing and clamouring against each other.

Noell's face twisted up at him, the flashlights from the room pushing shadows back and forth across his face. 'What… what are you *doing*?'

'Trying to save us both. The *files*, Noell. Christ, it's the best deal you're going to get.'

'They're going to bury you, Noell, or hand you over to the Ivans,' said Ganz. Reinhardt blinked a glance at him. He did not know if Ganz was playing his own game or not, but it was a welcome line.

'The Ivans? Why the…'

'Reinhardt!' Collingridge called. The American guard Collingridge had left shifted closer.

'Goddamn it, Noell. Just…' The frustration was tight, as if something was breaking through, inside. Like that feeling, the one he seemed to have more and more, of something coming up through the earth, something old and hoary, a darker nature, mud-smeared and with the mad rolling eyes of an animal gone wild.

'Hey, you. Y'all take it easy, now,' the American called out.

'Reinhardt! Stop it!' Ganz gripped Reinhardt's shoulders.

Reinhardt had his hands clamped around Noell's head. He had his thumbs in the man's eyes, and he had not even known it. He pushed Noell down and away, repulsed by his own lack of control.

'Reinhardt!' Collingridge called, again.

'Oh, God, oh…' Noell moaned as he curled away from Reinhardt.

'The *files*.'

'Yes. God. The files. The fi – Theo said he hid them… he hid them in the cellars… in the cellars of a factory. At Güstrow. Güstrow. Where the airfield was. The unit's airfield. It's near Rostock. It's there. It's all there. That's what he said. That's all I know.'

'Reinhardt! For fuck's sake, will you get in here?'

The room was a riot of shifting shadows, angles that lengthened and shortened as flashlights were waved around. The air was hot and humid with men's breath. Collingridge was kneeling by Kausch, whose hood he had removed. The Sturmbannführer glared pure hatred at Reinhardt.

'We caught a big one, Reinhardt,' Collingridge said. He waved a piece of paper in Kausch's face, an arrest warrant with a grainy picture of him in SS uniform. 'You sure you want to be making these threats, Sturmbannführer? The Poles would love to talk to you, and the Russkies even more. You might want to think about making me happy so I don't hand you over to them.'

'Be quiet, little man. I warned you, Reinhardt. I warned you.' Kausch's voice dripped venom. 'Not all of us came. In case something like this were to happen. The others have gone to your house, you traitorous piece of shit, because I knew you were not to be trusted. They've gone to your house, and by this time, they'll have killed your harlot landlady, and they'll have gutted your craven son, and they'll have taken care of that malodorous pile of rags you call a best friend. I warned you. I warned you. Treachery never pays, Reinhardt.'

Reinhardt and Collingridge exchanged glances. The American was tight around the eyes. 'Can you get me there? Can you get me home?'

Collingridge nodded. 'I'll drive you. Chief Inspector,' he said to Ganz, 'my men will secure these prisoners. We proceed as agreed with Noell. My men will help you, but he is not my concern. He's yours and Reinhardt's, so make your preparations accordingly. *Hillock! Choose out two more men. You're with us.*' Collingridge paused, then tossed a pistol at Reinhardt. 'Let's move.'

Collingridge drove them fast across Berlin, through the darkened streets, but Reinhardt's thoughts outpaced the Jeep's speed, outpaced the feeble glow of its headlights as they flickered the road into view ahead.

Arriving at Mrs Meissner's house, Reinhardt made to run up the short pathway, but Hillock stopped him dead with one hand on his shoulder, the other holding a Thompson submachine gun by its grip. It looked like a toy in his hand as he pointed it at the house, at the door where it hung ajar. Collingridge nodded Hillock and the other men ahead. Reinhardt crowded close behind Hillock's vast bulk, the American pistol an unfamiliar weight in his hand.

At the door, Hillock pushed it open with the Thompson, peering inside. Reinhardt, looking past him into the darkened house, saw a body in the hallway. He could not tell who it was.

'Friedrich?' he called. 'Rudi?'

Something moved in the kitchen and the light over the table came on. A man stepped into view. Reinhardt did not know who it was. The man stared down the hallway at them. He had a gun in his hand. A British Sten, Reinhardt saw.

'*Sir. I think they're here*,' the man called. In English.

Another man stepped into view, carrying a Sten, then a third. He was blocky and compact, and walked with a tight economy of movement as he limped down the hall, stepping over the body.

'Sorry about the mess,' Markworth said. Then he grinned.

'Oh, God,' Reinhardt breathed, tension flowing out of him. 'Oh, God.'

'He's got nothing to do with it. You can thank Sergeants Dudgeon and Northam,' he said, glancing at the other two men. They were flat-faced, expressionless men, cheeks smeared black and their hair hidden under tight-fitting woollen caps. 'Royal Marine Commandos. Handy chaps to have around. There's a couple more Nazis in the garden. One of them might even still be alive.'

'You did it,' Reinhardt breathed. He felt himself sinking and was not surprised to find himself slumped against the wall. 'You did it.'

'Of course I did it, Reinhardt. Of course I did. Why would I not?'

'Friedrich and Meissner?'

'Upstairs. Safe and sound. They've got Corporal Hilton for company.'

'Thank God. I didn't know… I didn't know if you would really help me. I couldn't trust… I couldn't trust the police, you see. Thank you. Thank you for the life of my son.' There were steps in the hallway, and Friedrich came outside. Reinhardt held out his arm and wrapped it around his son's shoulders. He felt his strength giving out, and he lowered himself shakily to the doorstep, Friedrich sitting next to him.

Markworth clapped his hand on Reinhardt's shoulder. 'It was my pleasure, my friend. A reminder of the good old days, if you like.' Markworth glanced up at Collingridge as the American lit a cigarette. 'You got the others?'

Collingridge nodded. 'Good work, here. I wasn't sure if Reinhardt's gamble would pay off, but it looks like it has. And we got something unexpected. Right, Reinhardt?'

'We got a pilot,' Reinhardt nodded.

'You got a pilot?' Markworth asked.

'One of those that Leyser's been after. You remember Noell? The first victim we found, when we found Carlsen? Turns out he had a brother. A *twin* brother. And he's a pilot.'

'What are you going to do with him?' Markworth asked.

'Have a word,' said Reinhardt, leaning his head back against the doorjamb. 'But we've got nothing on him. Noell's done nothing wrong, so we won't hold him, but I don't think he can really stay in Berlin. We won't be able to protect him, and the Soviets will want him.' He felt Friedrich stiffen against him. 'And Leyser's still around. Even if I don't see how Leyser can get to him, we're no closer to getting him either.'

'You're not going to give Noell to the Soviets, surely?' asked Markworth.

Collingridge shook his head. 'Not till Reinhardt's done with him, and even then, not if we can avoid it. We have a nice little haul of Nazis. It's been a while since we bagged a lot like that. We'll run Kausch and his merry men through CROWCASS, see if any of our side wants them. If not, we'll give Kausch to the Russkies. They'll want him, for sure. That should buy Reinhardt some time.'

'Reinhardt, you know the British are going to want to hear what Noell knows about the British connection. We will need to speak to him at some point. We're clear about that, aren't we?'

Reinhardt looked embarrassed, and it was Collingridge who spoke up. 'Look, Markworth. You'll understand if we want to give the German police some time with Noell. I mean, I understand your concerns, but Reinhardt's got some murders to solve. And as these murders have been occurring mostly in the American Sector, and that's where we caught Noell, the US authorities are happy to back the police on this.'

'Well, well. Are the Americans lining up with the Germans against the Brits then?' Markworth asked. His mouth carried a little smile, and his tone was ironic, but there was a hard glitter in the corner of his eyes.

'Of course you can speak to him,' Reinhardt said. 'We just need to speak to Noell first while his head is straight. Otherwise, you and then the Soviets will just confuse him.'

'I understand. I'm not so sure Whelan will, or any of the others. It's them you'll have to deal with, as I've got to go back to Bad Oeynhausen in the morning.'

'Thank you,' Reinhardt murmured, running a hand over his brow. 'I mean it. Thank you for everything.'

46

Once again, Reinhardt's sleep was broken and ragged. Too many thoughts, too many worries for anything resembling rest or even sleep that gave oblivion. He rose early, dressed mechanically, and went down to the latrine. As was his wont, he smoked a cigarette in the garden afterwards. The sky was a thunderous riot of clouds, their formations towered, banked, and buttressed like a fortress of the gods. The sky was about all he saw of nature these days, he realised, that one trip out to the Soviet Zone the exception, and he treasured those memories of fields and forests, matching them with other, older memories of Bosnia and the wild challenge of its mountains and valleys. Now, what he knew of the changing of the seasons and the year's march, he saw and read in the clouds and it felt wrong, it felt singular, as if a greater story was out there to be read if only the nature of the words could be revealed.

He realised, suddenly, he was not alone. Sergeant Dudgeon was standing statue-still in the corner made by the hedge and house wall. Their eyes met, and Reinhardt nodded to him and the man nodded back, gravely, the only move he made. Reinhardt finished dressing and left the house quietly, past Corporal Hilton, where he stood at the window of Meissner's old study. Outside, he took a couple of steps down the little driveway and Sergeant Northam seemed to coalesce from the early morning shadows, the leather of his jacket creaking softly.

'Going somewhere, sir?'

'I still have a job, Sergeant. I will be fine.'

'We'll keep an eye here the rest of the day, like Lieutenant Markworth asked.'

'I thank you, Sergeant, for my life and the lives of my son and friends.'

'A friend of the Lieutenant's a friend of mine, sir,' Northam said.

The Zoo Station's iron superstructure hung over the platforms like the grid of an immense board game. All the panes of glass that had filled the interstices in the structure were gone, or else they existed only as serrated fragments that caught the light that streamed and pillared through the roof's fretwork. Despite its damage, the station, for all journeys west, was a heaving and bustling hive, the same heaving and bustling hive it had always been, and a thriving black market hub as well.

Reinhardt nursed a cup of what had been sold to him as some kind of ersatz chocolate from one of the little kiosks that had reopened in the station's concourse. Even for Berlin's low standards, it was awful, but it was warm. The station carried the chill of metal and concrete, a chill that sank deep and could only be dislodged by moving around. All he could do was shift his weight from side to side, nursing the pain in his knee and feeling his feet go ever more numb with the cold as the crowds and noise throbbed and ebbed all around him. Farmers bartered jars of drippings or crocks of butter. He saw women selling jewels, someone else selling soap, and a man sold packs of cigarettes from a sack, two toughs flanking him. He knew that over on one of the farther platforms, false papers could be obtained or real ones altered. Children ghosted the crowds, heads and eyes alert for opportunities. Anything and everything was for sale except, it seemed, a way out.

Seeing what he needed, he left the kiosk and walked as quickly as his heavy feet and the crowds would allow to the ticket inspectors who controlled access to the platforms. He pushed through the Berliners who eddied along the line of platforms like forlorn waves upon a desolate shore, past men in cast-off military dress or in black coats with *PW* in faded letters on the backs, past women bundled almost shapeless in disparate layers. Most of them had no tickets, no hope of getting out of the city. The Allies were letting almost no one out anymore, not without special passes or permits, claiming the pressure on their Zones from the millions of Germans expelled from Prussia and from Eastern Europe was too great to allow more immigration. Reinhardt showed his police identification to the ticket officers, feeling the avalanche pressure of hundreds of eyes behind him, and slipped out onto the platforms, walking down past a train idling in wafts of steam to a man standing alone next to an open carriage door.

'I'm surprised you're not taking the plane from RAF Gatow.'

Markworth turned, the slight frown on his face washing away when he recognised Reinhardt.

'Trains give you time to think. And they're useful for observing what's going on in the Soviet Zone.'

'I came to say good-bye. And to thank you again for your help.'

'For my help, think nothing of it. I left word at your station. Someone on General Nares's staff will want to be involved in questioning Noell, then almost certainly some people in Bad Oeynhausen will want to speak with him. I'll have a word with them, see what I can do to give you some time.'

'Thank you. We will need it.'

'Still no sign of Leyser?'

'Nothing. But Leyser has nowhere to go now,' Reinhardt said. 'I wanted to offer you a last thought about him. It may be helpful to you in your inquiries in Bad Oeynhausen.'

'I'm all ears. I'd offer you a last molle to go with it, but I don't think there's either time or place.'

Reinhardt shook a cigarette out, nodding his thanks as Markworth lit it for him, and continued speaking quietly. 'You know we keep wondering at Leyser's state of mind. What he must be trying to say with his gestures. Wondering what must have happened to him to make him do what he has done.'

'I think its justice of some kind,' Markworth said. 'If I learned one thing during the war, it is that justice can be sought for the strangest things, and take the strangest forms.' His eyes met Reinhardt's, and he knew Markworth was thinking of Bosnia and of what Reinhardt had told him he had done with the Ustaše.

'But if it's justice, it's justice for something those being murdered don't even remember. None of the pilots remembers what he did. I'm sure of it. Not unless Leyser reminded them of it just before the end.'

'Maybe that's reason enough for him. Maybe it's enough the murders mean something to *him*.'

'Desert and sea,' Reinhardt murmured around a long pull on his cigarette. Whistles shrilled up and down the platform. People began to step up into the carriages, but Markworth stayed still, listening. 'Sand and water. That's what they symbolise. Desert and sea. Leyser is remembering his… agony… in the desert when he forces sand down the throats of those he murders. But those he murdered, he found, did other things, with other men. Experiments on humans. Experiments in water. Sand and water. Revenge and justice.'

Markworth blinked, nodded. 'I think you may be right,' he said, his words almost lost as whistles blasted anew.

'In Bad Oeynhausen, you need to look for men working on your denazification programmes, or something like that, who might have had access to information like Leyser seems to have had. It must not be a long list.'

'It should not be,' Markworth answered, his eyes alight. He clapped Reinhardt on the shoulder. 'Well done, man!' he exclaimed, waving away an irate platform guard. He pulled himself up into his carriage, leaning heavily on his good leg and angling towards the window, looking down as the train juddered into motion. 'I'll be in touch. Don't finish all this off without me, now, you hear?'

The late daylight did nothing for the ruins of the house on Sedanstrasse, leaving enough of the original construction's elegance to make its damage all the more evident. Reinhardt took the same staircase up to the floor where the Americans had captured Kausch, then followed a sturdy wooden staircase higher, his feet crunching in dust and plaster. The place stank of damp and mould, of wet and charred wood, of sewage and waste, the myriad tangle of odours and scents that a building gave up when it had been blown out and open.

He found the room on the top floor, where Brauer had said to look. He had to worm past a fall of wreckage where roof beams had pitched down into a corridor, splaying themselves like sheaves of wheat, and where the floor was holed like moth-eaten cloth. He walked carefully, watching crumbs and shards of debris clatter down onto the floors below, hearing them crack and bounce like pebbles. The door, when he reached it, was half-hidden behind another beam that lay athwart it, but if he angled himself just right, the passage past it was easy.

The room beyond was a tangled mound of debris. A huge wooden cupboard had been cracked in two, and its contents strewn across the floor. The windows were all smashed, only a couple of panes remained intact, but Reinhardt stood and looked and saw the order that emerged, slowly, as if submitting itself for his inspection. He saw the boards that had been cut to the size of the windows, and that could be locked into place if needed. He saw the metal curve of a lantern winking out from beneath a heap of rags, he saw the bed where it lay propped, as if haphazardly, across a jumble of bricks that were waiting to be stacked to support it. He picked up one of the cupboard doors, and his reflection wobbled and lurched back at him as he steadied it against the wall. Inside the cupboard, beneath a dusty swirl of rags and tattered cloth, he found tinned food, a mess kit, a small cooker and, searching further, a bundle tied with a leather belt. He unwrapped it, laying out on the bed a quilted jacket, of the type a Russian would wear, a shirt and trousers, a flat cap, and a pair of black boots with the leather scarred white.

Inside a packet in one of the jacket's pockets, he found a mix of objects, the significance of which escaped him before he realised he was looking at a kit to disguise oneself. A stick of charcoal, packets of gum that could be used to insert in the mouth and cheeks. A small mirror and set of brushes. A pot of paste of some kind, sticky to the touch. And lastly, in an empty tin of shoe polish, what looked like fuzz or hair, and which was, he realised, a set of fake moustaches.

'There's more.'

Reinhardt had heard the steps, recognised the rhythm, and was not startled when Brauer spoke.

'There's uniforms. All four occupying powers. Weapons. Knives, mostly. Garottes. Clubs. Silent stuff. Like what we used to carry in the trenches, eh?'

'That's in keeping with his training, I suppose.'

'God, this is very far from being nought-eight-fifteen, I can tell you. What must he have been thinking…?'

'I suppose it was a lair, of some kind,' answered Reinhardt, looking up and around, seeing the order amid the disorder.

'And now he's up and running. I wonder where's he gone to ground?'

'If he's as smart as I think he is, he's probably got a dozen places like this across the city.'

'Bit sentimental and risky of him to use his old home then, wouldn't you think?' Brauer speculated, idly tapping his boot against the skirting boards.

'What did you find out in Potsdam?'

Brauer nodded, and from the way his mouth moved, Reinhardt knew the news would be bad, or not what he wanted to hear. 'I found them. Like you said.'

'In the parish records?'

Brauer nodded again. 'The church in Potsdam was damaged, but the records were saved. I found them in the marriage registry. They had a church wedding, as would've been the norm back then.'

'And…?'

'As you suspected.'

Reinhardt tilted his head back. 'Ah, Christ,' he swore, quietly.

'I'm sorry, Gregor,' Brauer said, putting his hand on Reinhardt's shoulder. 'What about Noell?'

'He's told us what he knows. Which is nothing about Leyser.'

'So he's out?'

'He will be soon.'

'*Reinhardt!*'

'I'm coming, Ganz,' Reinhardt called back, distracted by the information Brauer had given him. 'We should go. Are you still with me?'

'Does a timid dog ever get fat? I wouldn't miss it for the world,' Brauer grinned.

Ganz was waiting on the street with a battered car huffing behind him, its engine giving off a reek of charcoal and seemingly on the edge of giving out with every stutter of its motor.

'We need to get moving, Reinhardt,' Ganz said, before stopping and peering more closely at Brauer. 'Good God. Is that Rudi Brauer?'

'Good to see you too, Ganz,' Brauer grinned.

'Dick and bloody Doof,' Ganz muttered, shaking his head, looking at the pair of them. 'Back together for one last show.'

'You've missed our Laurel and Hardy act, then, have you?'

'Like a hole in the head. I'd break out the beers, lads, but you've got problems, Reinhardt. Dommes said you were here.'

'What problems?' Reinhardt asked.

'Your baton's turned up. Covered in Stresemann's brains and whatnot. And I don't doubt it's got your fingerprints all over it.'

'Where? Where was it found?'

'At the Stresemann murder scene. They shoved a bunch of refugees from out east into the place, and the municipal authorities found it. The call came through the Neukölln station. Dommes took it, and she told me.'

'You're sitting on it?'

'For now.'

'What are you going to do?' Brauer asked.

'Now, that's an interesting question, Rudi. Reinhardt knows something of the answer. The easy option – the *survivor's* option – has me bringing you in to Linienstrasse for questioning, and they tend to get a bit nasty with their questioning up in Mitte, as you know. But quite frankly, I find it strange that the two times Stresemann's murder has shown up, it's been to trip you up, Reinhardt. I'm starting to suspect your theories are right. So you've got one shot at wrapping this up, tonight. Because tomorrow I'm going to have to do something about that baton, and getting rid of it's not an option.'

'One night's all we need,' Reinhardt said. He said it with far more confidence than he felt, and suddenly pieces shifted and he watched and felt them, carefully, testing the new shape as he talked. 'You said Linienstrasse. Take me there, instead. I can go straight in the front and out the back. It will look good,' he pressed, raising a hand to Ganz's and Brauer's objections. 'It will help if he thinks I'm in there, and out of his way. It will give him confidence. Otherwise, it's one of the holes in the plan. He needs to know where I am. You know it can help, so let's just do it, and make a show of it.'

Ganz drove, the car hiccupping and wheezing its sorry way through the darkening streets. At a street corner he slowed enough for Brauer to step out into the lines of shadow that cleaved the rubbled frontage of a block of ruins, then pushed on to Linienstrasse. Ganz parked on the narrow street and they waited, timing things for the shift change, and when they saw men beginning to drift into the building and others begin to drift out, he walked Reinhardt through the front entrance of Berlin's main police station, past the curious gaze of the police guard on duty. Inside, Ganz hustled him into the warren of cells along the building's rear, mostly deserted now at this late hour, and then out a small door into Lothringer Strasse.

'Go, quickly. I'll take care of the paperwork. It'll look like you're in here, but it won't hold up forever.'

'You're sure of things?'

'Yes, yes. Noell will be released in about half an hour. Unforgiveable. Really. I will need to have a word with Mrs Dommes about the state of administration. A real clerical balls up. The British will be furious and make a stink. Collingridge knows. He'll stand back and leave things to us. You need to move, *now*, so go.'

No sooner had Ganz closed the door behind him than Reinhardt was walking away fast down the darkened streets, moving quickly, block by shattered block, while the sun set and the ruins rose black and stark before him, as if carved from the bottom of the sky, like cut-out versions of themselves.

He walked until he found the address he needed, a hostel for refugees and displaced people from the east, a place that stank of dilapidation and damp and sewage, a place that belonged thirty years in the past when Berlin's working-class neighbourhoods squatted close around their collective stench and squalor.

Upstairs, in the chill dark of the room that had been marked out, he settled in to wait. He waited, until steps shuffled to a stop outside the door, and it opened, slowly. A man stepped inside. The two of them blinked at each other.

'I made it,' Andreas Noell said.

47

Late as it became, the place was noisy. Men's voices strident and loud, the accents of the east. Music coming from somewhere, the shrill notes of a violin. Children crying, screaming, playing. The noise of feet in the hallway all the time. Somewhere, bedsprings banged rhythmically. He sat in the dark – the room lit only by what light came through the windows, enough of it to coat the hard edges of what little furniture there was – and went over the case in his mind, over and over, as well as this arrangement he had made.

This *trap*, to call it what it was.

The room had two entrances: a door, and a window that gave onto a fire escape that itself dropped down into a narrow refuse-strewn alley. Reinhardt heard noises from outside from time to time, from the alley, but although each one made his nerves stretch taut, somehow he felt that Leyser – if he came – would come through the door, and do so openly. None of the murders showed any sign that the victims had struggled. Reinhardt felt they knew the man they opened the door to. That, or they had no reason to mistrust the type of man who came through it. That they had opened the door to the kind of man they would have expected to have knocked.

An expected guest. A hotel concierge. A policeman.

Or a postman, he thought, remembering the last proper investigation he and Brauer had made under the Nazis. Dresner, the Postman. Who would not open the door to a postman…?

The hours ticked by. The hostel quietened.

The knock at the door was firm. Not too loud. Authoritative. It jolted his heart from its well-worn track, froze him stiff in his seat with his skin feeling as if it had shrunk around him. Noell sat up in a sudden tangle of movement on the bed, saying nothing. The knock came again, and Reinhardt's heart shuddered back into rhythm, and he gestured at Noell to get up. Noell shuffled to sit on the bed. With his vision accustomed to the room's low light, Reinhardt saw Noell looking at the door with wide eyes. He blinked them at Reinhardt, who made an exaggerated nod with his head and hands, pointing at the door.

'Who is it?' Noell called, his voice faking that of a man just woken from sleep.

'Police,' came the muffled response. Reinhardt positioned himself to one side of the door, drawing the .45 Collingridge had given him but forgotten to take back. Noell unlocked the door, then stepped well back into the room. The door opened. There was little light in the hallway, but it carved form from darkness, and Reinhardt slitted his eyes to keep as much of his night vision as he could manage. A man came in, sculpted by shadow, a dense, compact man in a long coat and a hat pulled low over his brow. He moved smoothly, easily, his hands held at his sides.

'Who are you?' quavered Noell. 'What do you want?'

'I am Leyser.'

Without looking, the man pushed the door shut. There was a moment of stillness, then Leyser was moving, slashing into Noell, who cried out as he crashed backward. Leyser followed, seeming to flow over the floor, a blotch of darkness against the dimness of the room. Reinhardt waited, almost frozen with fear. Waiting for the next act in this awful drama. Waiting, hearing, as Leyser hauled a gagging Noell up onto the bed. The pilot was speechless, wheezing for breath and powerless to stop his hands being dragged up and tied to the bedframe.

'*STOP!*' Reinhardt cried. He thumbed back the hammer on the .45, the sound slithering mechanically across the room. Leyser froze, whirling in surprise. Reinhardt watched his form spring off the bed, lowering himself into a fighter's stance.

Reinhardt switched on a flashlight, aiming it square at Leyser. The light arrowed across the darkened room, lurched, steadied on his face. It bunched up, wrinkled into harsh incisions of light and shadow, and Leyser ducked down, showing the crown of his head.

'Look at me. Look at me, Leyser. Look at me. Or I will shoot you, and you will never have your story told.'

Leyser straightened slowly. He seemed to unfurl, little by little. His face came into view, etched, whittled from the darkness. Reinhardt needed more light, and he sidled over to the door and the light switch. The room's bulb flickered on, steadied, lighting across a blunt expanse of forehead. A slim nose. The dark line of a moustache. It was a forgettable face, and the differences were hard to see, what Reinhardt knew and what he saw overlaying each other, quivering like a rung bell. They were subtle. The cheeks bunched out and the skin darkened. The eyebrows thicker. The chin pushed forward. But there was no doubt.

'Take off the moustache.'

The man smiled, then peeled the moustache away from his lip, leaving a line that glistened and then faded.

'The cheeks.'

The man dug a finger into each cheek and pushed and spat out wads of gum. The face fell in, thinned, became something else.

Someone else.

It was Markworth.

'Don't move,' Reinhardt said, keeping his voice steady with an effort. Markworth was tense, coiled, ready to run. 'Kneel down. Kneel down with your hands beneath your knees. Do it.'

Markworth moved slowly, kneeling, his eyes never leaving Reinhardt's, who was terrified by the flat, implacable weight of them and the danger he represented.

'Noell? Noell are you all right?' Noell lay slumped half-on, half-off the bed, moaning as he clutched his chest with one free hand.

A bruised line lay heavy across his face, from forehead to nose to mouth, one eye already swelling shut.

'What are you doing, Reinhardt?' Markworth asked.

Reinhardt jumped, the words were so sudden. 'Putting an end to this, Leyser.'

Markworth frowned. He shook his head. 'You can't be serious.'

'You deny you are Leyser?'

'No. But you can't stop me. Honestly, Reinhardt. You came so close with your reasoning. You came to understand me. You must know that you cannot stop me. Not so near the end.'

'It's over, Leyser.'

'It can't be, Reinhardt.' Markworth's voice was implacable. 'You can't. I won't let it happen.'

'This is insanity, Leyser. Markworth.' Reinhardt could not call him Leyser. The name felt wrong. It was not the name of the man he knew, kneeling before him. 'Whatever your name is. It has to end. It makes no sense.'

'It makes perfect sense, Reinhardt. To me.'

'But to whom does it make sense? You are many things, Leyser. Markworth. I believe there were many choices open to you.' Reinhardt paused, remembering suddenly his conversation in Sarajevo with Begović, about what defined a person. 'You are a German. You are an Englishman. Your father's name was Leyser. Your mother's maiden name was Markworth. We found their marriage records in Potsdam. I think when you were captured in Tobruk, you offered your services to the British, I think out of disillusion, maybe out of a sense of atonement. I think that when this war started, you were unsure which way to fall, and you somehow fell into the Germans' ambit and you found yourself regretting it. You fell into the father's camp. It is so often the case. Am I right?'

'Your son didn't.'

'And to a young man like you, I think the German cause may have looked oh so attractive,' Reinhardt continued, ignoring that stabbing thrust from Markworth, hoping he did not show how close it had hit home. 'The chance for adventure. That would be the young man in you. The chance to right old wrongs. That would be the father. Do I wrong you, Markworth?'

'No,' Markworth smiled. 'To the point on nearly all points, Reinhardt. My father called me home in 1938. His discourse was always that of Versailles. And he was making a lot of money off the Nazis. For me it was an officer's uniform, men to command, special training. It was a heady mix, Reinhardt, I'll not deny it. But the darkness came out fast enough.'

'And your mother?'

'My mother stayed by my father's side throughout the first war, but she would not do so for a second. She saw through the Nazis quick enough. I suppose, in a way, we all did, except some of us allowed the blinkers to stay on. But this is all nice enough, Reinhardt, and so, now what?'

'Now, it's over.'

'No, it's not. You can't hold me. I am James Markworth. I am British. A member of the occupying forces.'

'You are Marius Leyser. A German.'

'You can't prove that, apparently. Nothing remains to prove that.'

'Your British masters know. Someone among them knows who you were.'

'Someone does. Someone far from here. That won't help you now.'

'It will be a shock to them. Who you are, what you've done.'

'They'll get over it.'

'I have Semrau.'

Markworth smiled, but the light in his eyes glittered hard, like glass. 'The archivist. Him… I could have killed him ten times over. I suppose I should have. But I don't regret leaving him alive. It was my choice. He was my proof I was no longer fighting the war, and he'll have to live with what he did. I chose those I killed. And why. If it were still the war, he would be dead. And so would you. And so we come back to it, Reinhardt. What do you do now?'

'The best I can, Markworth. Leyser. The best I can. I have caught a man who has murdered, by my count, fifteen men.'

'You've been counting.'

'Including the life of your friend, Carlsen.'

'Fifteen men used to be a day's work for us, Reinhardt,' but Markworth's eyes flickered at Carlsen's name, perhaps a sign of guilt, and Reinhardt fastened on it as a hook, as something to use against this seemingly imperturbable man.

'For you, perhaps. But that was then, and this is now, and what you did was premeditated.'

'"Premeditated", Reinhardt?'

'Prellberg was spontaneous, I think. He triggered something in you. But he led you to the others. Then you used the WASt, and when you could find no more, you created the Ritterfeld Association, and brought your victims to you. And when your friend Carlsen realised what you were doing, he tried to stop you.'

'Making me a "premeditated murderer". Don't the police have better names for people like me? And besides, where's your proof, Reinhardt?'

'I've got enough of it. I've got Semrau. I've got you in this room. And I don't doubt that when I search you, I will find a tube, maybe a rubber hose, and a box of sand.'

'You don't think a man of my ingenuity and training can explain that away?'

'I've got a concierge in the Hotel Am Zoo. I've got a war veteran in an apartment. I'll find Carlsen's evidence. And I've got Bochmann,' Reinhardt lied. Keeping the .45 on Markworth, Reinhardt shuffled over to the room's wall and rapped on it. Markworth's eyes followed him, narrowing, and Reinhardt watched his face closing in, a granite stillness coming over him, but Reinhardt was sure it betrayed rage. A rage so all-encompassing it consumed him. Markworth was right about one thing: Reinhardt had precious little proof, and it was unlikely in the extreme that he would be able to hold Markworth to account for his crimes. The British would take him and repatriate him, or something similar. The shape of Markworth's crimes shifted in his mind, the pattern of this investigation, and Reinhardt knew that any resolution or justice he could aspire to would be personal. The system would never allow him anything else. What little justice there would be would have to be found here and now, and might only mean something to the two of them. The hunter and the hunted.

'What you want is vengeance, but it's blind. Noell!' Reinhardt called. The pilot rolled over, moaning, blinking hard against his pain. 'Noell. Do you know this man? Do you?' Noell lowered his head, shaking it. 'Look closely, Noell. Look. This man, Leyser. Have you ever seen him?' Reinhardt shone his flashlight on Markworth, flicking his eyes between him and Noell. 'This man was the man Prellberg and Gareis attacked in Tobruk, in October 1942. In a hospital. Do you remember that?' Noell nodded his head, weakly. 'Do you remember why? Do you remember attacking a Berber encampment? Do you remember?'

'I don't… I think so. I don't know.'

'Did you know the encampment was not a Berber one? It was a German unit you attacked. A unit of Brandenburgers.'

Noell winced, shook his head. 'I don't know. I don't…' His face cleared. 'Yes. But, it was so long ago, and it was an accident.'

'It might have stayed that way,' Markworth grated, 'only some of your friends tried to kill me in hospital. And I remember the way the aircraft went round and round the encampment, making sure nothing moved… remembrance is a strange thing, Reinhardt,' Markworth said, and his voice was coiled tight like a snake's. 'I will show you something. You remember the scars I showed you. I said they were from the cannon of my tank.' He moved slowly, taking his hands out from under his knees. With his left hand he pulled back the cuff of his coat and then his shirt. 'They were from heat. That was no lie. But it was no gun.' The scars went all the way up his right arm, as far up as his clothes could be rolled. 'It was the desert sun. Where they left me alone. Wounded. Bereft of friends and companions.' He unbuttoned his shirt. His chest was covered in a mottled drift of scar tissue and skin blotched red. 'Days in the sun, Reinhardt. I don't know how many. I never recovered from the burns. The doctors did what they could. The British did a little better. But this is what I was left with. The rest of me too. Only my head, which I covered, shows no sign of the sun, but what the sun could not burn without, it burned within.'

'Noell doesn't remember, Markworth. Doesn't that mean anything?'

'It means nothing. They took everything from me, and they did not even know it. I was a speck of black upon the desert sand that they chased and machine-gunned. I was a mummy rolled in bandages in hospital and still they came for me. I was a fragment of myself, a kernel I held against the sun. And then, when I came across that first one – Prellberg – and I realised who he was and what he was doing, I was there again, on that sand, and they were above me, around me, and there was no escape.'

'Did he *remember*?' Reinhardt was mesmerised by the menace that Markworth gave off, and by the even roll of his voice. His German was smooth, fluent, the halting mispronunciations gone for the artful camouflage they had been. He knocked on the wall again.

'He said he did not. But he wet himself lying to save himself. He gave me Hauck. He knew where he was living. And he gave me the other one – Lütjens – as someone more deserving of vengeance. He told me about the test unit, what they did. That was justice. You were right, Reinhardt. I will give you that. It was about both. About justice and revenge. And you were right about consequences,' he laughed softly, as Reinhardt knocked on the wall a third time. 'No one remembers what they did, no one remembers the consequences of their actions. People walk uncaring into the future and have no idea of what bloody ties stretch out behind them, and isn't that part of the problem?'

The door opened, and Weber stepped inside. Reinhardt blinked at him, and Weber smiled.

'Expecting someone else?'

48

Two of the other young detectives followed Weber in. Schmidt and Frohnau, Weber's two shadows. Schmidt had Ganz, and he had a pistol on him. Weber had a pistol as well and he pointed it at Reinhardt, holding out his other hand for Reinhardt's .45.

'Weber. What do you think you're doing?' Reinhardt managed.

'I'm not that sure,' Weber answered. His cheeks were flushed high with excitement, but his skin was pale beneath. 'I overheard a rather lovely heart-to-heart. Something about justice and revenge. About Germans and British.' He looked at Markworth. 'Is this the one you've been chasing? Quite the catch for the one who brings him in. Which will not be you, I'm afraid.' Weber's smile, his self-satisfied smile, his mischievous smile, slipped, then faded under the withering pressure of Markworth's eyes. He swallowed, turned his eyes half on Reinhardt. 'Because aren't you supposed to be in a cell in Linienstrasse?' The three young detectives grinned at one another, Schmidt poking Ganz with his pistol. 'You're easy to follow, old man. And Reinhardt, you're under arrest, or at least under suspicion. Something about Stresemann's murder?'

'He had nothing to do with that.'

'It speaks!' Weber quipped, looking at Markworth. 'And how would you – whatever your name is – know that?'

Markworth looked at Reinhardt, and shook his head, a smile on the corner of his lips. 'He knows. He's the only one with a brain among the lot of you.'

'Weber. What are you doing?'

'Be quiet, Reinhardt. This is mine now.'

'Weber, you've no idea…'

Weber turned and cracked Reinhardt across the face with his open palm. The blow was hard enough, but it was meant to shock, not stun. The kind of blow made to make a point, put someone in his place.

'Weber…' he tried again and made no attempt to avoid the second slap. He felt his blood begin to boil at the humiliation, felt the animal desire to rip Weber's throat out, but he held himself still.

'Inspector Weber,' Ganz shouted, before Schmidt shoved his pistol into the back of the elderly detective's neck for emphasis.

'Quiet, I said.' Weber's colour was higher, his breathing quick. In the corner of his eye, Reinhardt saw Markworth tense, as if he sought to join his weight to this confrontation. 'And I told you, Ganz, it's not "inspector". It's Chief Inspector. Kommisariat 5.' Weber's eyes gleamed as his secret came out, and suddenly things made sense to Reinhardt. Weber's youth, his apparent self-assurance, where he might have come from: he was protected. That, or he was part of something that would cover him, and he knew that Collingridge's information of rumours of a new Soviet-backed secret police force was true, and he knew who it was who had spoken to Skokov of Reinhardt's activities.

'K5?' It was Markworth who spoke. His eyes pushed hard at Weber, flicked up and down him, steadied on Weber's face, and although Reinhardt could not see it, he knew Weber was flushing with embarrassment because Markworth had found him wanting.

'K5,' Weber blurted, as if too full of self-pride to keep the word in. 'A new police for a new era. A police force to stop any drift back to the ways of the past.'

'Same shit, different shovel,' Markworth said, and Weber jerked as if struck. 'Let me guess. You're one of those who came back from Moscow following the Red Army. Better yet, given your evident callowness, you were born there. Born in exile. I can hear it in your voice.'

'We shall love talking to you, Mr Markworth,' Weber hissed. 'We shall love putting you on display too. A Fascist officer and war criminal in disguise. A Fascist officer at the service of the West. Of the British. Hiding within their ranks. Or allowed to prosper. And I don't exclude you from all this, Reinhardt,' Weber said derisively, and Reinhardt knew he was remembering his humiliation at Reinhardt's hands outside von Vollmer's factory. 'You have a lot of explaining to do. Another Fascist officer, another little placeman showing his true sympathies.'

'Weber, you…' Reinhardt began.

'I suppose you had better bring me in then, young man,' Markworth interrupted, and the challenge was evident in his words. He held out his wrists to be shackled, but Weber shifted, and his companions shifted with him. 'What, no manacles? No cuffs? Not even a bit of rope?' he mocked them. 'Such foresight. You'll go far, young man.'

'Be quiet, pig, or I'll shoot you where you kneel.'

'And where's the glory and advancement in that, eh? And what about these pesky witnesses? One body you could explain. Three would be a bit harder, especially with the Americans about. For they are nearby, aren't they, Reinhardt?' Reinhardt could only nod, latching on to the hook Markworth was offering. 'That's Reinhardt's deal with them. He caught me, fair and square, and they're standing back for now, but they won't forever. So if you want me,' he said, raising one knee, and pushing himself slowly to his feet, his hands outstretched at his side, 'you'd better save the speeches for later and take me while things are quiet.'

How quickly the authority and initiative in the room had shifted, Reinhardt realised, wondering if Weber could feel it too. He glanced at Ganz and saw he had felt it as well.

'Hands up!' Weber snapped.

'They're already up, young man,' Markworth mocked him, his arms up and fingers linked behind his back. Weber nodded to Frohnau, and while he kept his pistol aimed at Markworth, the other detective patted him down, pulling, as Reinhardt had guessed, a bag from one of the pockets of Markworth's coat. He emptied it on the bed, a quick rush of sand and a length of rubber pipe. Reinhardt looked at Markworth, and he saw the twitch that went across Markworth's face, almost a snarl, as if of frustration at vengeance so nearly complete but frustrated. And he reminded himself – because he realised he had forgotten it – that before him stood a cold-blooded murderer. But Markworth was also a man he had come to like, even admire, and he was a man who was subtly engineering the present circumstances to some kind of advantage for both himself and Reinhardt. He was doing that, Reinhardt knew, but he was doing something else. He had done something else. Markworth had done something, right in front of them, but Reinhardt could not work out what it might have been.

'He's clean,' Frohnau said.

'Good. We're going downstairs. Me first, and our friend,' Weber said, looking at Markworth. 'Then you, Schmidt. Frohnau, you keep Reinhardt company.'

'What about him,' Frohnau asked, pointing at Noell.

'Cut him loose and leave him. We've got bigger fish,' Weber grinned.

Weber put his pistol to Markworth's back and pushed him out of the room, swearing at him to move faster as Markworth's limp had reappeared, much exaggerated. Schmidt followed with Ganz. Frohnau fumbled Noell's bindings loose, then pointed Reinhardt out.

'You can't just leave him here. He's not safe. And he's a witness.'

'Shut up and move,' was all Frohnau had to say. They caught up with the others as they clattered down the stairs after the first four, and found them on one of the building's lower landings as Markworth hobbled down slowly and with a group of men coming up the stairs. The newcomers had the hangdog look of exhausted men, covered in the dust and filth of whatever labour they had been able to find. They stood to one side as Weber waved them away, their eyes flat and lidded.

'What's going on then?' one of them asked, a man with white hair and white stubble that creased the contours of his weathered and lined face.

'Never you fucking mind. Just stay out the way,' Weber ordered.

'Big city manners, is it? And there I was, thinking people were more polite here.' By his accent he was from the east, and Reinhardt marked him as a displaced person forced out of his home by the war's end.

'Shut it, old man.'

'They're taking me back,' Markworth blurted. 'They're taking me back to Königsberg, and I've done nothing.' His accent was suddenly pure Pomeranian. 'I can't go back, I can't, I *can't!*' He had changed again, subtly. His posture, his voice, everything spoke desperation and terror, such that Reinhardt would hardly have recognised him.

'What you doin' with him?' one of the DPs demanded.

'I said shut it,' Weber snarled, shoving the man back with his free hand. The man allowed himself to be pushed, but his belligerence was plain.

'Sod that,' the man retorted. 'I put up with that enough back home from the fucking Poles and the fucking Ivans. I'm not fucking putting up with it here.'

'What?' Weber lashed, pushing his face into the other's. 'You think this place is some paradise for you lot to just waltz in, is it?'

'Do you have any idea what you're sending him back to?' the older man asked. 'And anyway, just who are you?'

'They're secret police,' Markworth wailed, his accent flawless to Reinhardt's ears. Weber tightened his grip on him, pushing the pistol harder against the back of his neck, but his face betrayed its fear and its indecision. 'Secret police, like the old days. They're sending me back. They'll send you back, too. I've done nothing *wrooong*,' he keened.

'Is it true, then?' the old man asked.

There was no answer, because Markworth was moving to his own rhythm in the distraction he had just made. He slid one leg back between Weber's and spun himself around so that Weber's pistol was suddenly pointing past his head, not at the back of it. Before Weber could do more than gape, Markworth had steadied him by his lapels and head-butted him. From farther up the stairs, Reinhardt heard the crack of bone. There was an explosion of blood, and Weber collapsed to the floor like a marionette with its strings cut.

Schmidt gurgled with fear as Markworth dipped his right hand into his left sleeve and pulled out a long, slim blade from what must have been a hidden sheath. Reinhardt recognised it as a British Commando knife, its steel a lustrous gleam as he cut it at Schmidt's face, and part of Reinhardt recognised it for the blade that must have killed Stresemann. Schmidt squalled and reeled backwards as the knife opened the skin across his forehead, and his face was flooded with blood. His pistol clattered to the floor as he flailed against the side of the stairwell, Ganz dropping his weight away to one side. Markworth flowed past them, his limp hardly bothering him, and there was death in his eyes for Frohnau beneath the Red Indian splash of Weber's blood across his forehead.

He was too far away, though, and Frohnau's pistol was coming up as he shoved Reinhardt to one side. Reinhardt grabbed it and pushed it hard into the wall, grinding his weight onto it, onto Frohnau's knuckles until his fingers spasmed open. He turned into the policeman and punched up and into his groin. Frohnau's eyes gaped wide like a fish's as the breath whooshed out of him. Reinhardt felt Markworth behind him, and fumbled Frohnau's pistol into his own hand, turning, ducking, but Markworth was too close.

The Englishman battered aside Reinhardt's arm, and there was a moment when their eyes met, just a moment, long enough for Reinhardt to know what was coming, and then Markworth's fist slammed into the side of his knee. Reinhardt screamed with the pain as it erupted up and through him, and maybe he screamed more with the betrayal of it, and the pistol fell away. Almost mute with the pain, his movements the flailing panic of a drowning man, Reinhardt scrabbled with his arms at Markworth's legs, thinking only to pull him down, but he was left empty-handed on the stairs as Markworth stamped upward, the DPs' shouts and Schmidt's screams following.

'Markworth! *Markworth!*' Reinhardt bellowed over his pain. Someone lifted him to his feet, pushed the pistol into his hands.

'Go,' Ganz wheezed, pushing him on.

The first steps up were agony, the remainder little better, as Reinhardt forced himself almost on all fours past the pain of his knee, the palms of his hands scrapping across the gritted filth of the stairs, and he knew he would not be in time. He reached the top floor with his breathing like a bellows, limping with his weight against the wall, pushing past people as they emerged from their rooms, and heard the cry from the room they had left.

'*Markworth!* Markworth, *don't!*'

He lurched into the doorway, saw Noell on the bed with his head twisted awry and sand scattered about his mouth, and the window hauled up and open. He fell into the window frame, one hand on the scarred wood for balance, looking out into the night. A hand gripped the collar of his coat and hauled him half outside, his feet scrabbling wildly inside the room. A blow to his elbow, and the pistol fell away into the night.

There was a small ledge outside, wide enough to walk on, coated thickly with dirt and grime. Markworth stood there, his knife against Reinhardt's throat. Reinhardt went as still as his breathing would allow.

'You cannot follow me, Reinhardt. I don't want to hurt you, but you can't follow me, and you can't stop me.'

'Markworth, this must end.'

'It has. I'm finished, now. Noell was the last.'

Reinhardt felt him move and closed his eyes, cringing from the blow that would come. Markworth hit him behind the ear with the pommel of the knife. Reinhardt's world went black, and he hardly felt it as Markworth shoved him back into the room. The blackness faded, starred agony replacing it. He heaved himself onto hands and knees, his cheek dragging wetly up the wall as he pulled himself up to rest his head upon the sill. His tongue lolled, and he felt like a dog that puts its head into the wind, mouth agape.

It was darkness down in the alley. He could not tell what was down there, or who, or how much time had passed.

'Br...' he croaked. 'Brra...' But his voice failed him.

Down in the alley something flashed, a stutter of light. Sound billowed up, the ripping crash of a gun and some distant part of him – the same part, perhaps, that had recognised Markworth's knife – recognised the noise of Brauer's Bergmann.

'Brauer,' Reinhardt whispered, then slid back down the wall into unconsciousness.

Part Five

The Devil Is Never So Black

49

On a cold and crisp morning a few days later, Mrs Meissner asked Reinhardt to escort her to Schlesischer Station. She was excited about her art commissions, about meeting up with former colleagues coming in on the train to discuss the hunt for looted treasures, but nervous about going into the Soviet Sector alone. There was a gleam in her eye, something pleasingly conspiratorial, and he smiled as he escorted her down the street, her hand nestled on his forearm. On the U-Bahn, he chased a pair of children out of the seats reserved for the elderly and wounded, and she sat primly, her hands folded over her handbag as the train bounced her along.

At the station, there was already something of a crowd, mostly elderly men and women, and she waved gaily to people of her acquaintance, colleagues and friends from the art world. Inside the station, policemen formed a cordon at the head of the platforms, and there was a welcoming committee of more people she knew. Mrs Meissner pushed a newspaper into Reinhardt's hands, and he drifted over to a bench as she joined her friends. He scanned the headlines, noting the arrival of a commission from Belgrade, in the new Socialist Federal Republic of Yugoslavia that Tito's Partisans had created from the wreckage of the war, come to inquire as to what it would take to hunt down and reclaim all the art and treasure the Nazis had looted from their country.

There was nothing, though, about an incident in a hostel for DPs, nor about the escape of a wanted criminal. That particular headline had been quashed. The case was done, though, and Reinhardt thought that so was he. Done with Berlin's police, all but persona non grata after the fiasco of the trap laid for Markworth. Not quite a fiasco, he corrected himself, noting his habitual introspection and slide into morbid self-analysis. The trap had worked, it was not his fault, nor Ganz's, that Weber's involvement had given Markworth the confusion he needed to make his escape. Weber was gone, and Reinhardt did not know where. Unmasked as a K5 agent, and thus as an infiltrator into a police force already thoroughly infiltrated with Allied agents of varying colours, Weber's usefulness was at an end. He had vanished upon his release from hospital, probably somewhere east. Schmidt was back at Gothaerstrasse, his head heavily bandaged, and Frohnau watched Reinhardt's every move with deep suspicion.

Most of the police looked at him the same way, with suspicion, or askance, maybe a few with admiration. Reinhardt had been subjected to the cold fury of Margraff at a meeting in his offices in Linienstrasse, but Ganz and Bliemeister, and even Tanneberger, had spoken for him, and at least there had been a suspect, even if he had escaped. Something of Reinhardt's old legend still clung to him, but he also knew none of them really trusted him, and he was sure there was little to no future for him in the force. Not in this city, not in these times.

'Give it some time,' Collingridge had urged him. He called Markworth a 'serial killer', and Collingridge's star had risen with the capture of Kausch and his band. The Americans backed him – he had even had the visit of Collingridge's superior, a veritable caricature of a cigar-chewing Texan – and Bliemeister had spoken to him about coming to work for him as an adviser, but it was hard knowing that your own people, your colleagues, the men who were supposed to go shoulder to shoulder with you, doubted your loyalties.

The British were furious, but more interested in covering up the involvement of one of their men in so many crimes, and in protecting BOALT from being mentioned too often and too openly. It was hard to know, though, whether Whelan and the British were more embarrassed by Markworth's betrayal of them – sporting analogies were much in use, 'just not cricket' heard once too often, 'bad blood will out' almost as much – or more angered by his activities under cover of the British Occupation authorities: murder and the encouragement of seditious activities in the formation of the Ritterfeld Association.

They were more afraid of being embarrassed, Reinhardt concluded, rattling the newspaper's sheets into shape as a train pulled into the station, of looking like fools in front of their peers. The Soviets were quietly content where they were not openly satisfied at the situation in which the British found themselves, but it was the opinion of only one of them that mattered to Reinhardt, as he folded the newspaper into his lap and lifted his eyes to the station's open roof, where the repairs had not yet reached.

Skokov had found the files, at Güstrow, where Noell had said they had been hidden. Reinhardt did not know what was in them, and could not have cared less. Although he had been unhappy with what had happened to Noell, the Soviet had been true to his word, releasing Friedrich from whatever bondage he had held him in.

'Be careful, Captain,' he had said, his eyes alight with sardonic amusement, 'that the past does not come to haunt you.'

'It haunts all of us,' Reinhardt had replied.

'Your son has nothing more to fear from me. What he carries within him, and what his comrades believe he has done, will matter more now. But in that, I can no longer help him.'

Rumours, and more than rumours, of the war in the east… That war that had sucked millions down into its maelstrom. Reinhardt still looked at his son and wondered, and the policeman in him longed to know, but the father in him could wait. One day, his son would speak of it. Reinhardt feared that day, and yet could not wait for it to come. On the way here, Reinhardt and Meissner had passed Red Army women on duty at a crossroads, stocky and blunt in fur hats, brown tunics, skirts and knee-high boots, with submachine guns slung over their backs. They carried traffic-control batons like lollipop sticks, directing vehicles. They were efficient with their movements, coming to attention whenever an Allied vehicle passed, rigorously checking the few German ones. One of the soldiers eyed him up as he passed, tapping her baton against the leather of her boot. She was a heavy, swarthy-faced woman with dark, slanted eyes over slabbed cheekbones and all unbidden, the opening lines of Blok's poem came tumbling up out of his mind.

Millions are you – and hosts, yea hosts, are we,
And we shall fight if war you want, take heed.
Yes, we are Scythians – leafs of the Asian tree,
Our slanted eyes are bright aglow with greed.

Some words, Reinhardt thought, were prophetic. He had thought it then, the first time he had heard the poem in 1919, still largely bedridden after the war with his injury, and he thought it now. They had thought they had the Russians bested at the end of the first war, thought they had the measure of a brave but fragile enemy, but Reinhardt remembered… he remembered the sense of vastness that loomed beyond the Russian front lines. He remembered nights of moonlit clarity, pushing his eyes as far as he could out and over snow-clad hills lined and rumpled across a far grey horizon. He remembered marching, marching over landscapes of devastating emptiness, through forests of pillared darkness that, despite the teeming multitudes that passed beneath and between their cathedral gloom, seemed never to have known the touch or sound of men. How could they have done it again, he wondered, thinking back to that expanse, that endless frontier that had almost swallowed his son, and swallowed so many other men. Swallowed nations and whole peoples. How could they have stirred that far horizon to anger?

How could they now regret what they had called down upon themselves?

People began filtering out from the platform where the train sat wreathed in steam. Men, women, children, farmers, the poor, the not-so-poor, more refugees from the east, Red Army men. The station filled with noise that was curiously empty, the cacophony of steps and sounds and words a crowd produced sucked up through the open roof, not reverberating back down and around. He rose to his feet to check on Mrs Meissner, seeing her still with her friends, and he moved slightly to keep her in view, leaning back against the wall and lighting a cigarette.

'I like trains. Did I ever tell you that?'

The voice came from behind him. It froze him solid, his cigarette spiralling smoke up into his eye. He swallowed, lifting a hand to it.

'You did. Once. I presume I should not turn around.'

'That's right,' Markworth said. 'Best you don't.'

'What are you doing?'

'Playing fool's games, Reinhardt. What else?' There was a light note to his voice. 'How's your head?'

'Sore. You're not going to hit me again, are you?'

'Don't worry. I'm not here to cause trouble. But I couldn't leave without knowing. What gave me away? I'm curious.' Markworth asked, as if there were no urgency.

'The tap,' Reinhardt said, as he drew deeply on his cigarette. 'The first time we met, when we argued about whether Carlsen had been in Noell's rooms. You asked me were his prints in the apartment? You asked, "Were his prints on the tap?" The one tap. How would you know that if you had not seen it, been there yourself?'

'That's it?' chuckled Markworth incredulously.

'The first thing. There were others. Your German kept giving you away. You asked what went wrong with "us" once. You hid it, but I know you meant what went wrong with "us Germans".'

'There's more?'

'You knew idioms. Sayings. Expressions. I reasoned only an Allied agent could move across Germany leaving all those bodies. It all built up. And you didn't react when I told you Noell had a twin brother, because you knew already. That was why you murdered Theodor Noell with water. You knew who he was.'

'What else?'

'The times the accusations of me murdering Stresemann, or having something to do with his murder, were the times I came close. You put Fischer up against me, hoping he would injure me enough to get me off the case. When that didn't work, you used my baton on Stresemann's body. When that didn't work, you arranged for the baton to be found.'

'I did. I'm sorry. None of it would've stuck, you know. And if it had, I'd have done what I could to help.'

'I know.' And Reinhardt believed it.

'Anything else?'

'The Royal Marines. How, I wondered, did a former tanker and now a liaison officer in the Occupation know where to find commandos?'

'When I was captured, the British did not hold me long. A Brandenburger's skills made a good match for a commando's.'

'You took a risk with them, Markworth. They might have talked.'

'You were a risk worth taking, Reinhardt.'

Reinhardt said nothing, holding himself still around those simple words.

'What a curious couple we made, Reinhardt. I wanted to congratulate you on the trap too. Releasing Noell, then making sure he went to where you were waiting so there was no need to tail him. You fooled me. Well done.'

'Was Carlsen really your friend?' Reinhardt asked suddenly.

'He really was.'

'Why did you kill him?'

There was a long silence, but Reinhardt knew he was still there.

'I did not mean to. I suspected he was on to me. He worked in the war crimes division, investigating men like Lütjens. He was angry when he died, and then when I killed another of Lütjens's team, he suspected foul play. Something I said must have put him onto me. We talked a lot, a bit like you and I did. About the past. About justice. About revenge. But I had no idea he had begun following me, or at least keeping track of where I went. He surprised me that night at Noell's apartment. I… I killed him without thinking. It felt… almost as if someone else did it.'

'Maybe someone else did. A man called Leyser.'

'What are you saying?'

'I make no excuses for you, Markworth. But I knew men in the first war. And afterwards. Their experiences… divided them… from the men they were.'

'You mean shell shock? You mean all this time it's a shrink I've needed, not revenge?' He was silent, and when he spoke again the levity had faded from his voice. 'Maybe you're right. Sometimes… sometimes I felt like two men. But I won't take that for an excuse. I knew what I was doing.'

'And now? How does it feel now?'

'How did it feel when you handed over those Ustaše to the Partisans?'

'It felt right,' Reinhardt admitted. Markworth said nothing. 'So you found Gieb and persuaded her to help in exchange for ridding her of Stresemann.'

'Carlsen already knew her. I simply convinced her to help, and then got her out of the city once she had done so. Her price was Stresemann.'

'Your one good deed. May I ask you a question?'

'Certainly.'

'Your limp. You limped as Markworth, not as Leyser.'

'Leyser was wounded when his camp was shot up, and wore a leg brace, my friend. Easier to move around that way. Leyser… I… removed it when…'

'… when Leyser became Markworth,' Reinhardt finished.

'God, maybe I am as much of a mess as you seem to think I am,' Markworth muttered. 'How is your friend?' he asked, after a moment.

'Brauer is fine. Annoyed you got past him a second time. Annoyed you knocked him out again. There's not many claim that distinction.'

'I'm honoured then. Give him my best regards.'

This was becoming ridiculous, Reinhardt thought, and maybe Markworth thought the same. There was another silence, heavier, and Reinhardt felt the distance beginning to sink in. He knew, by rights, he should turn. Turn and confront him. Call for help. It would be the right thing, but the wrong thing. It would be a gesture, nothing more. But then, were not gestures all that were sometimes needed? A man who stood up for a friend. A woman who brought a neighbour help in times of need. Someone who offered a seat on a crowded train to an elderly Jew. Someone who would not follow a law that made no sense. There had been a time and a place for all those gestures, and Reinhardt knew he had not made them as often as he should have, when the opportunity had presented itself. Was this, then, such a time, and if so, which way to fall…?

'Lift a drink for me one day, Reinhardt. Yes? Maybe in that bar. A molle, and maybe a toast. To times and men that might have been.'

He was gone, then. Reinhardt could feel it. He waited a moment, then turned, but saw no one and he knew Markworth could be anyone. He could have been that Red Army soldier tickling a little girl under her chin as he offered her an apple. Or he could have been that man who hunched his shoulders around as if lighting a cigarette. Or perhaps the blind veteran with a stick, sounding his way across the station's concourse.

Any of them, and none of them. He had faded away. As he was trained to.

Up at the barrier, Mrs Meissner was waving to him. A group of newcomers had gathered around her, people from the train, the commission from Belgrade in black coats and with bags lumped around their feet. Someone was reading a speech, and a little girl held up a bouquet of flowers to one of the visitors. Mrs Meissner was talking to a woman, and the woman looked across the concourse, searching, until she found Reinhardt. She walked towards him and took off her hat to reveal a spill of white-blonde hair, and Reinhardt's heart, which had broken on a sunny hillside in Bosnia, seemed to suddenly knit itself back together and began to beat again, to beat and fill all those places within him that he thought had withered and died.

Historical Note

Whereas I was fortunate enough to have lived in Bosnia for six years, and so was able to use much of what I had seen and learned and done in crafting *The Man from Berlin* and *The Pale House*, I was faced with a very different situation for *The Ashes of Berlin*. When considering occupied Germany and Berlin and the postwar years, the reader or historian can be overwhelmed by the quantity and quality of information.

The Ashes of Berlin does not aim to be a novel about postwar Germany: it is the story of one man's investigation through Berlin in early 1947. As such, I have related events through Reinhardt's eyes, resisting the temptation to wrap everything in allegory. There is no shortage of books, many of them excellent, on the situation in postwar Germany. There are so many that I will go into no great depth here on the overall situation, but rather attempt to add historical detail to those elements of the postwar context that Reinhardt was faced with in his investigation.

In early 1947, the time in which *The Ashes of Berlin* is set, the Second World War had been over nearly two years. Although the guns had fallen silent, the war's effects lingered on, and the peace had thrown up problems all its own.

Following Germany's unconditional surrender on 8 May, 1945, and in line with wartime Allied planning, the country was divided up into three Zones of military occupation, with the French Zone later added to make a fourth. The American Zone was centred on Frankfurt, the British on Bad Oeynhausen, the French in Baden-

Baden, and the Soviet in Berlin. Divided as it was into four sectors, Berlin was a microcosm of the Occupation itself.

In August 1945 the Potsdam Conference, the last time the leaders of the victorious powers met in person, addressed Germany's political future. The country would be run by an Allied Control Council in Berlin. This council was to be made up of representatives – mainly military, but some civilian – who would jointly develop and implement policy and issue laws. Various subcommittees were established, including the Public Security Committee, which, in October 1946, reformed Berlin's police force. Although the council functioned well enough initially, the tension between the Allies quickly began to come to the fore, especially concerning economic policy, denazification, and the devolution of powers back to the Germans. Some of these tensions manifested themselves in October 1946 in the first free and fair elections in Germany since 1933. Across Western Germany, parties of the social democratic type were largely victorious, often led by Germans, such as Konrad Adenauer, who had a history of resistance to the Nazis. In the Soviet Zone, the Socialist Unity Party – a Soviet-enforced merger of the Social Democrats and the German Communists – was victorious, largely because it had no opposition. In Berlin, however, it was trounced in a clear rejection of the Soviets by the city's inhabitants.

The elections, as well as the relations between the Allies, showed there were very different visions for Germany's future and the role of Germans in it. The realities of the peace could no longer mask the divisions that the alliance against the Nazis had papered over. The treatment of former Nazis was one such issue.

Denazification progressed very differently within the four Occupation Zones, with various degrees of intensity and various methods of application. The British and Americans initially proceeded with vigour and enthusiasm, but the sheer numbers of people potentially involved overwhelmed them, coupled with the need to cut the costs of the Occupation by getting Germany back on its feet and diminishing as well the potential for German revanchism. They were the first to hand responsibility for denazification back to German tribunals and panels in the late 1940s, a time when relations with the Soviets were deteriorating seriously and when it seemed likely the Germans would be needed as allies.

In the French Zone, partly because the French made little distinction between Germans and Nazis, and partly because many of the officials appointed to govern it had themselves been officials in the Vichy regime, denazification never became an issue. In the Soviet Zone, it took on dimensions of class warfare, with the Prussian aristocracy and officer class – men like von Vollmer – singled out for particular treatment. Their properties were seized and redistributed, and their traditional values of duty, obedience, and patriotism were considered as being coterminous with the Nazis' values, or at the least had done nothing to inhibit the Nazis' behaviour.

Tens of millions of Germans were potentially affected by denazification. It would have been impossible to judge them all. Many former Nazis, or men and women who had supported them, thus eventually found their way back into positions of public and private authority and even respectability under all four occupying powers. Over time, the perceived failure of denazification became a convenient, if self-serving, stick with which the Soviets and East Germans would beat the Western Allies and West Germany. The sad fact is that all four of the Allies were complicit in denazification's qualified successes, such as the Nuremburg trials of the major offenders, and its rather glaring failures, such as the ways in which some major offenders escaped prosecution while greater numbers of lesser offenders, or even people who had barely been complicit in the Nazi regime at all, suffered severe consequences.

As part of Germany's surrender, the Allies had access to all that country's patents and mined its technical expertise and intellectual development to the fullest. The boost this gave to Allied economies and companies was considerable. Of particular note is the race by all the Allies, especially the Americans and Soviets, for German scientists and know-how. Thousands of Germany's scientists, doctors, technicians, chemists, and physicists were prized and sought-after assets, wooed, cajoled, persuaded, hunted, or kidnapped and exfiltrated to the USA or USSR. The US-led Operation Paperclip, which brought hundreds of German specialists in various spheres to live and work in the US, is perhaps the most infamous example of the lengths the Allies went to, although the Soviets had a similar programme. Many of these scientists had been wholly complicit in the Nazi's terror, or at least fully aware of it, and the Allies knew it. Men like Wernher von Braun, the director of the Peenemünde experimental facility, an expert in rocketry and one of the fathers of America's future space programme, had his membership in the Nazi Party and the SS expunged and his war record altered in order for him to be brought to work in the United States.

The human cost of German wartime scientific and technical advances was high. More people, mostly slave labourers from concentration camps, were worked to death or killed building the V2 ballistic missile than were actually killed by the weapon itself. The Germans also used human experimentation during the war. These macabre and revolting trials on living humans such as prisoners of war, Jews, homosexuals, political prisoners, the disabled, and children, were designed to further aims such as Nazi racial theories and medical experiments, or to aid in the military effort by testing the effects of various weapons or experimental surgery techniques. The air force did indeed conduct experiments on freezing and altitude, some of which were led by Dr Sigmund Rascher at a facility in the Dachau concentration camp. Rascher and his experiments existed, but the squadron to which Andreas Noell was posted, that supposedly tested his findings, did not, although ones similar to it assuredly did.

Details of these experiments, and much else that the Nazi regime did, survived intact in records captured by the Allies or in the testimonies of survivors of the camps. The cliché of Germans' mania for paperwork and records has substantial basis in fact. The complete personnel records of the Nazi Party, much of the SS's records, as well as the records of dozens of Nazi-affiliated organisations were captured by American troops and placed in the Berlin Document Center. The armed forces' records – the WASt, the Wehrmacht Information Office for War Losses and POWs – were also captured by the Americans and returned to Berlin where they were placed under French control. The WASt remains to this day an amazing repository of personnel information, housing millions of records of servicemen of all three branches of the German armed forces – army, navy and air force – as well as information on prisoners, casualties, and war graves.

The divisions between the Allies were unfortunate because the tasks facing them were herculean and demanded cooperation and coordination. Destruction across the length and breadth of Germany was colossal. The Allies, particularly the Soviets, conducted widespread looting, expropriation, and dismantling of industry, indeed of anything of any value. Harvest and livestock were often requisitioned, leaving little for the population. Most of Germany's cities had been heavily bombed by the British and American air forces. Berlin itself had been shattered by the war and solely occupied by the Red Army from the beginning of May to the beginning of July 1945, when British and American troops entered the city. The city was thoroughly sacked during the Soviet assault, and the population – particularly Berlin's women – suffered the near-constant depredations of Red Army soldiers in the weeks that followed. Even today, traces of those last battles in April 1945 can be found.

The health and sanitation situation was grave as the country headed into one of the coldest winters in living memory. Diseases such as tuberculosis took virulent root, and there were outbreaks of cholera, typhoid, and diphtheria. Rations were insufficient and malnutrition was rife. Basic services such as water and power took time to restore. Law and order and functioning local administration had to be put in place while ensuring neither became refuges for former Nazis. There were millions of displaced people, such as slave labourers and prisoners of war, to care for and repatriate, not to mention the dire situation facing most Germans themselves. All this would have challenged any administration. As it was, and despite the genuine efforts of many Allied officials, the Occupation was marked by inefficiencies in administration, vagaries among the Zones, often strong degrees of callousness, with corruption a worsening element. Black markets were ubiquitous. The cost of Occupation was also heavy on the occupiers, particularly for the all-but-bankrupt British, and another imperative in getting Germany back on its economic feet.

Millions of German civilians had fled west to escape the Red Army during the last months of the war. The end of the war saw millions more, overwhelmingly women, children, and the elderly, expelled in horrendous conditions from eastern Germany, from land ceded to Poland, or from eastern European states such as Czechoslovakia. Eastern Germany had been heavily fought over by the retreating Germans, whose scorched-earth tactics and desperate measures had brought misery on their own people, and by the advancing Soviets, who were ill-disposed to show any mercy or forbearance to the civilian populations they encountered. Millions were killed, disappeared, or died of maltreatment, disease, and exhaustion. Women and girls suffered horribly, especially at the hands of men of the Red Army and their allies. Suicide rates soared. Refugees fled as far west as they could, into Berlin or into the British and American Zones, adding to the already dire humanitarian situation. But in the war's aftermath, Germans and their needs were low on the pecking order – of all the Allies – for protection, assistance, and justice.

The behaviour of Soviet soldiers could be highly unpredictable, with individuals capable of terrible brutality and callousness, but also of showing great kindness and consideration, especially to children, even if this aspect of their behaviour has been somewhat romanticised. The Soviet war memorial in Treptower Park has a monumental statue of a Red Army soldier cradling a child in its arms. The statue was inspired by the actions of Red Army Sergeant Nikolai Masalov, who, during the assault on Berlin, rescued a young German girl while under heavy fire. Accounts abound of the lengths to which Soviet soldiers could be tender with children, even to the extent that Berlin's women came to know that, if a child was with them, they were all but safe from molestation, and children became almost prized possessions, shared between friends and family.

As is so often the case with war and the population displacements that result, the burden of it fell unequally on women and children. Women and girls were the victims of horrendous levels of sustained sexual violence by the conquering powers, but the fate of their menfolk was playing out to its own drama. A huge percentage of Germany's men had served in the armed forces and were either dead, wounded, missing, or imprisoned. Due to traditional recruitment policies of the German armed forces, many of the survivors of the officer corps were refugees from eastern Germany, from provinces lost to Poland or in the Soviet Zone. Worsening matters, in August 1945 the Allied Control Council dissolved and declared illegal all German veterans' organisations, including the armed forces. Most dramatically, the law banned all organisation or association of veterans and revoked all their pensions, benefits, and rights, including for those who had not even fought in the war. At one fell swoop, this rendered all but destitute millions of men and the families who depended upon them. Veterans were widely distrusted and vilified. However, despite formal injunctions against organising themselves to claim their rights and honour, they quickly created informal networks and groupings. Von Vollmer's factory and its attendant association – albeit aided and abetted by Markworth's plotting – are a fictionalised example of how this could have been done.

The Allies did keep a close watch on veterans, as indeed they did on any group that could, it was felt, harbour Nazi sympathies or provide shelter and succour. One such group that never materialised, despite a high degree of propaganda and hysteria, were the 'Werewolves', which were supposed to have operated clandestinely within occupied Germany to resist the Allies. Another group that never existed was BOALT – the British Occupation Authority Liaison Taskforce – although something like it might have and maybe could have. The British and American armies had many Germans, or men of German ancestry, in their ranks, and many of them came back to Germany with the Occupation. Given the real need to feel the pulse of German opinion about the Occupation and the occupiers, a unit like BOALT would have found ample employment. The Brandenburgers did exist. An elite unit, similar in training and ethos to Britain's Commandos or the SAS, the Brandenburgers were proficient in languages, making them a dangerous force and lethal infiltrators.

A last word on the military concerns the vast numbers of prisoners of war captured by the Allies. All four of the Allies used prisoners to some extent as forced labour, for example to bring in the harvest, for rubble clearance, or for postwar reconstruction. Most prisoners were vetted and released relatively quickly after the war ended, the vast majority by 1946, although the Soviets did keep many prisoners into the early 1950s. Given the titanic struggle on the Eastern Front between the competing ideologies, the Soviets implemented indoctrination programmes with German prisoners and attempted to recruit some to their cause. These efforts had limited success, although several organisations were formed, such as the League of German Officers. By and large, these organisations had limited impact with most prisoners, who treated them as traitors. Paul Margraff, a German soldier captured at Stalingrad and Berlin's chief of police after the war, was one such officer, and there were others whom the Soviets placed into positions of authority in, for example, the police force. Margraff unabashedly promulgated pro-Soviet policies, turned a blind eye to Red Army excesses, and ensured Berlin's police toed the Soviet line.

With the German armed forces, indeed almost any organisation remotely military in nature, rendered illegal, this left the police as the only remnant of the German state capable of exercising control and upholding the law. The police, however, were powerless to prevent crimes committed by the Allies. Furthermore, the police leadership across the country had been replaced with men picked by the Allies for their loyalty. In Berlin, this saw the Soviets replace the entire police force with 'anti-Fascist' elements that often behaved as badly as, if not worse than, their Fascist forbears. Police officers were complicit in the harassment of non-Communist politicians and parties, and showed little cooperation with the Western Allies. Police command – the Presidium – was in Mitte in the Soviet Sector. Officers employed in the Presidium were compelled to live in the Soviet Sector, and officers in the Zones of the Western Allies were obliged to go to Mitte, where, it was suspected, they received instructions on how to behave.

Exasperated by Margraff's behaviour and the general attitude of Berlin's police, the Western Allies eventually negotiated a thorough reform in October 1946, which, among other measures, decentralised control of Berlin's police and introduced assistant chiefs of police for the police commanders in the four sectors. These assistants – one of whom was the Bruno Bliemeister who makes a brief appearance in *The Ashes of Berlin* – were former policemen who had retired before the Nazis came to power or who had been forcibly removed by them. They were nominated by the Allies to keep an eye on police operations, but they could not overtly interfere in them. Rather, they ensured that inter-Allied policies were implemented and, at least in the three Western Zones, diluted Soviet influence over the police as much as possible.

In writing this book, I would like to acknowledge the following works in particular:

Soldiers as Citizens: Former Wehrmacht Officers in the Federal Republic of Germany, 1945–1955, by Jay Lockenour (University of Nebraska Press, 2001)
Berlin 1945. World War II: Photos of the Aftermath, by Michael Brettin and Peter Kroh (Berlinica Publishing LLC, 2014)
The Long Road Home, by Ben Shephard (Vintage, 2011)

As well, I would like to acknowledge the assistance afforded by the National Archives at Kew, London.

As a human, I can only wish that we would treat one another better as a species. As a humanitarian worker, I know this sadly to be untrue, that since the end of World War II, the litany of man's inhumanity to man has been a long and bloodied one.

The arc of Reinhardt's story in and around the tumultuous times of World War II, from reawakening in *The Man from Berlin* to resistance in *The Pale House* to reconciliation in *The Ashes of Berlin* has now come to an end. Although Reinhardt will not march again – his days as a marching man are over – he still has stories to tell, and those stories will be found among the tides of people displaced by the war, and within the international relief operation set up to assist them.

About Us

In addition to No Exit Press, Oldcastle Books has a number of other imprints, including Kamera Books, Creative Essentials, Pulp! The Classics, Pocket Essentials and High Stakes Publishing > oldcastlebooks.com

For more information about Crime Books go to > crimetime.co.uk

Check out the kamera film salon for independent, arthouse and world cinema > kamera.co.uk

For more information, media enquiries and review copies please contact > marketing@oldcastlebooks.com